Freeman

MAY 2012 CH

A NOVEL

LEONARD PITTS, JR.

BOLDEN

AN AGATE IMPRINT

CHICAGO

Printed in the United States.

Library of Congress Cataloging-in-Publication Data

Pitts, Leonard.
 Freeman / Leonard Pitts.
    p. cm.
 Summary: "At the end of the Civil War, an escaped slave first returns to his old plantation and then walks across the ravaged South in search of his lost wife"--Provided by the publisher.
 ISBN-13: 978-1-932841-64-0 (pbk.)
 ISBN-10: 1-932841-64-4 (paperback)
 ISBN-13: 978-1-57284-699-9 (ebook)
 1. Freedmen--Fiction. 2. African-Americans--Fiction. 3. Reconstruction (U.S. history, 1865-1877)--Fiction. 4. Southern States--History--1865-1877--Fiction. I. Title.
 PS3616.I92F74 2012
 813'.6--dc23

                    2012009592

9 8 7 6 5 4 3 2 1

Bolden is an imprint of Agate Publishing. Agate books are available in bulk at discount prices. For more information, go to agatepublishing.com.

For Marilyn
(and all the Tildas everywhere)

His first thought was of her.

Outside, something heavy thudded the sky and the old house shuddered hard as if its floorboards had been stomped upon by giants. He put his book aside and swung down from the bed where he had been resting, fully dressed. Maybe it was thunder. The skies had been leaden all day.

But thunder rolls and this was a percussive boom such as he had heard many times on the battlefield. This was cannon fire. Then, overtop the cannons, came the sound of bells, every kind of bell there was, fire bells, church bells, school bells, all pealing at the same time in a perfect confusion of joy. And all at once he felt it, hope fluttering in his chest like a butterfly in a cage. It was difficult to breathe.

Lifting the oil lamp from the stand by his bed, he made his way down the dark hallway, down the stairs, each step taking him deeper into pure bedlam. When he emerged onto the stoop, he found his landlady, the widow Brewster, standing among a small knot of people, watching the crowded avenue flow by. Her face, usually so pinched with contempt for him and every other living thing, glowed with beatific light. Tears shone on her cheeks. At the sound of his approach, she turned and, to his great surprise, smiled. If he didn't know better, he'd have thought her beautiful.

"It's over," she said, and her voice trembled under the weight of just those two words. She said it again: "It is over."

His mouth fell open but not a sound came out. A trail of fire sizzled across the sky and broke high above them in a star of silver and gold. The impromptu parade surging past, the shopkeepers and floor sweepers, the countermen and maids, every Negro in Philadelphia, it seemed, all craned their heads as one to look, point, and exclaim. All of them chattering at once and waving tiny American flags. Someone lifted three cheers for the United States. Edwina Brewster hugged him. Actually wrapped her arms around his waist and squeezed. It was over. The war was done.

And his first thought was of her.

He had called her Tilda. She had called him Sam.

These were names they had given one another for their own private use and amusement and they were, he thought, the names truest to who they really were. But they'd each had other names.

When he was born, his mother—a careworn face, barely recalled—had named him Henry. The woman who bought him when he was seven had told him she already had a Henry on her place and did not want the confusion. She had named him Hark. When that woman died eight years later, leaving no heirs, he was sold at an estate auction and bought by a woman who disliked his name yet again. All her slaves were named after figures in classical Greek literature, she explained, not looking at him as a footman accepted her gloves and another unhitched the horses from her fine rig.

She appraised him with a brief glance, a gangly, frightened boy, lying manacled in the back of the wagon, hair unkempt and flecked with bits of straw. "You'll be Perseus," she announced. And then she walked away.

He was still looking after her when the footman produced a skeleton key and opened the ring of metal around his wrist. "You think that's bad," he grumbled. "She call me Zeus."

Later that same day, he was sitting in front of the cabin he had been given, wearing the rough clothes he had been issued, eating with his fingers from the bowl of cornbread and greens someone had handed him, when he felt eyes on him. He looked up and beheld her for the first time. He almost dropped his bowl.

She stood hip thrust with one hand akimbo. He judged that she was his age or close to it, but she already had a woman's curves, her thighs round and strong beneath the faded house dress, her breasts straining against the plain fabric. He felt a stiffening in his groin and moved the bowl to cover it.

"She call you Perseus, hmm?" Her smile was gentle and amused. "That woman and her Greek."

"What she call you?" he stammered. His throat was so dry it hurt.

"Danae," she said. "Do I look like some Danae to you?"

She looked like…beauty. Lush black hair plaited in a single braid that fell back from a dark, radiant face. Her eyes were almond shaped, her lips full, and, just now, pursed in thought. In that very instant, he loved her and knew that he would love her always.

"I'm gon' call you Sam," she said finally. "That all right with you?"

"Yes," he said, uncomfortably aware that anything she wished to call him would be all right with him. Then out of nowhere, he heard himself say, "And I'm gon' call you Tilda. You mind that?"

"Tilda," she said, contemplating the darkening sky. Then she looked at him and smiled. "No, I don't mind that. I kind of like that." And he felt something warm break open inside his chest.

"Well, I got to go," she said. "See you later, Sam." She turned to walk way.

He watched her go, his bowl of greens forgotten. "See you later, Tilda," he said.

It was fifteen years since he had seen her. He didn't know the last time he had thought of her. Sam had trained himself *not* to think of her, because thinking of her only made it hurt worse, only reminded him how far his poor life had meandered from everything that made living it worth the trouble. So he had learned to lie flat on his belly in an orchard, Minié balls chewing up peaches and men indiscriminately, and not think of her. He had learned to languish on a train, pulse thudding in his temples, fighting for breath, the air rent with the moans of dying men, and not think of her. He had learned to live quietly, to take his meals alone in a corner of Edwina Brewster's kitchen, to recline on his narrow bed in a narrow room on the top floor of a rooming house and read his books, not thinking of her.

Now a bonfire blazed to life at the end of the block, people dancing in golden light, now a parade carried Jefferson Davis by in effigy, a linen figure stuffed with straw hanging by the neck from a pole, now someone raised three cheers for U.S. Grant and bells tolled all over the city and flags fluttered and Edwina Brewster wept unreservedly and thinking of Tilda was all he could do. Tilda. His Tilda.

It was too much. Sam slipped back inside, climbed the stairs to his room, sat on his bed, and opened his book.

He tried to remember how not to think of her. It had been so long. Would she be thinking of him? He did not think she would.

Surely it would hurt her too much, not just the years they had been apart but also the years they had been together, the son they'd had. And lost.

Down went the book. He went to his window, where he was met by his own reflection: dark skin, a broad, strong nose, full lips, and deep set brown eyes. To his surprise, the sober, unrevealing face he had long ago trained himself to show the world, the *white* world in particular, had cracked open. Tears were running out.

The tumult from below came to him as an indistinct murmuring. Another string of fire flung itself across the sky to open in broad, bright tendrils of red. He saw it hazily through the tears. A quote came to him, the way quotes often did.

> *Now conscience wakes despair*
> *That slumber'd,—wakes the bitter memory*
> *Of what was, what is, and what must be*
> *Worse.*

John Milton. And the words were sour to him in their unutterable truth.

All the things he had trained himself not to remember came rushing in on him. He remembered how Tilda had looked, sweaty, exhausted, and aching from her labors, but smiling for him. He remembered how his son had looked, smudged with blood and afterbirth, hair matted to his scalp, eyes pressed closed. And he remembered how the boy had looked fourteen years later, lying with mouth agape in a muddy bog. You would have thought him asleep, except for the bloody red hole in his back. Ajax, the woman had called him, another of her Greek names. But to Sam and Tilda, he had always been Luke.

It confused him some at first. "Why I got two names?" he had asked one evening when they had all come in staggering from a long day in the fields.

The look Tilda gave him then caused him to shrink away. "*She* call you what she want," Tilda had said, jerking her head toward the big house. "But to us, you always be Luke."

Mistress was aware they had their own names for each other, but she never said anything about it. She was, Tilda always said, a good mistress, all things considered.

To which Sam had always replied, "Yeah, but she still a mistress." It was their one argument.

Enough, he thought, turning from the window. *Enough.*

Tilda was years behind him now. He did not even know where she was. Maybe still with Mistress. Maybe long since sold away. And even if she still belonged to Mistress, who was to say Mistress was still on the old place down in Mississippi? So many masters and mistresses had abandoned their properties because of the war, had taken their slaves and run to Texas.

There was no telling where Tilda was. She might be anywhere. She might even be dead.

Sam lay back on the bed. He did not pick up the book again, knowing it would be useless. Instead he lay there with eyes closed listening to the thump of fireworks and the muted cheers from the streets, trying to remember how not to think of her.

Sleep was long in coming.

In the morning, he walked through streets littered with tiny American flags and the charred remains of bonfires. The city was in a stupor of joy. He bought a paper from every paperboy he saw. The headlines shouted:

Victory!! Victory!!
Lee Finds His Waterloo
The Rebels Want Peace
The Nation's Thanks To Its Glorious Heroes

He read as he walked. Robert E. Lee had surrendered at a place in Virginia called Appomattox Courthouse. Gen. Grant had declined to take him prisoner. A day of thanksgiving had been declared on the recommendation of the governor. Churches were expected to be packed all day.

"I might have known," said Billy Horn, as Sam entered the reading room of the Library Company of Philadelphia. "War or peace, you will come through the door right on schedule with your head buried in a newspaper."

"Good morning," said Sam. The sight of a colored man reading was a never-ending source of wonder and consternation to his coworker. Sam set the papers on a counter.

Louisa Prentiss had thought the law forbidding slaves from being educated a foolish one and had made a show of flouting it. But no one bothered her about it. Mistress was the widow of a former Mississippi governor, the wealthiest woman in the county, and one of its most powerful people of either gender. It was generally accepted that she was "unconventional," and if she pampered her slaves, if she gave them fancy Greek names or allowed them to read books openly, or refused to sell them even when you offered her a fair price because she didn't believe in breaking up families—even *nigger* families—well, no one dared say anything about it. "Miss Prentiss's niggers," her slaves were called and it was generally understood that they were untouchable.

Nevertheless, Sam had been glad to land in Philadelphia, where, he thought, a colored man with a book in hand would be no particular novelty, nor incite sidelong glances of threat and hostility. He had been mostly right about that, but there were exceptions. Billy Horn was one of them. Sam hoped without any real expectation that the white man would have nothing more to say on the subject. But that was impossible, he knew, for this particular white man on the first day of peace.

Horn was a shaggy young man who had been one of the first volunteers to join the federal army, driven by a profound conviction that no state could be allowed to just pick up and leave the Union whenever it so pleased. He had lost an arm in the first big engagement at Bull Run, convalesced, and then returned to Philadelphia where he promptly lost his fiancée, who could not envision her prospects married to a man with one arm. But as far as he was concerned, the ultimate betrayal had come the next year, when Abraham Lincoln issued his Emancipation Proclamation.

"He turned it into a slavery war," Horn had groused darkly one day. He had been talking to a patron, but staring at Sam, who stood above him on the catwalk that circled the reading room, shelving books from a cart. "I did not sign up for that, sir. This was supposed to be a war to restore the Union, nothing more. I did not lose my arm for nigger freedom." He had raised his voice on the last words. People had looked around reproachfully. Mary Cuthbert, the no-nonsense spinster who managed the library, had called him into her office.

He would apologize the next day. He would say he had been drunk. Sam knew better. Billy Horn had been sober as a funeral dirge. He came around the desk now, grinning beneath the heavy underbrush of a brown beard, and clapped Sam heartily on the shoulder. "I suppose you are pleased," he said.

"We are at peace again," said Sam. "I would think we would all be pleased." He said it the way he said everything, especially to white men: his voice even and clear and free from any trace of Negro dialect. His enunciation was always pointedly correct. Everything about him was always pointedly correct. Especially with white men.

"You know what I mean," Horn said, leaning close. His voice was like metal scraping stone and Sam smelled the awful, fermented breath. There would be no need for Horn to lie about it this time.

"You have been drinking," said Sam.

"I have been *celebratin',*" said Horn. "I'd expect you would, too. The slavery war is over. The niggers are free."

Sam made himself smile, made his voice amiable. "Look, Billy, I have books to shelve."

Horn's face clouded. "Oh, now you think you're good enough to give orders to a white man, is that it? I guess I shouldn't be surprised. That's what comes of nigger freedom."

"You are inebriated," said Sam.

Horn's brow wrinkled as Sam had known it would. "Inny-*what?*" he demanded.

Sam smiled. He liked using big words, five-dollar words, on people who presumed to treat him as less than he was just because he was a Negro. He especially liked using them on white men like Horn, arrogant without just cause. It amused him to see them have to grope for the definition.

"It means you are drunk," he said, turning on his heel and walking away. Not only were there books to shelve, but also returns to sort through, floors to sweep, garbage to empty. He did not have time for this. Sam began to gather the books patrons had left on the table Saturday night at closing. It did not escape him that it had been Horn's job to re-shelve them before leaving work.

Sam got two tables away before Horn moved to intercept him. "Please allow me to pass," said Sam. He spoke politely, spoke correctly, and he tried to ignore the heat he felt spike in his chest.

"You do like giving orders to white men, don't you?"

"I have work to do," said Sam. "Please allow me to do my work."

"Free niggers," snarled Horn with contempt. The big right hand came up and he shoved Sam. The books fell from Sam's arms and he rocked back a single pace.

It was enough. Sam's hands came up and before he could think, his right fist shot forward and smashed the tip of the bigger man's nose. Billy Horn staggered, right hand coming up to catch the blood that gushed from his nostrils.

Sam was instantly appalled. He had just struck a one-armed man. Few things could be more despicable. He stepped forward, palms up, intending to apologize. But now Horn's one arm was coming toward him, the hand bloody and grasping. Sam leaned back out of range and the big man, drunken and overbalanced, stumbled and swept a stack of books to the floor.

"Free niggers!" he cried. "I'll show you."

"Mr. Horn!" A woman's voice stabbed the moment and the air rushed out of it. Mary Cuthbert was standing in the doorway to her office, cheeks bloodless, mouth compressed to a thin, angry line. Sam wondered how long she had been standing there, watching them. Long enough, he decided. She didn't even look his way.

"Join me in my office," she told Horn, and that voice would brook no dissent.

Horn's expression was that of a man just awakening and finding himself in a place he did not know. "Miss Cuthbert," he said, stupidly.

She wheeled about and he had no choice but to follow. The door closed softly behind him. Miss Cuthbert lowered her shade.

Sam busied himself picking up books from the floor and off the desks. He could see the shadows of them against the shade, Miss Cuthbert seated at her desk, leaning back, hands tented before her, Horn perching on the edge of his chair, his single hand gesturing wildly. Sam could hear their voices, but he couldn't make out the words. Not that it was necessary. The tone told him enough. Her voice was icy and sharp, his rose toward falsetto.

When the door opened five minutes later, Sam looked up in time to see Horn leave the room at something just short of a trot. He went straight for the front door, which closed behind him with a bang that made the windows rattle.

"Sam." Miss Cuthbert was at her office door, beckoning for him.

"I am sorry," he said, lowering himself into a seat that still bore the heat of its previous occupant.

She waved the apology down. "I saw it all," she said. "You were the soul of forbearance as you have been every time that loutish man has sought to bait you. I should have dismissed him long ago, but what with his arm and his service to the Union, well, I could not do it. I suppose I felt sorry for him."

"No one can blame you for that," said Sam.

"Yes, but I allowed that to blind me to what was best for the library. That was unfair to my other employees and to you in particular. I just wanted to let you know that you won't have to worry about Mr. Horn anymore. He is no longer employed here."

She picked up a piece of paper from her desk and lifted her reading glasses, which lay on her bosom, suspended from a chain. It was a dismissal. He didn't move. She looked up at him—a question—and he realized to his surprise that he had just made a decision.

"There is something I need to tell you," he said.

She frowned. "What is it, Sam?"

He had time to wonder if he was not about to do something he would regret for the rest of his days. Miss Cuthbert spoke again, her voice softer this time. "Sam," she said, "what is it?"

He gazed up at her. "I realize this is going to seem very sudden, and I apologize to you for that. You have been nothing but fair to me. You have given me every opportunity."

She leaned back in her chair. "You are leaving," she said. This wasn't a question.

"Yes, ma'am."

"Immediately?"

"Yes, ma'am."

"May I know why?"

For some reason, the question caught him off guard. "Well, ma'am," he said, "there was a…there was this…"

She smiled a thin smile. "There is a woman," she said.

He nodded gravely. "Yes, ma'am, there is. Or at least, there was. My wife."

"She was a slave?"

"We were both owned by the same woman, ma'am."

"Now you are determined to go find her."

"Yes, ma'am, I am."

"All the way to Mississippi?"

"Yes, ma'am."

"You do realize that's insane."

He had been gazing fixedly at her desk. Now he met her eyes. "I do, ma'am. But I still must go."

"You have not seen her in, what? Ten years?"

"It has been 15 years, ma'am."

"Fifteen years, then. And you will be travelling into what was, until just yesterday, enemy territory."

"Yes, ma'am."

"Sam, by this time, she may well have married someone else. She may not be in the same place. She might even be—I hate to say this, Sam, but it is the truth—she might even be dead. She may have taken sick or been killed in the war. You have no way of knowing."

"I realize all of that, ma'am."

"But that will not dissuade you."

"No, ma'am."

"She must be an exceptional woman."

He was not a man who smiled often, but he did now. "She is, ma'am. She is truly exceptional. Plus, well…I feel as if I owe it to her."

"Oh? Why do you feel that way?"

Tilda shrieking his name in hatred and fury. Him, chained to a whipping tree, wanting to explain, wanting to apologize. Not having the words, because the words do not exist. Then the whip knifing through the air, cutting his flesh. And her, cursing him.

"I made a mistake," said Sam. "I did something I should never have done. I hurt her."

"I'm sure she's forgotten all about that by now," said Miss Cuthbert.

"No, I can assure you she has not," said Sam.

"I see," said Miss Cuthbert. She drew a breath. "Well, then, the alternate might be true. She might not wish to see you. You might travel all that way and she might refuse."

"Yes, that is a possibility," said Sam.

"But you're going anyway."

"Yes, ma'am, I am. But I hate to leave you shorthanded." He liked Mary Cuthbert. He had met her when she was volunteering as a nurse, tending to the Union wounded at a makeshift hospital. He had not been wounded himself, had been loaded on the train with all his limbs intact, something not many in that ghastly rail car could claim. But he had been sick, suffering from one of the deadly wasting diseases so common in camp. He had fever, headache, delirium, and chills that shivered him so violently his teeth knocked together. He had lost 20 pounds, unable to keep food down.

The doctor had decided that he would die, and he had been left in a sunless corner of the hospital in Philadelphia where he might do so in peace. He didn't know this at the time. He learned it the day he awoke to find Mary Cuthbert reading to him. She nursed him to health, spooned a watery broth into his parched lips when he couldn't keep anything else down, offered to write letters for him (he had no one to write to), exactly as if he were white.

She was delighted to learn that he could read and was even happier to discover they had a love of books in common. She had told him that when he was well enough, he could come work for her at the Library Company of Philadelphia. "Founded by Mr. Benjamin Franklin," she had added, in a rare show of pridefulness.

Franklin, lips knotted in something that was not quite a smile, watched from a portrait over her desk now as she shook her head. "Do not trouble yourself on my account," she said.

"Yes, ma'am, but you have been more than fair to me, and I feel bad just leaving you this way."

"Sam, this library survived for many years before you arrived. It will survive without you. Finish out the day. You may draw your pay when you leave."

She lifted the glasses again. Sam stood to leave. His hand was on the doorknob when she called his name. He turned. She was gazing at him closely.

"Sometimes, you simply must follow your heart," she said. "No reasonable man can blame you for that." A smile. "No reasonable woman can, either."

"Yes, ma'am," he said. "Thank you, ma'am."

He felt oddly weightless and untethered as he closed the door to her office. It was as if saying it, speaking this sudden, up-from-nowhere compulsion aloud, had made it real when before, it had only been...what? Idle thought? Passing fancy? Well, if it had ever been that, it was no longer. He was actually going to do it, actually going to leave behind comfort and predictability—*home*, meager as it was—to go looking for Tilda. It occurred to him that he might truly be mad. He was surprised to feel himself smiling again.

The day passed in a blur, passed as so many of his days had passed in the months since he came here, in routine worn meaningless and forgettable by repetition. How many books had he shelved? How many floors had he swept? How many windows had he cleaned? It felt like thousands.

But he would miss this place. For a man who loved books, it was as near as earth ever came to heaven. He would miss Homer and Milton,

Aeschylus, and all the other poets and storytellers who had lightened his days while he was here. But he missed Tilda more.

When he was done working, he collected his wages, bid Mary Cuthbert a last farewell, and walked out into a fine, misting rain. For a moment, he simply stood atop the double stairwells that curled in opposite directions down to the street. A tradesman's wagon clattered by on the rough bricks. A Negro woman pushing a cart sang out, "Pepperpot, right hot! Who will buy some pepperpot?" Two white women walked past her, lost in conversation, not even noticing she was there.

From across the street, he could see through the trees the back of the old Pennsylvania statehouse where the founders had debated their Declaration of Independence and Constitution. He found himself wondering, as he often did when he contemplated this view, how they could have sat there, powdered and bewigged, debating the rights of man, yet never see the hypocrisy and irony of returning home to be tended by slaves. They had even written slavery into the great document for fear of offending delegates from the South. But the reckoning had come and now the country lay in smoldering pieces, and he had no idea if, or how, it could ever knit itself together again.

At that moment, as if Sam's thoughts had conjured him, Billy Horn stepped out from the trees behind the statehouse and walked toward him. Sam held his ground. His fists came up automatically when Horn was halfway across the street. But the other man tottered as if it required all his concentration just to stay upright, and his eyes were shiny as a new coin. Sam lowered his hands. He did not have to guess where Horn had spent the day.

"What do you want?" asked Sam.

Horn stopped, still a few feet away, and a humorless smile opened like a seam in the heavy beard. "What do I want? What do I want?" He turned the question over as if considering it closely. "I want a thousand Union greenbacks. I want a fetching wench or two to help me spend it." He barked in a sudden wild guffaw, but tears tumbled from his eyes. "I want the life I used to have," he added, softly. "I want my good right arm back, goddamn you. I would never have given it in the first place if I had known it was for the likes of you."

"You are"—the word *inebriated* came to mind, but Sam thought better of it—"drunk. Go home."

Horn shook his head sorrowfully. "I remember a time, and not so long ago, mind, you would never have dared talk to a white man that way. The world has changed, hasn't it? Just since surrender. The world has changed."

His eyes searched Sam's as if he really needed to hear Sam's answer. And Sam thought of how, that day, he had punched a white man in the face and renounced a job he loved in order to traipse to Mississippi, searching for a woman he had not seen, or even allowed himself to think of, in many years. "Yes," he said, with more tenderness than he'd have thought possible. "The world has changed." His whole life, everything he had ever been, everything he had ever known, thrown in the air like confetti, the pieces drifting down. *Changed.* And no one yet knew exactly what it was changing to. Drunken fool though Horn was, Sam did not blame him for his fear.

Horn nodded. "Well, I liked the world the way it was," he said, and added after a pause, "though I expect you did not."

It was, Sam knew, as close as Bill Horn could come to an apology. The white man's eyes held Sam's. He pursed his lips as if he were about to speak. Then he simply turned and stumbled off, disappearing into the foot traffic on the street. When he was gone, Sam turned up the collar on his frayed old Union coat and walked home to the boarding house off Lombard.

After dinner, he told Edwina Brewster he would no longer have need of her room. He told her to give away or sell his few meager articles of clothing and books.

Sam had no money. Mary Cuthbert had paid him $1.25 a day to work at the library. Edwina Brewster had charged him $5.00 a week to live in her boarding house. The difference had gone into clothing and books. So when he set out early the next morning, he didn't walk to the docks and he didn't walk to the train station. Instead, he walked until he reached the bridge that spanned the Schuylkill River. There, he paused and took in a breath. It smelled of chimney smoke, rotting fish, and the threat of rain. He had nothing in his hands, nothing in his pockets, nothing on his back except a shirt and a Union Army jacket, and he wondered again if he were not about to make the biggest darn fool mistake of his entire darn fool life.

And it occurred to him: yes. Quite possibly, he was.

Still, he shrugged and did the only thing that made sense to him: he started walking. He set off on foot in search of her.

Tilda. His Tilda.

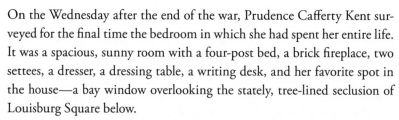

On the Wednesday after the end of the war, Prudence Cafferty Kent surveyed for the final time the bedroom in which she had spent her entire life.
It was a spacious, sunny room with a four-post bed, a brick fireplace, two
settees, a dresser, a dressing table, a writing desk, and her favorite spot in
the house—a bay window overlooking the stately, tree-lined seclusion of
Louisburg Square below.

On the floor at the foot of the bed sat a steamer trunk, the lid open,
already filled with dresses, bonnets, and shoes; a few treasured books; and
some other effects. Only one item remained to be packed before the trunk
could be sealed—a polished walnut box she took now from her writing desk
as she went to sit on the ledge of the bay window.

She did not open it right away. Instead, she ran a finger along the gleaming surface, knowing this would be difficult and, in some part of her at least,
wanting it just the same. A pair of carriages rattled past one another in the
street below, the faint clop, clop, clop of horse's hooves carrying to her ears.
Prudence felt a tear slip her eye. She let it fall.

On the night before the battle in which he was killed, Captain James
Kent of the 1st Massachusetts Regiment had written a letter to his new wife
back home in Boston. Now, two years later, Prudence steeled herself and
raised the lid of the box in which all of Jamie's letters were neatly stacked.
She lifted the envelope containing his final letter off the top.

Prudence unfolded it carefully; the creases in the paper were nearly
worn through from repeated handling and she knew that sooner or later

the letter would tear. There had been a time, especially in the awful weeks after his name showed up in the listing of the dead in the newspaper, that she had read this letter every day. It gave her comfort somehow, made her feel she was with him and he with her, still. Then time had passed, days piling into weeks and weeks into months, and months, finally, into years, and the need to read his words every day had dulled some. As had the pain.

But that need had returned today. So she held the letter before her, though by now she knew its every word by heart. The war was over, the cause won to which he had given his life. So it seemed right somehow, *necessary* somehow, to read Jamie's letter again, to hear his voice again in these first days of peace. She lifted the pages up to the light coming through the window. Jamie's manly scrawl was comforting in its familiarity.

The letter strove, as his letters unfailingly had, for a light tone. There was the usual effusive expression of his love for her, the usual reminder of how terribly he missed her. The following pages he filled with amusing anecdotes of life in camp; he recounted with horror the bumptious customs of the men from the rustic areas of the state, told how his days of marching had given him a new appreciation for the simple pleasures of a cup of tea, a good book, and a warm fire, and groused about the incompetence of a captain who marched his men 20 miles in the wrong direction.

Prudence's smile as she read these things was mixed with as much regret as amusement. She recognized it now, though she had not before, for what it was. He had been performing for her, minimizing the fear and the hardship so she would not worry for him.

In every letter, he had done this. And it wasn't until here, at the very end of this letter, that he allowed the façade to slip. It was as if he knew, his protestations to the contrary notwithstanding, that it would be his last. He wrote:

> *Now dearest, before I close, I must speak to you of a matter I fear you will find upsetting. I beg you forgive me. Were there any way I could spare you this, I would do so gladly, but it is important to me that you understand what I am about to tell you.*
>
> *Tomorrow, we fight a momentous battle against the rebel forces that have dared invade Northern soil and there is every expectation that our casualties will be heavy. Dearest, only God can know in advance who will be called upon to pay the ultimate price, but I honestly have no fears for my own safety. I simply do*

not believe I was born to die on a Pennsylvania field. We all have
a destiny and I do not believe that is mine.

And yet, dear heart, I would be a fool to deny the possibility.

The sound of laughter brought her head up from the paper. Down below, a young couple was walking in the little fenced park that occupied the
middle of the square. The woman held three fingers to her mouth, daintily
amused at something her beau had said. He was looking quite pleased with
himself. They held hands. To Prudence, they seemed so young. She, at 26,
had not felt young in years.

She returned to Jamie's letter.

I do not tell you these things to burden your heart, dear
Prudence, or to make you fearful, though I know that will be
the inevitable outcome. But facing such possibilities has a way of
concentrating a man in his whole mind and I realize that in the
event of the unthinkable, there are things I want you to know in
no uncertain terms.

The first is that I love you. Never doubt that, Mrs. Kent. I
love you more than words can ever say. My heart has ever, and
only, been yours.

The second thing I want you to know is this: If I should fall
in this crusade, I did not die in vain. I beg you do not mourn
me as one who lost his life senselessly. Do not let them say of me
that mine was a tragic death. Oh, Prudence, would that I could
convey to you how far from tragic, how far from senseless, such a
demise would be.

Please don't misunderstand me, dearest. It is not that I seek
death, nor that I would welcome it. It is, rather, that if I am to
surrender my life, I can think of no more glorious cause in which
to do so. You know that I hate Negro slavery with all my being,
Prudence. What we have done to that poor, unfortunate people is
a stain upon our national honor that will not be cleansed before
centuries were done. If they are the lesser race, it were our sacred
duty to lift them up, to civilize them, to instruct them to the limits
of their abilities. If they are not lesser, as I know you and some
others firmly believe, then our crime is so much the greater, for we
have done this awful thing to those who, but for the shading of
their skin, are exactly like ourselves.

Either way, Prudence, it is a sin before our Creator that some of his children are so haughty, so filled with grand opinion of self, that they have thought themselves justified in enslaving the Negro. Our Southern brethren forget that for all their humble station in life, for all their defects, the Negroes are also children of God.

I have long been on fire for the abolitionist cause, as have you. But I have always supported it from afar, always given my money and my time, but never my self. This war has changed all that, has given me the chance to support this glorious cause at the hazard of my very life. As a result, I feel more alive, more firmly centered in the rightness of my cause, than ever I have before.

So should I die, say only that I did so willingly. Say that I died in the service of that which I believe and, if given the opportunity, I would do so again. Say that I died fighting on the side of good and eternal God.

I am at peace, whatever comes. No man can ask for more.

Well, dearest, I must close now.

All my love, all my life.

Jamie.

He was killed twelve hours later in a place called Gettysburg.

Prudence refolded the letter and put it back in the box. She brushed at the tears on her cheek, noting absently that the trees in the square were leafing out quite nicely.

Tomorrow, she was going to the South. She did not know if she would ever return. The realization left her feeling oddly weightless, like a dancer suspended in mid-leap, not yet knowing where she might land. Her uncertainty must have shown on her face, because Bonnie stopped in the doorway and asked, "Are you all right, there, Miss Prudence?"

Prudence smiled. They were as unalike as two women could be. Bonnie was slender and pretty, with skin the color of walnut shells and a cautious, deliberate manner. Prudence's skin was pale and flawless but for a dusting of freckles on her cheeks. She had hair the color of October leaves and where Bonnie was careful and thoughtful, Prudence was driven by a native impulsiveness that (so she had many times been told) bordered on suicidal. Yet, for all their dissimilarity, there was no one in the world to whom she was closer. Not even her own sisters.

Prudence sat on the bed. "I am well, Miss Bonnie," she said.

It was an old joke between them. They had known each other since they were little more than toddlers, since the day Prudence's father, the late John Matthew Cafferty, had brought Bonnie home with him. The two girls had taken to one another from the start, had grown up together, roughhoused together, trusted one another with all the secrets of their hearts. But the Negro butlers and cooks and footmen who hiked over every morning from their side of the Hill to wait upon the wealthy whites on this side had seen this relationship and worried over it, wanting Bonnie to know that all white people—*most* white people—were nothing like the Caffertys.

So they had sought to school Bonnie in habits of deference, to prepare her to take what they assumed would be her place in the world. The result was that after a time, Bonnie had stopped addressing Prudence simply by her name and had begun calling her "Miss Prudence" instead, and nothing Prudence could do or say would make her stop. Finally, fed up, she had started calling her friend "Miss Bonnie" to teach her a lesson. *We'll see how she fancies it.*

As it turned out, she fancied it just fine.

Bonnie had never found that "place in the world" the colored servants assumed she would. Instead, she had remained in the Cafferty household all her life, becoming John Cafferty's fourth daughter in all but actual fact. But she and Prudence still used the stilted honorific in the privacy of their friendship; it amused them to do so.

"You do not look well, Miss Prudence," said Bonnie now.

Prudence smiled. "Is that so?"

"Are you troubled with second thoughts?" asked Bonnie. Her voice lifted with hope.

Prudence shook her head. "No second thoughts," she said. To emphasize the point, she closed Jamie's letter in its box and dropped it into the steamer.

"It grieves me to hear that."

"Miss Bonnie, this is something we must do."

"We," said Bonnie.

It was all she said, but it was enough. At Prudence's insistence, they were traveling south together, but Bonnie did not want to go. Young as she had been when she left there, she had no memories of the South, but what she knew of it, what she had read and been told, had filled her with loathing and primitive fear.

Prudence tried to jolly her. "You would have me go down there alone?" she said, fluttering her eyelashes like a coquette. "Fair and delicate flower that I am?" Prudence's lack of delicacy was legend in Boston society.

Bonnie would not be jollied. "I would rather if neither of us go down there, ever. The best day of my life was the day I left Dixie behind."

Prudence sighed. "And my father, who brought you out of Dixie, made me promise before he died that the moment the war was over, I would go down there and build a school for colored."

A lean, leathery face, a voice reduced to a rasp by the depredations of cancer, leaning close to her, the eyes alight, the stench of death on his breath. "Mark my words," he had said. "When this war is finished, when the Union is restored, this government will do nothing for the colored man. It will free him and then it will leave him to fend for himself in a hostile and resentful land. It will require people like us, people of means, to fill in the gaps." He had fallen back into his chair then, as if exhausted by his exertions. There followed a racking cough, and the sputum he spat into his handkerchief was flecked with blood.

John Matthew Cafferty had arrived in America penniless and alone as a boy, his mother having died on the journey from England. On his third night of wandering the docks, he broke into a warehouse, seeking only a warm place to sleep. Instead, he found a life.

He had awakened to find the warehouse owner hovering over him. John tried to run, but the man snatched him by the collar before he had taken the second step. His name was Cyrus Campbell and he was a genial free colored man who had become quite wealthy as a furniture maker. To the boy's great surprise, the black man didn't box his ears or call the law. Instead he took pity on him. Over breakfast, he offered him an apprenticeship.

"What do you think, lad? Or have you a better offer somewhere else?"

Campbell had regarded him with a puckish expression. The boy understood the man was having sport at his expense and he replied with grave dignity. "I have no better offer, sir," he said.

Cafferty remained with Campbell for 30 years, first as apprentice, then as an employee, and finally, as a partner and a kind of surrogate son. Several years after his benefactor died, John Cafferty, by now a wealthy man himself as the sole owner of Campbell & Cafferty Fine Furnishings, had gone to Buford, Mississippi, where Cyrus had lived on a cotton plantation until he escaped to the North, leaving his mother behind. Campbell had intended to buy her freedom, but had not been able to earn enough soon enough and never saw her again. So Cafferty had bought that plantation and freed every slave on it. And thus began a tradition: every year on the same day in June, in memory of Cyrus Campbell, he went back to Buford and bought a slave.

He could never say how he chose them. He simply waited for some look in a dark eye or tilt of a woolly head that gave him the sense that here was a woman or a man not yet crushed by a lifetime of being owned, one with gumption and guts who would, if set free in a free place, be able to make a life. Sometimes, he bought entire families on the basis of one woman's prideful posture, one man's fierce glare. Some chose to stay on in Mississippi. Those that so desired, he took to Boston, helped them find lodging and gainful employment, and set them free.

Twenty-six years before, the very first beneficiary of his largess had been a woman named Mildred. He embarked from Memphis with her and her daughter, but Mildred took sick on the journey and died, as his own mother had so many years before. He buried her near St. Louis and brought her baby with him to Boston, where he raised her as his own. Bonnie Cafferty—when she was 10, she had asked if she might take his name—had come to love the tall, raw-boned man like the father whose name she never knew, for saving her from a lifetime of scars. When he died, she had mourned him unreservedly.

But she did not want to go back to the South, not even to honor him. She hated the South. Even more, she feared it. Its current state of devastation and defeat did not change that. In some ways, she thought, it made it worse. What is meaner and more hateful than the haughty brought low?

"There must be another way," she told Prudence. "Find an agent down there you can trust. Why not volunteer for one of the schools organized by the Freedmen's Bureau? In that way, at least, you would act under the imprimatur of the federal government. You would have protection."

"That is not what my father asked," said Prudence.

"Well, he didn't ask me, Miss Prudence."

"I know," said Prudence. "*I* am asking. Will you deny me?"

Bonnie sighed. She sat on the bed beside Prudence. "I deny you nothing. You know that. But do you not think it foolish to rush down there so soon after the fighting has ended? Things may still be unsettled."

Bonnie shook her head. "We shall travel by steamship down the Mississippi River. The Mississippi has been in Union hands for two years now.

Any danger from marauding rebel armies is nonexistent, particularly with the surrender at Appomattox."

"We ought to be concerned about more than just the armies," said Bonnie. "What of the people?"

"What of them?"

"The people—the *white* people," she amended, "will be bitter because of their defeat. It might be wise to allow that news to sink in, give them more time to get used to the way things are now before we go gallivanting about down there."

"We do not gallivant, Miss Bonnie. We travel on a sacred mission. Do you really think we should delay simply because a few rebels may be walking around with bruised feelings and their lips poked out?"

"It is more than that, Miss Prudence."

Prudence went on as if she had not spoken. "And how long do you think we should defer to the rebels' tender feelings? Two weeks? Two months? A year?"

"You are sporting with me."

Prudence put a hand on her friend's shoulder. "Not at all," she said. "I just want you to see how impractical your suggestion is. We can wait. We can wait a month. We can wait a year. And while we wait, colored people will be suffering. Do you not care about that?"

Bonnie's dark eyes flashed. "Do I not care? Of course I care. How can you ask me that?"

"Why are you so reluctant, then? Is it just fear?"

"Perhaps," admitted Bonnie. "Perhaps it is. But if we are examining motivations now, let us consider yours. Is your haste to travel to Dixie just a sign of loyalty to your father? Or does not grief for Captain Kent also cloud your judgment?"

Prudence sighed. Something came into her eyes, then, something Bonnie could not read. "I loved my husband," said Prudence. "I grieve him still. You know that."

She did. For all the years Prudence had been courted by Jamie Kent, Bonnie had been her friend's confidant. It was Bonnie to whom Prudence had first confessed her feelings, Bonnie who had nursed Prudence through the inevitable spats, Bonnie who had been closer even than Prudence's two older sisters. "Of course I know," she said. Her voice was soft.

"One of the things I loved about him was his passion for the abolitionist cause. Other men went to war saying they fought only for Union. Jamie knew what he was fighting for from the beginning. He was fighting to free the slaves. You know what that means to us Caffertys."

Bonnie smiled, remembering a night as girls no more than five years old when they had snuck down a narrow passageway lined with garden implements and jars of preserved foods in the basement of the big house. At the end of the passageway, Prudence had given her a meaningful look, then took hold of a brick in the wall, pulling it to the right. To Bonnie's amazement, the very wall itself lumbered heavily open.

All she saw of them was eyes, three pairs of them, wide and frightened in the flickering light of the candle Prudence held. A woman, a man, and a boy, sitting—there was no room for them to stand—in a tiny compartment Bonnie had never known was there.

"It's all right," Prudence told them. "We are friends."

Bonnie gaped. "Who are they?" she asked.

The boy had piped up then. "We's run away from ol' Marse," he said.

"Father helps runaways," Prudence had said. And she had given her a look Bonnie had always remembered, a gaze clear as water and righteous as judgment itself.

Prudence gave her that same look now. "I know you think me reckless," she said, "but I promise you, I am aware of the dangers. A woman with a Yankee accent traveling with a Negro into the South to set up a school for free Negroes? I know there will be…objections. But the spirit of the two best men I have ever known compels me. Besides, as you well know, I can dish out trouble as well as receive it."

And at that, Bonnie could only smile. Prudence's father had often joked that his youngest child was the least-appropriately named person in all of Boston. She had been a tomboy when she was a girl, a scrapper, a marble shooter, a feared hitter in base ball. People who didn't know her were always surprised to learn these things; her features were delicate, and it was impossible to see in her the reckless, dirt-smudged girl she once had been. It made people underestimate her. She had learned to use that to her advantage.

"I know," said Bonnie, "you are not a frail little thing to be knocked over at the first stiff breeze. But those people,"—a pause, a look—"well, we will need to be careful. That is all I am saying. Not every place is like Boston."

"You said, 'we.'"

"Of course I did," said Bonnie.

Prudence smiled her relief. "Of course you did," she said.

And so it was the next morning that they stepped down together from the house where Prudence had lived her entire life, ready to leave the only city she had ever known. The tears had been cried, the farewells had been said. Now Bonnie watched as Prudence's sister Faith held both her hands and spoke earnestly while the third sister, Constance, directed Rogers, the houseman, in loading their three trunks on the wagon.

Constance, Prudence, and Faith, thought Bonnie with a private smile as she gazed upon the three auburn-haired women. Mister John had never been subtle about preaching the virtues of life. How she had twisted and fidgeted through all his long lectures about thrift and honesty, chastity and patience. How she missed him now. She had known no other family than the Caffertys. And she loved them as much as she could love anyone.

Still, she thought, and not for the first time, it would be nice if she had someone of her own who might be heartbroken by this leave-taking, someone who would miss her and mourn her absence. But there was not. Oh, there had been suitors from time to time, but nothing that ever threatened permanence. It made her wonder sometimes if there was something wrong with her. Other than the Caffertys, she was alone in the world.

"Bonnie? Have you heard a word I said?"

She started. Constance had been speaking to her. "Forgive me," she said. "I was preoccupied."

Constance sighed heavily at the prospect of having to repeat herself. She was the oldest sister—her husband, David, now ran the family business—and she took seriously (too seriously, Prudence often said) the responsibilities of her station. "I simply asked you," she said now, "to please govern Prudence. You know our sister can be"—a delicate pause—"headstrong. We shall depend on you to curb her reckless tendencies. And take care of yourself as well," she added.

Then it was Faith's turn. "In a way, I envy the two of you this adventure," she said.

"It is not an adventure," protested Prudence. "It is not a lark."

Faith lifted her hand. "I know that, sister," she said. "What I meant is, I admire your courage. Be careful down there. Return to us safely."

"This is not easy for us," said Constance.

Bonnie surprised herself. "This has not been easy for any of us," she said. "It has been difficult on all of us. The war, I mean. But something tells me the peace is going to be just as bad."

They looked at her. She met their eyes. Around them, the square went about its quiet business. A woman entered the park pushing a baby in a carriage. Two women wearing hoop skirts promenaded on the opposite side of the street. A wagon rattled past on Mount Vernon Street, going uphill.

"Well," said Constance finally, "let us hope you are wrong."

But they knew she wasn't. She could tell.

In the awkward silence that followed, Rogers opened the door of the coach and gave them his hand as they climbed inside. Bonnie and Prudence settled into the plush, upholstered seat. Rogers returned to the seat above, then flicked the leather reins lightly over the horses. The wagon rattled forward, and Bonnie watched as everything she had ever known disappeared behind her.

The woman lies atop a thin mattress on a dirt floor, huddled beneath a single sheet. She shivers in the cold and watches starlight through a gap where the wall doesn't quite meet the ceiling.

She has no idea what time it is. Shading toward morning, she thinks. The darkness is still but for the soft snoring behind her, Wilson and Lucretia, somehow managing to sleep. But the woman is too tired to sleep. Fatigue has soaked her bones. It is not simply the fatigue of work, though there is that, what with the endless hours spent clearing debris the Yankees left behind. But more than that, there is the fatigue of life.

Her own existence has become onerous to her and it is difficult to conceive that she was ever not cold, not old, not scared.

It is a moonless night. The stars are brittle white against the unrelieved expanse of darkness. There was a time, she vaguely remembers, when she stood beneath such a sky and talked to Jesus, just as naturally as talking to Wilson or Lucretia, and asked Him to save her. She had faith. Oh, Lord, such faith.

But He did not save her. And it has been years since last she stood beneath stars, looking up.

She takes an inventory of her pains. Her left buttock is still sore from when Marse Jim kicked her there because she did not fetch his shoes promptly enough. Her left cheek still aches from when Marse Jim hit her there with a closed fist. (She never learned what her offense was that time.) Her muscles are leaden from lifting and carrying. On top of it all, she has a bad tooth; it pounds like a hammer if her tongue so much as brushes against it. It's in the back, top right, and it's so rotten that it fills her mouth with a dead taste. As a result, she takes no joy in food, although food is so mean and meager these days she supposes no one does.

The one good thing about it: Marse Jim no longer finds her attractive. Even loaded up on that popskull he likes to drink, he no longer has the urge to crawl on top of her, breathing his fetid breath in her face, bristles of beard scratching her cheek as he pushes that hateful thing of his in and out of her until she considers her very beauty a curse. She is grateful to have lost it.

Lucretia, younger than she and still tolerably attractive, is not so lucky. When old Marse gets in a randy mood, she is the one called to satisfy him nowadays. But then, now that the woman thinks of it, even that hasn't happened too much lately. Apparently, Marse Jim himself cares little about rutting these days. With all the popskull, the woman wonders if he still can rut. Or perhaps he has simply lost interest, living with so much grief.

After all, his wife and his three daughters have been carried off by disease just since the war began. And his only son, Little Jim, was killed by the same renegade Yankee raiders who ransacked the plantation last month, who fired the barn and the house. You can still smell the smoke.

It shouldn't have happened. This area has been in Yankee hands for two years. Been peaceful most of that time. But then the Yankees got wind of some of Marse Jim's big talk, how he was going to raise a company of rebs and kick the federals out of this part of Mississippi, and sent a company of men to investigate. Marse Jim should have backed down from them, but he wouldn't. He cursed at the federals, then Little Jim threw a rock, shots were fired, and things got out of hand.

And when it was over, Marse Jim's home was gone. His home and his only son.

It was that final loss that seemed to unhinge him. He was never a good man, never a good master, but was he ever so hateful and mean as after he lifted his boy's bloody corpse from the dirt and cradled it, screaming curses as Yankees touched torch fire to his home?

Sometimes, it makes her feel sorry for him in spite of herself. She knows how it is to lose a son.

When the inky blackness above shades to a deep blue and the stars lose their hard edge and begin to seem unreal, she rises, wrapping the thin sheet about herself, and steps outside into the morning chill. A sudden blast of snoring shatters the stillness and she pauses and spares a glance across the path for the cabin that used to belong to Wilson. With the big house gone, Marse Jim sleeps there now, lies dead to the world, curled around the Sharps carbine that has become his only companion.

The woman waits—why, she doesn't know—but the sound doesn't come again. She moves on. In a pit in the yard, she builds a fire, heats a tin of water, and uses it to press together four patties of cornmeal. They are almost out of cornmeal. She wonders if there is any corn left to grind. The woman puts the patties on a shovel blade and places it across the fire so the cornmeal can brown. This is what they have to eat now. Corncakes and dandelion greens.

While she waits on breakfast to cook, she makes a morning visit to the privy. She returns to find Wilson and Lucretia squatting at the fire, eating their corncakes. They nod acknowledgment. It is too early for speaking. Breakfast passes in silence.

The stars disappear, the sun staggers above the horizon. Its light is meager and it falls on ruin. The kitchen is little more than black sticks, tumbling in on one another. The house itself is only a pile of blackened lumber. The barn is missing part of a wall and most of its roof. The blacksmith shop and the stable are ruined spots on the earth. The fields are leveled. Only the two slave cabins still stand mostly intact.

And Marse Jim thinks he can raise this place back to what it was with just the three slaves he has left, and two of those, women. As she does every morning, the woman gazes upon a landscape of shambles and wonders if the white man has lost his mind. Driven by a hellish, not quite sane determination to put things back as they were, he has them working sixteen-hour days clearing debris, plowing weed-choked fields, and hammering together the frame for a new house. Not undertaking one job, finishing it, and moving methodically on to the next but, rather, spending an hour clearing a field and then being ordered to pick up debris from the yard, to spend half an hour there and then being ordered at gunpoint to go up on the ladder and work at patching the roof of the barn.

It's as if his mind tumbles ahead of him, unable to settle, unable to focus. So much to do, so much to do. He runs along, trying to do it all, trying to catch up with his own thoughts and forcing them to do the same. The woman doesn't know how much longer she can keep up.

She was born a slave. She has been one all her life. It has never been easy. But it has never been as hard as this.

The woman hears stirring in the cabin Marse Jim has taken. He appears a moment later, a balding, burly man with red eyes and a ragged black fringe of beard. Wilson comes to his feet straightaway. "Marse Jim," he says in that voice of false cheer that white people somehow never see through. "Got breakfast for you, sir."

Marse Jim, pulling suspenders over a filthy undershirt that barely contains a prodigious gut, grunts his lack of interest, then staggers off in the direction of the privy. A moment later, there comes a long, guttural sound, *hrrrrrrk*. It repeats itself twice. Wilson, Lucretia, and the woman look at one another. No one speaks, though Wilson allows amusement to flicker briefly in his eyes.

By the time Marse Jim returns, they are working. Wilson is pulling charred timbers from the wreckage of the kitchen, his hands wrapped in rags to protect them. The woman and Lucretia are harnessing the plow to a cantankerous mule, made more stubborn—listless, really—by lack of feed. Its skin falls in sallow ridges against prominent bones.

"Not yet," says Marse Jim.

Wilson straightens. "Marse?"

His eyes are downcast, like a shy schoolboy, his lips moist and flecked with pieces of vomit. "I said, not yet," he says. And now he looks up. "It's been a month. One month today. Want you people to go up to the grave with me, pay respects to Little Jim. You should want to go. He was your young master, after all." He says this last through an accusatory scowl, as if they have already turned him down.

But for the woman, the calculation is a simple one. A morning spent at the dead boy's grave, versus one spent lifting lumber and walking behind a recalcitrant mule. There is no contest.

Wilson says, "Marse, we'd be honored to." He says this with false gravity and for a moment, Marse Jim regards him so intently that the woman wonders if he has finally seen through.

But Marse just says, "Well, all right, then. That's better. And maybe you could sing one of those darky songs."

Wilson says, "Darky songs, Marse?"

Impatience clouds the white man's red face. "Yes, darky songs! You know what I mean. All them moanin' songs you niggers sing down to the clearin' Sunday mornin's when you think nobody can hear you."

Lucretia shoots the woman a look. Wilson says with perfect earnestness, "Oh, yes, them songs. Yes, Marse. We be pleased to sing for you and young marse."

"Well, that's more like it, then," he says. "We'll go in a minute."

He lumbers back to the cabin and goes inside. Wilson waits until he knows the white man cannot hear him, then turns and says with the same perfect gravity, "Oh, yes, Marse, we be happy to go up top of the hill and sing darky songs for your dead boy. Why Marse, you ain't even need to ask. Nothin' give us more pleasure."

Lucretia risks a pretty laugh. "Shush, fool. Anything get us out a morning work, I'm happy to do."

"Ain't that the truth," says Wilson. "We sings them darky songs all day for you, Marse, you want us to. Sing 'em so pretty, make the angels weep in heaven." Lucretia laughs again.

"Both of you just hush up," hisses the woman. "It's nothing to fun about, losing a child. Even a child of his."

Wilson's smile is thin and cutting as a knife's blade. "We just have to disagree on that," he says.

The woman leads the mule back into its stall. When she returns, Marse Jim is there. He is wearing a rumpled shirt now and a slouch hat sits atop what remains of his coarse, black hair. His eyes glitter. The woman thinks he may be the most pitiful thing she has ever seen.

"Let's go," he says.

It isn't far. Thirty minutes, though all uphill, to the slope where the family graveyard sits, overlooking what once were fields of Jim McFarland's land, blooming white in spring. Fields black now and scoured of all life.

They walk single file behind Marse Jim. No one speaks. The woman brings up the rear. The sun feels good on her back.

She remembers Wilson's smile, that tight, secretive pressing together of his lips, so different from the open, show-all-the-teeth grin that white people never see through. It scares her some.

She is not sentimental about Little Jim McFarland. He was a devilish child who delighted in making life difficult for the slaves—he sneaked into his father's room and broke his father's things and blamed it on little black boys knowing they would be whipped for it, he lay under the house and chunked rocks at slaves returning from the fields, he thought it funny to hide in a tree and pee down on some poor colored man having his lunch below. She has no doubt that, had he lived, he would have grown up to be just like his father, if not worse. He was not a good boy and she does not miss him.

But that doesn't mean he deserved to get shot by some hot-tempered Yankee boy not too many years older just because he bloodied the Yankee's head with a rock. That doesn't mean his father's pain is not worthy of respect.

They reach the top of the hill. The little cemetery is overgrown with weeds. The older tombstones stick up from the soil at crooked angles, some of them cracked and broken. One of the Yankee boys did it, seemed to take pleasure trying to kick the grave markers to pieces before his commander stopped him. Just meanness, thinks the woman. Meanness, plain and simple.

If Marse Jim notices the condition of the graveyard, he gives no sign. He leads them past the broken and defiled markers for his father, his mother, his brothers, his daughters, his wife. Leads them to the far edge where there is a small wooden marker that was not disturbed by the marauders because it was not erected until after they moved on. It is lettered with charcoal, crudely drawn and unlikely to survive the next rain.

> *Here lies Jim McFarland Jr.*
> *Born Feb. 2, 1853*
> *Murdered March 14, 1865*

Marse Jim removes his hat, glares down at the marker. His thoughts are unknowable.

The woman turns from him, preferring to study the broken tombstones and burned fields. Sad sights, but preferable to seeing that narrow junction of dates on the boy's grave marker. Twelve years old when he died. Her own son was fourteen.

He loved mornings, did her son. Would get up at dawn just to see the stars disappear, the horizon turn from black to blue to pink to gold. He was smart as a whip, her son. He could read just as well as white boys, if not better. And he could cipher, too. Blue was his favorite color. And when Mistress—her old mistress, not Marse Jim's peevish wife—gave them a pig to roast for Christmas, he was always first to finish his plate. She misses him terribly.

She has at least that much in common with Marse Jim, understands at least that much about him. The woman wishes there was a way to say that to him. Maybe it would make it easier for him. Maybe it would make it easier for them all. But of course, there is no way.

"You all can sing now," rumbles Marse Jim.

Wilson, Lucretia, and the woman look at each other. And then, as if they shared one mind, they sing a song they have sung many times when moaning seemed the only sensible response to the meanness of life.

> *Father, I stretch my hands to thee*
> *No other help I know*
> *If thou withdraw thyself from me,*
> *Oh, wither shall I go?*

She closes her eyes, lets the words take her. How many times have they sung this song? Sung it through fire and flood, sung it through beatings and stillbirth, sung it to shore each other up, urge each other on. The song groans beneath the weight of their voices. They pull at the words, stretching them out til one syllable becomes two or three, becomes a perfect dirge bearing all their suffering and sorrows as a river barge bears its cargo toward the sea.

It is an awful sound. A sad, awful sound. That is the entire point.

Lucretia and Wilson, she knows, are singing by rote, pretending feelings they don't feel. You can hear it if you listen closely enough, see it if you only look: Lucretia's face a mask, a dead space untrammeled by emotion, Wilson's mischievous eyes rolling back in a perfect imitation of piety and pain. But Marse Jim will not notice this. Like most white people, he never truly looks at them, never really listens.

Three times they sing the verse, moaning more extravagantly each time. After the third, again as if they shared a single mind, they stop. There is a large quiet. Marse Jim touches two fingers to the crude marker. "I'm sorry, boy," he says. "I should've done better." His eyes are dry. His soft voice trembles just the least bit.

After another moment, he turns on his heel. They allow him to pass, then fall in line for the walk back down the hill. The woman is directly behind Marse Jim. His head is held so low it is barely visible beneath the rounded slope of his shoulders. It is a terrible thing to lose a child. Doesn't matter if you are slave or master. A terrible thing. They walk for a few minutes. Then she hears herself say, "I had a boy, too."

Where it came from, she has no idea. She only knows she is immediately sorry she said it. Sorrier still when he whirls on her like something dangerous coming up behind. "What did you say?"

She tries to swallow, but she can't. Her throat seems coated with dust. "I said, I had a boy, too," she says. "My boy died, too."

For a moment, he looks perplexed, looks as if she is trying to cheat him and he cannot figure out how. She braces herself for his fist because when he is confused, he hits. But in the end, he doesn't hit her. Instead, he snorts a kind of half laugh, as if in disbelieving contempt for all the damnable, eternal presumption of fool niggers. He turns without a word and continues down the hill at a faster pace.

She stands there. Lucretia and Wilson pass her. They shoot her looks that question and condemn. She cannot meet their eyes and finds herself staring instead up the path they have just walked, back up to the little cemetery at the top of the hill where a wooden marker sits atop a 12-year-old's grave.

"My boy died, too," she says, when they are gone. She says it in a voice both soft and defiant, to no one in particular and to everyone she has ever known. Then she follows Wilson and Lucretia down the hill.

When they get back to the house, they are surprised to find two men waiting for them. One is a Negro in tattered clothes driving a buckboard. The other is a white man sitting astride a magnificent bay horse. He is dressed in the uniform of a Confederate cavalry officer.

Marse Jim hesitates as he approaches, and the woman knows this is because he deserted from the rebel army last year, when he came home to take care of his boy after his final daughter died. He has lived in fear ever since that they would come and take him back. She imagines he wishes he had not left his rifle and pistols next to his bed.

The cavalry man sweeps his hat from his head. "Morning," he says. "Captain Augustus Chambers, late of the Seventh Tennessee Cavalry." He nods toward the Negro. "That's Nick."

Marse Jim has stopped well short of them. "What do you want?" he asks.

"We thought this place might be abandoned."

"Well, it ain't."

"So I see. Well, then, might we trouble you for some water?"

"You might as well know: if you've come to take me back, I'll just run off again, first chance I get."

Chambers is perplexed. "Take you back to what?"

"The army, of course. It wasn't cowardice caused me to leave, neither. It was my boy. After my daughter died, wasn't nobody to take care of him. Of course, he's gone now, I suppose I could go back—love nothing better than to shoot some Yankees for what they done to my place—except there's nobody to watch my niggers. They'll run off soon's I'm gone and I'll lose the last thing I have of value in the whole world. So you see, that's why you can't take me back."

He falls silent abruptly. It is as if the uncharacteristic speech has tired him out.

A sadness steals across Chambers's face. "I am not here to take you back to the army," he says. "There is no army to take you back to."

Now Marse Jim takes a step forward as if into a fight. "What? What in hell's name do you mean?"

"I mean that the war is over, sir. General Lee has surrendered."

"No." Disbelief escapes him in a hoarse gasp. "When did this happen? How?"

The captain dismounts. "I will tell you," he says, "but perhaps you will first be kind enough to allow a thirsty traveler some water?"

"Well's on the other side of the house," says Marse Jim, pointing. "I'll walk with you." He seems to remember them all at once. "You niggers get to work," he snarls.

"Nick, you help them," says the cavalryman.

Without a word, the Negro climbs down. He is very tall—well over six feet—and very lean. He walks with a limp. As the two white men disappear around the side of the house, the three Negroes wrap their hands in rags kept inside an upturned pail for just that purpose and begin pulling charred timbers from the wreckage.

"What happened to you?" Wilson asks.

"Took a ball in the heel," he says. His voice is deeper than any man's the woman has ever heard.

"You were fighting?"

An emphatic shake of the head. "*He* was fightin'. He took me along, said I'se gon' be his body servant to check his wardrobe, fetch his meals and like that."

Wilson laughs. "That's white folks for you," he says. "Even need servants when they go to war. I done heard everything."

The woman is impatient. "Is it true about the war?"

"Near as I can tell, it is. Telegram come in Sunday. Say Marse Bobby Lee give out in some place called Appomattox."

"So it's over?"

"'Pears 'bout. My marse been gloomy for five days, ever since he seen that telegram. I can't hardly read, so I don't know what it say, but I can tell by how he act. And he act like somebody died. They all do. Been on the road with him for three days and they all leavin' they camps and goin' home. Got they heads down, tails between they legs like whipped dogs."

"So what gon' happen to us?" asks Lucretia.

"Us?" says Nick. A shrug. "I guess we's free."

The woman has her shoulder beneath a timber and is grunting to lift it as he says this. Her gaze comes around to him because for some reason, it strikes her as the most absurd thing she has ever heard. She is surprised—no, *horrified*—to hear herself laughing. It starts small, but it grows like fire. She tries to control it, but that only makes it worse. It is hard to breathe. Her knees buckle and she feels the timber slide off her. It falls with a clatter.

Lucretia is appalled. "You better stop that laughing 'fore they hear you."

But now Wilson is infected with it and he is chuckling, too. "Hold on there, Lucretia. You can't tell no free nigger what to do."

At that, the laughter explodes out of her like water through a broken dam and she can't even try to hold it back. She collapses onto a pile of timber because isn't that just the funniest thing in the world, the idea that she, frightened and tired and bent beneath the weight of burnt wood, is free? Soon they are all helpless. Lucretia is the last to go. She keeps trying to protest, but giggles keep breaking through and at the end, she is not resisting anymore, just slapping her knees and leaning on Wilson, who staggers against her in turn.

The woman keeps waiting for it to pass. It feels so good to laugh, but she is distantly aware that laughter is dangerous, that if Marse Jim comes around that corner and finds them like this, there will be hell to pay. But the spell does not pass. She gasps for breath and it strikes her that laughter is a kind of madness.

"I've got to get away from y'all," she says, panting, "before we all get in trouble."

She rises on unsteady legs and walks toward the barn where the mule is tethered. Behind her, she hears them sniffling, struggling to master their laughter. They know the same thing she does: that if Marse Jim comes back and sees this, there's no telling what he might do.

"I'm sorry. I didn't mean to make you laugh."

She is surprised to find Nick at her elbow, following her to the barn. "It just struck me funny is all," she says.

"I suppose it is in a way," he replies. "But in another way, ain't funny at all, is it?"

It takes her a moment to respond. "No," she says, "I guess not."

"What you gon' do, now you's free?"

She doesn't know how to answer the question, so she deflects it. "What *you* gon' do?"

He scratches his chin. "Don't rightly know," he admits. "Marse been talkin' to me 'bout that very thing, but I can't make up my mind. Going home with him now, because that's where my children is. Got a boy and a girl. Their mama dead, ain't nobody but us and I promised when I left I'd be back for 'em. But after I get 'em, don't rightly know what I'm gon' do then. Marse Gus done asked me to stay on, say I can work like I always done and he'll pay me wages. Sound good but I keep thinkin', if I just stay where I always been, how I'm gon' know I'm free?"

They pause before the broken barn wall. "Don't know what to tell you," she says. "Never had such a problem."

"Well, you got it now, don't you? Same as me."

The woman thinks about this a moment. "No," she says, "not the same as you." She tries to imagine just walking away from Marse Jim, declaring herself free and demanding to be paid for her work. "Marse Jim would kill me dead if he thought I was even *thinking* about freedom."

"He can't do that."

A bitter chuckle. "You don't know Marse Jim."

"But all you got to do is get to the federals. They'll protect you."

"That's easy to say. We're way back here in the trees, a long way from any federals. We wouldn't even have known we are supposed to be free if you hadn't come along."

"But you can't just stay here and keep slavin'. Slave times is over."

"For some," she says. She steps through the broken wall.

Something is wrong. The woman knows it the moment she enters the cool darkness. It is a moment before she picks it up: the foul smell, the angry buzzing of the flies. When she gets to its stall, she is not surprised to find the mule lying dead, swollen tongue poking out of its mouth.

No more plowing for old mule. Worked to death. Starved to death. She hears Nick coming up behind her. "The mule's free anyhow," she says.

"That's a purely contrary way of looking at it," he says.

"It's the truth," she replies.

"What's your name, anyway?"

The question gives her pause. She hasn't had much use for a name in the four years since she was brought here by a mistress desperate to sell before everything she had was lost. Before that, well, she had a few names. She thinks about it, then gives him the one she liked the best, the one she used for a few years when she was, if not happy, at least at peace with her lot in life. It was such a long time ago.

"Tilda," she says. "My name is Tilda."

Tilda was coming in from the fields, pulling the burlap sack heavy with cotton. Her hair was gathered under a rag wrapped around her brow, her dress was stained and her expression bore no joy, no love, no hatred, no thing beyond numbness, a fatigue that settled in the cast of her mouth and sucked the very light from her eyes like marrow from the bone.

In this, she was no different from the rest of them, a mirror image of the 12 others who staggered in with her, released at last after 15 hours spent bent over beneath the indifferent sun, extracting cotton fiber from the boll, the hard brown shell of the plant which, if you are not careful—and even if you are—will cut your fingers so bad and so much you can't feel cuts any more.

From can't-see-in-the-morning til can't-see-at-night, this was how they worked. And they might as well be mirror images of one another because what was the difference between them? A name? After a time, you came to know that a name was but a fiction, a thing white folks gave you for their convenience, so they could call the one and not, by mistake, get the other. It allowed the pretense that you were an individual. But they were not individuals. You could see that in the sameness of them now, trudging in from the fields. They were all just pieces of the same evil machine. Just slave niggers.

And yet, if that was so, why did he wait there for her at the edge of the field? Why did his heart hammer and his breath come shallow when he saw her—*her* and not any of the others who looked just like her? Why did he rehearse his words while he waited for her to see him? And why did it all go away when she did see him, when she looked up from her own tired shoes and saw a man standing there, then realized who that man was? Why did he feel his past, his now, his every hope of the future riding on how she would respond? Her mouth opened and he caught his breath and held it tight as he waited to hear what she would say.

And she screamed.

No, not her. She was gone and he was...where was he?

It took a moment. He was not with her. He had not found her. Instead, he was lying in a field in the darkness of night. He had been walking for most of four days, had crossed meadows in the shadow of mountains, ferried across rivers, taken a ride with a friendly Negro farmer in exchange for helping unload his wagon. And it had brought him here to this field in the center of the capital city, this field where cattle slept, pigs rooted about for food, and a fetid and sluggish creek wandered past, emptying into a river. Sam had fallen asleep—how long ago?—lying on a slope in the shadow of a stubby marble structure someone had told him was an unfinished monument to General Washington.

Now the scream came again and he was surprised to realize it had not been part of his dream. And the cry resolved itself into a single word.

"Lincoln!" she cried. "Lincoln!" she moaned. "Oh, Lord, not Lincoln!"

His eyes found her standing in the flickering light of a street lamp. She was old, with skin the color of mahogany, her gray hair bunched beneath a dirty yellow scarf. Her face was awash with tears and she sagged as if her knees would no longer hold.

"They done shot my president!" she cried. "Lincoln dead!"

Sam rose. He trembled with a cold no breeze had imparted. An agonized groan rose from everywhere at once. Someone yelled, "No!"

"What do you mean?" some white man demanded with a white man's impatience. "How do you know this? Goddamn you, speak!"

"I heard it just now from a soldier," she cried. "They done shot the president. They done shot *my* president!"

"Who did it?" The same white man, his voice a bark of command.

"They say it was an actor. Booth."

"Edwin Booth has shot the president?" A laugh that tried to disbelieve.

"No, that weren't the name." The old woman closed her eyes, searching the darkness there for the name of the assassin.

The white man said, "You mean his brother, then? John Wilkes?"

She opened her eyes. "That's the one. Shot the president at the theater. At Ford's."

The white man turned from her without another word, his lips working furiously, no sound issuing forth. Another white man standing next to Sam spat, "That reb son of a bitch. Need to hang every last one of 'em, by God."

When Sam looked toward him, he snarled, "What the hell are you looking at, nigger?"

Sam glanced away.

He did not know what to do with himself, but he knew he could not simply stand there, still, as if nothing had happened. It seemed important to walk. Many in the crowd had already begun to move. Sam joined them. They walked as if drawn by something nameless and inexorable, something that required them to stand in the awful presence of the awful thing, for themselves. Something that required them to bear witness.

All about him, candles were being lit, lamps were being lit, stricken faces were appearing from the darkness of an evening in spring turned suddenly grim as a morning in winter, to ask, "Is it true? Did it happen?" People nodded or said yes. The crowd swelled.

"You a soldier?"

It took Sam a moment to hear the question, a moment more to understand it was meant for him. He turned and found himself walking beside a dark-skinned Negro, maybe a few years older than himself. Sam stood six feet; the other man was a few inches shorter. His face was carved deep with lines, and his scalp was smooth, a landscape unbroken by so much as a single hair.

"I said, you a soldier?"

"Yes," said Sam. "At least, I was."

The man nodded toward the faded Union Army jacket Sam wore. "I thought so," he said. "And you got that soldier's walk," he added. "Straight up, chest out. Need to watch that. That walk get you killed, you ain't careful."

At Sam's questioning look, he gave a tight smile. "I served, too," he said. "Company E, 4th U.S. Colored Infantry. We defended this here city." The tight smile became a grimace, as if he were sucking on something profoundly distasteful, and he added, "Leastways, I thought we did. If what they sayin' about the president is true…" He allowed the thought to

evaporate. After a few moments they turned onto Tenth Street. And the
tiny hope Sam had allowed to live inside him died, gasping.

The street was madness. By the light of a gas lamp in front of the theater
he saw hundreds of people standing about, choking the muddy, rutted road.
Their faces were uniformly stunned. When they moved, they seemed to
stagger, as if walking was somehow new to them. But they did not move
much, other than to clear a path when some soldier or official came bar-
reling through, crying "Give way! Give way!" Otherwise, they stood, their
attention fixed on a narrow house across from the theater.

A Negro woman waited in back of the crowd, her hands pinned beneath
her arms, tears gleaming on her cheeks. Because he did not know what else
to do, Sam approached her. She did not seem to notice, but when he drew
close enough, she spoke without turning. "I seen him," she said. "He look
more dead than alive. They carried him right out the theater." She pointed.
"Right up into that there house."

"It's true, then?"

The question came from the Negro soldier who had walked alongside
him. Sam was surprised the man was still at his elbow. And what a foolish
question. But then, he thought, the man probably just needed to say it out
loud, for himself if for no one else. Saying it helped to make it real. The
woman nodded.

"Is there any hope?" asked Sam.

Now she turned toward him for the very first time. She was young and
she was pretty in a heartbreaking way, her eyes round, and red from crying.
"I seen 'em stop twice," she answered, and her voice was loose and fluttery, "there and there." She pointed toward the middle of the street. "They
reached into his brain and they pulled out the clots of blood."

Sam swallowed.

The other man said, "I need a drink."

A smirk from the woman. "They done closed all the taverns by order of
the government."

"Good thing I carry my own," said the man. A flask was in his hand. He
unscrewed it and took a long pull, then extended it to Sam. Sam hesitated
only a second—he was a man for whom exhibiting correct behavior was
very important, especially in public. And drinking from a stranger's flask in
the middle of a muddy street, well, it was hard to think of any behavior that

was less correct, less reflective of the sort of man Sam considered himself to be, wanted others to see in him.

But the president...

He accepted the flask and threw back a healthy swig. He felt it burn a path to his stomach, where it glowed like embers.

Now he hesitated again, unsure what the etiquette was, whether it was proper to pass the flask on to a lady. She solved his dilemma for him, reaching boldly to take the flask and tip it. She passed it back to him, he passed it back to the other man.

They waited.

Sam had not liked Abraham Lincoln much at first. Lincoln had always struck him as a coarse Westerner, too timid and accommodating on the evil subject of slavery. His famous Emancipation Proclamation had only infuriated Sam. After all, Lincoln had ordered the slaves freed in Southern lands where he had no jurisdiction, but left them untouched in lands where his word was still law. But though he had not liked the president, Sam had come to respect him if only because in the end, he had allowed Sam—and thousands of other former slaves—to go fight for their freedom.

Had someone asked how he felt about the president even a few hours ago, that's all Sam would have said, that he respected the man. But standing here in the muddy ruts of Tenth Street, watching a nondescript brick house, waiting for what, he did not know, was more than respect. The thought that Abraham Lincoln might be dying, might already be dead, made something flap loose in the very bottom of his stomach. It had never occurred to him that you could shoot a president like you could any other man. But apparently, you could. Black was white and up was down and right was left and the president of the United States lay in a nondescript house on a nondescript street, dying of a gunshot wound to his brain. Sam felt again what he had felt standing on the library steps: as if his very life, the whole *country's* life, had become confetti, floating down, and all he could do was wait to see where it would land, what the new order of things would be. Or if, indeed, there would ever be order again.

He waited.

It seemed to him incomprehensible that he had walked and ridden so far, crossed rivers and meadows and woods, only to reach this city on this awful night.

He waited.

"My name is Lucy," said the woman at some point.

"Sam."

"Ben."

She ignored Ben. "You from around here, Sam?"

He shook his head. "I am from Philadelphia."

"Ain't never been there. 'Course, I ain't never been nowhere."

A moment passed. She said, "You just get into town?"

"Yes," he said.

"You got business here?"

He shook his head. "I am just passing through on my way south to Mississippi. "

"I see," she said. It was clear from her tone that she did not.

"I was a slave," explained Sam, "years ago. There was a woman I knew who is still down there."

"You going to find her?"

"Yes."

"Same thing I'm doing," said Ben. "Goin' back to my wife. Her name Hannah. We got us a daughter, too, little baby gal. Ain't seed her in seven years, though, ever since I escaped Tennessee. I guess she ain't a baby no more."

Sam looked at him as if seeing him for the first time. "Long way to go," Lucy said.

"Yes it is," said Ben.

"You got a horse?" the woman asked Sam.

"I am on foot," said Sam.

"Me too," said Ben.

She shook her head. "Long way to go," she said again.

There was a silence. Then she said, "This ain't such a bad place to live, you know. Washington? It ain't so bad."

Sam looked at her. Earnest eyes above tear-stained cheeks. He knew what he was being offered. And he could only guess at the loneliness and fear that motivated it. Especially tonight. "No," he said, "I am sure it is not a bad town at all. But it is not the town I am looking for. That town is in Mississippi."

She met his gaze. She turned away. "Then Mississippi where you need to go," she said.

They waited.

Hundreds of them, they waited. Mostly colored, they waited. The sun rose. The sky was filled with clouds. The day was the color of nickel. It began to rain. They waited.

Sometime around six, the door opened, and an odd-looking white man with a fringe of white beard and goggle eyes stepped onto the porch. He seemed surprised to see the crowd. Sam knew him at once. Father Neptune, the president had called him: Gideon Welles, the secretary of the Navy. He walked through the crowd. They pressed him. "How is the president?" yelled Sam, above the tumult. "Is there any hope?"

He told them there was no hope.

They waited.

Was it an hour later? Two hours later? People began filing out of the house, men and women with glittering eyes and drawn faces. One of the last was Mary Lincoln herself. And as she climbed into a gleaming black carriage, she glared across the street with unmistakable malice at the theater where her husband had been killed.

And the people knew. They knew.

The carriage clattered away. They waited.

A group of soldiers turned onto 10th Street carrying a pine box. And now an anguished moan went up from the crowd. Sam clasped his hand to his mouth. His tears flowed freely. His voice was strangled, guttural, without words.

The soldiers carried the box up the stairs and into the house. Not a proper casket, but just a box, a shipping crate. Moments later, they brought it out again. They strapped it to the back of a horse-drawn wagon. The driver touched the horses lightly with his reins and the wagon began to roll. Soldiers and officers fell in behind the wagon. A crowd, most of them colored, fell in behind that. Lucy walked among them, her head down, crying inconsolably.

Sam took a step, two, as if the carriage were a ship and he was pulled irresistibly in its wake. Then he stopped. He stood watching the tragic procession until it was gone.

"What you suppose they do now?" Sam started. It was as if Ben had read his mind.

"I have no idea," said Sam.

"I pray to God they catch him. Want to see him strung up good."

"I agree with you there," said Sam. He started walking. Suddenly, he wanted nothing so much as to leave the capital city behind. Ben fell into step beside him.

"You say you lookin' for your wife?" he said.

"Yes."

"What her name?"

The question brought a soft smile he had not intended. "Tilda," said Sam. "At least, that's what I called her."

"Must be some kind of woman," said Ben.

"Why do you say that?"

"See it in your face when you say her name."

They stepped around a hog, snuffling and grunting in the mud. "Me, I can't wait to see Hannah and my little baby girl. Leila her name. Prettiest little thing in the world. Wasn't even walking, last time I seed her."

"I hope you find them," said Sam.

"Maybe we might travel together?"

"I beg your pardon?"

"Make sense, don't it? We both goin' the same way, lookin' for the same thing. We maybe might could help each other. Maybe might need each other."

Sam looked at him. "No, I do not think so," he said. "No offense."

Ben nodded. "None taken," he said. Then he said, "How you come to talk like that?"

"What do you mean?"

"You sound like you 'most white."

"I am sure I have no idea what you are referring to," said Sam. "I strive to speak proper English, nothing more."

Ben responded with a smile Sam couldn't read, and Sam was grateful when they parted company at the corner. He walked back the way he had come, head down, lost in reverie. Around him, the city was already wreathed in black bunting and American flags.

"Is it true? Is the president shot?" A white woman, old and stooped beneath her black shawl, intercepted him. Her voice was a whisper. Her eyes shone with the hope he would say no. And with the dread that he would not.

"Yes," he heard himself say. "He died just an hour or two ago."

She began to cry. "What will happen to us now?" she implored. The question wasn't rhetorical. She stared up at him with gleaming eyes. She waited for him. She needed his answer.

"I do not know," he said. He walked on.

All about him people were beseeching one another for news. Women cried. Men did the same.

Someone brandished a newspaper. "It says here he was shot last night. Maybe he is only wounded."

"No," cried another man. "He died this morning."

"Stop saying that!" ordered the first man. "Stop spreading rumor." He pushed the second man, but it was a weak and peevish gesture and the second man did not respond.

"That's what I heard," the second man protested. "I heard that he died."

Sam found it unsettling, this new idea that a president could die, that an entire nation could be left abruptly leaderless, rudderless, like an un-captained ship drifting on mountainous seas. He paused a moment to find himself and realized that without meaning to, he had returned to the field where the unfinished monument to Washington jabbed a stubby finger toward the sun. The White House was just visible through the trees to the north. Sam could only imagine the scene inside.

He wandered south, looking for a bridge to cross the river. "Is it true?" Another woman approached him.

"Yes," he said. He barely slowed.

What would happen now, he wondered. It was Lincoln who had pros-ecuted the war in the face of epic resistance and hardship. With him dead, would the war flare up again? Would the Negro be enslaved again? And if so, was Sam unknowingly walking headlong back into the old life he had found so intolerable, the life where your goings and comings, your very personhood and dreams, were circumscribed by another? He should turn back. Common sense and self-preservation demanded it. He could be back in Philadelphia in a few days, back at work in his beloved library by Thursday, surrounded by books, by knowledge, by the accumulated wisdom of a thousand great men.

He continued south. Tilda pulled at him.

At length, he came to a bridge spanning the Potomac River. The river was broad and placid here, lapping peacefully at the pilings below. Two

Union soldiers watched him approach. "What is your business?" one challenged when he stood before them.

"Nothing," said Sam, surprised. "I am just walking."

"What's your name?"

Sam stiffened. His head came up. "My name is Sam," he said.

"That's all? Sam?"

The soldier—a boy, really, shaggy blonde hair, chin whiskers still wispy—was spoiling for a fight. Sam considered his responses carefully. He thought of saying he was Sam Wilson, after the man who had owned him last, but something in him fumed against the thought. He had a self and it was one he wholly possessed, one that was not tied to a white man who had once considered him his property. Otherwise, what was the purpose of his escape to freedom? What was the purpose of these last four years of slaughter and privation? What was the purpose of the president's murder? He was an individual, not a nameless, interchangeable part of some infernal white man's machine.

So he looked the white boy quite deliberately in the eye. "Free man," he said. He pronounced the syllables separately, distinctly, stopping between them, making them a statement in themselves. "My name is Sam Freeman."

The boy's eyes widened, then hardened. The next thing Sam knew, he was lying on the wooden planks of the bridge, his hand to his bloodied mouth, his eyes flashing light that was not there. Instinctively, Sam reached behind to push himself back up. He stopped when he saw the pistol leveled at him, the boy's hand so tight on the trigger that in some part of his mind, Sam marveled that he was not already dead.

"You sassin' me, nigger?" From somewhere beyond the pistol that filled his vision, the white boy's voice came to him, high and shaky, as if the boy could not suck in enough breath.

All at once, Sam's bladder felt urgent and full. He fought down an urge to let it go. He would not give them the satisfaction of urinating on himself like a baby. What had he said that was sass? What had he said that was anything but true? This was a new day. He was a free man. Did they expect him still to cower? To duck his head and grin like a child? No. He had done enough of that. He had done years of that.

"You asked who I was, sir," he said, and was pleased to hear that his voice was quiet and reasonable and did not shake. "You asked my cognomen. You asked my appellation." Big words the boy soldier would not know.

"I asked your *name!*" the boy thundered, and Sam was distantly grati-
fied by this unwitting confirmation of ignorance.

"And I gave it to you," he said. "My name is Sam Freeman." He spoke
evenly. He did not separate the syllables this time.

"Jakey, what are you doing?" The second soldier, a voice from far away,
attempting to soothe his friend. "Put the gun down!"

"Did you hear him?" Jakey's voice had risen yet higher in indignation.
"That's what it's going to be like from now on, don't you know? You mark
my words. Niggers sassing white men, putting on airs."

Sam ventured to speak. "I was not sassing you, sir."

"You shut up!" The gun hand jerked. Sam flinched instinctively, hands
leaping up of their own accord. It was a moment before he understood that
there had been no shot, that he was still alive.

"This is what Lincoln has loosed upon us, you know," the one called
Jakey was saying. "Niggers will think they're good as white men from now
on. That's what comes from all this. I tell you, Matthew, that's not what I
signed up for. That's not what I fought for."

"Jakey, put the gun down. Come on, now."

The gun came closer. It shook. "You can live with 'em treating you like
there's no difference. I'll be damned if I will."

"Marse?"

A new voice had entered. Sam risked turning ever so slightly to find
the source. His gaze fell upon a dark-skinned Negro who approached cautiously, palms up. It was Ben. He was smiling. His smile was blazing, teeth
dazzling white and every last one on display.

The gun swiveled toward him, returned to Sam. "Who are you? What
the hell do you want?"

Impossibly, the smile broadened. "You ain't want to shoot ol' Shine, sir.
Shine, that's what they calls me. And I was just trying to explain, this boy
here ain't meant no harm. No, sir. See, family he used to belong to, they's
called the Freemans. But they's a white family, you see? Lives down near
N'awlins. He just figure, with the fightin' over, he go down there, see if they
got any work for him. 'Cause he miss the old place, you see. Miss his white
folks. Plumb sorry he ever run off, that's what he told me."

"Is that true?" the boy soldier demanded of Sam.

"'*Course* it true," said Ben. He was next to Sam now, had his hands
under Sam's armpits and was pulling him to his feet. He never stopped talk-

ing, never stopped smiling at the boy soldier. "We was traveling together, in fact, but Sammy here, he walk so fast, he so impatient to be there, he run off and left me. Ain't that right, Sammy?" He smiled up expectantly.

It took Sam a moment. "Yes," he finally managed. "Yes, that is right."

Shine clapped him on the back hard enough to jar his bones. "See? There you go. This weren't nothin' more than a little misunderstandin', is all."

The soldier Jakey regarded them dubiously and for a moment, Sam was sure the lie had not worked. Then the second soldier took over and waved them through. "Go on, get out of here."

"Yes, sir," said Shine promptly. "Thank you, sir." And, clasping Sam's neck as if he were a troublesome child, he steered him past the guard post.

He let his hand fall away a moment later, but the two men did not speak. They walked in silence for long minutes as the bridge fell further behind them. Finally, Sam spoke. "I want to thank you for what you did."

Ben snorted. "You mean, you couldn't get yourself out of it with your 'proper English' and talkin' like you got marbles in your mouth? No, I expect you couldn't. Like to got yourself killed back there, mister *free man*." He drew the syllables out scornfully. "How long you been a nigger anyway, mister *free man*?"

"I have never been that," said Sam, not bothering to hide his scorn.

"You know what I mean," insisted Ben. "You just woke up black this morning for the first time? Only thing I can figure for how you think you gon' look that white boy in the eye and tell him you's a free man."

Sam felt his temper rising. He fought it down. "Well, as I said, thank you."

"Old Abe a blood sacrifice, way I figure. Like Marse Jesus." Sam looked at him, not comprehending. "Jesus, he died for the sins of the world," explained Ben. "This man died for the sins of this country. Ain't fit to waste such a sacrifice on no foolishness."

It was not foolishness, Sam wanted to say. He let it go. "Why did you give him that name, Shine? Why not give him your real name?"

"That one real enough." He chuckled softly. "Ain't you never had to put white folks on? White folks likes a name like Shine, *free man*. Puts 'em at ease."

"It seems to me that a man's name should do more than just put white folks at ease."

This earned him a sly glance. "How you talk, *free man*. You ain't careful, your name gon' get you killed."

They were silent together for a moment. Then Ben glanced up. "So, *free man*, I ask you again: you want to walk along here together for awhile? Like I told you, seem to me, we maybe might need each other."

Sam nodded. "Yes," he said, "maybe you have a point."

And maybe they both were fools. This whispered up from some dark and frightened place in his heart before he could think to tamp it down. It was a ghost of a thought, gone almost before it was there. But it was there. Had been, off and on, ever since he left Philadelphia. More than once, he had thought of Cervantes's Don Quixote de la Mancha, and the mad adventure he'd set off on that existed mostly in his own mind. More than once, Sam had decided to turn back.

But he pushed on. He had no choice, felt himself drawn toward her in some fundamental, mysterious way impossible to understand or resist. He had to see her. He had to know. It was as if he could not go on until he had heard her verdict on his life.

Sam had no idea what that verdict would be. Probably, he thought, she would hate him. And how could he blame her? He was responsible for the death of their son. If he had not been so determined, if he had not been so mule-headed, if he had simply *listened* to her, the boy would be alive to this day—indeed, the boy would be a man, maybe with children of his own—and they might all have been together right up til the emancipation, owned by a mistress who was good enough as mistresses went, who didn't allow beatings and didn't believe in separating families.

And it would have been all right. He could have lived on that. It hadn't seemed so at the time, but now he knew: he could have lived on it.

Instead, he had filled the boy's head with freedom. The boy had listened. And the boy had died.

And now, Sam was going back for the first time since it happened. To say what? That he was sorry, though Lord knew he was? To ask forgiveness? To say he never meant it to happen? To tell her that he never once, not for one moment in all those years, stopped loving her? The Lord knew that all this, too, was true, but what did it matter? What could he say, what words existed, for when he laid eyes on her for the first time after so many years?

None. None at all.

And what words existed for a world that had changed so profoundly as to be unrecognizable in the space of just days? They were free now. *Free*. And yet, if freedom didn't mean you could choose your own name or walk where you wanted without challenge, then what did it mean? If it still required you to smile smiles you did not feel, to duck your head like a bashful boy and to put white folks on, maybe it had no meaning at all.

Just then, Sam and Ben had to jump into the mud by the side of the road to allow a calash to rush by, a well-dressed white man at the reins, chattering amiably with a woman at his side. Shine smiled that smile that made it seem as if a lamp had been lit inside his skull, then touched his forehead in greeting. Sam stared at his new companion in wonder and distaste.

If the white couple noticed either of them, they gave no sign.

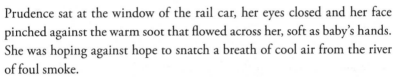

Prudence sat at the window of the rail car, her eyes closed and her face pinched against the warm soot that flowed across her, soft as baby's hands. She was hoping against hope to snatch a breath of cool air from the river of foul smoke.

They had been traveling for two days. She shuddered to think how many depots they had seen, how many trains they had changed. Boston up to Rutland, Vermont, down to Schenectady, New York, crossing into Canada north of Niagara Falls, through the province of Ontario back into the United States at Detroit. Now the farmlands of Indiana rushed by in a blur. Somewhere ahead, Chicago awaited. From there to St. Louis and then by steamship down to Memphis.

Prudence had never traveled across the country before and it was, she found, a perfectly awful experience. Hard seats, overflowing spittoons, dirty boys in and out of the car hawking newspapers, quack medicines, sandwiches, and mushy apples, passengers forced to crowd on and off the train for meal stops that lasted barely 20 minutes. A perfect cacophony.

Or at least, so it had been yesterday.

Today, the president was dead. The news had reached them in Detroit. Lincoln had been shot the night before. He had expired that very morning.

The news had turned the entire train inward. The conductor's stride was softer and less imperial, the dirty boys were sullen, the passengers gazed about with eyes that did not seem to quite see.

She remembered how exasperated Jamie and her father had been with Lincoln when the new president was inaugurated for the first time. His abhorrence of slavery, they agreed, was real enough, but at the same time, he seemed unwilling or unable to act on it. John Cafferty had read the text of Lincoln's inauguration address with his face congealed in a frown before passing the newspaper on to Jamie.

"The man is a ditherer," he complained, "begging the Southern states to turn from this foolish course they have set themselves on, plying them with promises to leave slavery alone if they would just consent to remain with the Union. The time for pleading with those people is over. Why not simply blockade their harbors, lay siege to their cities, stand up for right and do the Lord's work without fear or compromise?"

"He is not much," Jamie had agreed, "but he is all we have."

Like Jamie, her father had not lived to see the end of the war. But he had seen enough. And through years of horrifying headlines, years of watching young men ground up and spat out by the thousands in places like Chickamauga, Antietam, Cold Harbor and, of course, Gettysburg, her father's opinion of the president had changed, skepticism yielding to a grudging respect. "I cannot begin to imagine the pressures on that man," she had heard him say once over dinner the day casualty reports came in from a battle in a place called Shiloh. "Twenty-three thousand men," he said. "My God."

The man across from him, a shipbuilder, had barked a laugh of surprise. "Well, that is a change," he had said. "Words of sympathy for Lincoln? From you? It wasn't so long ago, John, you were complaining that the president was a timid mouse frightened of his own shadow. You said he lacked the necessary resolve."

Father had fixed his friend with a grave expression. "I have learned better," he said simply. "The president does move slowly and in his own time. But when he moves, by God he moves."

And now he was gone. That poor, homely man, she thought. What would the country do without him?

"You're thinking about Lincoln," said Bonnie, reading her thoughts. Somehow, she had always been able to do that.

Prudence nodded. "Yes," she said.

Bonnie closed her eyes and began to recite in a soft voice. "'Fondly do we hope, fervently do we pray, that this mighty scourge of war may speedily pass away. Yet, if God wills that it continue until all the wealth piled by the bondsman's 250 years of unrequited toil shall be sunk, and until every drop of blood drawn with the lash shall be paid by another drawn with the sword, as was said 3,000 years ago, so still it must be said 'the judgments of the Lord are true and righteous altogether.'"

Bonnie's eyes came open. "When he spoke those words at the inaugural last month, I wonder if he could have known some of that blood would be his."

Prudence was about to reply when she became aware of a woman across the aisle staring in open-mouthed fascination. Caught, the woman colored, touched her chest and began to stammer. "I do apologize," she said, speaking up to be heard over the clatter of the rails, "but your girl is so bright. I don't know many *white* people who could memorize and recite so well."

Automatically, Prudence stiffened in anger. "She is not—"

She stopped when Bonnie grabbed her hand, squeezing it tightly enough to hurt. "Miss Prudence," she said sweetly, very sweetly, "we talked about this."

And so they had. Bonnie had vowed to catch the first train back to Boston if Prudence did not curb her sharp tongue. Bonnie had insisted that while they traveled, she would present herself as Prudence's handmaiden. Her "girl." It was, she had said, the only way to travel together unmolested. So Prudence gritted her teeth and tried to pass it off as a smile. "Yes," she said, "my girl is very bright."

The woman's nod was dubious. The moment she turned away, Prudence snatched her hand back and massaged it angrily. "I suppose I should be grateful you did not break a bone in my hand," she said.

"No, you should be grateful if I don't break a bone in your *neck*," hissed Bonnie. "I told you how it would be, did I not? I warned you, did I not? We are not even in the South yet, and already you forget."

Prudence's only response was a grudging sigh.

"If this mission is to have any chance of success, Miss Prudence, you must learn to hold that temper of yours in check. We are a very long way from Beacon Hill. Nobody out here knows you, they do not know who your father was. And they will not tolerate your...eccentricities."

"But Miss Bonnie—"

"No." Bonnie shook her head and her voice was firm. "I am just Bonnie."

Prudence folded her arms. "Fine, then," she said.

A silence intervened between them. In it, people read their papers, a boy walked through hawking an elixir guaranteed to cure miasmas and low spirits, and a girl three seats behind them yelped as a cinder found her neck. Prudence felt a touch on her arm and looked over.

"I am not ungrateful," Bonnie said, "and I apologize if that is the way I sound. I *am* grateful to you, to your father, even to that old Negro furniture maker. Without him, your life—and thus, my life—would have been dramatically different. But what I am trying to remind you is that most of the country does not feel as you do. If this mission of ours is to have any hope of success, you must understand that. And you must take care that you do not underestimate the amount of bitterness and anger we will encounter where we are going."

"You need have no fear on that score," said Prudence.

Bonnie studied her. "Are you certain?"

"Yes," said Prudence.

"And you agree with me that we must do nothing to unduly antagonize the people we encounter."

"Yes," said Prudence. And when Bonnie didn't turn immediately away, she repeated it. "Yes," she said. "I assure you, I understand."

Bonnie watched her a moment more, saying nothing. At length, she leaned back upon the seat and closed her eyes.

They reached Chicago that afternoon. The city was wreathed in black bunting and American flags and its people all bore the same expressions of heartbreak and disbelief. The next train wasn't until morning. Prudence hired a wagon to transport them and their bags to a nearby hotel. She secured a room for the two of them, but when they came down for dinner, the hotel manager insisted Bonnie would have to eat in the servants' quarters.

"She will do no such thing," said Prudence. "She will eat with me in the dining room."

"Madam, we have our policies," said the manager, smiling, hands pressed together, bowing slightly.

"Devil take your policies," said Prudence.

The words made Bonnie lower her head, unseen by Prudence or the manager. It was as if their conversation this very day had never happened, as if she had not explained to Prudence patiently and lovingly why she must govern her temper and hold her impulsive nature in check, as if Prudence had never nodded and said she understood. "*I assure you,*" she had said.

But then, thought Bonnie, although temper and impulse loomed large in her best friend's character, they were not the only traits that defined her.

No, when you got down to it, Prudence Cafferty Kent was simply stubborn, the most mulish, headstrong person Bonnie had ever known. When her dander was up, everything else was forgotten and she became the immovable object daring the irresistible force to budge her. Obstinacy had served her well for a lifetime in Boston. Of course, everyone in Boston knew her or knew her father and it had become something of a joke, in her circle at least, for people to indulge the willful young woman with the eccentric behavior.

But what Prudence didn't understand, or *refused* to understand, was that they were no longer in her circle, no longer in Boston. They were in a far place with many miles yet to go.

The manager straightened and his smile went away. "I beg your pardon?" he said, regarding Prudence balefully.

They were still arguing when Bonnie walked away. She was halfway across the room when she heard Prudence call her name. She didn't stop.

"Bonnie!" called Prudence, louder this time. "Where are you going?"

And now she did stop, half turning toward an expression she knew all too well—lightning flashing in Prudence's eyes, righteousness tightening the line of her mouth, caught right in the middle of her favorite pastime, scolding someone who had been foolish enough to make her angry. Bonnie felt her shoulders slump. She was miserably aware that the room had gone still, that forks were paused in midflight, that waiters had frozen with plates halfway to tables, that every eye in the dining room was upon her and Prudence and the bizarre tableau now unfolding.

"I told you, didn't I," she said. "Did I not tell you?"

"Bonnie, this is only a trifle. This man just needs—"

"Just leave me alone, please," Bonnie heard herself say.

The face softened. "Bonnie." It was an entreaty, all the weight of all their years together behind that single word.

"*Please*," repeated Bonnie and that, too, was an entreaty. "Just leave me be."

"But where will you go? What will you do?"

Bonnie didn't answer. She walked away, listening for Prudence's steps behind her as she did. But to Bonnie's relief, Prudence did not follow. Bonnie walked out of the hotel alone and into the unknown streets.

For a time, she moved through the city without knowing herself, without seeing where she was going—the going itself being the entire point. Carriages and streetcars clattered past, chattering crowds parted around her, paperboys yelled of Mr. Lincoln's death.

Time passed. She did not know how much. But eventually, she found herself standing at the entrance to the train depot, hands clasped before her, gazing up at the sign over the door, trying to decide. So focused was she upon her own thoughts that it was a moment before Bonnie realized she was being watched. He was a small, gray-haired colored man in a porter's uniform and he leaned against the wall, smoking a pipe and regarding her with frank curiosity. She approached him on impulse. "I beg your pardon," she said, and she almost had to yell to make herself heard above the clatter of a train pulling into the yard on the other side of the building. "Would you kindly tell me when the next train might depart for Boston?"

"You got to connect through Detroit," he yelled back in a thin, tart voice. "But won't be no train out for Detroit til tomorrow."

"I see," she said. She thought for a moment, then said, "Well, can you tell me where a colored woman might go for a meal and perhaps a bed to sleep in?"

The face turned kindly. "Ain't too many of us here, tell you the truth. But I know a widow lady, a Negro, never turn a hungry traveler away. Come on with me. I'm goin' that way myself."

By the time Prudence lay down in the bed and pulled the covers up, her anger had burned itself down to simple sorrow. Bonnie was her closest friend. The thought of losing her was too much to bear. Prudence had no idea how she would go on without her. She feared being so truly alone in the alien place she was going to.

Why was Bonnie so stubborn? Why had she made such a scene over a trifling matter that could be swiftly resolved?

Where is she?

This last thought echoed in her. Chicago was a big, unknown city and doubtless contained more than its fair share of reprobates and malefactors. God grant that Bonnie would be safe among them.

It took her a long time to fall asleep.

She awoke with the light of the new day, heart fluttering with a hope that was promptly crushed. Bonnie had not come in during the night.

Prudence considered this for a moment. But what could she do? What choice did she have? She would have to press on alone. She settled her bill at the hotel and found a taxi back to the train station. The driver drove his horse at a crisp pace down busy streets Prudence did not see. She was busy telling herself that she absolutely would not worry about Bonnie. If Bonnie had chosen to abandon her like this, so be it. If Bonnie was truly determined to return to Boston, she had the funds to do so. Prudence was equally determined to carry on her father's wishes.

But she would miss her dearest friend. Truth to tell, her only friend.

And even as she sat on the train waiting to get underway, Prudence scanned the bodies moving back and forth on the platform for any sign of her. She would be easy to spot if she were there. Bonnie was a tall woman, her eyes clear and direct, her bearing straight—except, now that Prudence thought of it, for when she had stood there last night before that horse's ass of a hotel manager. Then Bonnie had playacted, allowing her gaze to cloud over and then diverting it altogether, standing stooped with her head down. It was as if she had become—had made herself become—someone else entirely.

Prudence was puzzling over that when she felt weight settle on the seat next to her. She turned gratefully to greet Bonnie. Instead, she found herself being admired, rather frankly, by a man twice her age at the very least. His sideburns were fashionably long and shiny with oil and he was chewing a wad of tobacco that made one cheek bulge like a tumor. He doffed his derby and gave her a smile that revealed brown teeth.

"Traveling alone, are we?"

Prudence sighed. She smoothed her skirt—it was long and straight, as she refused to wear the monstrous crinolines that took up so much space and made it almost impossible to move about. Then she adjusted her cornette and retied it carefully beneath her chin. The man grew impatient. "Didn't you hear me, miss?" he asked, and his voice was oilier than his hair. "I said, 'We're traveling alone, are we?'"

Finally, Prudence looked at him. The brown smile widened in anticipation. She said, "I know not how 'we' are traveling, sir. I know how I am traveling, but I fail to understand why that would be any concern of yours."

Now his smile shrank down to almost nothing, only to be reborn as a little smirk. "I see you're a real spitfire," he said. "But that's all right with me. I like a girl with spirit."

He patted her hand as he said it. She pulled away and he laughed. Prudence sighed. There were always some who were more difficult than others. Always some who refused to get the message.

He replaced the derby. "Name's Logan, honey. Marcus Aurelius Logan from New York City. I'm a manufacturer. Going down to Dixie to make my fortune. Lot of money down there right now for a man knows where to look. How about you? What are you going down for?"

She pinned him with a look. "Again," she said, "I fail to understand why my plans should be any concern of yours."

And now the smile died altogether, replaced by a hard look such as you might give a cur that has bitten you after you have fed it. "I'm just trying to be sociable with you," he said. "Pass the time of day. But it appears to me you're in dire need of someone to teach you some manners."

Prudence smiled sweetly. "And would that person be you?"

He returned the smile, scooted closer. "It just might be, if you play your cards right."

"Thank you for the offer," she said, "but I would sooner leap from a bridge and dash my brains out on the rocks below."

His fleshy face went cold and dark. He leaned in close. His breath was a sour mix of tobacco and mash, his voice became a guttural whisper. "Look, you highfalutin' New England bitch, I tried to be nice to you, but I'll be damned if I'm going to let some skinny strumpet talk to me like...like..."

He paused in confusion, looking down to discover what it was that was pressing into his left testicle. Prudence had produced a derringer and was holding the barrel against him.

Marcus Aurelius Logan looked up, forcing a smile. "You really think you can hurt me with that toy gun, honey?"

Prudence gave him another sweet smile. "It is small," she admitted, "but I believe it is positioned where it can do the most good."

"You wouldn't," he said. "You don't have the nerve."

"I suppose there is but one way to find out," she told him.

She held his gaze. He blinked, blinked again, then finally pulled back. Watching her warily, he stood up, announcing loudly, "I'm certain I can find more congenial company elsewhere." She watched him exit the car, his gait stiff-legged and quick. Only when the door had closed behind him did she replace the weapon in her bag.

Prudence was startled by the sound of hands clapping. She looked across the aisle and saw a small young woman with dark eyes applauding her. Prudence nodded acknowledgment. The other woman glanced at the man next to her. His head was back, his mouth had fallen open, and he had shoved his hat down over his eyes. She stood, hiked up the hem of her crinoline, and stepped past him and across the aisle. The woman landed heavily next to Prudence, her hems rustling. "I was about to wake up Stephen—that's my husband, over there—and send him to your aid. But then I saw you had the situation well in hand. Bravo." She clapped again.

Prudence felt herself blushing. "That was nothing," she said. "He just needed persuading."

"Nothing? Don't underestimate yourself, my dear. It is not every member of our sex who would have the courage to travel alone—or the presence of mind to know how to handle threats to her virtue. I salute you." She stuck out her hand. "I'm Dolly," she said.

Prudence spoke her own name as she took the proffered hand. "I hope you'll forgive me for imposing myself on you," said Dolly, "but Stephen is hardly the most amusing company. And you are, as I said, traveling alone."

"I did not start out that way," said Prudence. "I started out with a companion. But we became separated last night. In fact, I was just looking for her when the gentleman sat down."

"Her?" The woman seemed confused.

"A friend," said Prudence.

"I see," said the woman, though her expression suggested clearly she did not. The notion of two women traveling together seemed to strike her as even more outlandish than one. At length, she said, "Stephen and I are going to St. Louis. His father owns a meat-packing company there. He has promised to give Stephen a stake to start his own business. May I ask where you are going?"

"To Mississippi," said Prudence. "I was told it was impossible to take the train down there because the war has left the tracks in disrepair, so we—that is, I—will go to St. Louis and arrange passage on a steamboat."

As she spoke, there came the clatter of bells. She heard the conductor yell, "Booooard!" And then the train began to move slowly forward. The finality of it settled over her like a mourning shroud. So that was that. Bonnie was going back. She was going forward. It stung.

"To Mississippi?" The woman pronounced the word as if she had never heard it before. "What on earth for?"

"I am going to open a school for the freed Negroes."

Dolly regarded her with an expression Prudence could not read. "That is rather…bold of you, my dear. To be a woman traveling alone—or even with another woman, which is essentially the same thing—on such an enterprise, is commendable and all, but I doubt the Southerners will greet you with open arms. To tell you the truth, I'm surprised your husband is allowing you to go."

"My husband is dead," said Prudence. "He died at Gettysburg. But he would have approved. In fact, he would have expected it of me."

"Oh?" said the other woman, arching an eyebrow. "So, your husband would have expected his wife to travel alone into hostile territory to do a thing that can only inflame the local population?"

"Why not?" said Prudence. "After all, that is exactly what Moses did. Except, of course, that Moses was not a woman."

"Moses had God on his side," Dolly reminded her.

"I believe I do as well," said Prudence.

"With all due respect, dear, we must serve different gods."

Prudence said, "I would not be at all surprised if that were true."

This earned her a withering glance. There was a silence. Then Dolly said, too brightly, "Well, I suppose I should be returning to my seat."

"It was good talking to you, dear," said Prudence as the other woman stood and made her way cautiously across the aisle.

Alone again at last, Prudence folded her arms across her bosom and closed her eyes. She supposed she would have to get used to people like Dolly—and much worse. Dolly was only a busybody constrained by conventional ideas. The people she would encounter as she traveled south would be desperately poor, their farms burned, their cities leveled, their livelihoods gone. And they would be embittered, having discovered that all their hubris, all their daring and all their élan were insufficient proof against the superiority of Yankee steel, Yankee determination, and Yankee numbers. Bonnie was right about one thing: There would be hostility. She must anticipate that.

Then she corrected herself. There would be hostility from *some*. The newly freed slaves, she imagined, would welcome her mission with gratitude, would crowd into her school, eager for the education she could bestow. And that would be enough. With that, she could validate what Jamie and her father expected of her.

And then again, she felt weight settling on the seat next to her. Apparently, the man was a slow learner. Prudence reached for her derringer even as she opened her eyes. But it wasn't Marcus Aurelius Logan who sat next to her. It was Bonnie.

Prudence couldn't help smiling. "I thought you had left me," she said.

"I should have," said Bonnie. "If I had any sense, I would have. But I owe your father more than that."

"I was worried about you. Where did you go?"

"I found lodging with a Negro woman, a widow who lives near the river."

Across the aisle, Dolly cleared her throat loudly. "Excuse me," she said, and there was confusion in her eyes, "but is that the 'friend' you were referring to?"

Prudence regarded Bonnie for the briefest moment. Then she gave the other woman the sweetest smile she could muster. "No," she said, "of course not. This is just my girl."

Free? The word rattles in her thoughts, untethered, unattached, uncon-nected to any thing she has ever known or lived before.

Free?

It comes upon her at the oddest times. Using the necessary, fixing a meal, strewing cottonseed along a row.

Free?

It had seemed a thing too ridiculous and large to take seriously at first, a thing so outlandish that the only proper response was to laugh. But that was three days ago. The men who brought the troubling word with them, the tall colored man Nick and the white man who used to own him, have long since moved on. And Tilda is not laughing anymore. Suddenly, that word is all she can think about.

She finds herself trying to imagine it, define it, comprehend what it might mean.

Wilson and Lucretia struggle with it, too. Sometimes, during the day, her gaze will catch his or hers and the silent understanding will pass be-tween them and they will know they were both thinking the same thing just then: *Freedom. What does freedom mean?*

At night, with Marse Jim lying in the next cabin snoring loud enough to silence the crickets, they have talked about it, tried to decide what to do with it. Lucretia and Wilson are sweet on each other, have been since they were children, and Tilda can tell they are intoxicated with the prospect of going somewhere, finding someplace where they can be together, alone, and never again answer to any master's order, any master's bell, any thing in the world but their own desires and needs. Eve and Adam back in the garden, that's what they want to be.

Tilda is older. She knows better than they how life can work, how cruelly and capriciously it can treat your hopes, your wants and your innocence, until you come to realize that it is better not to have those things anymore, better to leave them behind you, because all they do is get you hurt. She is not sweet on anyone. She cannot even remember how that feels.

Standing there in the doorway of the barn, the man, Nick, had touched her arm. "What you gon' do, Tilda, now you free?"

"I'm gon' clear timber for Marse Jim," she said.

"But you free now," he said.

She gave him a look. Let him see in her eyes what she thought of fancy men spouting nonsense.

"You don't believe it?" he said.

"I believe what I can see right in front of me," she told him. "And right in front of me, there's burnt wood Marse Jim says he wants me to clear."

"You could come away with me," he said.

"I don't even know you," she said.

"Ain't much to know. I could make you happy. Shucks, I could make you love me."

He grinned at her. Tilda had time to wonder what this man was sniffing around her for, tired as she was, ruined as she was. She shook her head. "I don't think so," she said.

To her surprise, he flashed her another smile. "I ain't done with you yet, Miss Tilda," he said. "I'll be back. Ain't gon' stop tryin'."

She shrugged. "Love is long suffering," she said. "Says that in the Bible."

His eyes tightened with confusion and she could tell he was about to ask her what that meant. Then she heard the rumble of Marse Jim's voice in the yard and went to tell him the mule was dead. And that ended all talk of freedom.

She is careful about that dangerous word, wary of it, the way you would be of a snake in the garden or a rat cornered in the shed. Still, she is intrigued—she can't help it—and when they talk about it, the three of them whispering together in the darkness of the cabin, she can't stop herself from imagining how it would feel simply to walk away from here and find some place wholly her own, where she might make her own orders, set her own priorities, belong only to her own self.

But always, the soft fantasy of it runs up against the hard reality of the slouch-bellied, sour-breathed white man who owns her—owns her even though, if Nick is correct, nobody owns anybody anymore. Tell that to Marse Jim with his flinty eyes and his guns always near at hand, Marse Jim who heard what the reb officer had to say and then went right back to ordering them to go here and do this and fetch that, just like always, just like nothing at all has changed.

And maybe nothing has.

They are still colored, after all. Nobody has freed them from that.

For her, that decides it. Freedom is just a word. Oh, it sounds good. Sounds fine. But still, no more than a word, carries no more weight than that. It is a dreamy flight of fantasy. And she has no time for that. She has to live on the hard shores of reality. She has to *live.*

It surprises her some that she clings so fiercely to living after all that has happened, after all the reasons she has been given to loosen her grip. But there it is. Living is a hard lot. But, she supposes, it still beats the alternative.

"We's done decided."

This is Wilson, a disembodied voice in the darkness of the cabin, one night around midnight.

"Decided what?" she asks, although she already knows. It is six days now since the dangerous word was first spoken.

"Decided we's gon' be free."

"Oh?" She lies on the narrow corn shucks mattress that might as well be ground for all the comfort it gives.

"Yes," says Wilson, and from his voice, he is sitting up in the corner.

"Leaving tonight," says Lucretia, and she is at his side.

"Ain't no moon tonight," says Wilson.

Tilda's heart jumps. So soon? To make the decision, announce it, and then act on it all at once? Is that what freedom is? Just an excuse to be rash and reckless? "Marse will kill you," she says. "He will catch you and he will kill you, sure as you're sitting there. You know that."

"Don't know nothin' of the sort," says Wilson. "He ain't but a man, same as me."

"He's a man with a gun," says Tilda. "That is not the same as you."

Wilson does not answer. After a beat, Lucretia pipes up, her voice tremulous. "We wanted you to come with us."

"She won't come," says Wilson. "She scared."

The contempt in his voice amuses Tilda. "Yes, I'm scared. You would be, too, if you had any sense."

"You mean, if we was old like you?"

"*Wilson!*" Lucretia is scandalized.

"What? It's true, ain't it?"

Before Lucretia can answer, Tilda does. "It is true," she says. Well over forty years lie behind her. If that isn't old, what is? She is old, all right. Old enough that she cannot remember when she was ever as young as these two foolish children speaking to her out of the dark.

"I told you this was a waste of time," Wilson says. His voice is bitter with reproach.

"Tilda, you don't want to be free?" Lucretia sounds like a child. Innocent. Uncomprehending. Too young to know what happens when fantasies collide with realities.

"No," says Tilda. "Marse will never allow it."

"Waste of time," repeats Wilson. Tilda has the impression he is pulling on Lucretia.

"All right," Lucretia says. "All right."

For a few minutes, the only sound Tilda hears is the two of them moving about, gathering their few meager things, she supposes. Then the door creaks open. The cold enters.

"You sure you won't come?" There is a hopeful note in Lucretia's voice that could break your heart if you let it.

Wilson cuts off any reply. "We got to go," he says. And then, to Tilda: "You ain't gon' wake that man up soon's we gone, is you?"

"How am I going to do that?" asks Tilda. "You didn't tell me your plans and you slipped out of here while I was sleeping."

He gives a grunt of satisfaction. The door closes.

She listens as their footfalls fade. She thinks of praying for them, the way she used to pray for everything. In the end, she doesn't. She doesn't want the prayer to fail, doesn't need a new reason to be angry with God.

Tilda cannot even imagine taking the risk Wilson and Lucretia are, cannot imagine being so young, so in love, that crossing Marse Jim begins to seem a sensible idea. She cannot sleep. She doesn't even try. She simply waits. When the sun burns darkness from the sky, she rises with a soft grunt, wraps the thin sheet around herself and goes outside. She builds a fire. Tilda uses the last of the cornmeal to make corncakes. She makes four of them, like always.

After a while, Marse Jim stumbles out of the cabin. He staggers off without a word to use the privy, returns, and draws up short. "Where are they?" he asks.

Tilda, sitting at the fire eating the last of her corncake, shrugs. "I don't know. I haven't seen them this morning."

He grabs her arm, yanks her to her feet. "Don't lie to me," he says.

"I'm not lying," she says.

He punches her in the face. She sees lightning, crumples to the ground, hands covering her bleeding mouth. The bad tooth in the back falls into her throat and she chokes on it. She is on her knees desperately harking at the tooth as he stalks off. She hears him inside the cabin, muttering angrily to himself. "Think I'm a fool? Think I'm a fool?"

Tilda spits out her tooth as Marse Jim steps out of the cabin. He has the slouch hat pushed down on his head, two pistols wedged crosswise in his belt, the Sharps carbine in hand. She is still on the ground. She is afraid he is going to shoot her. He doesn't look her way. "Been expecting this," he says, cracking open the breech on the carbine, dropping a cartridge in. "Ever since them two came through here the other day talking about nigger freedom, I been expecting this." He is speaking to himself. He is speaking to the morning.

"Marse?" She has clambered to her feet. Her bones ache. "What are you going to do?"

"Goin' after them, of course." Bending down, he grabs up the three remaining corncakes from the shovel blade she cooked them on, slips them into his pocket. "Come on."

"What do you mean, Marse?"

"You don't think I'd leave you here by yourself, do you? You'd run away just like they done."

"Oh no, Marse. I'll be right here waiting on you when you return."

"I'm not a fool," he says. "Man comes through here sayin' the federals have won, you think that means I'm supposed to just give up my property without a fight? Well, I don't know if the federals won or not. Lot of rumors go round in wartime and most of 'em's bullshit. But this much I can promise you: I ain't gon' just stand by and lose what's mine."

She has never heard him give a longer speech—or bother explaining himself at all, for that matter—to a Negro. Might as well explain yourself to the dead mule, that's how he thinks. He motions with the rifle barrel. "Let's go," he says. She knows better than to say another word. Her jaw aches where he hit her. She leads him out to the main road. The footprints are fresh and clear in the soft soil. She is glad she didn't pray.

How many hours ago did they leave? Six? Maybe seven? Is there a town six or seven hours from here? Some bustling place Wilson and Lucretia can lose themselves and hide out from Marse Jim? Otherwise, they have not a chance. He will find them and he will beat them without mercy before he drags them back.

They walk a footpath through a forest of loblolly pines. After an hour, it carries them out to a main road rutted by wagon wheels and pitted with footprints. She has not been this far from the main house since the day she was brought here, years ago. She allows herself to hope Marse will lose the trail on a busier road, but he does not hesitate even an instant, trudging forward with his head down, reading the road, muttering to himself occasionally. "I see you," he whispers to the road. "I see you there." She believes he does see them. He is like some implacable thing, immune to the doubts and needs that might slow other men, less determined men. He just keeps on going.

She wonders if he was like that in the war, moving forward no matter what was exploding around him. Or did he hunker behind breastworks, did he tremble and wet his pants when the order came to advance across some field toward some copse of trees thick with Yankees? She does not think so. She cannot imagine him trembling or unsure.

Not a word passes between them. The first hour becomes the second, becomes the third. When the sun stands high in the sky, he stops at a freshwater pond, sits on a fallen tree and produces the corncakes from his pocket. He eats one, places the other two beside him.

Tilda is so hungry her stomach is on a first name basis with her backbone. He has not said she can have one of the corncakes, but he has not said she can't, either. She gathers herself and takes the risk, walks up to where he is sitting and picks one up. She has to eat, doesn't she? She deserves to, doesn't she, traipsing about out here God knows where?

He doesn't so much as look her way. But as she is walking off with her prize he says, "You didn't go with them." Not a question.

She calculates quickly, decides it is safest to stay with the lie. "Didn't know they was gone, Marse," she says. "They slipped out without telling me."

He grunts in response. After a moment he adds, "You were smart."

It chills her. She waits, but he doesn't say more. Instead, he finishes the corncake, cups his hand to the pond and takes a drink, then starts off without a word. She takes a drink, then follows him.

After two hours, they reach a town. This is Buford. She remembers this place. She was auctioned here, sold off by a woman who had always claimed she didn't believe in selling her people. She always called them that—her people, not her slaves or her niggers. Of course, she reconsidered her refusal to sell when money grew tight. Suddenly everything was open to negotiation. So it was that Tilda had wound up the property of this shambling trash-heap of a man, had gone from a place where she was allowed, once chores were done, to sit with a book and read, to a place where chores were never done and there was not a single book in the house.

Marse finds his way unerringly to a tavern, tells her to wait for him outside. "Don't you get any ideas," he says, index finger pointing in her face.

She swallows. "I won't," she says.

She doesn't.

For two hours she sits out there, listening to the clink of glasses, the braying laughter of white men. It turns cold, begins to rain. She huddles beneath the awning, watches white and colored come and go. A group of federal troops wanders by, laughing at some joke between them. They stand taller, straighter, than any men she has ever seen and she has to fight down an urge to run to them, tell them everything, beg them to take care of her. But what if they send her away? What if freedom is only a lie? Then she would have only committed suicide, wouldn't she?

As if in answer to the unvoiced question, the tavern door swings open and Marse comes through, swaying like a tree in a storm. "There they go," he says, staring after the departing federals. His voice is thick and mushy like porridge. "There they go, the rascals who killed my boy."

His voice rises on the last words and for a crazy moment, she is afraid he is about to raise his rifle and shoot one of the federals in the back. Instead, he watches after them with his filmy eyes until they are gone. Then he shakes his head and steps down from the porch without a word. Tilda follows.

The rain has turned the street to mud. Tilda thinks it will be impossible for Marse to trail them now. She is wrong. Even though he totters like a baby on new legs, he still does not hesitate. They walk for hours. The rain stops. She builds a fire. He goes out with his rifle, hunting dinner. Running doesn't even cross her mind. At length he returns, a rabbit's bloody carcass hanging by the ears from his fist. He hands it to her without a word, followed by a knife, settles himself against a tree, and closes his eyes.

She takes up the knife and goes to work skinning the hare. After a moment, Marse Jim begins to snore. The sound draws her and she pauses in her work to look. His chest rises and falls with a steady rhythm and she marvels that he can hand her a knife and then fall asleep, as if it has never even crossed his mind that she might bury the blade in that heaving chest all the way to its hilt. Then she realizes: the thought has not crossed her mind either, has it? Not a flicker of temptation, not an instant of inducement. Nothing. And he knew this about her, didn't he? Knew it before she did. This is why he could give her a knife, then go to sleep.

She returns to her work, hands working with a brisk, mindless efficiency, lopping off the head, cutting sinew, separating fur from flesh. She is angry with herself, embarrassed by herself. When did she become so old? So old and riven with fear? She knows she has not always been this way, but she cannot recall when she was something other, cannot even remember what it must have been like.

Marse wakes to the sizzle of fat dropping into the flames. When the food is done, she hands him the makeshift spit. Without a word, he pries off a large piece of meat. She eats what remains. They sleep that night on the dirt.

The next morning, they come upon Wilson and Lucretia. They are sleeping in a clearing, curled together against the cold. Marse Jim raises his rifle. Tilda follows. Her throat is stiff like parchment. Her stomach is a rock. Wilson and Lucretia begin to stir at the sound of Marse Jim's approach, slowly at first, then all at once as realization arrives like a thunderclap.

Wilson taps Lucretia's shoulder. "Marse Jim," he says, and there is gravity in his voice, none of the false cheer he usually uses to put white people at their ease.

"Think you can run out on me?" Marse Jim growls from behind the rifle.

Wilson says, "Marse, we is free now." He is coming to his feet as he speaks. He never gets there. The rifle barks and the blast hurls him against a tree. He does not move.

Tilda does not realize she is screaming until the white man slaps her. "Shut up, goddamn you!"

He has thrown the rifle down, pulled a pistol from his belt and trains it now on Lucretia. She is shrieking, crouched over the bloody dead thing that was her Wilson less than a minute ago.

"Marse, don't!" cries Tilda.

He does not acknowledge her. They stand frozen in that blood-stained tableau for a long moment, until finally Lucretia turns on Marse Jim. The hatred glares from her eyes with a force that is almost physical. "You ain't had to do that," she says. Her voice is scalding.

"Think you can run out on me?" he repeats.

She stands with deliberate slowness. "We's *free* now," she says. "You heard it same as we did."

"Yankee lies."

"How you talk? Wasn't no Yankee told you that. Was a reb, one of your own kind."

"Yankee *lies*," he insists. "How are they goin' to free *my* niggers? How are they goin' to take from me something I paid good money for, something I bought fair and legal? I *own* you."

"Don't nobody own nobody no more. That's the law now."

'You think I won't kill you, just because you're a woman?"

"You can kill me," she says, and her voice is level, "but you can't kill the truth. We is *free* now."

His mouth works soundlessly. Then he shoots her. She looks down at the red hole blossoming in her stomach, then back up at him. She seems surprised. Her gaze falls on Tilda and there's something else there. To Tilda's horror, it is accusation. And then, close on that, pity. Lucretia's legs give way and she crumples. Her eyes are still on Tilda. And then, they are on nothing.

"You didn't have to shoot them," Tilda hears herself say.

He brings the gun around. "Are you next?" he says. "Are you plannin' to run out on me, too?"

It takes her a moment. Finally she says, "I'm just saying you didn't have to shoot them, that's all." She resists an urge to squeeze her eyes shut against the coming muzzle flash.

It doesn't come. He stares at her a long time. A very long time. Then he lowers the gun. "We're goin'," he says. He stoops to recover the rifle.

"We're not going to bury them?" She is appalled that they will go to eternity with no one to speak words on their behalf.

"We're goin'," he repeats.

Still she does not move. "There was too much work on that place for four people," she says. "How are we supposed to manage it with two?"

"We're not goin' back there," he says, walking away from her.

"What?"

"We're goin' west," he says. "Someplace new. I will not live in a country dominated by the Yankee race." He is already halfway across the clearing.

She stands there for a long moment after he has disappeared, wrestling with the implications of what he has said. She is so tired. She feels as if the ground has risen up, taken her by the ankles, and will not let go. What a wonderful thing it would be to stop fighting it, just to stand here and never move again.

She looks around her. Wilson lies with his head against a tree, his chest a bloody mess, one leg drawn up in a grotesque posture of repose. Lucretia's head lies at his feet, her eyes still staring down infinity. Tilda kneels and gently, gently, lowers Lucretia's lids. Her hands linger there a moment, soft against the cooling skin. Then she stands and follows her owner.

It rained a lot.

It was a mean, cold rain that sent fingers of ice trickling down your back, into your shoes, that turned the roads into swamps. You had to make sure your shoes were tightly laced or the mud would suck them right off your feet, like meat right off a bone. The calendar said spring had arrived, but winter clung hard to the land. As did the war.

They began to see it as they inched south. The cratered farm fields, the black trees, the fields still so littered with Minié balls they crunched beneath your feet, the decomposing hand sticking up from a shallow grave as if the occupant were trying to claw himself free, eager to join one last doomed charge against one last sunken road. They saw it, too, in the mean, miserable eyes—white people's eyes—that sometimes marked their passage, eyes that had taken in defeat and humiliation and hunger and did not yet know what to do with them. These things were still too new, too raw.

Resentment of those things leaked out of a white man who watched Sam and Ben go by from atop his roof, then went back to hammering wood across a hole left by shell shot. Out of a white woman with a plow who watched them pass, then went back to following a rangy mule across an unkempt and overgrown field. Out of a white boy who stood by the road, barefoot and dirty, in clothes that were little more than tatters, his eyes following them down.

A man approached them once, an imperious white man on a horse, with a Spencer carbine hanging from his saddle. His beard reached to the middle of his chest, his teeth were the color of bark. "Who you niggers belong to?" he demanded.

"We belong to no one," said Sam.

Ben got in front of him, blazing a path with that smile. Sam was coming to hate that smile. "What he mean to say is, us used to belong to the Pattersons down in Mi'sippi. Yankees come an' got us. We tryin' to make our way back there now. Get back to our white folks. Only true home us know."

"I've some work needs to be done on my place," said the man. "Hauling and patching and like that. Couple weeks worth. Pay you a dollar a day. You can sleep in the barn, take your meals on the back porch."

A bow. "We thank you kindly for the offer, suh, but us is pow'ful eager to get back to Mi'sippi. See the Pattersons."

The white man gave them a hard look. Ben smiled into it. Finally, the white man's mouth twisted and he spurred the horse so abruptly Sam had to jump aside. "Free niggers," the man muttered as he rode away.

At night, they found somewhere just off the road and made camp, eating whatever they could catch in the woods or beg from somebody's back door. They rubbed and wrapped their feet, which had become hard where they were not blistered, the toenails turning black and peeling off, a hard ache hammering from inside the very bones.

And as they sat there they talked, mostly about how it would be, the things they would do, the lives they would build themselves, in this brave new time when nobody owned anybody anymore. It would be better, Sam said. Yes, white people would need some time to get used to the new order of things, but soon enough they would accept it. What choice did they have? Federal troops would be there to enforce federal authority. So while white people might not like it, they would soon enough get used to it, soon enough begin making work contracts with the people they had owned until just a few weeks ago. A black man would have a chance to put some money in his pockets, advance as far as his strength and ingenuity would carry him, sell his services to the highest bidder, move around as the mood struck him, maybe save and buy a piece of land all his own.

It would be good, he said. Ben would see.

"You still plannin' on bein' a Negro in this here new world?" Ben asked him one night.

"What do you mean?"

"I mean, long as you's a Negro you best get over this idea white folks gon' ever treat you like a man."

"They will give you the treatment you require of them," said Sam. "Carry yourself as a man and they shall have no choice but to treat you as one."

"You must done met some different white folks from the ones I been dealin' with all my life," said Ben. He chased it with a laugh.

The laugh irked Sam. He did not like being mocked. Then he thought of Billy Horn, and of the white man who snapped at him the night was Lincoln was shot, and of the boy soldier on the bridge. He said nothing.

Ben annoyed him sometimes, but on balance, Sam was grateful for the company. Sam Freeman was not the most voluble or social of men. Still, it was unthinkable to him that he might have spent these long hours trekking across unfamiliar woods and meadows and mountains and valleys with only his own company to entertain him, only his own thoughts to hear. Having Ben along made the journey easier.

Ben had run away from a plantation near Nashville seven years before. He said he had done it for his baby girl. Born and raised a slave, he had thought he'd made—*peace* wasn't the right word, he said, but it was about as close as he could come—peace with his lot in life, with waking in the dark and returning in the dark and, in the hours between, being treated like a beast of burden. He had been, he said, sold like a horse, whipped like a horse, and worked like a horse. And he had accepted it, had taught himself to think as a slave must if he is to survive: expect nothing, want nothing, hope for nothing.

Then Leila was born and he made the mistake of holding her, of watching her stretch, tiny little hands balled into tiny little fists, then yawn and fall asleep, content, in her father's arms. And his reserve broke, cracked open like river ice in the spring thaw. Because he could not abide the thought of her ever learning to expect, want, hope for, and get nothing.

He ran away a year later. He planned to find work in the North, save his money, and buy freedom for his daughter and her mother. Then the war came.

"If I only knew," he told Sam. They were sitting at the fire, having eaten an evening meal of salted meat from Sam's old haversack. "If I only knew. I would never have left them. I would have stayed there. I would have waited. We could have been together all along and then freed together. If I only knew."

Sam recognized in the other man a guilt all too familiar to him, because he saw it reflected whenever he caught his own image in some pane of glass. It was a guilt that isolated you, made you alone. But Ben was not alone, was he?

"You left your child," Sam told him softly. "I killed mine."

Ben had been staring into the fire. Now, slowly, he raised his eyes. "What did you say?"

Had it really been 15 years? Suddenly it seemed like last night, the details crisp as fall leaves. The boy, watching from corners as his parents argued over freedom. Tilda asking why Sam couldn't leave well enough alone. They had a better life than colored had any right to expect, had plenty food to eat, a mistress who didn't curse them or require inhuman amounts of work from them, who made sure her people were adequately fed and clothed, who didn't believe in whipping and selling or separating families, who even taught her slaves to read and allowed them access to books.

Tilda, pleading. Talk to slaves from any other owner, she said, and they would tell you how rare that was. "We have everything here," she said.

And himself, how smug he was. "Everything but freedom," he replied. The boy, still watching silently from corners, looking so much like his mother, nodding sagely at that.

Sam answered Ben. "I said, I killed my boy," he said.

"How?"

The boy, coming to him the damn fool night before he did the damn fool thing, declaring himself. Saying, "Papa, I want to be free, too." Looking up at him with Tilda's eyes.

"I had the same plan you did," Sam told Ben. "To run away, save some money and buy my family. But my son—Luke was his name—wanted to come with me. I should have told him no."

"But you didn't."

"I did not. We argued about that, his mother and I."

Tilda, eyes flashing. "Are you out your mind? He's just a boy."

"What she say?" asked Ben.

"She said he was too young."

"What you say?"

The question brought a rueful smile. "I said, 'No man has received from nature the right to give orders to others. Freedom is a gift from heaven, and every individual of the same species has the right to enjoy it as soon as he is in enjoyment of his reason.'" He smiled again, this time at the confusion on Ben's face. "A fellow named Diderot said that," he explained. "He was French. Tilda and I...she was like me when it came to reading."

"I see," said Ben. "And readin', I guess that explain why you talk like you do. 'Most white."

"Our mistress had very...radical ideas. She allowed Tilda to learn to read. Tilda taught me. We quoted books to each other all the time."

"And did this French man you quoted her, did he make her change her mind?"

Sam's hand, flying to his cheek, cupping the sting.

"She slapped me," he said.

"But that ain't stop you," said Ben. He was feeding branches and twigs onto the fire.

Sam shook his head. "No. She begged me not to take him, but that also failed to persuade me. He was 14 and I felt that was old enough for him to know what he wanted to do, old enough to decide if he wanted to make a try for his freedom. She said..."

For a moment, he couldn't go on. He paused, looking back 15 years into her desperate eyes. They were pleading with him to listen. Just, for once... *listen.* But he couldn't do that. Not him.

Sam broke away from her eyes, forced himself back into the here and now, forced himself to finish the sentence. "She said I was going to get us both killed." What followed came out of him in a whisper. "Sometimes, I wish I *had* gotten us both killed, instead of just him."

The words fell into a silence broken only by the hiss of the damp wood— the rain had finally stopped—feeding the smoky fire. What was there to say? Hadn't she said it all so long ago? Wasn't the truth of it proven now, irrefutable now?

Of course, he hadn't known that then. He had been wounded by her prediction, had drawn himself up and said righteously, "He's dying every day, just being a slave. If I have to choose between dying slowly as that woman's property or dying fast trying to be free, I'll chose the last one every time."

He had stared at her, daring her to respond, but she had not. For a long moment, they had only watched one another from either side of this gulf that had suddenly opened between them. After a time, she folded her arms over her heart and walked away.

And that had been that, effectively the last words that ever passed between them: her awful prediction, his smug reply. They were still not speaking to one another shortly after midnight that same evening when he gathered their son and slipped away with him, the two of them melting together into the impenetrable darkness of the moonless night. At the last moment, Sam glanced behind him to see her, just a shape, just a different shade of shadow in the blackness, standing in the doorway, arms still barricading her chest, watching them go.

"We ran away that night," said Sam.

"You weren't afraid the boy would slow you down?"

"Initially I was. As it turned out, I should have been worried I would slow him down. Luke could run for hours and never get tired. He wanted his freedom, you see. He desired it as deeply as I did, perhaps more."

"How long before they come for you?"

"Two days." Pause. "It was the best two days of my life."

He remembered thinking that he had never really known his son before. How could he? When had he had the time? Sam working the fields all day, his son a houseboy waiting on Mistress and her seven children til all hours of the night. When had they had the time to be just father and son, fishing, talking, roughhousing with one another?

So it was hard not to smile some at the memory of those days alone with his boy. Running for their lives, mind you. Running to escape. But they had laughed as they had never laughed before, Luke imitating Mistress and all those children and their airs and pretensions with devastating accuracy. Late on the night of their second full day of freedom—the *last* night, as it turned out—they had even wrestled upon a carpet of fallen leaves to settle the question of which of them was the strongest. Sam had been surprised at the strength of his young son's limbs. Just yesterday, the boy had been thigh high and clinging to his mother's skirts. Now look at him, tall and straight and strong enough to make his father sweat a little, to make the veins pop out on his father's arms, before finally giving up. And Sam looking down at him and smiling a private smile, knowing all at once it wouldn't be long before he wouldn't be able to pin the boy anymore.

Afterward, they had talked as they lay on their backs and watched the stars make their nightly pinwheel across the heavens.

"Where are we going to, Papa?"

"North."

"Where in the North, Papa?"

"The Ohio River. You cross that into Ohio."

"Ohio is in the North?"

"Yes. It's free there."

"How long will it take us?"

"Long time. We have a long way to go."

"But we'll be free there?"

"Yes."

He was increasingly confident about that. Sam had forged traveling passes to help him get past any skeptical whites who stopped him and demanded to know what he was about. He had started out on a Friday night and it wouldn't be until Monday that Mistress could place an advertisement in the paper or have handbills printed up. And it was whispered that there were white people who would help you, who would hide you in their homes, transport you in their wagons. There was said to be such a man in the next county north. Sam just had to find him, that's all. It was the great unknown of this entire gamble, but if Sam could solve it, he thought they had a reasonable chance of getting away.

"Papa?"

"Yes?"

"What are you going to do when you're free?"

Sam had felt himself smiling in the dark. "Find work," he said, "and save some money."

"You're going to get Mama?"

"Yes," he said. "Mind you, it's going to take a while, take a long time. But I'll save some money and we'll go back for your mother."

"Why didn't she want to come with us?"

The question made Sam's chest tighten. "She was scared," he said. "She thought we might get caught."

"She likes it there."

It took him by surprise. "No," he said, "that is not it. She just...it's just... sometimes, it is easier to stay with something you know, even if you don't like it. It can be frightening to change."

"Papa?"

"Yes?"

"Are you scared?"

He considered this a moment. "A little," he finally said, "but I'm excited, too."

"Papa?"

"Yes?"

"I'm glad you brought me."

This struck some deep chord in him. "I am, too," he said. "Now, go to sleep." And they both did.

"The dogs woke us up the next morning," he told Ben, and it seemed he could still hear them baying in the distance, still feel the freezing sweat that coated his skin in the early chill. They never had a chance. By the time he shook Luke awake and came to his feet, they were surrounded by white men.

There were six of them and they looked enough alike—dark hair, long noses, close-set eyes—that Sam knew right away they were related. A family of slave catchers. Four of them were on horseback and the other two held the leashes on a brace of bloodhounds, the dogs straining forward, barking excitedly. Three of the men on horseback held pistols trained on Sam and Luke. The oldest of the group, the one Sam took for the father, had his pistol holstered and sat his horse as casually as if he were bored.

Luke said, "Papa..." His eyes were wide and panic edged his voice.

"You had a good run, Perseus," the older man told Sam. "Time to go back."

"No!" The defiance in Luke's shout took Sam by surprise. "No!" he cried again, "we're not going back!"

Sam put a hand on the boy's shoulder. "Luke, hush," he said. "We haven't any choice."

The man said, "You should listen to your daddy, boy. He knows what's best."

Luke turned to him then, and Sam knew the boy was waiting for him to give the word, tell him what they would do, tell him they would not just give in. His son's eyes right then broke Sam's heart forever. They searched him and did not see what they were looking for. They searched him and found him wanting. The failure melted them, urgency puddling into disillusionment.

The boy didn't understand. You don't resist when there are six men with guns and horses and you have nothing in your hands but the flesh that covers them. Sometimes, the only thing you can do is submit. Sam wanted to

say this to his son, wanted to say *something* to his son. He hesitated, looking
for words. And then the chance was gone.

Luke ran.

It was a forever moment, one that stretched from then til now til always,
one Sam still saw in dreams. The boy, arms and legs churning toward the
trees, the dogs barking and pulling at their leashes, the gun coming up, Sam
crying his son's name, turning to go after him. In dreams, sometimes, he
made it. In dreams, sometimes, he got there in time, brought Luke down
before anything could happen. In dreams, sometimes, he saved his son's
life.

But in memory, there was a shot that caught Luke in midstride. One
instant his arms and legs working in coordination, carrying him away. Then
a bang that echoed, that made birds on the high branches take wing, and
each of Luke's arms and legs was on its own, out of sync, flying in different
directions from the center mass of him.

Sam was running before his son hit the ground.

Oh Lord, no. Oh Lord, no.

Oh, Lord.

But there it was, right between the boy's shoulder blades, a tiny, ragged
red hole. Sam turned his son. The life was already draining from the boy's
eyes like sand. "Luke, I'm right here."

The eyes found him. Luke said, "Papa…" Then the eyes lost their focus
and Sam was looking down on a dead thing that one breath ago had been
his son.

It would not register. His mind would not take it in. He kept working it
like it was a math problem and he couldn't get the sums to line up properly.
Sam shook his son, gently at first, then insistently, then desperately, crying
out his name. Behind him, the slave catchers cursed at their brother.

"Goddamn it, Zach, how many times we have to tell you to think before
you act?"

"But he was gettin' away."

"You damned fool! He ain't had nowhere to go!"

"You know how much you get paid for a dead nigger, Zach? Nothin',
that's what! Do you know how much money you just cost us?"

As they argued and cursed, the older one, the father, nudged his horse
forward. He came up quietly behind Sam. "Time to go, Perseus," he said.

Sam looked around. The sun was behind the white man on the big horse, casting them both in silhouette. "My son," said Sam, helplessly. He could say no more.

"I know," said the man, and his voice was oddly gentle, "but we can't help that. We got to go."

"They tied my hands," Sam told Ben, "and made me walk behind the old man's horse. They left my son lying right there in the woods. They did not even allow me to give him a burial."

"That's the way they do, ain't it?" said Ben. "Once a nigger dead, he ain't got no more value to 'em. Might as well leave him to rot in the woods."

"It took two days to get back. They kept arguing with the one who shot Luke over how much money he had cost them. I remember, we came to this spring and they untied me so I could get a drink. Instead, I made a grab for the old man's gun. I did not get two steps before one of his boys clubbed me upside the head with a gun butt and I fell into the water. I still have the scar. The boy said, 'He was trying to kill you, Pa.' And the old man said, 'No. He would have used the gun on himself.' He was right. I have felt that way a little bit ever since, I suppose."

Ben spoke gently. "Sam, you can't..."

"I killed my son," said Sam.

And what could Ben say to that? After a moment, he got up and put more wood on the fire. It crackled and a thin plume of smoke rose. He sat down.

Sam said, "It was middle of the day when we got back to the quarter. The old man—Ames, was his name—went to the house to report to Mistress. The boys tied me straightaway to a tree. There were no whips on the place. Our mistress didn't believe in whipping slaves. So one of the Ames boys had to go and get a whip off his horse. Couple of the others went and called all the slaves in from the field. After a moment, I heard Tilda crying, 'Where's my son? Where's Luke?'

"She ran up to the tree where I was tied. 'Where's Luke?' she asked me. 'What happened to Luke?' Before I could respond, one of the Ames boys snatched her away and threw her down to the ground. And I was glad of it, because it spared me from answering her. How do you tell a woman you have killed her son? How do you say that?"

A single tear overflowed his eye. He swatted at it impatiently.

"I know not how to say that," he mumbled. "I was glad I did not have to. Of course, she figured it out on her own when she could not find him. I heard her shrieking and crying behind me. I could not see her, though. I was unable to turn my head, so closely had they pressed me against the trunk of that tree. Then the Ames boys ripped off my shirt and started laying on the licks. And you know, I did not even feel it. I could not even tell you how many times they hit me. I know they hit me; I still bear the scars from that, too. But I had all the pain I could handle, just hearing Tilda cry."

Another tear. Another impatient swipe.

"When they were done, they threw me in the pest house to heal up. They would not let anyone in there except an old blind woman, Mammy Sue. She tended my cuts as best she could. Once, I asked her how Tilda was doing. 'Not good,' she said. I said, 'Would you tell Tilda something for me? Tell her I'm sorry.'"

Sam's laugh was bitter as unripe fruit. "Are there any two words in the English language more useless than those?" he asked. "'Sorrow makes us all children again.' Ralph Waldo Emerson said that."

"What *she* say?" asked Ben.

"I asked Mammy Sue the next day when she came in to apply the poultice to my back. She told me Tilda said nothing, not a word. She said it was as if she had spoken to the tree. As I said, the word is useless."

'Yeah, but wasn't too much else you could say," said Ben.

Sam looked at him. "As soon as I was feeling better, Mistress sold me. One day, she walked into the pest house; it was the first time I had seen her since they brought me back. She faced me with me a sorrowful countenance as if to express to me how profoundly I had disappointed her. She said, 'Perseus, I never would have thought it of you.'"

"What you say?"

"I said nothing. What am I supposed to say to that? Then this white man entered behind her. He looked me up and down as though appraising a horse. He said to her, 'Yes, he'll do just fine.' That was when I realized I was being sold.

"An hour later, I left there, tied in the back of his wagon. It rolled past the fields where the slaves were working, chopping cotton. Some of them stopped to look as I went by. Tilda never lifted her head, never even looked my way. I wanted to cry out to her, but it would have been useless, and besides, what could say? I saw them telling her I was leaving, I watched them point toward me. She never stopped what she was doing."

"Angry," said Ben.

Sam nodded. "She had a right to be."

"So why you going back?"

Sam pondered this a moment. Then he said, "I do not rightly know. I suppose I just feel there must be something more I should say, some word I can find that will be more meaningful than *sorry*."

He pulled out his watch. It was getting late. "I am going to retire for the night," he said. He found a likely spot and lay down on the thin spring grass, clasping his hands behind his head as a pillow. Ben did the same and after a moment, Sam heard the other man's breathing grow steady and deep. Only then did he allow himself to weep. The tears fell silently, his body shaking. He covered his mouth with his hand, lest any sound escape.

Regret ate him like cancer. It gnawed at the very gut of him.

His son, his only child, the quick and lively boy who had looked like him and walked like him, even stood like him…and his Tilda, who had adored him and nurtured him, who had given shape and meaning to his days…why hadn't that been enough? Wasn't it more than many men had? Wasn't it more than he even had a right to hope for? Why, then, had he risked it and ruined it? Why did he need all that, and freedom, too?

God, he had loved her.

Not just because she was beautiful, not just because her thighs were round and strong and her hair thick and long. No, he had loved her laughter. He had loved the quiet moment lying together on a mattress of corn shucks after a hard day, not speaking and not needing to. He had loved holding her hand and watching the rain from the front door of their cabin. He had loved watching her nurse their son, watching the boy tug greedily at her nipple while she gazed down on him with all the tenderness in the world. He had loved reading a book and handing it to her saying, "You should read this," and then talking about it with her afterward. He had loved her.

He still did.

The knowledge of it brought tears rushing in fresh sheets of pain down his cheek. He wept in silence.

And it began to rain.

They left the steamboat at Memphis in the bright heart of the morning. After two days floating quietly down the sleeping river, they were jolted by the cacophony waiting at the end of the landing stage: whistles and curses, the bleat and squeal and mooing of livestock and the song of Negro stevedores, toting cargo onto and off of the ship. Prudence hired two wagons—one for them, one for crates that had been shipped ahead—and they set off traveling south. On the cusp of twilight they arrived in Buford, an ugly little town of mud streets and clapboard dwellings squatting toad-like against the eastern bank of the Mississippi.

This was where Bonnie was born. But Prudence saw no soft gleam of sentiment in her best friend's eyes as she gazed about. No, Bonnie's eyes weighed and judged and, finally, disdained. Something about it made Prudence sad. It was, she thought, as if Bonnie had somehow been separated from herself.

Overhead, a hawk circled lazily in search of a late-day meal. In the homely streets below, one barefoot white boy chased another, their steps landing like hammer blows on the wooden planks of the sidewalk. They barely managed to dodge around two pinch-faced white women who never even saw them, who stared up at the passing wagons with eyes demanding answers.

At the very end of town, just before Main Street surrendered itself to cotton fields, the driver brought the lead wagon to a stop. Time, sun, and rain had scraped most of the paint from its weary boards, but the warehouse was still imposing, lording it over a row of tiny shotgun houses that cowered in its shadow. The warehouse was a remnant of prewar times, when there was commerce here. But commerce had long since died in this part of Buford. Across the street stood what had been a livery. Now boards were nailed across the door and the grass grew tall as a small child around it. Next to that, shadowed and abandoned, stood a stable and harness maker, next to that a cotton broker, next to that a tobacconist, all of them shuttered and abandoned.

Commerce was just a memory. Now this part of town belonged solely to the Negroes who, as if on some silent signal, came to their front doors, gathered in their meager yards, and converged on the two wagons. Curiosity burned in dark faces. No one spoke. Bonnie gazed down at them, eyes still weighing and judging. Prudence did not like that look.

She climbed down from the wagon without waiting for assistance and went to gaze up at the warehouse. It would do, she decided. Not that its fitness had ever really been in question. Her father had chosen it, after all. Still, it was good to see for herself.

Prudence turned, surprised to find the Negroes pressing closer. All she saw of them was eyes, patient, waiting.

She spoke with voice raised, looking from one to another to make sure she encompassed them all. "My name is Mrs. Prudence Cafferty Kent," she said, "and I am from Boston."

"Is that in the North?" A little boy gazed up at her from the shelter of his mother's dress.

Prudence smiled. "Yes," she said, "Boston is in the North. My father— my late father; he died last year—was a man named John Matthew Cafferty. Some of you may know him, or at least know of him. He owned a plantation south of town where there were no slaves. Before the war, it was his custom to travel down here once a year. He bought slaves, and even took some of them back to Boston, and set them free. That is Bonnie in the wagon," she said, nodding. "Her mother was the first slave he bought." They all turned to look. Bonnie's gaze flickered and became unfocused for a moment. Then she gathered herself and stared resolutely forward.

"On his last trip down here," Prudence continued, "my father bought this building. He knew the war was coming and he felt certain the North would win. But he was concerned that after the war, when you all were set free, the government would not provide you with opportunities to better yourselves, to learn. So he intended this building to be a school for you all. As I say, my father did not live to see the end of the war, so we are here to carry on his dream. This will be the Campbell and Cafferty School for Freedmen. Miss Bonnie"—she caught herself, glanced at Bonnie, went on—"and I will be the teachers and it will be open to all who want to come."

"Why you pappy do this for us? Out the goodness of his heart?" The man's voice was a singsong of mockery, his chin was lifted, and his eyes were twin coals, smoldering in a deep, dark pit.

Someone else said. "Don't talk like that 'bout Marse Cafferty. I knowed him. Took my brother with him one year to the North."

Another voice said, "I knowed him, too. Worked on that place of his for a while, me and a bunch of others. Might've made a go of it, 'cept white folks wouldn't sell us no supplies, nor leave us alone to farm in peace."

Prudence leveled her gaze. "My father came to this country as a small boy from England. His mother died on the ship and when he disembarked in Boston, he was all alone. He might have died but for a colored man named Cyrus Campbell, who took him in. He was an escaped slave from right here in Buford and he took my father on as an apprentice. He had a business making furniture and years later, he made my father his partner. Father became a wealthy man and he always felt that he owed his life to Mr. Campbell. So when Mr. Campbell died, Father decided he would—"

There were white people in the crowd. It stopped her. She saw them all at once, two white men standing in the back, smirking at her. They were watching and wanted her to know. Prudence swallowed.

"When Mr. Campbell died," she went on, "Father decided he would free slaves and build a school here in honor of the man who had saved his life."

The angry man's mouth twisted, but a general murmur of approval lifted from the crowd. Prudence glanced up at Bonnie, who gave her a nod and a tight smile of encouragement.

"Cyrus weren't no runaway slave." It cut through the murmur like a wolf in a herd of sheep.

Prudence was alarmed. "Who said that?" she demanded.

In response, the crowd shifted itself around for a moment until it disgorged her, a tiny, ancient, mahogany-skinned woman. Her faced sagged in as if it was about to be sucked into her toothless mouth, her scalp peeked through the thin white crown of her hair, and she leaned on a stick for support. But her eyes were clear for all that, and they regarded Prudence now with defiance.

"Knowed Cyrus," she said. "Knowed him from a boy. He weren't no runaway slave. I know you just saying what you been told. But it ain't the truth. Ain't even close to the truth."

Nothing ever surprised Prudence. She prided herself on that. A thing might be unexpected, but she always rose to it, always met it head on, never let it push her back. But this.... Her mouth was open and filled with silence.

"Who was he, then?" Bonnie, still sitting atop the wagon, rescued her.

The old woman bared her gums in what Prudence supposed was intended as a smile. "He were the devil, that's who he was."

"I do not understand," said Prudence.

"Expect you wouldn't," said the woman. "Cyrus were Marse Josh Campbell's son."

"He was the *master's* son?"

"Yes'm. But ol' Marse Campbell, he owned up to him. Lots of white mens, they wouldn't do that, but Marse Campbell did. His wife ain't give him nothing but daughters, you see. Seven girls. But they was this slave he owned named Ginny, she the one whose door he be knockin' at after midnight, thinkin' nobody know. She give him a son. And Marse Campbell, he loved that boy like he were mos' white. His only son, you see? He ain't never had much use for girls."

"I see," said Prudence. She was distantly aware of Bonnie, climbing down now from the wagon, coming to stand by her. Somehow, Bonnie always knew when she was needed.

"Sometimes, I think Cyrus thought he was mos' white hisself. Even though he could have seen different in the mirror. Raised up in the big house, you see. Never slaved a day in his life. Now, how Mistress and all them girls felt 'bout that, livin' up there with Marse's black bastard son, I couldn't tell you. Don't think Marse much cared what no women think no way. And that boy was mean as a snake to the slaves. Mean just for the fun of it. Cussin' at 'em, orderin' 'em around, hittin' 'em, siccin' the overseer on 'em for no good cause. He even treated his own mammy that way, you hear me? She were my mammy, too, so I knew."

"Cyrus was your brother?"

"Yes'm. I were six year old when he were born."

"Oh, my goodness," said Prudence. She felt ill.

"Cyrus, he near 'bout 24 when Marse Josh died. And in his will, Marse give Cyrus his freedom." She sucked at her toothless gums. "Set him free, yes he did. Give him a piece of land and his pick of the slaves. But like I say, Cyrus ain't knowed nothin' 'bout handlin' no slaves. Knowed about furniture like you say. His daddy taught him that. But he ain't knowed nothin' 'bout handlin' slaves. He just like to whip on 'em, is all. Hated anything black, that boy did. Black as he was, he hated anything black.

"Finally the slaves, they got tired of it. Tried to kill him. Twice. Way I heard it, one tried to chop him with a hoe. Cut him pretty bad, then run into the woods. They ain't never caught him. Two weeks later, somebody took a shot at Cyrus. Nobody know to this day who done it. But that when Cyrus decided he had enough. He hired hisself a caretaker to run the place and skedaddled up to the North. That's the last I heard of him til you just ride up here now. And I'm sure you mean well, Miss, but I want you to know, Cyrus weren't runnin' from no slave catcher. He were runnin' from *slaves*."

Prudence's thoughts spun like a wheel on a muddy road, seeking traction and unable to find it. The kindness of Cyrus Campbell, the compassion of a genial colored man who took in a frightened little boy who had nowhere else to go, was the story on which her family was founded. She supposed nothing the old woman said changed that story. It had not become a lie. Yet at the same time, it was no longer quite the truth. The gentle benefactor was a cruel slaver who had victimized his own. And if he was no longer what she had believed him to be, how could the Caffertys still be what they were? Cyrus Campbell's good deed was the reason the Caffertys were who they were and did what they did. But apparently the thing she had thought bedrock was really only sand.

"No reason for you to know," said the woman, as if Prudence had spoken her confusion aloud. Pity softened the deep lines of the old woman's face. She regarded Prudence for a moment, then looked beyond her. "So, this gon' be a school, then?"

Bonnie answered for her. "Yes," she said, "this will be a school. Though I am no longer sure it will have Mr. Campbell's name on it." There was satisfaction in the old woman's laugh.

"What y'all gon' do 'bout them cots in there?" This was the man with the burning eyes.

"Cots?" asked Prudence. "What cots?"

"In the war," said the man, "the rebs used this place. Made it a hospital for they wounded. When the feds come, they 'vacuated out in a hurry, left all them cots in there. We feared to touch 'em, 'cause we ain't knowed if the rebs might come back. So them cots been in there, I guess, two years or more."

"Show me," said Prudence.

The man shouldered forward through the crowd, went to the loading door, and pushed the handles in the center. The two sides of the massive door fell inward, hinges creaking in complaint. Hot, stale air rolled out, covering the street like a blanket.

The space Prudence and Bonnie stepped into was cavernous. And just as the man had said, the light that entered from the windows at the top of the wall just below the ceiling fell in stripes across four endless rows of cots, all with bedding in disarray. The sight of them whispered a story: men had lain there and there and there, bandages on their heads, bloody stumps where their arms and legs had been, the air rent with their dying cries. The floor was strewn with clothing, most of it stiff and brown with blood, and with saws, books, pencils, pipes, glasses. There was a bucket in the center of the floor. It was filled with feet and hands, some of them already gone to bone, others with scraps of flesh still attached.

In unison, Prudence and Bonnie crossed themselves. Bonnie said, "My sweet Jesus." Then a rat, gray as rainclouds, waddled out from shadow. It stood in the light near the skeletal hands, lifted its head, watching them. Prudence was seized with the sudden queasy realization that the missing flesh of the dead limbs had not simply decomposed. After a moment, the rat scuttled heavily away, disappearing beneath a stairwell that climbed up from the warehouse floor to a loft and what had once been a suite of offices.

"We shall have need of a cat," said Bonnie, standing beside her.

Prudence shivered. "We shall have need of a great many things," she said.

She had thought herself prepared, had thought they would sweep some floors, knock down some cobwebs, have the school open in a matter of days. Now she knew she'd had no idea of the difficulty that awaited her. And she had only been here 20 minutes. Twenty minutes, and everything had changed. What would it be like after 20 days?

"Miss, where you want us to put your things?" The drivers were standing in the warehouse door, just back of the crowd.

Prudence said, "In here, I suppose."

The man grunted and, with his partner, got to work unloading the wagons. There were a dozen crates, all bearing unassembled desks from Campbell & Cafferty. There were several trunks filled with books. There were clothing and personal effects. All of it to be stacked into the musty space with—it dawned on her all at once—not even a lock on the door.

"So," said the black man with the livid eyes, "What you gon' do with them cots?"

Prudence stirred. "Discard them, I suppose."

"Discard? You mean throw 'em out?"

"Or we could give them away, Miss Prudence," said Bonnie, her tone one of helpful deference that irked Prudence's ears and made her glance over. But there was no deference in her friend's eyes. Instead, Bonnie's eyes implored her. She understood the message. *Take charge. Take charge or everything is lost.* This crowd was judging her in this moment and the success or failure of everything they were here to do rested upon what happened now. Who would believe in her or her school if they thought her only a ditherer, made helpless by every surprise, reversal or misfortune?

"What is your name?" she asked the man with the fiery eyes.

He smiled the easy, beneficent smile of someone who has won a victory and can afford to be magnanimous. And Prudence realized he knew what she was about to ask and had been waiting for it. "My name Paul, ma'am. Paul Cousins."

"Paul, I need a man to help me get this building together, dispose of these cots, find a mouser—no, two—to get rid of the rats, clean up the place, and then help to maintain it. Would you like the job?"

He grinned, made a show of scratching his chin. "Well, ma'am, that's right nice of you to offer, but I don't know."

Prudence smiled a cutting smile. He had overplayed his hand. "Very well," she said. "Is there another man who would like to earn two dollars a day?"

Every man's hand bolted into the air at this. The offer was twice the going rate. Paul Cousins panicked, his hands coming up in a gesture that begged her to wait. "Ma'am, I ain't said I don't want the job."

Prudence was aware of Bonnie turning aside to hide a smile. "Well, do you or do you not?" she asked Cousins.

"Yes ma'am," he said. "I do. I do indeed."

"Then I shall expect you to start first thing tomorrow. I will see you here and we will work out details."

She addressed herself then to the mass of them. "We are going to begin classes here one week from today at eight o'clock in the morning. As I told you a moment ago, I am Mrs. Prudence Kent and this is Bonnie. We will be offering instruction in reading and arithmetic initially, with other subjects to be added. We will teach any and all who wish to learn. My father believed with all his heart that the enslavement of your people was an evil crime, in part because it deprived you of your God-given right to educate and better yourselves. Now that the war for your freedom is over, we are here—*I* am here—in hopes of restoring that right to as many as want to seek it. If you would allow it, we would like to be your teachers. Those who agree to that, please signify it by raising your hand."

A little boy was the first, his hand shooting into the air, straining toward the ceiling. Then one by one, other hands joined his: men, women, little boys, little girls, some shooting up in the air like fireworks, some rising hesitantly as if weighted down. In the gloom of the old warehouse, hands kept going up.

Prudence said, "Bonnie, would you please get some paper and take down their names?"

Bonnie gave her a look and Prudence knew she was feeling it, too, despite herself. Satisfaction. A sense that somewhere, John Matthew Cafferty was proud.

"Y'all gon' need a place to stay." To Prudence's surprise, the old woman was at her elbow.

"I suppose you are right," said Prudence.

They had thought to sleep in the offices upstairs; one of the crates from Campbell & Cafferty contained cots and bedding. But she wouldn't sleep in here until the place had been cleansed of rats and ghosts.

"Y'all stay with me," said the woman. "Since my sister died, I got a extra room. My house just a few doors down. It's the one with the flower garden out front. Probably not nice as you used to, but it keep the rain off. You come on when you finish here. I'll have supper for you."

"Thank you," said Prudence. "I shall be pleased to pay you for your trouble."

The woman shook her head emphatically. "No," she said, pointing to where Bonnie stood surrounded by people waiting to give her their names. "The way you pay me is: you put my name on that list. I wants to learn, too."

The sparkle in her eyes made Prudence smile. She was so old. How much longer could she expect to live? A year or two? Five maybe? But she wanted to spend those years seeking what she had been denied all her life. The dignity of her own humanity. She would learn vowels and consonants and numbers and calculations, the knowledge that proved she was not and never had been the dumb beast of burden she had so long been assumed to be.

Prudence had thought she had some notion of what it would mean, bringing education to former slaves. She realized now she'd had no idea. When it came to so many things, she'd had no idea. And for the first time in her life, she felt the simple contentment that comes from knowing bone deep that you are where you were meant to be, doing what you were meant to do.

"Ginny," said the woman. "That my name, just like my mammy. Make sure she get that down on that paper there."

"I will," said Prudence.

A tart nod. "Then I see you when you done here."

She moved away with her painful gait and Prudence watched her go. The drivers were still stacking crates. The crowd pressed eagerly toward Bonnie, and she had to ask them several times to be patient. Prudence was smiling, still glowing with the simple rightness of it all. Then all at once, she realized something, and for reasons she could not articulate even to herself, it iced her chest with foreboding.

The white men were gone.

They were walking through a grove of cottonwood and hackberry trees on the banks of a muddy river, when Sam's right foot lifted out of his shoe like a snake shedding skin. When he knelt to examine the shoe, he found it split open at the seams, coarse white threads visible in the gap. Its mate was in much the same shape.

Ben sat next to him. "Guess you gon' be barefoot for a while." He produced two pieces of dried meat he had brought with him from Washington and passed one over. "Last we got," he warned.

"Do you not think we should save it, then?" said Sam.

"No, I do not," said Ben, as he tore away a chunk of the salty beef. "Hungry now. 'Sides, something turn up." He showed Sam the glaring smile, made his voice a darky rasp. "De Lawd gwine make a way," he said.

Sam said, "Let us hope you are right." He threw his busted shoe. It arced high above the trees, landing with a satisfying splash in the water beyond. Its mate followed just seconds behind. He removed his socks, rolled them together, and stuffed them into one of the pockets of his coat.

Ben pointed. "They's a town yonder," he said. "Just across the river. You see it? We might maybe could find somewhere to get you a new pair."

"I doubt it," said Sam. But he stood up anyway, pocketing the beef.

"You don't believe in de Lawd?" asked Ben, eyes shining mischief.

"I am not hungry," said Sam. Which was a lie. He simply couldn't bring himself to eat the last food he had in some airy faith that something would magically present itself when they got hungry again. "Let us go see what they have down there."

Half a mile down the river, they encountered an old white man, hair gray and long and sprawling from his scalp in dirty tangles, who agreed to row them across in his skiff. They paid him ten cents each for the ride.

After a few moments, as the old man grunted and sweated and pulled the far shore closer, they began to make out the town. Even from a distance, they could see that it was dead.

Fragments of wall unconnected to other walls rose from the earth with the grim singularity of tombstones, the names of businesses still visible on the brick. Livery. Harness maker. Dry goods. It went on like that for blocks. They watched in silence, the only sound that of water smacking the skiff.

Moments later, the old man left them standing upon the far shore. The earth was packed mud, cool beneath Sam's bare feet. In silence, they climbed the embankment from the river, in silence they walked into the center of town, passing through the shadow of tombstones that had once been places, businesses, offices. Now doorways fed into space, windows that had once looked out upon sky and trees and people going to and fro lay smashed in the mud, walls towered nowhere for no purpose. It was a cloudless day. The sun shone down, pitiless. The scrape of Ben's shoes on the dirt seemed unnaturally loud.

And then there came a squeal of laughter.

Sam looked up in time to see two Negro boys darting across the street, a little one chasing a bigger one toward the shadow of half a building. The bigger one disappeared, but at the sight of the two strangers coming toward him, the smaller boy stopped. He stared intently, as if he had never seen men before. Then the bigger boy reappeared. His eyes bucked at the sight of them and he grabbed the little one by the hand and yanked him away.

A moment later, Sam and Ben drew abreast of the remnants where the two boys had disappeared. They found themselves facing the two boys along with a man and a woman, standing in the middle of a de facto courtyard, staring. The boys were in front, the bigger holding the smaller with a protective palm splayed across his breastbone. The man was taller than Sam, muscular, head smooth as a brown egg, just like Ben's. He had a rifle held casually across his shoulder, the muzzle pointing into the sky, a warning held in abeyance.

Sam said, "Good morning." He touched his hat.

Ben said, "How y'all?"

The one with the rifle called out, "Passin' through?"

"Yes," said Sam.

"Ain't much here."

"Yes, I can see that," said Sam.

"You don't mind my askin'," said Ben, "what y'all doin' here?"

The woman spoke up. "We used to belong to Marse Morrison. He the biggest planter around these parts. We left his place when we heared them firin' off for surrender."

"Y'all are livin' here?"

"We waitin'," said the woman.

"What are you waiting for?" said Sam.

"Federals, I s'pose. Wait for the federals, find out what we s'pose to do now."

"Anything in this town?" asked Ben. "Somethin' to eat, maybe? Or someplace my friend can find a pair of shoes?"

"Don't know nothin' 'bout no shoes," said the woman, "but we got venison. Brother here shot him a deer yesterday. You welcome to some stew."

The one she called Brother gave her a disapproving look, his lips drawn up until they were just a knot of flesh almost touching his nose. Sam heard her say, "Shush that. We got plenty."

Sam was about to beg off, but Ben moved forward, smiling at them. It was a real smile, not the strained parody of a smile he saved for white people. "Well, thank you," he said. "Stew be just fine."

Brother lowered the rifle from his shoulder as they passed. "Sorry 'bout that," he said. "Can't be too careful, nowadays."

They entered an open space where a rough lean-to had been built from the detritus of destruction, planks of broken wood angled against the brick wall. It was, thought Sam, enough to keep the rain off, no more. The woman pointed and they sat at the entrance. Sam glanced inside and was surprised to see four or five books next to the bedrolls lying open on the dirt.

The woman introduced her family. The one with the gun was named Eli. She called him Brother because he was her brother. Her name was Sarah, but he called her Sister for the same reason. The boys were both hers. "They daddy got sold away a few years ago," she said softly, pausing for a moment to watch as the boys chased one another through the open space where the building had been. "Don't rightly know where he is now. They uncle they daddy now, I expect."

"Not knowing where family is," said Sam, "is something I am sure many of us have experienced."

"Whoo, how he talk," said Sister with a laugh. "He talk 'most white, don't he, Brother?"

Brother ignored her. He regarded Sam with a sharp expression. "You lookin' for someone?"

"We both are," said Sam as he accepted a steaming plate ladled from a stewpot. "He is trying to find his daughter and her mother and I am trying to find my, well, wife, I suppose you'd say."

"You *s'pose?*" said Brother, not bothering to hide his scorn.

"Well, there was not any real ceremony. There was nothing to make it legal."

There was something almost cruel in the smile that curled Brother's lips then. "You need some white man with a Bible to tell you who your wife is?"

Sam considered this. He thought of Tilda as she had looked holding their son, a contentment stealing across her face such as he had never seen, as if she could live in that moment the rest of her life and it would be enough, would be all she needed, ever. "No," he said, "I do not."

"Yeah," said Brother, "I didn't neither."

"Guess ain't a one of us ain't lost somebody," said Ben, quietly. He blew on a spoonful of stew.

There was a moment. Then Sarah said, "Sam, you don't mind my askin', do you know where your wife is?"

He shook his head. "The last time I saw her was on the old place in Mississippi. That was a long time ago."

"I knew where Fletcher was, I might try to find him," she said. "'Course, I got the boys to think of."

"Need to give that up," said Brother. His voice was granite, a cudgel dashing hope to death like some small furry animal.

"I know," said Sister, her voice small, ashamed of itself. Sam had the sense he had wandered into the middle of some argument that had been going a long time. Would be going a long time yet.

"I just miss him sometimes," she said. "That's all."

Ben had been chewing thoughtfully on a mouthful of venison. Now he nodded at the books. "Y'all likes to read?"

Sister smiled bashfully. "Naw, we can't read. Them for the boys, for them to learn on."

"Took them from Marse," said Brother. "From his library. Him and Missus done run off, scared of the federals, so we took the wheelbarrow, put some books and things in there 'fore we lit out."

"Don't know what we gon' do with 'em," said Sister, laughing. Her teeth were brown, with wide gaps between them. It occurred to Sam that she was probably not nearly as old as she looked, that she might even have been pretty once. "We sure can't traipse around the countryside pushin' no wheelbarrow."

"Man owed me that much, though," said Brother, and his voice had narrowed to a thin sliver of ice. "All them years I worked for him, he treated me like some kind of mule or horse or somethin'? He *owe* me that much and a whole lot more."

Sam said, "Do you not fear that he will come after you?"

Brother cast a meaningful glance toward the rifle, leaning against the brick wall within easy arm's reach. "I hope he do," he said. "You can see books ain't all I took from him."

"Brother angry," said Sister.

"Damn right I am," said Brother. The curse caused Sister to suck in her breath. He cut his eyes toward her and after a moment he said, "Sorry about the language, Sister, but it the truth."

Suddenly, Sam was eager to get going. He forked up the last of the venison. The meat had a dark, full taste, and it occurred to him that he had not eaten so fine a meal in a very long time. He held up his plate. "Is there someplace I can wash this for you?"

In response, Brother snatched it from his hands and flipped it back against the brick wall, where it broke in several large pieces. "Missus's plates," he explained. "We put some of them in the wheelbarrow, too."

Ben looked from Sam to Brother, carefully speared the last of the meat from his own plate and put it in his mouth, and then tossed the plate casually against the wall, where it shattered, the pieces landing atop the remains of Sam's plate. They all looked at him. He gave them back a blankness that made them laugh. "Hell with 'em," he said.

Brother nodded, still laughing. "Hell with 'em all."

"Hell with 'em," said Sister, eyes shining with her own mischief, one hand covering her mouth as if to hide the profanity that had just slipped out.

Sam was more certain than ever that she had, indeed, been pretty once. "To hell with them," he said, completing the circle.

As the laughter renewed itself, he wondered if this wasn't all a kind of madness, this idea of being free, of being governed only by your own wits and wants, of saying to hell with white people. A glorious madness.

It scared him a little. "We should be going," he said. Ben, wiping amusement from the corners of his eyes, nodded. They thanked Sister and Brother for the meal and walked on, leaving the family standing before the lean-to in the shadow of a brick wall that had once framed a building that was no longer there.

"Hell with 'em," said Ben, softly reminiscent.

"That is easy to say," said Sam.

After a moment, Ben said, "Yeah."

The street was packed mud, a gift from a recent rain, cool underfoot. But Sam knew he had to find something for his feet soon, else the miles and the rocks would tear his skin and leave him hobbling. He could not hobble all the way to Mississippi.

"Maybe shouldn't of been so quick to throw that shoe away," said Ben, as if he could just pluck Sam's thoughts from a stack in his mind. "Might maybe could of fixed it someway."

"Maybe," said Sam, not liking the idea that his thoughts had somehow become transparent, "but there is nothing to be done for it now." He found himself almost whispering the words. Something about the stillness of the dead town, the vast emptiness of it, seemed to demand that reverence. Not even birds flew overhead. As the business district gave way, they entered an area where houses had been reduced to frames, the wood deeply scored and still stinking of fire.

"They burned all the secessionitis out of *this* town," said Ben. Sam didn't answer, his eyes slowly searching the ruined landscape.

"Look there," he said, pointing. It stood on the next block, the one house among dozens that was more intact than not. The front of it had been smashed, probably by a shell, and was collapsing in on itself like a drunkard. But the rest of the house was untouched. Even the paint looked fresh.

"You think maybe they some shoes in there?" asked Ben.

"There is only one way to find out," said Sam, starting forward so abruptly that Ben had to hurry to keep up.

The front door was impassable. Sam walked slowly around. The windows were open. From the rear, it looked as if the owners had simply been called away and might return at any moment. Sam paused, fighting himself, wrestling down his own intuition.

The two men mounted the steps to the rear porch. Sam pushed at the door. It swung inward easily and without sound.

They found themselves in a parlor that smelled of smoke and shadows, of air that had known neither light nor movement in a very long time. The shades were drawn. It was hard to tell in the darkness, but the walls looked to be a sunny, incongruous yellow. The furniture was sturdy and serious. Decorative vases lined the shelves. Framed photographs watched the darkness. Sam took one down. He found himself staring into the face of a white woman, her eyes kindly above the hint of a smile, as if something unseen by the camera amused her greatly. She was seated. Towering behind her was a man, heavily bearded and with piercing eyes, one large hand resting proprietarily on the woman's shoulder.

In her lap was a baby. It had moved before the exposure time lapsed, rendering its face an indistinguishable blur. You could not even tell if it was a boy or a girl. The child looked like a ghost of its own self, like a presentiment of death.

Ben was on the stairs. "Come on," he said. "They gon' have any shoes, they most likely be up yonder."

His voice was unusually taut and Sam knew he felt it, too, the whisper of wrongness stirring the hairs in his ear at every step. Someone—someone *white*, even worse—had lived here not so long ago. The furnishings the two men walked among, the things they handled, the very air they breathed, *belonged* to someone. And though it was unlikely those people would choose this precise moment to return to their ruined home, there was, nevertheless, a sense of invasion in walking in their places, touching their things, being here when they were not.

Sam nodded, replacing the photograph on the buttery yellow shelf and following Ben. The stairs did not creak at the weight of them. The silence felt unnatural. It made you want to speak, want to snap your fingers or knock on wood just to hear the noise it made, just to assure yourself you still were there, still real.

"Don't like this," said Ben.

"Nor do I," said Sam.

"We find you some shoes, you better hold on to 'em this time."

It was a feeble joke and Sam knew it for what it really was. A need to throw words against the silence.

"I will," he said. "You may depend on it."

The stairwell gave onto a hallway that crossed it at a perpendicular angle. There were windows at either end. Someone had pulled the shades here, as well.

There were five doors, three lined up on the opposite side of the hall, two flanking the stairwell. Ben moved to his right, toward the first door. Sam followed.

Ben turned the knob, pushed the door open. This was a bedroom, a boy's bedroom, to judge from the troop of painted wooden soldiers encamped on the gleaming wooden floor at the foot of an unmade bed. Clothes littered the room, spilled from the open top drawer of a dresser. There would be no men's shoes in here. Sam and Ben backed out of the room, Ben pulling the door closed behind him.

"Look like they had to leave in a rush," said Ben.

"Perhaps," said Sam and his voice felt loud. "However, it could be the boy just isn't very tidy."

He tried the door across the hall. The handle was slimy in his sweaty fist. The door swung open into the cool darkness of what had apparently been a reading room. Books crowded the shelves. The rocking chair next to the oil lamp was inviting. Despite himself, Sam stepped forward, intending to read just a title or two. Ben caught his arm. "Can't wear no books on your feet," he said.

Sam looked at him. Sweat beaded his bald scalp. Ben's mouth was a line strung taut between his cheeks. Sam nodded and they left this room, too. There were three more doors to check. Sam led them down the hall to the middle door. He tried it, it opened.

This was where the shell had hit. Most of the far wall was gone. Half the floor had collapsed into the porch below. A bed and a dresser lay strewn on their sides like the contents of a pocket dropped onto a table at the end of a wearying day. Ben pressed him from behind, but Sam warded him off with an arm and closed the door. "There is nothing in there," he said. "The room was destroyed by the same explosion that destroyed the porch down below."

Ben released a sigh that was almost a groan. "Two more," he said.

They moved down the hallway to where the last two doors faced one another. "You take that one," said Sam. "I will take this one." Ben nodded, stepped into the other room. Sam tried his door. It swung open easily. Then his throat constricted and for a moment, he could not speak. His hand came automatically to his face to cover the smell.

She was there, the woman from the picture. She lay on the bed, fully dressed, staring at him with eyes that had been dead so long they had retreated into their sockets like some beast into its cave. There was a hole in her chest and her blouse was stiff with blood that had dried brown. The man lay on his back across her legs, his arms flung out from the great mass of him, as if to shrug at eternity. A black pistol lay on the floor where it had fallen from his left hand. The gunshot wound was in the temple. You could see chunks of desiccated tissue in the dried spatter on the wall.

"Oh, my God," said Sam.

"Lord Jesus," said Ben, suddenly at his side.

Sam had seen violent death before. He had seen it take men in mid-stride so that suddenly they flew backwards as if they had struck something human eyes could not see. He had seen it corkscrew men down to the ground, spurting blood and crying for their mothers. He had seen shells explode and men fall to the earth in pieces and chunks, like bloody confetti from some devil's parade. But that was the battlefield—that was men contesting with other men and every man holding onto his life against other men trying to take it.

He had never seen death where a man brought it into the ordinariness of his very bedroom and inflicted it upon his wife and then himself. It was a species of horror he had never imagined.

"They seen the end comin' and knowed they was gon' lose," said Ben. "They couldn't stand it."

"Yes," said Sam, "but to take their own lives...?"

"Guess they rather that than live under 'nigger domination,' as they say." Ben had moved past him and now flung open the closet. It was as empty as the dead woman's eyes. "Somebody already been here," he said. "Cleaned everything out."

He went around the side of the bed, knelt near the dead man's feet. Sam noticed for the first time that they were bare. "Ain't gon' find no shoes in here."

"What do you suppose happened to the little boy?" asked Sam.

Ben shrugged. "Hell would I know? If he smart, he a long way from here. Just like we need to be. Come on."

And that was when they heard the pop. It was a flat, distant sound, but it was unmistakable. Gunfire. Sam got to the window just as the second pop reached his ears.

He saw it immediately, a puff of smoke lifting above the fragment of brick wall where they had left Brother and Sister. Six meanly dressed white men in identical gray slouch hats sat their horses opposite the opening of the makeshift courtyard. The one in front was holstering a long-barreled revolver.

Brother staggered into view, hands clenched around the rifle he had shown them so proudly. The white men did not react. Brother went down on one knee, looking for all the world like a supplicant before a monarch. Sister rushed forward, her mouth contorted around a shriek Ben and Sam could not hear. As she knelt next to Brother, he pitched forward, the rifle spilling from his hand. The white man with the pistol climbed down from his horse to claim it. He said something to Sister. Whatever it was, it was lost on her. She was bent low over Brother, whispering something in his ear. But even at this distance, Sam could see that Brother did not hear her and never would again.

"Why in the world would they shoot him?" Sam said.

"For being a Negro with a gun, I expect. Maybe for stealing from that master of theirs. They don't need no reason."

The white man was back on his horse. With a last glance down at the body in the mud, he swung the beast's great head around and the whole group of patterollers ambled slowly toward the river. Behind them, Sister had collapsed into the dirt next to the corpse that had been her brother just moments ago. The two little boys were crying.

"We should go back there," said Sam.

"Why?" hissed Ben. "What we gon' do? We gon' go after them patterollers, the two of us? We gon' cry with that woman or find some way to bring that man back to life?"

The hostility of it took Sam by surprise. "They fed us," he said. "They were good people."

"I know that," said Ben. "But what that got to do with it? What we gon' do for them people? Ain't nothin' we can say, nothin' we can do. Can barely do for our ownselfs."

"It does not seem right just to leave them."

"What 'right' got to do with any of this?" demanded Ben. His voice was a lacerating whisper. "When the last time you seen 'right?'"

The two men stared at one another for a long, airless moment. Then Ben gave a sigh and it seemed to take something more out of him than just air. His shoulders rounded, his eyes softened. "Look," he said, "you want to go back down there, you do it. I can't stop you. But I'm out here trying to get back to Hannah and my little girl. That's what matter to me."

With that, he spun on his heel and left the room. Sam heard his feet knocking on the stairs, and then the bang of the back door. Back at the encampment, the little boys tried to help their mother to her feet. They couldn't. She sagged between them like a sack of flour.

From the bed, the dead white woman watched him with her shrunken eyes and her blouse brittle with brown blood and her dead husband lying across her legs, arms flung wide.

Sam backed out of the room slowly. Then he trotted the stairs, running to catch up.

For most of her 26 years, her days had been filled with nothing more strenuous than piano lessons, walks in the Common, recitals, and teas. While Prudence had chafed under the decorous conventions that framed their lives as young women of means, while Prudence had hidden under the stairs when it was time for piano lessons and preferred the company of the maids to that of the maidens who sipped tea in the parlor, Bonnie had relished every second of their privilege.

Oh, there was the sense sometimes of being too much on display—the living embodiment of the Caffertys' eccentric insistence upon the social equality of Negroes. There was the annoyance of having to smile graciously and express gratitude on behalf of the entire colored race whenever some smitten young white man felt the need to express with too-forceful earnestness his abhorrence of slavery. But always, that pinprick of irritation was counterbalanced by the remembrance of how extraordinarily blessed she was to be in a drawing room in Boston and not a cotton field in Buford.

Sometimes, though, it nagged her heart when she glanced up from conversation with some heiress or lawyer and it struck her that she and some stooped and wrinkled maid, moving about soundlessly, invisibly, while filling tea cups and taking up empty plates, were the only colored people in the room. It gave her an odd feeling, like looking at another self. In the color of their skin, the cast of their hair, the shape of their noses and lips, they were so much alike, and yet at the same time, they were nothing alike at all.

Once, the maid caught her looking and Bonnie snatched her eyes away, feeling like a picklock caught at the window. But not before the maid had given her a smile that unsettled her, that made her feel as if she were a fraud and only the maid was aware, as if they alone were in possession of a great and damning secret the others could not begin to guess.

All her life, Bonnie had felt that way, felt as if she were getting away with something. In the last week, that feeling had vanished like ice under the summer sun. In the last week, she had gotten away with nothing. She had spent those days in the first hard physical labor of her entire life.

Now, sweat trickling down her brow, her hair fuzzy beneath an old flowered scarf, Bonnie leaned on her broom between the big doors of the old warehouse, open to admit a breeze, and gazed back at what she, Prudence, and Paul had accomplished. The cots were gone, given away to colored families. The bucket of limbs had been buried in a field, the rats had been routed by an aggressive tabby they called Prissy, the detritus on the floor had been discarded, the chairs and long tables had been uncrated and assembled, the walls had been whitewashed, and she had just finished sweeping the floors.

Bonnie felt an unfamiliar pride swell her chest, a sensation wholly different from that she had felt when she mastered a difficult piano part or moved with seamless elegance through some Boston tea. This was a sense of...*accomplishment*, a sense that she had *done* something. The warehouse, which had become first a soldier's hospital and then a derelict husk, home only to rats, cobwebs, and ghosts, had been transformed by their hands into a classroom. A hand-painted sign on the front of the building made it official: "Cafferty School For Freedmen." Bonnie could not help smiling.

Prudence, seeing her there, seemed to read her mind. She stopped shelving books and came to join her. "Well, Sister," she said, "look what we have done."

"Indeed," said Bonnie.

"You did not think it possible, did you?"

Bonnie shook her head. "I had my doubts."

"And now?"

"We have accomplished a miracle."

"That we have," said Prudence. "And just in time."

She called out to Paul Cousins, who was in the back of the room, testing one of the last chairs to make certain it was sturdy. "Paul," she said, "come here a moment."

He looked confused. "Yes'm, Miss Prudence?"

"Join us," she said. "We were just admiring our own handiwork."

"Miss Prudence, I ain't got time. Still got one more of them chairs to put together."

"Shush," she said. "It will hold. Come look."

So he came and stood next to Bonnie. After a moment he said, "We done a lot here, that's for certain. More'n I thought we could, tell you the truth."

"We are ready," said Prudence, and her voice held a touch of wonder. She turned to Bonnie and repeated it. "We are ready."

Bonnie felt herself smile. "Yes, sister, I'd say we are."

"Y'all always call each other that," said Paul. "Y'all ain't really sisters, are you?"

Bonnie laughed. "No, not really," she said.

Prudence spoke solemnly. "Yes, really," she said. She looked at Bonnie. "We *are* sisters. We simply had different parents."

Bonnie squeezed Prudence's hand. "Well yes," she told Paul, who looked confused, "when you put it that way, I suppose we are sisters at that."

There was a moment. Then Prudence said, "Come. That's enough work for today. Miss Ginny has promised us a sumptuous meal to celebrate the completion of our labors. I told her I would bring some rice from the general store. Why don't the two of you walk with me and we can make an excursion of it? It is a lovely afternoon."

She gave them a sweet smile, but Bonnie knew Paul would not see the mischief shining at the edges, would not know Prudence was only scheming to throw the two of them together. She had whispered just the night before, as they lay abed in the darkness of their room, that she thought Paul was smitten. Bonnie had laughed and called it the silliest thing she had ever heard.

Now, as he nodded too eagerly, a broad grin splitting his dark features, she was not so certain. "Why sure," he said, with rather too much casualness, "that be right fine."

He was, Bonnie had to admit, not bad looking in a rough-hewn sort of way. But she could not imagine herself with someone just days removed from slavery, someone who said "Marse," and who lowered his eyes when he addressed white people—even Prudence. Someone who could not read.

For some reason, she thought again of that maid, looking at her as though they shared a secret. But they did not, she decided. Though they were both colored, they shared nothing else.

"Prudence," she said, "we have so much work yet to do. Besides, I am in no fit condition to be seen in town. I am dusty and my hair is unkempt."

"As am I," said Prudence. "What of it? We are not going for a promenade in the Common, sister."

"I think you look right fine, Miss Bonnie," said Paul. And the eyes that had seemed lit by fire a week ago now ducked bashfully when Bonnie looked at him.

"You see?" said Prudence. "Mr. Cousins thinks you look right fine. That settles it." Her eyebrows lifted playfully, daring disagreement. It was an expression of triumph Bonnie knew well from their years together. Prudence usually got what she wanted.

"Very well," said Bonnie.

Her expression must have promised dire retribution, because Prudence reflected back eyes so rounded by blameless innocence it was all Bonnie could manage not to laugh. Paul, oblivious to the entire exchange, rolled his neck and made a show of stretching the knots out of his back. It was a warm afternoon, the breeze carrying just the barest warning of the chill to come when the sun left the sky. "Nice day," he said.

And, thought Bonnie, it was. It really was.

They closed and locked the big doors, closed and locked the smaller door on the side of the building, and set off up Main Street walking three abreast, with Prudence on the inside and Bonnie in the middle. Miss Ginny was sitting on her tiny porch in a rocking chair, smoking a corncob pipe. She waved as they passed.

"Y'all gettin' along all right with Ginny?" Paul asked.

"Oh yes," said Prudence. "She was very kind to take us in. Do you not agree, Bonnie?"

Bonnie smiled an inward smile at the obvious attempt to draw her into conversation. "Yes," she said, "she was most kind."

They passed two little colored children, a boy and a girl, going the other way. "We see you in school Monday," the little boy sang out. The anticipation suffusing his voice warmed her.

"So tell us about yourself, Mr. Cousins," Prudence said, looking across at him.

"Well, first thing to tell you is, ain't no 'mister.' I'se just plain Paul." He had been trying to talk Prudence—and Bonnie—out of the formality for days.

"Tell us about yourself," Prudence insisted, and Bonnie knew this was for her benefit. "Were you born here? Are you married? What do you intend to do, now that you are free?"

"Aw, miss, ain't much to tell 'bout ol' Paul. Done chopped cotton most of my life for Marse Angus Dunbar. He got a big place couple mile or so from here. When the freedom come, I mostly thought I just make the contract and stay on his place. I ain't come to town for nothin' but to look around, see what town look like, 'cause I ain't never been before. But I always planned to go back, you see? Go back and chop cotton like I always done. 'Course, that's before I seen you and Miss Bonnie come to town. Y'all done changed all my plans." He was looking at Bonnie as he said it.

"Oh?" said Prudence. "How did we do that?" Her voice was honeyed like a beehive. Bonnie bit her lip, fighting an urge to jab Prudence with her elbow.

"How y'all change my plans?" repeated Paul. "Ever' which a way, I suppose. Tell you this much: ain't plannin' to go chop cotton for Marse Dunbar no time soon. Figure to stay 'round here long as y'all have me." Still looking at Bonnie.

Prudence said, "As long as you are going to be around the school anyway, why not allow us to teach you? We shall have an adult class in the evenings and you are welcome to attend."

Bonnie had asked him the same question the day they hired him, as she stood there taking down names and he stood a few feet away, watching her warily. In response, he had smiled abashedly. "No, ma'am," he had said. "I don't think so."

He did the same now. "Well, it's like I told Bonnie," he said, shoulders hunched, grinning like a bashful child, "ain't no use y'all tryin' to get no learnin' into my ol' head. Y'all best to concentrate on them young 'uns. They the ones you need to help."

Bonnie surprised herself. "Paul, you are not that old," she said. "There are people much older than you who have signed up. Look at Miss Ginny. If she is not too old, you certainly are not."

"Yes, ma'am. But still ain't no use. They's some you can teach and some you can't."

Bonnie pressed it. "How do you know if you have never tried?"

The grin closed over, disappeared as if it had never been. "Ma'am," he said, "I know." It was the sound of a closing door.

They fell silent. Around them, Main Street changed. Street lamps appeared and the shotgun houses of the Negro district became the tree-shaded front yards and two-story homes of the white district. After another couple of blocks, the street changed yet again, giving way to stores and the town's few other remaining commercial interests as they drew closer to the river.

It was a Saturday afternoon and the street was busy. Women walking together, boys racing about, a small group of Union soldiers watering their horses, a pair of white men sitting on a bench, spitting juicy brown streams into the dirt. Bonnie felt people's eyes on them, marking their passage. She knew what they were thinking: *Here came those two Yankees, the outsiders from up North who were set to open that school for the freedmen.* Bonnie glanced up at Paul. His face had gone rigid. He sensed it, too.

"We seem to have attracted quite a bit of attention," said Prudence, and now it was unanimous.

"I had no idea we were of such interest," said Bonnie. They had spent the entire week getting the school ready. This was their first venture to the west end of Main Street.

A towheaded little white boy with bare feet and patches on the knees of his jeans ran up alongside them. "Y'all the ones openin' that school for the niggers?" he demanded.

"We have opened a school for freedmen," Prudence told him. "And I must say, young man, that I do not approve of that sort of language."

The scampering boy stopped short, puzzlement creasing his eyes. "What you mean?" he demanded. "What language?"

They left him there. Bonnie was glad he didn't follow.

"'Pears we got more trouble," said Paul, nodding.

Ahead of them, a group of four young men—little more than boys, really—had assembled abreast the walk. The one in the middle—dirty blonde hair straggling from beneath his cap, something that would someday be a moustache dusting his upper lip—lifted his chin in challenge. "I expect you all are the Yankees everybody's talkin' about," he said through a pleasant smile. "Out for a stroll this fine afternoon?"

"Let us pass," said Prudence.

He looked around, playing for the crowd that had materialized out of nowhere. Women with crimped, judgmental mouths, men with mean, poor eyes. "Why, ma'am," said the boy, loudly, so everyone could hear, "that's right unfriendly of you. I just asked you a simple question. Y'all are the Yankees, ain't you? The ones opening up that school down yonder for the niggers?"

Prudence stepped forward until she was staring down into his eyes. "Who we are and what we are doing is hardly any of your concern," she said, and her voice was wintry and formal. "Now please, step aside and allow us to go on our way."

For the first time, the boy looked uncertain. His Adam's apple bobbed. He smiled again but it had a rather sickly cast. "Why of course," he said. "Just tryin' to pass the time of day is all."

He nodded at one of the other boys and they stepped to the side, the barrier of them opening like a gate. Prudence, Bonnie, and Paul walked through single file, Prudence leading the way, her chin characteristically high. Paul brought up the rear, glancing nervously about.

The store stood a block from the river. Its green awning announced that the proprietor was one A.J. Socrates and that in addition to selling groceries, he maintained a telegraph office and postal services. Inside, the shelves were lined neatly with food in boxes and cans. It was the new way of selling groceries, but Bonnie didn't fully trust it. She had never understood how people could be expected to buy food they could not see and inspect.

The store was empty but for the shopkeeper himself, who stood behind his counter, leaning on his fists as if to brace himself for the group's arrival. A.J. Socrates was a tall, thin man, his face sallow and shrunken. "What do y'all want?" he demanded, his voice hard like drought soil.

"We would like to buy a small sack of rice," said Prudence.

He nodded toward a far wall. "Right there behind you," he said, in the same terse voice.

Bonnie was nearest, so she reached for it. And then she stopped. A delegation of women had entered the store. There were four of them, four matrons who lined themselves up expectantly, hands folded before them. You could read the hardship of the war in the fraying of their dresses, the thinness of the fabric, the stony grimness of their eyes. But their proud bearing suggested these had once been women of means.

Seeing Bonnie pause, Prudence turned. Bonnie noted with alarm that a crowd had gathered around the door. They were trapped here. She glanced at Paul. His face had turned to stone.

"I've wanted to meet you," said one of the women. "You are the Yankee teacher?"

"I am Prudence Cafferty Kent," said Prudence. "I am headmistress of the Cafferty School." Automatically, she extended her hand. The other woman did not deign to see it.

"Why are you doing this?" she demanded. "That's what we want to know."

Prudence drew back her hand. "Because we are out of rice," she said. Bonnie winced.

The woman's mouth shrank until it was only a thin, bloodless line. "Don't toy with me, dear. I assure you, I'm not some beardless boy you can cower. You know very well what I am asking. We are beaten. We all know that. What we can't understand is why you all seek to rub our noses in it. Are all Yankees so petty and cruel?"

Prudence's back stiffened. "I can assure you: we do not seek to rub your noses in anything, madam."

"You are trying to raise the niggers above us," said the woman. "What do you call that?"

At that, a whoop went up from the crowd outside. "You tell her, Millie!" cried a man's voice. People slapped at the window in their approval. "Hey, now, get away from there!" yelled Socrates.

A second woman spoke up. "Do you think we gon' just stand around while y'all try to raise the niggers up?"

The third woman cut spiteful eyes toward Bonnie as she spoke. "You may believe in treatin' 'em as equals, sweetie, but that don't mean the rest of us cotton to it. That may be how you all do things up North, but you ain't up North no more."

The fourth woman said, "You all need to go on back where you come from and let us deal with our niggers as we see fit. We know how to handle 'em. You all don't."

"I am here to teach! That is my only interest." Prudence's voice was raised and she bit off each syllable into its own separate little chip of ice.

1

1 FREEMAN

The third woman laughed. It was a nasty sound. "Honey, you can't teach 'em!" she shrilled, as though Prudence had said something unforgivably naïve. "They're *niggers!*"

Prudence faced her, her features placid in that icy calm that sometimes overtook her when she was seething. "In that case," she said, "you have nothing to worry about, do you? In that case, I am wasting only my own time and money, neither of which should be of any concern to you."

The woman colored. The first woman, the one someone had called Millie, spoke up. "We dislike the precedent," she said. "We dislike people such as you putting ideas in their woolly heads. That does nothing but ruin them and leave them unfit for performing their natural function."

"That function is to serve their white superiors," said Prudence. It was not a question.

The women all nodded. "Well of course," said the first woman, Millie.

Bonnie had time to realize what would come next, time to mourn the passing of a lovely afternoon when they had walked to the store just for the pleasure of doing so. Prudence faced the woman squarely. "You truly disgust me," she said, the syllables again bitten off in slivers of ice.

The woman's color drained. The entire room seemed to gasp. "I beg your pardon?" she said.

"I believe I spoke clearly," Prudence replied. "You disgust me, all you lords and ladies of the benighted South, in all your delusions of your own superiority. If you truly were superior, we would not be having this conversation." Bonnie grabbed Prudence's elbow. Prudence jerked her arm away, her eyes never once leaving Millie's.

"You are not superior," she said. "To the contrary, were I ever given to choose, I should prefer an afternoon spent playing checkers over a cracker barrel with the meanest, most unlettered Negro tramp to a high tea in the company of any one of you."

A huge moan went up from the crowd outside as if a great blow had been struck in a boxing match. As, thought Bonnie, perhaps one had. Millie's hand flew to her chest and she glared at Prudence. People banged harder on the glass.

"You all need to get," the shopkeeper told them. He was, Bonnie saw, frightened for his window.

"How we s'posed to get?" asked Paul, his eyes on the mob massed in front of the store.

"We shall not leave without what we came to buy," announced Prudence, whipping around. "They will not chase us off."

Her right hand, Bonnie saw, was inside the dress pocket where the little derringer resided. How quickly this day had turned. She was relieved to see the Union soldiers just then, moving toward the crowd. "What's going on here?" she heard one of them demand.

"You lot move along," ordered another.

As the soldiers waded into the crowd to disperse it, the shopkeeper stared at Prudence with eyes that judged her to be mad. Then he came around the counter, brushed past the three of them, stabbed his hand out and grabbed the rice Bonnie had been reaching for. He shoved it in Prudence's arms. "Get out," he said, retreating once again behind his counter.

"What is our bill?" asked Prudence, setting the sack on the counter and reaching for a little coin purse.

"Nothing," he said. "Take it, and get out of here. And don't come back. Tell Ginny if she needs something from now on, she can come get it. Or she can send one of these niggers. But"—a quivering index finger aimed at Prudence's face—"you are not to come into my establishment ever again."

He pushed the sack at her. Prudence didn't move. Finally, Paul stepped forward and took it. Still Prudence didn't move. She stared at the shopkeeper and for a moment, Bonnie feared what her sister would say. But Prudence only looked, only let him see that she was not cowed—not by him, not by these women, not by the whole rebel army if it should encamp right outside this door. When she was satisfied he understood that, she wheeled around to go, her steps so brisk Millie had to dodge out of her path.

The soldiers had succeeded in clearing much of the crowd away from the door. The rest simply scrambled from her path as quickly as they could. Bonnie didn't blame them. Prudence's eyes were a cold fire. She walked as if she might walk through you. Bonnie and Paul found themselves rushing to keep up.

Already she could hear the buzz of conversation building behind them. Bonnie looked back. White people clotted the street, eyes following them back toward the Negro district. But nobody chased after them. They had had enough of Prudence to last them awhile.

Bonnie trotted up on Prudence's right. "Slow down, sister," she said.

Prudence looked at her, sighed, then slackened her pace. "The nerve of them," she said. "The absolute *nerve* of them. They believe they have a right to interrogate us? To intimidate us? Because we are opening a *school*? Never in my life have I seen such prideful, infuriating, *ignorant* people."

"I told you, did I not? I have been telling you all along. But you were too stubborn to listen."

"I listened," protested Prudence.

"No," said Bonnie. "You *say* you listen, you *always* say you listen. But then, in the end, you always do exactly as you please."

"That was a right foolish thing to do," said Paul. He had come up on her left.

Prudence stopped. They all stopped. "I beg your pardon?"

He swallowed, but held his ground. "I said it was foolish, Miss Prudence. You catch more flies with honey, my ol' mammy use to say."

"Mr. Cousins, what in the world are you talking about?"

"I'se just sayin', with them kind of folks, you got to know how to jolly 'em. You got to go along to get along. Can't always say what you want to say, especially when they got all the power on they side and they's more of them than they is of you."

And even though she felt the same way, even though she had just said as much to Prudence herself, something about Paul's words vexed Bonnie Cafferty. "Is that what we are supposed to do?" she demanded. "Smile at them as they insult us and belittle us? Nod our heads and shuffle our feet as they threaten and try to intimidate us? I am sorry, Paul. Maybe you find that easy to do, but I fear we do not."

The hurt that crumpled his face made her sorry she had said it. Almost. She looked at Prudence and found eyes she could not read. "Come," Prudence said, "Miss Ginny will be waiting for us."

They walked the rest of the way in silence, the street changing in reverse, livery stables and dry goods stores becoming two-story houses with white children playing in the yards, becoming little shotgun houses crammed with colored. At the end of the block, at the very end of the town, towered the warehouse. And what they saw as they approached it made them bypass Miss Ginny's and go to stand out in front under the sign that said "Cafferty School For Freedmen."

The big splash of whitewash staining the wall was fresh, still dripping. The splatter was stark against the near-black wood of the old building. It obliterated the sign.

They stood there a moment, watching streaks of paint race once another to the ground. Nobody spoke. Finally, Prudence stepped forward to test the lock on the big doors. It was sound. She went to the side of the building and checked that lock as well. Apparently satisfied, she came back around to where Bonnie stood, fighting back frustration tears, and where Paul kept shaking his head.

She looked at them. "We shall require a new sign," she said. "Mr. Cousins, please see to it."

Sam and Ben sat together as they had for hours, in a long line on a long bench in a long and darkened hallway. They were just outside a tall wooden door upon which was painted in flaking gold letters the words "Mayor's Office." But it was not the mayor's office and had not been ever since the federals seized the town. Now it was the office of the provost marshal and the entrance was flanked by two soldiers, one of whom stood aside as the door opened and an old colored man shuffled out. He was sucking at toothless gums in apparent dissatisfaction with the justice he had received inside.

"Next," said the soldier, and a young colored man next to Sam sprang to his feet, hat in hand, and went inside.

"'Bout time," said Ben.

They had lost the better part of a day in this valley town in the extreme southwestern tip of Virginia and he was not happy about it.

"We need to tell someone in authority what we saw," said Sam. He said it patiently. He had been saying it for days.

"Been pert' near a week ago," said Ben. "You think it still matters?"

Sam shrugged. "I am sure it matters to Sister. I am sure it matters to those children. 'I slept, and dreamed that life was Beauty; I woke, and found that life was Duty.' That was written by a woman named Ellen Sturgis Hooper. It means we have duties in this life, Ben, obligations to more than just ourselves and our interests."

Ben stared at him a long moment. Finally, he growled frustration, crossed his arms over his chest, found something at the far end of the hall to look at. A man came up the stairs opposite them. He groaned when he saw the length of the line. Then he took a seat at the end.

Sam drew his right foot up to massage the agony that now lived there. It was another reason, if he were honest about it, that he didn't mind spending most of the day waiting to see the man in charge of this district of Virginia: it meant that he could rest. He had caught a thorn in the ball of his right foot days before, and even though he had pulled it, the foot was now swollen and discolored, the wound oozing white pus that had turned to mud on his dirty skin. The foot throbbed like a tooth.

"That foot don't look like it gettin' any better," said Ben, watching him.

"I know," said Sam.

Somewhere near the end of the line, a baby bawled, screeching out its frustration with life. A woman in the middle of the line coughed a thick, wet cough, then leaned her head back against the wall, eyes closed, tears leaking. There were about 30 of them in all waiting there, and except for a few murmured conversations, they waited in silence. To glance down the line was to stare into unrelieved negritude, wide, solemn brown eyes in dark faces, looking out upon a world gone suddenly, abruptly, unknown. What in all their lives had ever been more frightening or unsettling than freedom?

Up the stairs came a colored woman dressed in rags—a head wrap and a thin old dress covered with patches, all of them in different colors, as though stitched together by a magpie. Her hopeful smile revealed teeth that were discolored and few. Her eyes, shiny with rheum, lit on Sam. She approached him without hesitation and for an instant, he wondered absurdly if he knew her. But there was no recognition in those eyes. Just something eager and heartrending.

She spoke without preamble. "I'se looking for my daughter," she said, in a voice rough like burlap. She took Sam's hands in her own and lifted them. Hers were bony and cool. The nails were jagged.

"I beg your pardon?" said Sam.

"I'se looking for my little girl," she said. "Is you seen her?"

Sam was confused. "Ma'am, how would I know if I have seen her or not? I do not know your daughter."

She shook her head, smiling her wet smile to assure him. "Oh, you'd know her if you saw her," she promised. "She was such a pretty little thing, prettiest baby you ever did see, I expect."

Sam felt something cold flow through him, as though his blood had become ice water. He was aware of Ben, staring. "Baby?" he said.

She was still smiling, but now some irreducible mourning crept in from the edges of her gaze. "Marse sold her from me, pert' near 20 years ago, I reckon."

"Do you know who he sold her to? Do you know where she is?"

The woman shook her head vigorously. Then she grinned. "But I'se bound to find her. Yes, sir, I is."

It struck Sam that the war had left the slaves a nation of mad women and men, rootless, homeless, wandering about, looking for wives, looking for children, trying to get back that which could never be retrieved, put back what once was, and never mind that you knew (though you would never admit it even to yourself) that this was not possible. You tried anyway and sometimes, as now with this wretched woman, the trying left you broken. A loathing climbed through him like rising water for white men and all their cruelty and arrogance. Look what it had done. To him, to her, to this line of negritude stretching to the end of the bench, the end of this broken country.

He was surprised to feel tears forming in his eyes. The woman watched him quizzically. There was something delicate and birdlike in the way she cocked her head to regard him from different angles with her merry eyes. Sam coughed to steady his voice. He spoke gently. "I shall look for your baby girl," he said. "If I see her, I will tell you."

Her face brightened. "You promise me?"

Sam gave the bony fingers a soft squeeze. "I do promise," he said.

She nodded. Then she was standing in front of Ben and lifting his hand. "I'se looking for my little girl," she began.

"I heard," said Ben. "I'll let you know if I see her."

And on she went to the next person in the line. "Poor old woman," said Ben when she was out of earshot. "Feel sorry for her. I surely do."

"Are we so different?" asked Sam. This earned him a sharp look. He shrugged. "You and I are out here just as she is, searching for what we will probably never find."

"Speak for yourself. I got enough sense to know my daughter ain't no baby no more. Got to be near 'bout seven, eight year old by now. And I know where she is, too, or where I left her, anyway. She in Tennessee with her mama."

"Yes," said Sam, "but what I mean is, even if you find her, even if I find Tilda, it is not going to be as we remember it. Time does not stand still. They have changed, we have changed. You cannot return to what used to be."

"You sayin' you ready to give up then? Go on back up North and forget all about it?" The question was a challenge.

"No," said Sam, "of course not."

"Then hush up about it. Don't nobody need to hear that kind of thing." His words were hard, but his voice was not. His voice was imploring, the voice of a man who desperately does not want to hear his fears spoken aloud.

Sam said, "Perhaps you are right." He went back to massaging his foot.

Moments later, the door opened and the young colored man came out, his expression grim with satisfaction. Sam had time to glance at Ben. Then the young soldier said, "Next," and they stood together and walked into what had once been the office of the mayor.

The provost was an Army colonel, a big man with a drooping moustache and the black stump of a dead cigar in his teeth. He sat writing at a table in the middle of a vast room illuminated by light from a pair of tall windows. At the sound of their entrance, he flicked them with a glance, then went back to his writing. "And what is it I can do for you boys?" he asked. His words were light, but his voice was leaden with tedium.

Sam and Ben exchanged another glance. Then Sam said, "We saw a killing."

This brought his head up, narrowed his gray eyes. "You saw what?" he asked around the dead cigar.

"We saw a killing," said Sam.

"Who is it you're saying was killed?" He produced a fresh sheet of paper and began writing.

"He called himself Brother. His name was Eli."

"White? Colored?"

"He was colored. The man who shot him was white. We saw them, but they did not see us."

An eyebrow lifted. "Them?"

"It seemed to be some sort of rebel posse. There were six men in all."

"When did all this happen?"

"It happened five days ago."

The colonel stopped writing. "Five days? And you are just reporting it now?"

"It happened in Forsyth," said Sam. "It took us that long to get here, as we are traveling on foot."

The pen went down. "There's nothing in Forsyth. Town was blown to cinders."

"There are a woman and two children. They are the dead man's family."

"I suppose what I mean to be saying is, I've enough trouble right here without sending men on a daylong ride to investigate something that happened five days ago. That is six days, all told. You think we will find any of them still there? The woman? The posse?" He snorted. "Even the dead man is gone by now."

"So you shall do nothing?"

"There's nothing I *can* do."

Sam felt himself getting hot. "It does not concern you that there is a rebel militia operating up in those mountains and that it is killing people?"

Ben hooked his forearm. "Come on now, Sam. We done took up enough of the colonel's time." His face was split wide by that idiot grin, that grin of deference and obsequious entreaties and shuffling feet. Sam was learning to hate that grin. He wrenched his arm away.

The colonel made a scornful sound. "Six men a militia? I do not think so."

"It is not my purpose to debate terminology with you, sir," said Sam stiffly. "You are a Union soldier, are you not? If you are, it seems to me you have a duty here. Would you apostasize from the cause to which you once swore fealty?"

Sam heard Ben behind him, struggling with the word. "Apostasize?" he pronounced uncertainly.

But to Sam's surprise, the soldier simply smirked at him in response. "It means to betray an allegiance," he explained. "Your friend here is accusing me of being untrue to the Union cause. He further wishes to make it understood that he is an educated Negro." The colonel's mouth twisted as he added, "That is the most troublesome sort of Negro in my experience."

Sam said, "My point is simply—"

The colonel ignored him, swinging his gaze pointedly toward Ben. "Where are you boys headed?" he asked.

"He goin' to Mississippi," said Ben. "I'm goin' to Tennessee."

"Family?"

Ben nodded. The smile was gone. "He lookin' for his wife. I'm tryin' to find mine, too, and my little girl."

The colonel removed the cold cigar from his mouth, looked at it for a moment. "Starting to get a lot of that," he said. "Boys like you, walking long miles, trying to find family, knowing they probably won't. It's sad, really. Don't know how you do it." A silence intervened. Then he looked up and his gaze encompassed both of them. "Look, I know you think you are doing the right thing in reporting what you saw."

Ben said, "It *was* bad, sir. Shot the man down like he were no more than a hog."

"I do not doubt that it was bad. Just as I am aware there are still a lot of rebs out there that don't know—or don't care, more likely—that the surrender was signed and the war is over. We'll get them all eventually, including the ones you say shot down the man in Forsyth. Of that I am confident. But in the meantime, I were you, I would be careful out there."

"Is that it?" demanded Sam. Ben had his arm again.

The colonel's expression was mild. "Boy, what I do is, I sit at this desk day in and day out and I play Solomon. This one has been cheated out of wages by a master who promised to pay him and then refused. That one says the free man sassed him and he don't take kindly to sass from niggers. It is my job to sort it all out, to keep the peace between a bunch of no-account white men who resent the very air I breathe and a bunch of slaves—*former* slaves—still trying to figure out what it means to be free. I must keep them from each other's throats. And then here you come, wanting me to drop everything and go scouring the mountains for some posse of rebels who killed a man *five days ago* and a hundred miles away." A hardness had crept into his voice. "Yes," he said, "that is, indeed, it."

Ben tugged on Sam's arm. There was a moment, Sam staring into the white colonel's eyes. Finally, he allowed himself to be pulled away. He didn't want to, but what else was left to do? What was left to say? "You boys be careful," said the colonel as Ben pulled the door open. He had his head down and was writing again.

The line of negritude was looking up at them on their exit, staring as if answers might be written on their faces. The soldier said, "Next." Ben trotted down the stairs. Sam followed him. They left the building, emerging onto a portico ringed by white columns chipped and scarred from small-arms fire. Official notices were tacked there—curfews, wanted posters, proclamations. The sky hung low, the clouds pressing their swollen black bellies against a landscape of wooden shacks and hog pens, a livery stable, a tavern, a bank. A flash of white light blasted the world, gone before it was there. Then the sky let forth a guttural roar and it began to rain, a sudden torrent of water rushing down. Like it had been waiting for them. Like God had held His fire until He had them in His sights.

"Shit," said Ben. "Goddamn it to hell." He pulled up his collar, hunched his bald scalp, and stepped down into the deluge. Sam followed him and they trudged down the middle of a street suddenly slick with mud and horseshit. They had already lost five hours waiting in the hallway outside the mayor's office in order to go inside and accomplish nothing. There was no thought of lying under a wagon to wait out the storm. No thought of anything but walking.

Sam found himself grateful for the rain. The mud was cool and easy beneath his bare feet.

They would walk until the light failed, then do as they had done many times before: find some old man or widowed woman willing to trade a meal of pinto beans or sowbelly and a night in a stable or shed for a few hours spent chopping wood or mending a fence. Often, that would be their only meal of the day. Sam had always been a sturdy man, not fat, but solid. Now he could feel his pants growing too big for him.

They walked in the rain, forks of fire arcing down from the clouds, thunder vibrating the earth. After a few moments, the last of the town was behind them and they were walking a dirt path under an awning of trees. It was a little less wet in here. The rain whispered to the spring leaves far above. They walked in silence for an hour.

Finally, Ben spoke. "Lost a lot of time back there," he said.

"Do not start," said Sam.

"Just sayin'."

"Say something else."

"And you," said Ben with a cutting laugh, "tryin' to use all your high-falutin' words to show that man you's special so he won't treat you like he treat the rest of the niggers. Guess he showed you."

"I refuse to allow people to treat me as a 'nigger' because I am not a nigger," said Sam. "Perhaps you are, but I am not."

Ben stopped. "What the hell that s'posed to mean?"

Sam stopped. Thought for a moment, then opened his face into a strained grin, bucked his eyes as if he were trying to see all creation at once. "Yassuh, Marse," he said. "How us feelin' today, Marse? No need to worry 'bout ol' Shine, boss."

Ben's smile was surprisingly easy. "That all you talkin' 'bout? Shit, that just pretendin'. You tellin' me you ain't never had to put white folks on?"

"If you pretend long enough, it ceases to be a pretense," said Sam. "If you keep pretending, it becomes your identity."

The smile twisted. "You ain't seemed to mind my pretendin' when that soldier boy on the bridge had that Colt in your face, 'bout to blow you to hell. Your big words ain't helped you much then, did they? You liked my pretendin' just fine, then, ain't you?"

Sam could not answer, which infuriated him. He started walking again. Ben followed, chuckling softly.

After a moment, Sam said, "It is a new day. That is all I am saying."

Ben didn't bother to hide his contempt. "That's where you wrong," he said. "Ain't no new day. War over, I give you that. Slave times gone, I give you that, too. But you still a Negro and they still white. They still got the power and they still don't care no more 'bout you than they care 'bout a dog or a horse. That's why I told you it be a waste of time, sit up in that country town, wait to tell that provost what happened in Forsyth. What he care? He white, Brother a Negro, so what he care? Told you that."

"We had to at least try," said Sam. "It is bad enough that we ran and did not try to help her."

"How we gon' help her? What we gon' do? We gon' bring that man back to life? We gon' take care her and them chil'ren? Can't hardly take care ourselves! We done the only thing we could. We got out of there 'fore them white mens come after us, do the same thing to us they done to Brother. Wish you get that through your head. We done lost best part of a day 'cause your conscience botherin' you for doing the only thing made any sense."

"Conscience is what makes us human," said Sam. "We had a duty to Sister. You ever hear of Henri Benjamin Constant de Rebecque?"

Ben rolled his eyes and appealed to heaven. "Oh, Lord," he said, "you 'bout to tell me somethin' else you done read in a book?"

Sam spoke right through it. "He was a Frenchman," he said. "And he wrote, 'Where there are no rights, there are no duties.' You know what that means? It means if you really are a dog or a horse, then you do not have to worry about it. If you are nothing but an animal, you do not have to concern yourself with anything beyond your own needs: eating and sleeping and rutting around, that is it. But we are not animals, we are *men*!" declared Sam, slapping his chest hard for emphasis, "and if you are a man, if you have claimed for yourself all the rights of a man, then you must accept the duties of a man."

Ben stopped again, glaring at him. "Why you always do that?" he demanded. "Always quotin' books at me?"

Sam paused, met the angry eyes. "There is wisdom in books," he said.

"We don't *live* in no book!" To Sam's surprise, Ben shouted it. "Why you always think I'm gon' care 'bout what some white man who wrote a book think about what I do? You talk about duty? I got one duty in this life: to get back to my wife and my little girl, what I ain't seen in seven years. *You* ain't got but one duty: get back to Mississippi and find that Tilda you always talkin' 'bout. That's what we got to do, Sam. That's our duty. And we can't put up with anything take us away from that."

They looked at each other for a long moment. Then Ben gave a small shrug as if to say reasoning with Sam was like reasoning with a cabbage, and started walking again. Sam followed him and they came out from under the cover of the trees into a clearing. He didn't know what to say.

Sam was a man for whom words were water and air, necessary to his very being, necessary to his very sense of self, so not knowing surprised him. Then he realized: it wasn't that he didn't know what. It was that he didn't know how. He had read the great books, absorbed the great ideals—not simply for the value of the ideals themselves, but for what knowing them said about him, what it told Billy Horn and Jakey the soldier and anyone else who looked at him with contempt or presumed to judge him as something less because he was black: *I am here. I am a man. Your scorn and your hatred cannot diminish me.* He would make them understand that through the very force of his excellence and will.

I am here.

I am a man.

And yet...

"You are right," he heard himself tell Ben. "But do you not see—"

And then somebody shot him.

It happened just like that. He was speaking, Ben was turning to listen. Then all at once, a flat cracking sound, like a tree branch breaking, a stabbing pain, blood all over him. He had time to see Ben's features widen in shock. Then he was lying in wet spring grass, his own breath hot and loud in his ears, and he could hear more gun fire, bullets whizzing above like angry bees. Just like in the war.

He tried to get up, to claw his way upright, but his body would not obey. It was as if everything below his head had become a separate country. He looked down at himself. There was so much blood. Where was he hit? How bad? He wanted to fumble for the wound, *tried* to fumble for it, but his hands just lay there, useless.

Lord, if it was his gut… Don't let it be his gut.

He felt nauseous. He felt himself slipping, sliding, going.

His eyes closed. He saw Tilda's face. And then he saw nothing.

The little boy's forehead furrowed like corduroy. His mouth twisted and he pushed at the page with his index finger as if he could will the unfamiliar symbols to become a recognizable word.

"The," he said, finally. And then, "cat," he said.

Bonnie put a hand on his shoulder. "Take your time, Bug."

They called him that because the boy's distended eyes gave him an expression of perpetual surprise. Bonnie had refused to use the name at first, thinking it cruel. She had insisted on calling him William, his given name. But after a few days, he had come to her in distress, asking, "Why you don't call me Bug like everybody else?" To her surprise, his birth name made him feel more singled out than his nickname did. It was neither the first nor the only time her best intentions had produced consequences she did not intend.

The school had been open for just under two weeks and she found herself doing as much learning as teaching. She was becoming vaguely ashamed that she had fought so hard against coming here.

"Ran," said Bug, then began stammering his way into the next word. Two rows back, a little girl's hand bolted into the air, her arm going back and forth like a flagpole whipped in a stiff breeze.

"Put your hand down, Adelaide," said Bonnie, without looking.

Somewhat to her surprise, she was a good teacher. They crowded in to the old warehouse six days a week promptly at nine, ragged little boys and ashen-kneed little girls poring over the McGuffey primers she and Prudence had brought down with them from Boston as though the mysteries of the universe might be decoded in their monosyllabic tales. What was more surprising was that each evening, after hard hours spent plowing and chopping or sweeping out stores or just waiting hand and foot on white people, their parents, even grandparents, folded themselves onto the same tiny, child-sized benches their children had used that morning, opened the same primers, struggled over the same words.

"To," said Bug. Then his frown deepened and Adelaide's hand went up again. She was sitting cross-legged on the floor with about a dozen other children. The school had run out of benches. Today, once she was finished teaching, Bonnie would walk to A.J. Socrates's store and send a telegram to the Campbell & Cafferty warehouse in Boston ordering more desks, including some large enough to accommodate adult bodies. The school had doubled in size in just two weeks and there was every indication it was not finished growing. Negroes were said to be coming from farms five and six miles away on the news that here was a school where they could be taught.

"Ann," said Bug.

And now, having crossed the finish line, having reached the period at the end of the sentence, he looked up at her, face shining with triumph. As he did, Adelaide's hand fell as if someone had tied a heavy stone to it. Bonnie rubbed the boy's head. "Very good, Bug. *Very* good. You are making splendid progress."

The word rubbed new wrinkles into his brow. "What splen-did mean?"

"It means good," said Bonnie, smiling.

"Miss Bonnie?" Ivey, a tall girl, painfully thin, had her hand up, but she didn't wait for Bonnie to acknowledge her. "Why you talk like that?" she asked.

"Like what?" asked Bonnie.

"Like you white," said Ivey.

"No, it ain't just that," said Bug, and he was regarding her thoughtfully now. "We got a plenty white folks 'round here, and they don't talk nothin' like that."

"My Pa say it's 'cause she a Yankee," said Ivey, triumphantly.

It made Bug look up at her with those amazed eyes. "Is you a Yankee, Miss Bonnie?"

Bonnie smiled, amused to find herself a curiosity. "I come from a city called Boston. That is in the North." Hearing herself speak made her painfully conscious of how tart and plain her voice must sound in this place where mouths lingered languidly over words, as if to hold on to them that much longer.

"That mean she a Yankee," said Ivey.

"She ain't no Yankee," declared a little boy sitting next to Adelaide. "My marse told me Yankees got tails and they got a hoof like a cow."

"Yo' marse lyin' to you," said Ivey, indignant. "He lyin', ain't he, Miss Bonnie?"

Bonnie said, "We shall discuss that tomorrow. Put your readers away. We are finished for today."

The groans of disappointment rising from that announcement were, invariably, the most gratifying sound she heard each day. These children would stay here into the night if she allowed it. Bonnie unlocked the big doors and swung the left side open a few feet. She stood there and, as was her custom, hugged each one of them as they left.

Prudence came down from the loft upstairs where they had their office and stood next to her as the last child waved over his shoulder before trotting out to the fields. "How are they doing?" she asked.

"Splendidly," said Bonnie. The word made her smile softly to herself.

Prudence regarded her. "You seem to be doing rather splendidly yourself, Miss Bonnie." They often used the old nicknames in the privacy of this place.

"I enjoy the work," said Bonnie, "more than I thought I might. They are so hungry to learn. It is as if you cannot teach them fast enough."

"I know what you mean," said Prudence. "When I teach arithmetic, there is one little girl whose hand is constantly waving in the air."

"Adelaide," said Bonnie, and they both laughed.

"She is a whip," said Prudence.

"She will be teaching us before long," said Bonnie, and the laughter renewed itself. It felt good, standing in the sun together and laughing, the unseen hand of a spring breeze ruffling their hair. It felt good, knowing that Bug's and Adelaide's lives, Ivey's life, all their lives, would be different from what they might have been, that destiny itself would be rewritten, because of what they did here. The knowledge filled Bonnie like cool water in a crystal vase. It made her feel complete. And it struck her as she put on her straw hat and tied it beneath her chin that this must mean she had been incomplete all those years, that there had been something missing from her life and she hadn't even known it.

"You are going to send the telegram?" asked Prudence.

"Yes," said Bonnie. "Mr. Cousins will walk with me."

Prudence leaned toward her. There was something playful and sly in her eyes that reminded Bonnie of when they had been girls together. "Shall I come along as chaperone?" she asked.

"That will not be necessary," said Bonnie.

"You will be careful?" Prudence asked, serious now.

"You may depend on it," said Bonnie.

They had an unspoken understanding, after the incident at the store, that Prudence would no longer venture down the street to the west side of town. Whatever needed to be done down there, whatever business had to be conducted, Bonnie would do it.

She hated doing it. When she was here on the east end of the street, when she was teaching or preparing lessons or chatting at dinner with Prudence and Ginny, she could almost forget where she was, forget that Buford, Mississippi was a beaten place and that the white people here hated her for it.

She had raised no weapon against them, manned no artillery, occupied no territory. They hated her for existing, she supposed, hated her deeply yet impersonally, hated her before they knew her, before they saw her, before she uttered a single breath in their presence. But the problem was, they hated Prudence even more.

After all, the thinking went, Bonnie was a just a nigger—despicable, yes, but in the final analysis, beneath contempt. Prudence was the white Yankee who had put ideas in her head, who had induced her out of her natural place, who was a traitor to her own race, starting that school at the edge of town and teaching *their* niggers to read and write and calculate and maybe even to believe themselves every bit as good as white men. Worse, Prudence was the one who, when they tried to confront her about it, had responded with impudence.

So it was left to Bonnie to conduct their business, to do their shopping, pick up their mail, send their telegrams. But she knew Prudence, so she knew her sister would not long accept that arrangement. It was not in her nature. And this meant another confrontation was inevitable.

But that, decided Bonnie as Paul Cousins came walking toward her, was a problem for another day. To her surprise, he was wearing new store-bought clothes—a dark serge coat and a matching tie knotted in a neat bow. Prudence smiled, eyes still dancing. "Are you going to church tonight, Mr. Cousins?"

"No, ma'am," he said, removing his hat. His voice was as stiff as his posture in the unfamiliar garments and Bonnie found herself hoping Prudence wouldn't tease him anymore.

She didn't. Instead, Prudence said, "Well, I will see the both of you when you return." She gave Bonnie a meaningful look Paul Cousins didn't see.

"Yes, ma'am," he said solemnly, replacing the hat.

Bonnie shook her head, smiling despite herself, wondering again how it was she could have been incomplete and never even known.

"How them children comin' along?" he asked when they were halfway down the block.

"The children are doing quite well," said Bonnie.

"They seems to enjoy it. They likes you a lot."

"It is learning they like," said Bonnie, shielding her eyes from the afternoon sun and waving at a group of her students walking home on the other side of the street. "I am going down to order new benches because we no longer have room for all our students. You know, you are still welcome to join us in the evening class, Mr. Cousins. I could tutor you privately to help you catch up with the lessons you have missed."

She hoped the lure of spending time alone with her would be enough to make him reconsider his refusal to join the adult classes. The man was too proud for his own good.

For a moment, she thought he would accept her offer. He was certainly tempted. She could see that in his eyes. But then he smiled. "No," he said, "ain't no use you tryin' to teach me nothin' new. I'm an old dog. And besides," he added, "ain't I asked you to stop calling me Mr. Cousins? My name Paul. Gon' make these white folks think I'se puttin' on airs, you and Miss Prudence keep up."

Bonnie smiled right back. "I suppose I am just an old dog, too," she said.

It took him a moment. He blinked twice. Then the laughter cracked his face and broke out like water from a cistern. "'Old dog,'" he said. "All right, must'a had that comin', I expect."

Bonnie had had a few beaux in Boston, though not many. Eager and ambitious young freemen, smitten and bashful young white men, they had plied her with sweet cakes and sweet talk. But she never had been in love with any of them. That realization usually arrived when she found herself out for a ride or going to the theater with one of those young men and trying to imagine herself still with him in five years, three years, two years, one. She never could.

At 26, she was, she supposed, of an age where she must begin to contemplate her future seriously or risk dying a spinster. She wondered sometimes if that were not preferable to marrying a man with whom she could envision no tomorrow. She remembered how lost and awash in Jamie Kent Prudence had once been. Bonnie had never felt like that for any man. She did not know if she could.

But there was, she had to admit, something engaging in Paul Cousins. He was not eager or ambitious or especially young, nor even learned. There was, however, an openness to him. He had not an ounce of pretension in him. He was what he was, with neither apology nor regret. Somewhat to her surprise, she liked him. She did not know if her feelings could ever become anything more than that.

It took them 15 minutes to reach A.J. Socrates's store. A lanky white man with a long beard sat outside, aimlessly whittling a piece of wood into chips. He stopped what he was doing and watched with frank interest as they walked past him into the darkness of the store. Socrates glared at them with his customary hostility. Bonnie had the sense they wronged him simply by existing. "What y'all want?" he demanded.

Paul swept his hat from his head. "Like to send a telegram, Marse."

Marse, she thought.

The man's shirt was soiled and torn at one cuff. His thinning hair was unkempt, and he had yet to shave that day. This miserable wretch had never mastered anyone or anything, himself included. But he was white and they were not and nothing else mattered. He reached out a hand. "Well," he snapped in a brittle voice, "don't just stand there like a lump. Give me the message."

Paul's hand went inside his coat pocket and fumbled out the paper on which Prudence had written the note to her sister's husband at Campbell & Cafferty, requesting that he ship more desks and chairs. Socrates snatched the paper away. His eyes widened as he read. Then he looked up, shaking the paper in his fist like a rag doll.

"Do you know what this is?" he demanded. "This is trouble, that's what. Folks around here been plenty patient with you, boy. You and that Yankee wench. She shouldn't ought to press her luck."

Paul turned the hat slowly in his hands. He kept his eyes on the floor. "Yes, Marse," he said. "I just...that just the message they wants to send, is all."

The white man's eyes darted. He regarded Paul, he read the note again, then he fixed a baleful stare on Bonnie. Her eyes brushed his for not even a second before she remembered to glance down. But she could feel the hateful touch of his gaze even so. He said, "More chairs and benches, huh? So I guess you all will have every woolly head in the county crowded into that place now. Well, no skin off my nose." He placed the paper to the side of the telegraph as he began to key in the message, then added, "But people ain't going to like it, I can promise you that."

And how would people ever find out? Bonnie thought this, but did not say it. It would not be wise and besides, she already knew the answer. This slimy little man with the sinkhole cheeks and yellow eyes, with his ratty shirt and his five strands of hair across the bald expanse of his scalp, would run and tell them as quickly as he could.

Bonnie was seized with a sudden need to be out of there. It was all she could do to hold herself in that spot, the room silent but for the clicking of the telegraph, and not go running back to Memphis as fast as horses could hurtle, grab the first steamboat, and return to Boston where, it was true, white people called you nigger sometimes and acted like their white skin was some benediction bestowed directly from the hand of almighty God himself, but at least the colored person who sought an education was not a threat to the very foundations of the community.

She allowed her glance to graze Paul's face and was instantly sorry she had. His bottom lip was held fast by his teeth, his jaw was locked like a vault, his downcast eyes were searching some inmost vista and she knew the proud man (*too proud for his own good*) was engaged upon some awesome and awful struggle he would not want her to see. Would be ashamed for her to see.

Bonnie looked at the floor instead.

She looked up when the telegraph stopped clicking. The white man had his hand out. Paul placed three dollar coins in it, then lifted the paper with Prudence's message on it off the counter. "Let's go," he told Bonnie, his voice almost too soft for hearing. She followed him to the door.

The white man's voice followed them both. "Hope you all know what you doin'," he said. "Hate to see y'all get y'selves in a bad way."

His voice followed them out. The man carving wood chips looked up without interest. They walked together. Paul still had his hat in his hand, crushing the brim in his fist. When the white side of town fell behind them, Bonnie breathed for what felt like the first time in an hour.

"Mr. Cousins," she said, attempting a light tone, "I do not think—"

That was as far as she got. "Done told you before," he said, in a featureless voice, "ain't no 'Mr. Cousins.' Just Paul, you hear? That's my name, just Paul. Ain't no 'mister' nothin'. That's for white mens and I ain't no white man."

The resulting silence sat hard between them. It had, she realized, cost him something to hear himself treated—and find himself forced to behave—like a small child in front of her.

In front of her. Her mind repeated this last part belatedly, a sun dawning slowly. It almost made her smile, but she didn't. There was nothing here to smile about.

He spoke. She had to incline her head to hear. "I ain't had no call to snap at you like that," he said. "I ain't meant it. It's just…"

"I know," she said and touched his hand.

He looked at her. "I just don't know why white folks got to treat us so mean," he said.

She swallowed. "Not all of them are that way."

He studied the wooden planks passing beneath his feet. "Hard to remember that sometime," he said.

Silence sat between them again, but not so hard now. It was easier to take now.

The warehouse came in sight and Bonnie allowed herself to think ahead to the adult classes she and Prudence would teach tonight, one in the north corner of the warehouse, the other in the south. Miss Ginny would be the first to arrive, sitting proudly on a bench right in front. The adults were as eager to learn as the children, maybe more so, but they were more difficult too, more easily discouraged, more apt to take offense at the barest hint of condescension.

The voice brought her head up sharply. "Come on, honey, why won't you let *us* enroll in your nigger school?" Oily as axle grease it was, coming from just inside the big warehouse door. She saw her alarm mirrored in Paul's eyes. Then they were running.

There were two of them, two young white men. They had Prudence backed against a bench, where she could retreat no further without falling. Her chin was up, her right hand in her pocket, and Bonnie knew that meant she was clutching the derringer. One of the white men glanced around at the sound of running feet. Pale blue eyes in a blandly handsome young face regarded them with scant interest. "Are these two of your niggers, honey? Why don't you send them away until we're done?"

"For the last time," said Prudence, "I am asking you to leave."

The other man, a shorter, even younger version of the first, cackled at that like a bird on a wire. "Ooh, Bo, she askin' us to leave. Guess we better leave, huh?"

"I am goin' nowhere, little brother," said the older one and he leaned so close he and Prudence were breathing the same air. "Ain't goin' nowhere til I get what I come here for."

"Go on and kiss her," said the younger one.

"Think I'll do that," said the one called Bo. With his left hand, he took her face between his left thumb and forefinger, squeezing until her lips came together in a grotesque parody of a pucker. He planted his right hand on her breast like a plow handle and mashed it hard. "I never kissed a member of the Yankee race before. Like to see what they taste like."

"Let go of me!" she tried to cry, through her constricted lips. Bonnie saw the hand with the derringer coming up from the folds of Prudence's dress.

"Marse?" Paul's voice was fluttery, as if something was rattling loose inside his throat. "Marse Bo, Marse Vernon, what y'all doin' here?" His mouth was smiling a strange smile his eyes knew nothing about. They were frightened wide.

The older one's gaze narrowed. "I know you, boy?"

"I knows your pappy," said Paul in his odd new voice.

The one called Bo snorted. "Everybody knows my pappy. Charles Wheaton owns half the county."

"Yes, sir, I knows that." Eyes still wide, mouth still trying to remember what a smile looked like. But he took a step forward anyway. "I knows ever'body know who Marse Charles is. What I means is, I knows *him*. Use to shoe his horses back 'fore the war. He always brung 'em to Marse Dunbar, on account he had no blacksmith on his place. He always right sociable to me. How Miss Annie, by the way? She still fixin' to marry that Wiley fella?"

Confusion darkened the pale blue eyes. "You know my sister?"

The thing Paul's mouth was doing that wasn't quite a smile grew wider.

"Oh, no sir. Only by your pappy talkin' 'bout her. He proud of her. Proud of all his chil'ren, tell you the truth. He used to say that to me all the time, say, 'Paul, ain't nothin' better in this life than chil'ren who you do you honor.' That's exactly what he used to say."

And now Bonnie understood: Paul was shaming them. And threatening them. All without doing either.

Vernon pulled on Bo's sleeve. "Come on, Bo," he said, worried eyes darting toward Paul. "Pa'll be lookin' for us."

Bo stared hard, his expression that of a man who knows he's being fooled, but can't figure out how. He released Prudence's face and breast, shoving her away from him for good measure. She fell against the table. "Maybe you're right," he told his brother, eyes still fixed on Paul. "What I want with some stale Yankee widow anyway?"

His eyes roamed desks and tables and neat stacks of McGuffey primers and his lips curled. "Nigger school," he said. And he harked and spat on the floor. "That's what I think of your nigger—"

He stopped. The muzzle of the little derringer was pushing into his cheek. Prudence held it with both hands, her arms fully extended, her right index finger curled around the trigger. Bonnie scarcely recognized her face, a contortion of outrage and tears. "Don't you ever put your hands on me again," she said. Her voice sounded like a pot just as the last of the water boils out, an angry scorch of steam.

All at once, Bonnie couldn't seem to get enough breath. "Miss Prudence, you put that away," she said.

"You should listen to the nigger," seconded Vernon.

Bo Wheaton's palms came up and he looked cautiously left to the gun pressed into his cheek and the unnatural glare beyond. He smiled. "You gon' shoot me with that toy, honey?"

"You think I won't?" Her knuckles were white.

He appeared to consider this without much interest. "I think you might," he said. "And you know what'll happen then? My pa'll go to the military governor and swear out a complaint. Yankees are the only law in these parts right now, sad to say. They'll come take you away. Probably hang you. And what'll happen to your school then? Who you think will teach your niggers then?" The oily voice was calm, an undisturbed pond in the solitude of first light.

Paul had gone silent as a post. Bonnie stepped forward, hands raised as if in a holdup. "Miss Prudence, I am asking you to consider what your father would want. What would he tell you to do?"

Prudence didn't even look her way. "You touched me," she said. "I am not some piece of meat you may paw with impunity. Do not *ever* touch me again."

His eyes still tilted left. He smiled as if at some joke only he understood. "Ma'am," he said, "I never will. 'Sides, that was just a distraction. Wasn't the reason I dropped by at all. See, the real reason I come was to tell you: this school? Folks don't like it. Some of us think it'd probably be a good thing all around if you all hightailed it on back to your own country 'fore somethin' happens or somebody gets hurt. That's all I really wanted to tell you. The rest was just…funnin'."

She pushed the gun hard into his cheek. "Are you threatening me?"

"No, ma'am. Just statin' fact is all."

It hung there for fully half a minute, the five of them frozen in place like statuary just inside the warehouse door. Bonnie's throat was painfully dry. She needed badly to relieve herself. She had never been more terrified.

Finally, Prudence shoved the gun barrel against Bo Wheaton's cheek hard enough to break the skin. "Get out," she said.

Another smile. He wiped at the tiny cut, glanced at the smidgen of blood he found. "Whatever you say," he told her. He touched his hat and moved slowly away.

Bonnie didn't breathe until the two men had cleared the door and Prudence allowed the gun to drop. Then Bonnie rushed to her friend and they embraced. Prudence was weeping, shuddering. "I need a bath," she said. "I can still feel his hands upon me."

"I know," said Bonnie. "But you should not have done that."

Prudence pulled back. "You think I was obliged to let him paw me? No. You know me better than that."

She looked as if she was about to say more. Then her eyes caught sight of something over Bonnie's shoulder. She motioned with her head and Bonnie turned.

A few feet away, Paul Cousins was standing in the doorway with his back to them, one hand ceaselessly massaging the other. His shoulders shuddered violently. Prudence's eyes told her to go to him. She did.

Bonnie put a hand on his arm. She didn't speak. After a moment, Paul looked down at her, his eyes moist and anguished. "Man raped my sister," he said.

"What?"

"Back in slave time. I'm shoein' his daddy's hoss, he find her out back of the cabin working in the garden. He took her and he done his business with her. She weren't but 14."

"Paul, I am so sorry."

"It *ain't* easy, you know."

"Beg pardon?"

"The other day when you said I must find it easy to smile at 'em while they say things and threaten us? It *ain't* easy. Not by a fair sight."

She was stricken. "Paul, forgive me. I never should have said that to you."

He regarded her for a moment with fathomless eyes. Then he turned away. After a moment, she heard him say, "So, you really think you could teach me how to read?"

She has lost track of the miles.

Miles mean nothing anymore, anyway. Miles are just something somebody made up to measure distance, so that when so-and-so says he's traveled thus and so many miles, everyone will all have the same idea of what is meant. But how can anybody have any idea of miles when you have walked so many of them, when your skirt tail is caked with mud and your feet are crusted with blood and you have cramps in your legs sometimes so bad they just give out and you fall onto your face and the few blessed moments of lying there makes it seem worth the heavy foot that comes prodding you and then kicks you in your behind while a voice above rages, "Get up! Get up, goddamn your sorry hide!"

And even though you don't think you can, you get up anyway and you walk.

So yes, she has lost track of the miles.

She does know they are in a place called Arkansas. She gleaned this from Marse Jim's conversation with the ferryman who took them across the Mississippi River, not, heaven knows, from anything he said to her. He does not speak an extraneous word to her, says nothing beyond "Get up!" or "Walk faster!" So thoroughly does he ignore her that sometimes she wonders if she is still there or if she has not become a figment of her own imagination.

He has taken to explaining to anyone who asks that he is a veteran of the late war, walking home with a faithful mammy who insisted on joining him in the field to make sure he had enough to eat. He says this with a catch in

his voice and a gleam in his eyes that never fails to touch whoever is listening, says it so earnestly that she thinks he has come to believe it himself.

When he tells them this lie, people gaze upon her with raw adoration and gush fulsome praise for her faithfulness. She looks away and they
always take this for modesty, which only makes them glorify her more. It
surprises her that they believe such foolishness, but they do. They *need* to,
she thinks. And Marse Jim seldom has to tell the story more than two times
or three before finding some poor widow so moved by it that she will give
them biscuits or sowbelly and a place to spend the night.

She has her chances to run from him. At night, him sprawling against
a bale of hay in someone's barn, legs drawn up crookedly, mouth gaped in
a rasping snore, she could easily get up and slip out into the night. Maybe
even get away. Instead, she squats there as if rooted, as if she were something
growing up from the very soil, and watches him sleep. She wonders why.

Maybe it's because she has nowhere she could go.

Maybe it's because she knows he would find her.

Maybe it's because she remembers. Wilson flying backward from the
explosion, landing against the tree like a sack of flour. Lucretia, gazing at
the blood-oozing hole in her stomach, then up at Tilda, right up at Tilda,
spearing her with accusatory eyes.

"*We's free now,*" she had said. *Insisted.*

"*How are they going to free my niggers?*" Marse Jim had said. "*How are
they going to take away from me something I paid good money for, something
I bought fair and legal?*"

And then he shot her, and she died.

"Little Jim liked cane."

The voice jolts her in her reverie, brings her back to herself. She is sitting
near him under an old oak tree at the edge of a sugarcane field. His voice
is so unexpected that she glances around to see who he is talking to. When
she sees no one else is there and that the words must have been meant for
her, she grunts an acknowledgement, not knowing what else to do.

He barely notices, rubbing a stalk of cane contemplatively between
thumb and forefinger. "Brought him through this way once, must have
been about six years ago, on a trip to see some niggers this fellow had for
sale. Stopped somewhere 'long in here for the night and the owner of the
place, he give Little Jim a piece of cane to chaw on. He ain't knowed what it
was right away, but once he took him a chew, you never saw a boy so happy."

He seems to be waiting for her to respond, but what is there to say? She shrugs. "He really liked it, did he?"

It sounds weak to her ears, but apparently, it is response enough, an invitation to speak aloud about his dead son, because he immediately turns to her. It takes a moment to realize the thing on his face is a smile. "Oh yeah," he says. "It's sweet, you know, sugarcane. Just got to peel the skin back and there you go. Little Jim, he worked on that thing all that day. Always promised him I was going to bring him back here for another taste, but then the war come and I never got to do it."

His eyes are shining and she wonders again what it is she is supposed to say. And then, all at once she knows, and it is surprisingly easy to say because it is the truth. "I'm sorry they killed your boy. The Yankees had no call to do that."

He turns away and she gets the sense it is because tears are falling and he doesn't want her to see. "Damn right they didn't," he says, and his voice is harsh. "Damn right."

It is a hot day. The tree shade is a welcome mercy, the wind breathes softly on her cheek. She can't figure what it is that gets into her at that moment. She knows better, doesn't she? And if she didn't before, she surely does now. But she can't stop herself. She isn't even sure she wants to.

"My boy died, too," she says.

There, she said it. Same thing she said walking down the hill from Little Jim's grave, same thing that made him snort at her presumption, made Wilson and Lucretia give her that hard look as they trudged past. Same thing. But why should she not be allowed to say it? It's true, isn't it? Lord knows it is.

Still, she is braced for his cursing, even braced for him to hit her for her insolence. Instead, he looks at her. Looks at her for a long time. Finally he says, "What happened to him?"

She swallows. "Got shot. Same as yours."

He nods, seeming to think this through. "Runaway?" he asks.

"Yes," she says.

"Shouldn't of run," he says. "That's bad business, niggers running." He is silent for a long time, staring down the road they have just walked. Then he says, "But they ain't had to shoot him, I expect. Some of them nigger chasers, you know, they just plain don't think. All they want to do is bring the nigger back. Don't occur to them that you got to bring him back alive. Otherwise, what's the point? What's the value of a dead nigger?"

She absorbs this torrent of words, more than he has spoken all together in the last five days, stoically. She wonders if some rough nugget of empathy is supposed to lie buried in them. Then she decides it doesn't matter. She doesn't care. "I miss him," she says. "I miss my son."

He gives her that look again. Then he looks away. "Miss mine, too," he says. "Son shouldn't die before the father. That's just wrong."

"Shouldn't die before the mother, either," she says, wondering where this boldness is coming from. Wondering where her sense of self-preservation has gone.

But he only nods. "Shouldn't die before the mother," he agrees.

The silence that follows feels almost companionable, except that she knows it isn't. Even in the silence, he is still Marse Jim, and she is still just a nigger he owns. So they sit there another moment, together but not. And when he decides they have been sitting long enough, he stands without a word or even a backward glance, hoists the rifle to his shoulder, and starts walking. She follows.

She stares at the back of him as she has now for more days than she can remember, his balding head hunched down, his potato-shaped body pushed slightly forward, like a man walking uphill against a wind. And she wonders what this is that just happened between them, what it means that they just talked about their sons.

It is confusing. Because she is just a thing he owns. She knows this. She has always known this. But do you speak to the things you own about your son? Do you meet with them on the common ground of loss?

You do not. So maybe she is—maybe *he* knows she is—something more. She wants to ask him about it, but she doesn't know the words to do so. And even if she did, it would be useless. He would just stare at her and shake his head if she were lucky. Slap her so hard her ears would sing if she were not.

They walk for two hours through cane fields, Marse Jim dragging the rifle by the barrel. Abruptly he stops, one hand on his chest as if he is taking a pledge. She pauses, not quite abreast of him. Stands there and waits.

"Gon' stop here for the night," he says, without turning around.

She looks. "Here" is a cabin, on the edge of a row separating two cane fields. The door is open and it looks abandoned, perhaps by some slave who has run to seize his freedom. Tilda is confused. "Here?" she says. The sun is still high. Usually, they never stop until it sits low on the horizon and their shadows stretch long behind them.

He thunders at her. "Yes, damn you. Can't you hear?" Then he winces as if thundering has caused him pain. She can hear him breathing, the air creaking in and out of him in labored sighs. He nods toward the cabin, speaks in a tired voice. "Go look inside," he says.

She does. No one is inside except a mouse that bolts between her feet and off the step in a flying leap the moment she pokes her head in the door. She sees a cot with a thin, raggedy mattress, corn shucks peeking through the holes. There are shelves, but they are empty. A hook where no shirt or dress hangs. A table with nothing on it. All of it coated with the dust. The room is filled with absence.

"Nobody here," she calls, "for a long time."

He nods grimly, walks toward her. Halfway across, he seems to stagger a bit. "Marse?" she says. He glares at her and she swallows her question. He brushes past her and into the muggy darkness of the room.

He lowers himself carefully onto the cot and the corn shucks make a dry, crisping sound beneath his weight. She settles onto the floor. Through the open door, she can see the sun standing high above the cane. They had another two or three hours of light at the very least. But here they are, already bedding down for the night inside a cabin some slave once called home. And apparently, they will not eat tonight, either. Indeed, food seems to be the furthest thing from his mind as he reclines with a weighty grunt, the rifle on the bed between him and the wall, one forearm thrown over his face. He closes his eyes.

She stares, boldly. Something is wrong with him, she decides. But she doesn't know what.

Suddenly his eyes are on her and he has grabbed her forearm in a grip that radiates pain down to her fingertips. She didn't even see him move. "Don't get no ideas," he growls. "You try to get away, I'll kill you." He doesn't say it in the overheated way one speaks a threat. He says it in the way one explains a certainty, a simple mathematical calculation. Two plus two is four; try to get away, I'll kill you.

She starts, because it's as if he has read her thoughts, read her recognition of his vulnerability, and leapt ahead of her to the obvious conclusion. And she cannot shake her head vigorously enough. "No, Marse Jim. Wouldn't do that, Marse Jim. Ain't got to worry none, Marse Jim."

He looks at her for a long moment before he releases his grip. She flexes fingers she cannot feel. He leans back and closes his eyes. After a few moments, he is snoring loudly, breath leaving him in a whistle. She sits awake for long hours, stomach gnawing hungrily at itself, watching through the door as darkness rises from the rim of the world to catch the falling sun.

In the morning, he is worse. His mouth droops open as if he lacks the strength to keep it closed, and perspiration stands in little bubbles on his brow. He sits up on the edge of the bed, weaving as if the floor were dancing beneath him. She pulls herself into a sitting position, back aching from a night on the hard wood.

Marse Jim glares at her as if trying to remember who she is. Abruptly, he rises to his feet. It is an effort, she can see that. And once there he holds his head for a long moment, occasionally wincing and cursing with the pain. After a few moments of this, he walks out on wobbly legs. A minute later, she can hear his piss hitting the ground behind the shed. Then he appears in the doorway, motions with his head. And they are off walking again.

It is difficult for her to keep behind him. His determined gait has become a leaden shuffle, inching him doggedly across the Arkansas countryside, and she keeps catching up, despite her best efforts to trail. For two hours they walk like this, their progress painful and slow. Then, just as the cane fields deliver them to the edge of a tiny settlement, his strength fails him altogether and he slips down to the ground.

"Marse Jim!" she cries.

There is no answer from the disheveled heap lying in the center of the road. She edges toward him, feeling panic rising in her chest. "Marse Jim?" Still only silence. She is standing over him now. His cheek, what she can see of it through the coarse black bristles of his beard, is flushed and damp. His eyes are closed. Tilda reaches a hesitant hand out and shakes his shoulder, gently at first, then vigorously. He does not respond. She doesn't know what to do. The panic in her chest has risen so high she can feel herself about to drown.

"What's wrong with him? Is he dead?"

The woman who asks is white, standing at the front gate of a neat clapboard house, drying her hands on an apron.

Tilda hunches her shoulders. "I don't know, Miss. We walkin' along and he just fell over. Been sick for two days now."

The woman comes over to take a look. "He's poorly, all right," she says. "Let's get him in the parlor."

They each take an arm. It is not easy. They are only women and Marse Jim is a great vast bulk of a man. But eventually, they wrestle him out of the street and up onto the porch and, finally, onto a high-backed couch in a genteel parlor with paintings on the wall and a piano in the corner by the window. Soon, he is resting as comfortably as they can manage and the two of them stand near the couch, facing one another.

The woman says her name is Mrs. Lindley. She asks how it is that they have come to be in the lane before her house. Automatically, Tilda tells the story of how she and Marse Jim are on their way home from the war, Tilda having gone with him to make sure he was cared for in camp. "Where are you from?" asks the woman.

Tilda answers without thinking. "Mississippi," she says.

The woman's brow wrinkles. "But you were walking west," she says. "Mississippi is the other way. East."

Tilda manages an awkward smile. "Marse must have gotten confused," she says. She can see by the look in the white woman's eyes that Mrs. Lindley doesn't quite believe her. She allows the moment to breathe, then lifts her chin in the direction of the unconscious form on the couch. "Do you know what's wrong with him?"

The woman nods. "We used to treat soldiers here, before the war was lost. I've seen this many times. Your master has pneumonia."

Tilda is perplexed. "Pneumonia? What is that?"

"It's a sickness in his lungs. He will probably get better, though I've seen some die. I'll have to give him some brandy and quinine. It may be necessary to employ scarified cupping."

Tilda's confusion must show on her face. "Bleeding," the woman says. "To improve the blood flow, let the sickness out of him."

"You've done this?"

"I've helped doctors do it," she says. A moment passes during which the only sound in the parlor is the air laboring in and out of Marse Jim's lungs. Then Mrs. Lindley says, "Is it true, the two of you are going back to Mississippi?"

She is, Tilda decides, probably in her middle thirties, hair a nondescript color going over to gray, pulled back now into a bun. There is frank intelligence in the eyes that wait on Tilda's reply. They are blue and clear as water.

"No," says Tilda. "That's just what Marse Jim has been telling everybody."

Mrs. Lindley's mouth tightens with satisfaction. "That's what I thought," she says. "So where are you going, then?"

"I don't know," says Tilda. "He has not told me. We left Mississippi after two runaways. We found them, he killed them, and we have been walking ever since."

"Killed them?" Her hands hang clasped before her.

Tilda nods. "Shot them down," she says.

"But there are no more runaways. There are no more slaves. Haven't you heard? You all are free."

Tilda hopes she is not smiling. "Marse Jim doesn't see it that way," she says.

"I see." A pause, and then: "You know, you speak very well for a nigger."

"My previous mistress, the woman who owned me before Marse Jim, didn't believe in the laws against teaching colored to read. She made sure all of us knew how."

"I'm not surprised. You seem very intelligent. For a nigger, I mean."

There is no way to answer this. Tilda doesn't try. After a moment, Mrs. Lindley says, "You know he's not going to be in any shape to travel for a week, probably two. You could take your leave and have plenty of time to get away from him."

Tilda is confused. "Ma'am?"

"You could be *free*," she says. "There is no way he could stop you."

"I could do that?" She is surprised that the thought hasn't even occurred to her before this.

"Of course you could," says the white woman. "Don't get me wrong, I am no abolitionist. But the war is over and the Yankee government says you're free. I think that's a blessing in disguise for us down here. As you are free of us, so we are free of you. Whatever benefit you may have brought in terms of keeping house and working the fields was more than offset by the trouble that came along with you—your thieving, your running away, your laziness, the way you tempted our men into immoral behavior."

Her eyes seem to have caught fire, though Tilda supposes that might just be a reflection of the noon sun glancing in through the window. "I for one am happy you are free," she says. "Nothing could please me more than to see the whole African race leave our country. Go live with the Yankees, since they love you so much."

Tilda is taken aback by the sheer fury of her. "Yes, ma'am," she manages to say.

Mrs. Lindley seems to catch herself all at once. There is a moment. Then she says, "Do as you please. I'll go get the brandy."

As she leaves the room, Tilda's eyes fall upon a small picture hanging on the wall near where Marse Jim sleeps his noisy sleep. It depicts a man in a Confederate cavalry officer's uniform who stands, facing the camera. He has a Vandyke beard, his chin is slightly elevated and his hair sweeps back heroically from an ample forehead. One hand rests lightly on the shoulder of a woman seated below him. Mrs. Lindley gives the camera her clear-eyed gaze, and she is almost smiling, as if on the day the portrait was made, she was satisfied with the world and her prospects in it.

That night, Tilda lies on the floor beneath that portrait, unable to sleep. It is not Marse Jim's raspy breathing that keeps her awake. She is used to that. It is the thing the white woman said: She can be free now if she chooses.

There will be hardship, yes. She has nothing. She doesn't know where to go. She doesn't know what she would do. But would the hardship be any worse than what she is enduring now? At least she would not have to walk each day to exhaustion. At least she would not have to live in constant expectation of being cursed and hit. At least she would be the owner of her own self for the first time in her life. At least she would be free.

She sits there.

The moon is full and the light of it bathes the room, cutting oblong shadows onto the wall. She can see Marse Jim's chest rising and falling unsteadily.

She sits there.

Mrs. Lindley smiles down on her from the portrait on the wall. A clock ticks loudly in the darkness.

She sits there.

She stands up. Her legs shake. She ignores them. Glances over her shoulder at Marse Jim lying there, sweating and unaware. Vulnerable. She could give him what he deserves. It would be easy. But she is no killer. She is…

What?

Maybe that's the point of being free, she tells herself. A chance to find out.

As if in a dream trance, she moves toward the door. Moves through Wilson's body lying against the tree in a ghastly caricature of repose. Through Lucretia's blood-soaked dress and accusing eyes. Through her own fear, so powerful it clenches her heart like a fist even now, forbidding it to beat, sucks the air from her lungs, forbidding them to breathe. Her legs are so unsteady she is afraid she will fall.

She opens the door. The night is warm. A thoughtful moon has lit her path.

And there it is, freedom. One step away, two at the most. She could run down from this porch, run down that road. She could disappear and then...

And then...

And then.

Nothing. She cannot imagine, cannot see in her mind, what would happen next. Cannot *trust* what would happen next in the way you cannot trust jumping from a high bridge into cold, deep water. And she needs that, needs to be able to trust.

She tries not to need it. She commands her foot to take a step. For a moment, it actually hovers in midair over the threshold of Mrs. Lindley's front door. Then it comes down, right where it was.

Tilda turns away from the door, closes it behind her. She is cursing herself, raging at herself, wondering when and how she became this weak, timid creature she now seems to be. She wasn't like this always. What happened to her? What went out of her? Where has it gone?

She has her head down, but all at once, she is aware of being watched. Tilda raises her eyes and there is Mrs. Lindley, standing at the bottom of the stairwell. She carries a candle in a candleholder and by its light and that of the moon, her face is easily visible. Disgust and, Tilda thinks, disappointment mingle there.

She shakes her head and breathes a single word. "Niggers," she says. And then she turns and climbs the stairs, leaving Tilda alone with Marse Jim and the moon.

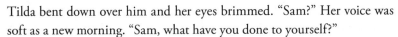

Tilda bent down over him and her eyes brimmed. "Sam?" Her voice was soft as a new morning. "Sam, what have you done to yourself?"

He tried to answer, but dust was lodged in his throat. He coughed, made himself swallow. "I have not done anything to myself," he said, finally. He spoke in a grainy whisper. "Someone did this to me. Someone shot me."

"You should be more careful. What were you doing out there in the first place?"

"What do you *think* I was doing?" He coughed again. "I was looking for you."

Her eyes grew even more tender. "Oh, Sam," she said. She touched his cheek with the back of her hand. He *felt* this, her touch cool and dry against the side of his face. "Oh, Sam," she repeated. "Is that what you're doing? You poor man. You're never going to find me, Sam. Go back home. You're *never* going to find me."

He became angry with her for saying it and that started him coughing again, a violent hawking that made his chest ache. "Do not say that," he said. "I will find you. I *will*."

She shook her head, and her brow creased as if disagreeing with him caused her pain. "No you won't," she said softly. "You were mad to think you would. You'll never see me again."

"Do not say that!" He was crying and didn't care. "Tilda," he said. He tried to reach out to her, but for some reason, he could not. He settled for repeating her name. "Tilda."

She stood erect, gazing down on him. "And look what you've done to yourself," she said with faint reproach.

"What do you mean? What have I done?"

In reply, she only nodded toward the left side of him. He looked. His arm was gone.

And he didn't care. "Tilda," he said, turning back to her. "Tilda." But she was gone, too.

Sam awoke stretched out atop a long wooden table in a room that stank of food, urine, and unwashed men. No light entered. He had no idea when it was. Sam tried to rise and discovered that he couldn't. It was as if body and mind had become disconnected somehow. The thought washed a wave of panic over him and he fought it down. Panic would accomplish nothing. He forced himself to assess himself and his surroundings. He found he could move his head, so he did that. First to the right, where a blackened pot hung suspended above the embers of a dead fire. Then straight above him, where heavy black timbers supported a roof.

A voice said, "Look like your friend is awake."

The voice came from his left and Sam's head came around, looking for its source. He tried to speak, but his mouth, too, seemed disconnected.

Just as Sam felt the panic rising in him again like bile, Ben's face swam into view. Ben was smiling and Sam knew instinctively that it was false, for his benefit. Worry pinched the edges of Ben's eyes. "Mornin'," he said. "Had us worried about you."

Where am I?

Sam heard the thought clearly in his mind. His throat produced only a raspy croak. "Easy now," said Ben. "Don't try to speak."

"Where...?" Finally the croak resolved itself into a word.

"You was shot," said Ben.

And now, another face came to hover above him. This face was dark like Ben's, but younger; it had a moustache and was topped by a thick ruffle of curly black hair. "Can you talk?" the new face asked. "How you feeling?"

"This here Josiah," said Ben. "He helped me get you here."

The other man opened his mouth to say something to Sam, but didn't. Instead, he told Ben: "I don't think he listening no more."

Sam wondered what he meant. Then the world shimmered and turned gray, and it was as if he were watching them through a rain-streaked window. Darkness fell.

Sam could not say how many hours more had passed when his eyes came open again. He lifted his head, grateful that he could. Ben, who was sitting in a chair next to the table, saw this and called out, "Josiah! He awake again."

"Where am I?" asked Sam. He was pleased this time to hear himself speak the words out loud, albeit in a voice so raspy he barely recognized it as his own.

Ben smiled. "Ain't rightly sure, tell you the truth. Might maybe still be in Virginia. Might be done crossed over into Tennessee."

Sam heard the other man enter the room. "Y'all in Tennessee all right," he said, standing opposite Ben, both of them looking down at Sam. "This here used to be slave quarters on the Jameson place. Him and his missus run away to the west in the war, took they slaves with 'em. Nobody seen 'em in a couple years. Whole place abandoned. You ought to be safe here for a while."

"Safe from what?" asked Sam. His voice felt a little stronger.

"Well actually," said Josiah, "not so much you as me. Ain't nobody huntin' you. It's me they after."

"Why are they after you?"

A grimness came into Josiah's affable eyes then. "Told your friend here earlier, while we's waitin' for you to wake up. I slaved over on the next place, Marse Edward's place. And his old mean wife tryin' to keep my daughter, even though slave times is over. They don't mean to give her back to me."

"What are you talking about?"

"Just that. Durin' the war, I run away with the Union when them soldier boys come through here and I fought with them. When I come home after surrender, first thing I done was go to Miss Polly—she Marse Edward's wife, the one who had my daughter. Woman was always crazy for Lizzie Sue for some reason. Never had no girls of her own, only them six devil boys. Kept my Lizzie Sue in that big house of hers like a pet for years. Hardly never let her even come to see us—me and Nettie, that's my wife.

"So the day I come home from the war, I rides up to the house and I knocks on her door, nice as you please. Miss Polly opens it and I tells her I'se come for Lizzie Sue. I says, 'Time for her to be with her mama and me now. We's free now, Miss Polly. Her belong to us.' And you know that woman wouldn't give me my child? First she try sweet-talkin', beg me to let her keep her 'little nigger.' That's what she call her. Say, 'I take care of her like she my own, educate her and everything.'"

Josiah imitated the white woman's voice as a thin, grating whine. "She tell one of them sons of hers, 'Go fetch my little nigger one of them blue-back Websters so I can teach her to read.'"

"But you told her no," said Ben. It was a statement, not a question. His jaw was clenched and Sam knew he was thinking of his own child.

"'Course I did," said the other man. "And that's when them sons of hers—like I say she had six, but the war left her with three—they come to the door with they guns and run me off. We been shootin' at each other ever since. I got one of them—Matthew, that's her youngest. He tried to bushwhack me when I come back to the house a second time. Took a shot at me, but he missed. I shot back and I ain't missed. Killed him dead. So they really means to get me now. And I means to get my daughter."

"Don't blame you," said Ben. "Ain't nobody with no sense could blame you."

"Yes," said the other man, "but it done got bigger than I ever thought. Mos' part of a week now, we been fightin'. That's how you got shot," he told Sam. "They seen you poke your head out them woods, thought you was me. You might have bled to death, 'cept I heard the shot and went lookin', found your friend draggin' you back through the trees. Got you back here and sent word to Mose—that's a colored man I know used to help a reb surgeon during the war. He come out here and fixed you up best he could. I'se purely sorry you got hurt so bad 'cause of me. Nothin' I can do about it, but I'se sure sorry."

"My arm," said Sam, abruptly remembering Tilda. He looked over and it was true. His left arm ended at the elbow, the stump of it wrapped in white cloth spotted with blood. The sight was plainly impossible. It could not be and yet, there it was.

Half his arm, *gone.*

"Mose said they was no way to save it," said Josiah. "Said them Minié balls, when they hit a bone, they just tear it up something fierce. Said only thing you could do is just cut it off."

"But I can still *feel* it," said Sam. Indeed, close his eyes and it might still be there. It prickled like he had laid on it for hours, crimping the blood flow. Occasionally, a sharp pain even stabbed through it. But how could that be, if it wasn't even there? Sam wondered if he was going mad.

No, not "going." He wondered if he had already made the trip.

"They say that happen sometime," said Josiah. "Cut off a part of the body and it's like your brain don't know it's gone yet. Mose said that'll go away. Just take a while."

Sam felt nausea bubbling in his throat. He felt tears sliding soundlessly down his cheeks. "Came through the whole war without a scratch," he managed to say. "And now look at me."

Ben put a hand on his shoulder. "It's gon' be all right," he said.

Sam flinched from the sympathy. "Don't," he said. And then: "Help me up."

So Ben extended a hand and Sam took it and drew himself upright. The room moved, circling around him as if trying to get a better view, and he gripped the table and willed it to stop. Josiah saw. "That's gon' pass in a minute," he said. "Mose also said tell you get some shoes for them feet. Said that infection in your right one look to be clearin' up, but you get infected again, you might could lose it, too."

Sam glanced down. His foot was swollen and torn, shiny with smears of some kind of liniment. "Tell your friend I have no choice," he said. "I lost my shoes a long way back. I have not been able to find a replacement and like you, there is someone I am looking for, someone I am determined to get back."

Josiah grinned. "Ben told me you talk like you 'most white. I ain't believed him, but I see he weren't lyin'. Hell, you sound mo' white than most of this white trash 'round here, tell you truth."

"He read a lot," said Ben. "Know everything in them books." The admiring note he heard in Ben's voice took Sam by surprise.

"Well," said Josiah, "I wish you luck with findin' who you's lookin' for." He slipped a forage cap on his head, the brim pulled low over suddenly intense and purposeful eyes. He slung an Enfield rifle over his shoulder, its strap crisscrossing the strap of a bag filled with powder and shot. A soldier returning to war.

"Where are you going?" asked Sam. He knew it was a stupid question the instant it left his mouth.

Josiah pushed a pistol into his waistband. "Where you think I'm going?" he said. "Been here with you two days. Now that you's awake, I need to get back out there and settle this. Take my daughter home."

"They are going to kill you," said Sam.

He nodded. "Good chance of that," he said, and it was as if he were ac-knowledging a good chance of rain. "But I don't see where I got no choice. What kind of free man I'm gon' be if let 'em take my daughter away and don't do nothin' 'bout it?"

"You could contact a provost marshal and have the authorities go in and get your daughter for you."

Josiah didn't bother to hide his disdain. "You think they gon' let me go after I done killed Miss Polly's youngest boy? Don't talk like a fool." He chased it with a smile to soften the blow, but Sam knew he was right. The man's only chance was to somehow spirit his daughter away from that house and then run somewhere they could not find him. And that was no chance at all. Josiah moved to the door.

He looked back at Sam. "You remember what I said about them feet," he said. "Mose say it's a miracle you got this far." He nodded to them. "Good luck to y'all," he said. And the door closed behind him.

For a moment, Sam and Ben just looked at one another. They didn't speak. They didn't need to. Sam brought his right hand to where his left arm had been. The stump was tender to the touch. What would he do with-out his arm? He remembered all the hollow-eyed men he'd seen in hospitals and tents, limping about, missing hands, arms, legs, and feet. He'd always felt a vague sorrow for them, never wanted to look at them too closely for fear they might be harbingers of his own fate. He had been elated to get all the way through with every limb intact. What a cruel joke to lose his arm after the fighting was done.

Or maybe that was wrong. Maybe that was the lesson here: that the fighting wasn't done, after all. Maybe it never would be.

"Wish we could have helped him," Ben said.

"I do too," said Sam, gazing up from reverie. "But you were right."

Ben's gaze narrowed. "When was I right?"

"In that house in Forsyth when the paterollers killed Brother and I wanted to go down there and you did not. I said it was not right for us to just run away. And you looked at me and said, 'What does right have to do with any of this? When was the last time you saw 'right?'"

"I was just talkin'," said Ben. "I was just mad."

"No," said Sam. "I thought about that for days. And you know, I cannot remember the last time I saw right. Truth is, I do not think I have ever seen right in my life."

Ben sniffed. "Well, what you expect? You's a nigger, ain't you?"

Sam considered the question. Finally, he said, "No, I'm not. As I told you before: I am a Negro. I am a colored man."

A smile. "A *free* man," said Ben. After a moment, the smile softened, like a balloon with the air leaking out of it. Finally it went away, and a speculative look came into Ben's eyes. "You think they ever gon' let us be free men, Sam? I mean, really free?"

"I do not know," said Sam. "It seems unlikely, does it not?"

Ben shook his head. "Sho' do. White folks been on top so long, they don't know no other way. You can see it in the way they look at us everywhere we go, them hard, mean looks like, 'What you doin' walkin' 'round down here like you think you somebody?' You can see it in the way they shot Brother down like he were a mad dog."

"You can see it in what happened to Josiah," added Sam. "A man should not have to fight a war just to get his daughter back. It is as if they think the man has no right to his own flesh and blood."

Ben's laughter was bitter as unripe fruit. "You might maybe want to change your name, then. Maybe you should be 'Most-Freeman. Someday-Freeman." He laughed again, but the eyes that beheld Sam were shining and bruised and had no laughter in them.

Sam didn't even try to laugh. He pursed his lips. He regarded his missing arm, the stump of it hanging there, useless. "No," he said, "I think I will stay with Freeman. At the very least, it will give them notice of my intention."

Ben appeared to ponder this for a moment. Then he nodded slowly in agreement. "You know what I'm intendin'?" he said. "Find Hannah. Find my little girl. Maybe hire on to some farm where the marse ain't too mean. Save some money, send her to school, learn her to read and talk pretty like you can. Maybe then *she* can work in a library in Philadelphia or some such," he added, teasingly. "Won't have to slave and stoop like her pappy."

He smiled, enjoying the thought. After a moment, the smile turned tentative and he gazed at Sam. "What you intendin', Mr. Free Man?"

For a time, Sam was silent. Then he looked up. "I'm just intending to find Tilda," he said. "I have not thought beyond that."

They stayed in the cabin three more days while Sam rested and regained his strength and allowed his foot time to repair itself. On the fourth day, they set out.

The morning was cool and damp and fog hugged the trees. It lent a ghostly aspect to the woods. There was no sun to navigate by and Sam feared they might get lost. But Ben swore he remembered the way Josiah had brought them and Sam was content to let him lead. The forest was dense with sycamore, ash, and pine trees. The dogwoods were still in bloom. Birds fluttered in the canopy of leaves overhead, and their morning songs trailed after the two men below.

Sam followed Ben down the dirt path that wended through the trees. They had not gone far before his foot began to ache and it was as if he had never rested. After about a mile, he saw that he was leaving droplets of blood in the dirt. Sam didn't say anything—what was there to say? He walked. But he had begun to wonder how much longer he could go on.

Eventually, they came to the edge of a clearing and Ben paused. It all seemed very familiar and Sam wondered why. Then he knew. It was here that he had been shot. Ben studied the trees on the opposite side of the field, which were difficult to see in the fog. Sam realized he was looking for the glint of steel.

When Ben was satisfied, he turned back to Sam. "House up there a ways," he said, pointing to their right. "We got to go straight across." Now he pointed directly ahead of them. "Don't want to see you get shot again in case them boys is out. I expect we ought to run. You up to that?"

Sam nodded. "Lead the way."

"Let's go, then."

And they ran.

Ben sprinted out ahead. Sam kept up as best he could, but his feet were bad and his missing arm threw off his stride, so his gait was lumbering and slow. His breath tore out of him in ragged exhalations, and he could feel his heart stomping heavily in its cage. And all at once he was back in the war, charging some damnable fort again and again, seeing men go down to the left of him and the right of him, running through explosions and seeing hunks of bone and flesh cartwheeling prettily through the air before landing with a sickening thud in the grass and wondering when it would be his turn and what that would be like.

But it had never been his turn, had it? He had slid through war as a fish through water. But peace was another matter.

Five strides ahead of him, Ben plunged into the shelter of the trees on the far side of the meadow. Sam clenched his teeth, lowered his head, and dug in. Until the last second, he expected the crack of rifle fire. Then he was in the trees, and he would have whispered a sigh of relief, except that suddenly Ben was right in front of him, too close, not moving, and Sam was coming up on him too fast. He stumbled and skidded, trying to avoid a collision.

"Watch out!" cried Sam. In the same instant, he brushed heavily against Ben, who staggered, regained his balance, but otherwise did not respond. Momentum took Sam a couple more feet before he regained control. "Why did you stop like that?" he demanded, walking back.

Ben pointed, Sam looked. And he stopped breathing. "Oh my Lord," he whispered.

There through tendrils of fog, he saw it—a body, a black man, hanging in a tree, the weight of him making the branch sag, his neck bent at an angle impossible for living flesh and bones to achieve. They walked toward him slowly. His eyes were distended as if about to pop free of their sockets, a grotesque parody of surprise. His tongue poked through lips that had gone gray like spoiled meat. Dried blood streaked the rags that had been his clothes. The skin on his right arm was torn as if dogs had been at him. The rips were deep enough that you could see his bones. And there were bullet holes in him. So many holes.

Ben wept. "All he wanted was his daughter," he whispered as tears made shiny trails down his cheeks. "She his own flesh and blood. Why they couldn't let him have her?"

"They are white," said Sam. "That is why." As he said it, a twinge of... *something*—lament, perhaps apology—passed through him for Mary Cuthbert, a white woman who had read to him while he lay in a darkened corner waiting to die.

"This ain't right," said Ben.

At that, Sam shot him a hard look, a look that demanded. Questions pooled in Ben's eyes. Then recognition chased them away. He shook his head again. "Don't think I ever seen right in my life," he said, dully parroting his own words.

"Exactly," said Sam. "Now let us go. For all we know, those boys may still be about in these woods."

Ben regarded Josiah's body, turning slowly at the insistence of a gentle breeze as the rope creaked softly against the branch above. Ben nodded and they took off at a trot.

All at once, they stopped. They spoke for a moment. Then Sam returned to the spot. He looked into Josiah's bulging eyes. "I need these," he whispered. An explanation. Or perhaps, an apology. And then, with his remaining hand, he began to unlace the dead man's shoes.

It happened shortly after dawn as they were walking to school. The smell was the first thing they noticed, a reek of blood and putrefaction that made their hands fly to their mouths.

Bonnie said, "What *is* that?"

Prudence could only shake her head. She couldn't imagine. They edged forward slowly, all thoughts of lesson plans and grades driven from them by the stench of decay.

It wasn't until they drew closer that they saw the tiny lump of her, lying there in front of the school. "Oh no," said Prudence. She felt sick. It was the cat, Prissy, and she lay hard against the big doors, yellow eyes open and vacant. A long slit had been cut into her side and she was in a pool of her own blood, grown tacky overnight. A bustling line of ants trailed away from her. For a moment, Prudence could not take it in. For a moment, she was without thought.

Then she saw the square of paper nailed to the door just above the little carcass. She snatched it off and brought it to her face. In a careless scrawl, it said simply: "Sometimes the mice fight back."

Bonnie took the note from her and read it, hand still pressed to mouth against the stench. Prudence stared, anger boiling up in her like steam in a kettle.

"Who could do such a thing?" gasped Bonnie.

"You know who could have done it," said Prudence. "Any one of them. Any one of them in this entire godforsaken town."

A tiny breeze blew and the doors moved, creaking slightly. Only then did Prudence realize they weren't locked. She looked closer. The latch was splintered. Cold dread flooded her thoughts. "Sister," she said, touching Bonnie's shoulder. Bonnie saw.

"They have been inside," she said.

"Yes," said Prudence. "Perhaps they still are." She stood, one hand in her pocket feeling for the little derringer. She took the right side door and pulled it open. Bonnie took the left and did the same. The cat was shoved aside in a smear of blood.

It was just after dawn and the light that entered the school was meager, but it was enough. Whoever they were, they had run riot in the school. Not a desk or a chair stood upright. The floor was a carpet of papers—pages ripped from McGuffey primers, work turned in by children, lesson plans. Whitewash splattered the floors, the furniture, the torn pages.

"Oh my God," said Bonnie.

"God had nothing to do with this," said Prudence. Fury coursed through her, a runaway train on straightaway tracks. She could hear her own blood humming in her temples. Prudence bit her lip hard, hoping the pain would distract her from the angry tears she felt building. She had no time for tears.

"What happened?"

They turned, and there was Bug standing behind them with his father, Big Will. The boy sometimes came in early for extra help with his reading. It was he who had spoken, the distended eyes even wider than usual. His father had no need to ask. He took in the ugly tableau with eyes that already knew.

Prudence hoped her voice was level. "Some bad people broke in and vandalized the school," she said.

"White people," said the boy.

It was not a question, but Prudence nodded. "Yes," she said, "in all likelihood they were white."

Big Will seemed embarrassed. "Miss Prudence, he ain't meant—"

Prudence waved the apology down. "I know what he meant," she said. "Besides, he is right, is he not?"

Bonnie was kneeling above the torn remains of one of the primers. "I feel as if I could gladly strangle whoever did this with my bare hands." Her voice was a knife's blade.

"You must calm down," said Prudence. She was distantly amused to find herself cast as the voice of reason.

Bonnie's head came up. "Calm down?" Her brown eyes, normally so thoughtful and warm, burned with a fire Prudence had never seen. In response, she made herself breathe, concentrated for a moment on nothing except the sensation of air coming in and going out. One of them had to stay calm enough to do the thinking here and it was obvious that, for once, it would not be Bonnie.

"There will be no strangling," she said finally. "Here is what we must do: Bonnie, when Paul arrives, you and he set about cleaning up this mess. Let the children help you. I would like to be able to hold classes here tomorrow, if that's at all possible. When you are finished, please go down to the telegraph office and order a new set of McGuffeys and anything else we will need."

"And what will you be doing?" asked Bonnie.

"I will be going to the county seat to speak to the provost marshal. I will implore him to send a troop of soldiers down to help us. I just need to find a way to get there."

Big Will brightened. "Preacher Lee goin' up there tomorrow to pick up some supplies. He gon' have use of Marse Joe's wagon."

"Do you think he would mind if I rode with him?"

"We can go ask him," said Will, "but I'm sure he be happy for the company."

And so it was that the following morning a wagon driven by the Reverend Davis Lee, a stocky, balding former slave with a thoughtful air and a slow, generous smile, pulled up before the county courthouse, an imposing structure sitting at the top of a flight of white stone steps. "Thank you," said Prudence as he helped her down.

He touched his hat in response. "I'll be back in an hour," he said, as he climbed back up on the wagon. As it went clattering away, Prudence asked a Union soldier for directions. She ended up waiting nearly an hour in a darkened corridor to be admitted to the provost's office. Inside, she found a thin man with a slight build, who regarded her with a sour smirk over his half-moon glasses as she told him what happened. She told him about the school. She told him about the vandalism. She told him about the cat. "We are at our wits' end," she said. "We need soldiers to protect us."

"Is that so?" he said, mildly. He had his glasses off and was wiping the lenses with a rag.

"Yes," she said. "The people in that town are determined to drive us out."

"Well, what did you expect?" he asked.

This stopped her. "I beg your pardon?" she said.

"Surely you apprehend the feelings of white men in the South on the subject of educating Negroes," he said. "You must have expected some resistance."

"Of course," said Prudence, "but—"

"We can barely protect the Freedmen's Bureau schools, Mrs. Kent," he interrupted, "and those are open under the auspices of the United States government. There is very little we can do for people, well-meaning though they are, who come down here on their own and traipse around, stirring things up."

Prudence stiffened. "So you are telling me, sir, that these people are free to do whatever they will to me and my school and you will do nothing about it? I need to be clear on this, because I have some friends in the North who will be most concerned to hear that."

He regarded her for a moment, his expression so pacific she could not have sworn he'd heard her. "What I am telling you," he said after a moment, "is that it would be difficult to catch and apprehend the vandals since vandals, by their very nature, operate under cover of darkness and catching them would be a task better suited to a guard or a detective than to the Union Army. Do not bother threatening me with your friends, Mrs. Kent. I am well aware that you are a woman of means and I am certain you have influential friends. I am but an Army colonel who answers to a general. But unless your friends are of such rank as to countermand a general, I am afraid there is but little they can do for you."

"But the town—"

"The town of Buford is a small place and has been mostly quiet since the fighting ended in this part of the country two years ago. The darks and their white folks got along reasonably well and managed to stay out of one another's way until *you* came along. So perhaps the problem is not the town at all, is it?"

He replaced his glasses and favored her with a bright, brittle smile. "Is there anything more?" The interview was over. Prudence was dismissed.

She stood, feeling like a leaden thing. He put his head down, pretending profound interest in the paper on his desk. She looked at him for a moment, memorizing the bald spot on the top of his head, trying to think of something else to say. But there was nothing. So she turned and made herself leave the room without a word. It was one of the hardest things she had ever done.

Preacher Lee was standing alongside his rig, smoking a pipe. Without a word, she gave him her hand and he helped her climb onto the back bench of the wagon. Lee took the driver's seat, flicked the reins lightly over the horses, and they started the two-hour journey back to Buford. Bonnie was grateful to see the hated courthouse slide out of her sight. A moment later, the town itself was only something remembered.

"Expect you didn't get what you wanted in there," said Preacher Lee, after a few moments.

"The man could not have been more obstinate and uncaring."

"Was you surprised?"

"I was. I should not have been, I suppose."

"No, you shouldn't. Mrs. Kent, the moment you come down here and opened that school, you cast your lot with the Negroes. Way they feel, if you cast your lot with us, they gon' treat you like us."

"I don't know how you can joke about it," she said.

"Ain't jokin'," he replied. Preacher Lee took a long, thoughtful draw on his pipe, let a cloud of smoke leak out. "You know," he said, "us colored ain't really knowed what Yankees was when the old masters and missus started talkin' about 'em. Some thought they was monsters with hooves and long hair and eyes in the middle of their foreheads."

"I have heard the children say such things."

"Yes," he said, "and some of us thought they was like Moses in the Bible, sent down here to lead colored children to the Promised Land. Thought we'd see the light shining under they skin and the halo floatin' over they heads."

"That is what you thought?"

"Some of us, yes."

"And now?"

He turned, so Prudence could see his disillusioned little smile. "Now we see Yankee ain't nothin' but a different kind of white man. Treat you better than the rebs, some of 'em, that's true enough. But still, he ain't nothin' but another white man. And like any man, he ain't gon' do but so much for you. Some things, you got to do for yourself."

"What are you saying, Preacher Lee?"

The smile turned sly. He returned his eyes to the road. "Got me an idea, is all. Have Ginny bring you to my church Sunday. We can talk about it then."

She wondered what he meant, but she knew from the puckish light she had seen in his eyes that he would not answer her, so she didn't bother asking. Instead, she settled back on the hard bench as the wagon jostled painfully over the rough road. They didn't speak much for the rest of the trip.

Four days later, Prudence stood in the bedroom she shared with Bonnie, regarding herself in the mirror and wondering yet again if a spoon bonnet with a nosegay of carnations were not too saucy for church. From beyond the closed door of the tiny bedroom, Miss Ginny's voice intruded upon her deliberations. "Come on, now. Paul like to be here any second."

"Coming," called Prudence. She checked the mirror one last time, decided the nosegay looked just fine. Her dress was a long and rather dowdy affair, lacking bustles, ribbons, and color and therefore suited, she thought, to a colored church out in the country. The hat was her only concession to style.

She opened the door and went to join Bonnie and Miss Ginny in the parlor in front. They sat together on a tatty gold settee that, like the other pieces in the room—two chairs and a table—was the castoff of a white woman Miss Ginny had once cooked for. As Prudence entered, Bonnie took one look at her. "Lovely hat," she quipped.

The older woman chuckled softly. "Now, you leave her alone," she said.

Out of Miss Ginny's line of sight, Prudence made a face at Bonnie—a favorite child taunting a less-favored sibling. The laughter that followed felt good after the trouble of the last few days.

Presently, there came a knock at the door. Miss Ginny opened it and there was Paul. "Mornin', ladies," he said. He lifted his hat and smiled a jaunty smile. "Miss Bonnie," he added.

Prudence was quietly amused. For the last couple of weeks, Bonnie had been teaching Paul to read. The affection between them was becoming obvious, though Bonnie denied it every time Prudence tried to bring it up.

It was a hot day, the air thick and close. They walked in a companionable silence toward the edge of town. When they passed the warehouse,

Prudence could not help herself. She looked over, half expecting some new outrage. But the building stood silent and unabused. She exhaled a breath she had not known she was holding.

Then a gleaming black wagon clattered to a stop beside them and she started. Bo Wheaton was at the reins and he spoke without preamble, without giving her three companions so much as a glance. "My pa wants to see you, ma'am," he told Prudence.

She felt their eyes on her. "I beg your pardon," she said.

"My pa sent me to get you," he said.

"If your father wishes to see me, I am at the Cafferty School six days a week. I am certain he knows where it is."

The blue eyes darkened and then, to her surprise, he smiled. "Yes ma'am, but he'd count it as a personal favor if you would call on him up to the house. My father, he's, well...an invalid since the war. Lost both his legs. It would be a great hardship for him to come over here. If you're worried about missin' your church service, well, I promise I'll have you there before the last amen."

"What does he wish to see me for?"

"Ma'am, I purely don't know. He just sent me to get you, is all."

"Well, if I go, my friends must go with me."

For the second time in less than a minute, he surprised her by smiling. "Ma'am, you're not from around here, so I guess you wouldn't know, but in this country, white people do not entertain niggers in their homes. Tell you the truth, it's not that common they entertain Yankees." He spoke patiently, as if instructing a child.

"So you expect me to just ride off with you alone?" said Prudence.

He nodded. "Yes, ma'am. And if you're worried about your personal safety, my pa says that I am to apologize for my"—and here, his smile bent with distaste—"boorish behavior last time we met, and to give you his personal assurance no one will bother you while you are in his care. Plus, I'm sure you still have that little pea shooter of yours."

He spoke to Paul without looking at him. "Tell her if my pap's word is good or not, boy."

She heard Paul say, "It's good." His voice had gone dead.

She glanced the question at him. He met her eyes and repeated. "It's good. Marse Wheaton set a great store by his word."

Prudence was curious. She had to admit that to herself. She turned, seeking out her companions, wanting their opinions. Miss Ginny and Paul held their heads down as though Bo Wheaton were the sun, too bright for direct viewing. Bonnie was staring at her, eyes widened. "I already know what you are going to do," she said, her voice softened by wonder and disbelief.

Prudence nodded, knowing it herself only in that instant. "Very well," she told Bo Wheaton. "Let us go see your father."

He answered her with a curt nod. Paul helped her climb up into the rig behind the driver. She was barely seated before Wheaton flicked the horses with the reins and the wagon started forward with a lurch that pushed her back against the plush leather seat and brought her hand to her head to hold the spoon bonnet in place. Wheaton turned the wagon in the middle of the street, bringing her back past Paul, Bonnie and Miss Ginny, who stood there on the boardwalk watching after her. They looked small and forlorn. She smiled to reassure them. And then they were gone.

Wheaton kept the horses at a brisk pace, just short of a trot. For long minutes, there was no sound except those the wagon made, the striking of hooves against the dirt, the jingling of bridles, the turning of wheels. They drove west toward the river, then turned north. The movement of the wagon stirred a hot breeze that flowed back against Prudence's face. The sun highlighted ripples of water that unfolded across the broad, brown back of the Mississippi.

"I meant what I said, you know." Bo Wheaton spoke without turning around.

The sound of his voice surprised her. "Beg pardon?" she said.

"About my behavior last time. My pa was right. That was boorish of me. Can't blame you for pullin' out that little pea shooter. You got sand for a Yankee gal. I'll give you that."

Prudence kept silent. She wished she had the derringer with her now, but she had thought it improper and unnecessary to go armed to church. Assuming her safe return from this trip, she would not make that mistake again. In this country, she told herself—no, in this *part* of the country—it might be necessary to go armed everywhere.

"I couldn't help myself," said Wheaton, as though she had spoken. "I've always had too great a fondness for drink. My father, my brother, my sister, they all say that. And of course, drink causes a loss of control. You're very pretty, ma'am. You must know that." Here, he glanced over his shoulder at her and the smile he gave was almost bashful. Prudence turned away. He went back to watching the horse's rumps.

"But the thing I can't understand," he went on, "the thing none of us can understand, is how you can come down here and do what you're doin'. You have to know—even a *Yankee* has to know—how wrong that is, ma'am. And not just wrong, but dangerous."

He looked back at her again, as if waiting for agreement. Prudence studied the river. Wheaton sighed as if fatigued and went back to the horses. "That's all I'm sayin'," he muttered. He did not speak again for the balance of the journey.

After a few more minutes, they arrived at a large house that sat on a bluff at the end of a long, tree-shaded lane. When the wagon clattered to a stop, a Negro man and woman appeared as if by magic. The man, stiffly formal and dressed in livery, placed a step stool for her convenience. He touched her elbow lightly as she climbed down from the rig. Then he went to tend the horses. He never spoke.

Prudence found herself standing beneath a columned portico beside a short, plump colored woman whose hair was gathered beneath a kerchief. Prudence smiled at the woman, who only bowed her head in response. "This here is Sassafras," said Wheaton, coming around to Prudence's side as the footman led the horses away. "Call her that on account of she's so sassy whenever anyone dares intrude upon her kitchen. I have some work to do. She'll take you to my father." He lifted his hat. "Ma'am," he said and then lowered the hat and sauntered toward one of the outbuildings.

"If you please come with me," said the colored woman.

She led Prudence through the front door and into a hall that rose two stories above her. From either side, stairways curled along the wall up to the living quarters above. A massive chandelier hung suspended overhead. Prudence wondered idly how long it took to light all the candles.

The woman led her through an equally elegant parlor and dining room, where the table looked long enough to accommodate 20 diners with ease. A door from here led to a wide, covered porch that wrapped around the back of the house, looking down upon the river. A steamboat was just passing by, heading north. Its decks were crowded with soldiers.

"What is your real name?" Prudence asked the colored woman as the latter gestured toward a chair positioned next to a round table, facing the view.

"Sassafras real enough," the woman said, and Prudence felt chastened, abruptly reminded of her place in the grand scheme of things. Why had she thought this woman would allow herself to be drawn into conversation with a white woman she did not know? It was vanity, that's all it was.

Prudence sat. There was a pitcher of lemonade in the center of the damask-covered table. It was flanked by two drinking glasses, one of which Sassafras now filled and placed next to Prudence. She pointed to a tiny bell that sat on the table.

"Marse be with you in a minute," she said. "You need anything, you give that bell a ring." And with that, she disappeared back into the mansion.

Prudence drank her lemonade. It was cool and tart and a welcome antidote to the oppression of the heat. In silence, she took another sip as the river rolled past below her. Despite herself, she was enraptured by the view.

A few minutes later, the sound of metal wheels turning against hardwood brought her around to see the door open and a balding, legless man in a wheelchair pushed through it by a young Negro man. How many servants did these people have?

"Well," said the man, as he was wheeled to a position opposite her. "I see you appreciate the view. I am pleased to think we have that much in common at least. I am Charles Wheaton," he said, without extending his hand. "You would be Mrs. Kent. I am pleased you accepted my invitation to come up here, especially on such short notice."

"Your son was rather insistent."

"Yes, he has that quality."

"Perhaps you would be so kind as to tell me why you wanted to see me," said Prudence.

He cut her a glance. "We are to be direct with one another, then? Good. I much prefer it that way. I grew up here, Mrs. Kent. I love this town. I am certain even those of your race can appreciate what it is to be attached to a place. This is my home, and I don't want to see it harmed."

"I do not follow you," said Prudence.

His smile just then was shrewd and mean. "I suspect you do," he said. "I want you to shut down that nigger school."

Her chin came up. "Mr. Wheaton, I will thank you not to use such vulgar language in my presence. I had taken you for a gentleman, sir."

It stung him. She could see that in the way his eyes went out of focus for just a second. Then they turned hard, little pellets of metal embedded in the fleshly folds of his face. "I want you to shut down that school," he repeated.

"I will not," she said.

He went on as if she had not spoken. "Ordinarily in this situation, I would strike a bargain to buy the building at a price that allowed you to make a handsome profit, on the condition that you go away and stir up no more mischief. However, I happen to know that your father left you a tidy sum—a furniture maker, wasn't he?—so I don't expect you would be subject to the ordinary temptations of money."

"You are quite right," she said.

"However, I thought you might listen to an appeal on simple moral grounds."

"Moral grounds," she said. It was not a question.

He sighed and did not speak for a long time, staring out at the lazy Mississippi. Then he said, "Mrs. Kent, do you believe in God?"

"I do," she said.

"As do I," he said, glancing at her. "And I believe God has set in place a natural order for all creation. He set white men on top of that order for a reason."

"Is that what your Bible tells you, Mr. Wheaton?"

"It is also what the evidence of my eyes and plain common sense tell me, Mrs. Kent. In physical deportment, intellectual capacity, and moral integrity, white men were set apart from all the other races of the world. That includes your red man, your yellow man, and most certainly, your black man."

"Most certainly," said Prudence, not bothering to hide her smile.

"I assure you it is not a joke, Mrs. Kent. There is an order to creation, and when all accept their places in that order, it works as God intended and every man is happier. But when people meddle with that order, when they sow confusion and discontent, dire consequences must naturally follow. Consider the late war as proof. Consider the fate of your president."

"Are you threatening me?"

Frustration blew out of him in a heavy sigh. "I am trying to *instruct* you, Mrs. Kent. As you can see, I am hardly in a position to do you any harm. I lost that ability, along with my legs, in a Yankee bombardment at Vicksburg. And I can further promise you that no one of my household or in my employ will do you harm, either. But Mrs. Kent, I cannot control what other people will do."

"You cannot or you will not? It is my understanding you are the most powerful man in this town. I find it difficult to believe there is much that happens in Buford you do not control."

"You give me entirely too much credit," answered Wheaton through a tight smile. "I do not control. But I do predict. This is cotton country. In a few months, it will be picking season and our planters will again be obliged to suffer the indignity of hiring labor they formerly owned outright. People will find that difficult enough to stomach. But if you, through your misguided efforts, give their labor force some foolish notion of moving beyond their station in life, if you interfere with the planters' livelihood..." He spread his palms as if to say the rest did not even bear speaking.

"Your townsmen have already been quite busy, Mr. Wheaton. They have threatened us. They have vandalized our school."

He waved at her words as one would a bothersome fly. "Those are just pranks, Mrs. Kent. They are getting their nerve up. If I were you, I would be braced for much worse."

"And yet these are the people you say God has ordained at the top of the natural order."

The flat of his palm slammed the table so fiercely that lemonade sloshed out of the pitcher. He roared, "Yes, by thunder! That is *exactly* what I am saying!"

He took a moment. She could see him struggling to master himself. Down below, a scrawny white boy, barefoot and bare-chested, wandered along the banks of the river. Prudence watched him until he was almost out of sight.

When Charles Wheaton next spoke, his voice bore only the remnants of his sudden rage. "Do you know that if it were not for a handful of investments in some northern firms that predate the war, I would be wiped out right now?"

"What is your point, Mr. Wheaton?" asked Prudence.

"We have lost so much, Mrs. Kent," he said. "This is what I am struggling to make you see. We have lost our homes and other property. We have lost our dignity and pride. We have lost our way of life and we have lost our country. By the holy God, how much more can you Northern people expect us to lose? Would you have us surrender our sacred place in the very order of creation? We will not meekly accept that. We cannot, if we wish to still consider ourselves white *men*. You will not prop the Negro up as our social or political equal. We will resist that with every means at our disposal, Mrs. Kent. We will resist for a hundred years, and more."

He regarded her for a long moment. Then he made a weary sound. "But you are going to do it anyway, aren't you? You are going to continue teaching them at that school of yours."

"Yes, I am," she said.

"You will not even consider locating your school elsewhere, perhaps in another town where the people are less likely to take offense?"

"And where would such a town be?" asked Prudence.

His eyes filmed over and he stared at the river. "Too bad," he said after a moment. "I had hoped I might be able to make you understand. Of course, I should have expected your response. I had a similar discussion with your father when he thought to buy a piece of the old Campbell place and loose a plague of free Negroes in our midst. You remind me of him. He was an idealistic fool, too. He had to learn the hard way, too. It mystifies me that neither of you can comprehend elemental truth. You are white, after all, even if you are from the North."

"I suppose that makes all the difference," said Prudence.

"I suppose it does at that," he said. "I am just sorry we could not come to terms. There has already been such suffering. Too much, really."

"On that much, we can agree," said Prudence.

He gave her one last speculative look, then nodded curtly, as if to himself. "Very well, then. Sass will show you out. Beauregard will take you back." The young Negro man reappeared on the porch as if by magic. He took the handles of the chair and wheeled the old man away.

Prudence was alone. She sipped her lemonade. After a moment, the large, dark-skinned woman stepped out of the house. "Come with me, ma'am," she said. Prudence stood and the woman led her back through the large, silent house. They stood together under the portico a moment without speaking. Then the woman said, "My name Colindy."

Startled, Prudence said, "Beg pardon?"

"You asked my name before," she said. "My name Colindy. Sass, that's just something they calls me. They think it's funny."

Before Prudence could respond, the wagon rattled to a stop in front of them. Bo Wheaton came around and offered a perfunctory hand as

Prudence climbed up. From her seat, she regarded Colindy closely and the colored woman watched her just as intently, eyes large in a face void of expression. As Bo clambered into his own seat, the black woman said, "You take care of yourself, ma'am. You hear me?" Still nothing showing on her face.

Prudence had a bare second to nod, then the wagon moved forward with an abrupt jolt. Colindy watched her go, then turned back toward the house.

"You turned him down," Bo was saying as the wagon flew at too great a speed down the long lane.

"I did," she said.

He turned to show her a smirk. "I told him you would," he said. "I bet Vern half a dollar you would. It's too bad. Like I told you, you got sand for a Yankee. I can't say much for your common sense, though."

"Fortunately, your opinion does not matter to me." Prudence spoke with an assurance she did not feel.

In silence, they rode back through town, past Miss Ginny's and the school, out into the country. They passed a cotton field. It occurred to her that Charles Wheaton had been right about one thing, at least. In another few months, the field would be a blaze of white and she would have to close the school down for a few weeks to give the children and adults time to pick the crop.

Finally, Bo brought the wagon to a stop next to a little whitewashed building that sat alone in a clearing. He came around to help her down. "This here is their church," he said, her hand resting in his. Then a sour smile bowed his lips. "Or I guess I should say it's you-all's church," he corrected. "You're pretty much a nigger yourself now, ain't you?"

Prudence pulled her hand from his in disgust. "You are a truly despicable man," she said.

He just laughed as he climbed back up on the wagon. "We are going to be friends someday, Mrs. Kent," he told her. "You watch and see." The wagon turned in a great clatter of wood and bridles and horse's hooves and he rode off the way he had come.

When she was sure he had gone, Prudence pushed open the door of the church. Heads turned at the intrusion. Murmuring voices fell silent. Eyes studied her. It came upon her all at once, fell down on her from nowhere. Prudence had never felt so white. White with all whiteness's burden of privilege, and history of cruelty, showing on her lone face. White with the expectations of others piercing her bosom like arrows. It wasn't simply that hers was the only white face in the room. That had happened before. She had spoken before abolitionist meetings, after all, and now she taught at a school for colored just a few miles away. But those things, she understood suddenly, had put her at the center of events. On those occasions, colored people came into her places, places she controlled.

This was the first time in her life—the realization came as something of a shock—*the first time in her life*, she had been alone with a mass of colored people in one of *their* places, where she was only a guest and controlled nothing. Prudence looked back into that sea of dark eyes, dark hair, dark skin, and felt heat rising in her cheeks. Though he had spoken crudely, Bo Wheaton had spoken truthfully in a way. She *had* cast her lot with them. And she had not understood until this very moment exactly what that meant.

It meant that she had thrown away prerogatives she had not quite realized she had, prerogatives she had always taken for granted, because they were as much a part of her as the skin on her face. This was what the Wheaton men, each in his own coarse way, had told her. And now, realizing the truth of it all at once, Prudence felt unmoored, felt as if she held herself to the earth only by sheer force of will. She searched the crowd for Miss Ginny and Bonnie, hoping the familiarity of their faces would keep her from floating away. She found them sitting near the front. Miss Ginny was smiling.

Bonnie did not smile. Her eyes were large and tentative, her mouth a grim line in the middle of her face. After a moment, she turned away. She held herself more erect than seemed absolutely necessary, her hands clasped together in her lap as if glued there. Prudence realized with a shock that Bonnie was feeling what she herself was: her own outcast singularity.

Bonnie was a Negro, but she had been raised in a white man's home in the North. She had never known Southern Negroes, had never been alone with them in their places. In her outlook and her deportment, Bonnie was more like Prudence than them.

For some reason she could not name, Prudence found that vaguely distressing, but she did not have time to wonder about it. From the pulpit, Preacher Lee welcomed her with a smile. "Mrs. Kent, please come on up here," he said. "We just been talkin' about you."

Mildly surprised to find that gravity still held her fast, she did as she was asked. She felt the touch of eyes upon her as she moved through them. Every eye except Bonnie's. Bonnie stared resolutely ahead.

"We understands Marse Wheaton sent one of them boys to get you," said Preacher Lee when she was standing next to him. "I expect he asked you to shut down the school you and Miss Bonnie there opened for colored."

"Yes, he did," said Prudence.

"And what you tell him?" The smile, broad and expectant.

"I told him no."

She flinched at the cheer that went up then, sudden, lusty, and full. People slapped one another's backs, clapped their hands, laughed uproariously. Preacher Lee let the sound wash over her for a full minute. Finally, he raised his hands and appealed for silence. As the last of the laughter was snuffing itself out, he said, "Did y'all hear that? She told him no."

Amid general murmurs and cries of assent, he turned to her. "We was sayin' before you arrived how grateful all us is for you and Miss Bonnie to come down here and start this school. Y'all ain't had to do it. We know that. You could have stayed up there in Boston, comfortable and snug. But y'all come down here to see about us, come down here to *help* us, and we thank you for it. We thank *God* for it."

There was another uproar. People shouted "Yes! Yes!" Some old woman moaned. It was a mournful, wordless sound. Prudence found Paul Cousins, sitting in the row behind Bonnie and Miss Ginny. His face reminded her of Colindy's. It bore no expression, gave away no secrets. Prudence wondered idly how colored people could do that so easily, could command their feelings to hide.

After another minute, the preacher raised his hand. "We know them devils already been causin' trouble for you. And we know the Yankee army refuse to help. I was with you when that happened. So here's what we proposes to do, Miss Prudence, if you'll let us. *We* gon' post a guard at the school to protect it and to protect you and Miss Bonnie. We got it all worked out. We'll set up shifts so somebody's always down there, every night, watchin' out for them rascals. All you got to do is give us the word."

Instinctively, she looked toward Bonnie. The warning in her best friend's eyes was clear as water. Don't do this, the warning said. It might be dangerous.

But Bonnie had not felt that creature's hand mashing at her breast. She had not gone for help and been turned away with a self-righteous smirk, as if she were the cause of her own troubles. She had not met Colindy or seen the look in her eyes. And she had not sat on that porch overlooking the Mississippi River and heard that bitter old man say that the natural order of things was for him to be on top and to keep his foot on the necks of people like Miss Ginny and Paul and Bonnie herself.

She met Preacher Lee's eyes. "Yes," she said. "I consider that a most excellent idea."

"Surprised you're still here. I thought you'd have run off like the rest of 'em." Marse Jim says this as he accepts a bowl of soup from her hand. He is on Mrs. Lindley's couch. It is the first time in ten days he has been able to sit up under his own power.

She wonders what she is expected to say. "No, Marse," she tells him. "Ain't run off." Confirming the obvious, adding nothing.

He works his tongue around inside his mouth like he's chasing a piece of gristle, his eyes speculating. "Can see that," he says. "Just surprised is all. Those others, they'd have been in the wind a long time ago, knowing I was down and can't do nothin' about it."

He eats some more, spooning soup into his mouth quickly, loudly. Flecks of chicken dot the unruly tangle of his beard. She stands there, waiting for him. He finishes quickly, reaches the bowl out. When she tries to take it, he holds it a moment extra, so that for just that second, both their hands are on it. He looks at her. "I guess every nigger ain't treacherous after all," he says. And releases the bowl.

It is supposed to be a compliment, she knows. "Yes, Marse," she says. "I expect not."

They set out again two mornings later when he judges his strength has fully returned. "Want to thank you for taking care of me," he tells Agnes Lindley. "Don't know what would have come of me if you hadn't been there." He is soiled and unshaven and Tilda wonders if Mrs. Lindley will ever get the smell of him out of her couch.

But Agnes Lindley gazes upon him as adoringly as a young girl in first love and clasps both his rough hands in her tiny ones. "It was the least I could do," she says, "for someone who fought for our nation."

His eyes crinkle. "Yes," he says in a strange, hoarse voice, "we did have ourselves a nation, didn't we?"

They stand there a long moment like some grotesque parody of courtship. Then he nods, as if wakening himself from a dream. "Well," he says, and he pulls his hands back. "Thank you."

Awkwardly, he doffs the hat she has given him—it belonged to her late husband, she says—and motions toward Tilda. Tilda crosses the threshold behind him—she tries not to remember the humiliation of standing on that spot, unable to do so simple a thing as take a step—and walks down into the day. The air feels like steam and it is not yet eight in the morning.

The sun on their backs, they walk to where the town ends. Then they walk into the fields beyond. An occasional wagon prattles past. Hours go by.

"Yeah, most niggers would have run." Out of nowhere, Marse Jim picks up a two-day old conversation.

She knows what he wants. He wants the why, the reason. But how can she give him what she doesn't have?

No, that isn't true. She does know the reason, but it humiliates her too much for speaking. She has become some weak and beaten-down thing, unable to imagine herself in any other life, unable to imagine herself free. Worse, she has become the hateful thing he always calls her, always calls every colored man or woman. He has beaten *nigger* into her, hammered it deep into the soft tissues of her very soul. And she doesn't know if she will ever get it out.

All at once, she is aware of him looking back at her, waiting for an answer. "Didn't want to leave you like that," she manages.

Scorn edges his voice. "You care about me," he says.

"You're my master," she says.

He appears to consider this for a moment. Then he turns back. "It's a good thing you didn't run," he rumbles. "Good thing for you. 'Cause I'd have found you, two weeks head start or not. I'd have found you and I'd have done to you like I done them other two." He pauses and when he continues, his voice is smaller, as if he is speaking to himself as much as to her. "Wouldn't want to do that," he says. "You deserve better than what they got. You been faithful. More'n you can say for most, white nor black."

It is, she knows, another intended compliment. She wonders if he knows how much his compliments make her hate herself. But of course, he has no idea. "Yes, Marse," she says.

He doesn't speak again. They spend the morning traversing fields of cotton and corn. Shortly after noon they stop in the shade of a tree and he breaks out some of the cold chicken and boiled eggs Mrs. Lindley has packed for them. He passes her the canteen full of water the widow has given them—for some odd reason Tilda has never understood, Marse Jim doesn't mind drinking after Negroes—but she mishandles it and it falls, spilling water into the dirt. She snatches it up. He glares at her and instinct winces her eyes closed against the coming blow, the only question being whether his hand will be fisted or not.

But he doesn't strike her. "Don't be so damn clumsy," he snarls.

She opens first one eye and then the other. This, she realizes all at once, is her reward for the humiliation of staying with him. To anger him and be cursed for it, but not hit. It is a small gift, but it is a gift nonetheless and she resolves to appreciate it. When life gives you little to be grateful for, you cherish the little.

"Yes, Marse," she says. He gives her a reproachful look as if reconsidering the mercy. She drinks from the canteen, thankful it gives her something to hide behind. He snatches it from her before she is done.

For the remainder of the day, the space between them is filled with silence. The walk is punishing, the June sun pounding down on them like retribution. Hours later, when their shadows drag long behind them, they are lucky enough to find a farmer who allows them use of the hay loft in his stable. Marse Jim breaks out the last of the chicken and boiled eggs— tomorrow, they will be back to begging and foraging, she supposes—and they have supper in the fading light of another lost day. When she is done eating, she lies back upon the straw, massaging a knot of pain in her right calf. A sigh slips out of her.

"Are you tired?" he asks.

She could not be more surprised if he had sprouted wings and circled the barn. "Yes," she says.

"Don't blame you," he says. "Long day. Another long day tomorrow." And he grunts and lies down opposite her, pulls the hat low over his eyes, and crosses his hands upon his chest.

Her thoughts are running laps. All his awkward advances, his lumbering attempts at conversation, point in a direction she cannot get her mind to follow. She feels the same confusion she felt the day they spoke about their sons. *She is a thing he owns.* No more than that, no more than a table, a hog, a chair. But you don't ask a chair if it is tired. You don't warn a table that tomorrow will be a long day. So perhaps—and her mind drags toward this with the stubbornness of a mule that has decided it is done plowing for the day—perhaps he has begun to see her as something other than a thing. Not a person, certainly. That would be too much. But yes, something other than a thing.

In the fading light, she can see the rise and fall of his chest. But if she truly has become something other than a thing, perhaps that is her chance to ask him the question that has bedeviled her all the long weeks of their wayfaring, the great mystery of this entire enterprise. She clears her throat to warn him the question is coming, piles her courage up as high as she can make it, then stands atop it and opens her mouth.

"Marse?"

He grunts.

"Marse, can I ask you a question?"

He grunts again and she takes this for assent.

"Marse, where are we going?"

He lifts the hat now, raises his head to get a look at her, as though her aspect might have changed somehow in the few seconds since last he saw her. As though she might have become something wholly new. She doesn't know what he sees when he gazes across at her, but he answers. "Going someplace a white man can be treated like a white man," he says, "and don't have to kowtow to Yankee domination. That's where I'm goin'. I have no desire to live under the thumb of them what killed my boy."

She considers his words, decides to push her luck. "Yes, Marse," she says. "But where is that?"

For the second time in as many minutes, she is shocked by him. He laughs. It sounds like pebbles rattling together in an old pipe. She hears anger in the sound. And sorrow, too. "Can't say I rightly know," he says. "California. Mexico, maybe."

"We are going to walk that whole way?"

"I expect we will," he says. "Get there or die in the tryin'. You think that's mad, I expect."

She knows better than to answer. He knows she knows and chuckles again. "Got no other choice," he says. "You don't understand that, I suppose, but it's truth. Man's got a right to live free, otherwise he can't be a man at all. That's something your Yankee government just don't believe, so I can't believe in it."

Man's got a right to live free.

It marks itself in her mind—her slave's mind—indelibly as ink. *Man's got a right. To live free.*

What about a colored man? Does that go for him, too? What about a woman? A colored woman? Does it go for her? She knows the answer, of course, but for a crazed, vertiginous moment, she stands on the precipice of asking anyway. Just to hear it spoken. Just to know what he might say.

But she knows she has already pushed her luck beyond the rim of common sense. She was foolish to push it that far. She would be doubly foolish to push it further. So she lies in silence and after a moment, his breathing turns to a loud rasping that makes the whiskers around his mouth shiver.

She watches him until all the light is gone, then gets up and climbs down from the loft. The world is the color of pitch and she is careful on the ladder, fearful of stumbling and breaking her neck. When she feels the floor beneath her she dismounts and walks slowly through the dark, hands stretched out before her, navigating from memory. Somewhere in the darkness, she can hear the farmer's horse, nickering softly. After a moment, she reaches the doorway and passes through it. She finds herself in a grassy field—she can feel it scratching at her ankles—beneath a canopy of stars.

She sits in the grass, drawing her legs up, like a child. She wraps her arms around them, then uses her knees as a platform for her chin. She makes herself as small as she knows how and watches as infinity wheels slowly above her. Does it see her, scarred and weary little black thing sitting in the tall grass of some farmer's field somewhere in Arkansas? And if infinity sees her, does it care?

She falls asleep looking up.

It is four days later that Marse Jim finds what he is looking for. That place he was looking for, that place a white man can live in freedom, turns out to be not California or Mexico, but a forest in Arkansas. They are walking through a tangle of trees, following a footpath that has a disconcerting habit of narrowing and disappearing in the underbrush, and Marse Jim is in a foul mood as a result, cursing up a fury and casting worried glances overhead in search of the sun so he can navigate. But the sun hides its face as often as not and she knows he fears them lost.

Then a boy's voice says, "You best stop right there, or I'll shoot."

He surprises them. He is standing in the gnarled, moss-covered limbs of an old live oak that bends toward the ground like an old woman stooped by time. He has a rifle trained on them.

Marse Jim is unimpressed. "Is that a fact?" he says.

"That is, indeed, sir." He is probably not yet 18, has something that aspires to be a moustache overtop a few chin hairs sprouting from skin as virginal and white as fresh fallen snow. He watches them from beneath a rebel's kepi.

"And just who is it that's givin' these orders?" Marse Jim asks.

The boy's voice is thin and reedy, but his response is crisp. "Private Virgil Goodman, sir, Monticello Artillery, Howell's Battery." She has the impression that a salute would ordinarily follow this.

Marse Jim grins, amused by the boy. "Well, Private," he says, "I am Captain James McFarland, Company H, Second Mississippi Infantry Regiment, and you ain't got no need for that Spencer you got trained on us. We're on the same side. I seen the elephant too, same as you."

It is the boy's turn to be unimpressed. He hops down from the low branch, his eyes never leaving them, motions with the barrel of the rifle. "I expect that'll be up to Colonel Moody to judge. Y'all want to walk straight through there. But first, I'll be needing your firearms, sir."

Marse Jim complies, handing over his rifle and the pistol in his belt, then lifts his hands and shakes his head, still amused, and walks where the boy has pointed. She follows him, the boy follows her. Occasionally, he pokes her in the back with the rifle to make her walk faster.

There is no hint of a trail here. They make their way through an old forest, detouring around trees and climbing over roots half as tall as a man. The ground is spongy with generations of dead leaves. The air is clammy and close. The sun does not penetrate.

Marse Jim says, "You've got a company of men back there, I expect?"

The boy says, "You'll see soon enough."

Marse Jim says, "Swear, you're the most close-mouthed pup I ever did see."

The boy doesn't respond.

She hears a dog barking a few moments before they emerge into a clearing. In the middle sits a large, rudely constructed cabin, ringed about by the stumps of trees. About 15 men are there. Some are sitting beneath trees, cleaning their weapons. One is perched on a railing on the porch, reading a letter. A few are chatting quietly together. They all seem older than the boy, most of them tall and rangy with heavy beards and a leanness in the eyes that suggests a long time between meals. Those lean eyes come up and all conversation stills as Goodman's captives precede him into the clearing.

"What you got there, Virgil?" asks a man with a yodel in his voice. He hooks a pair of spectacles over his ears and adjusts them so he can see better.

"Found these two skulking around over by Pike's Farm," yells Virgil.

The man laughs. "They hardly look like Yankee spies, Virge."

"Boy always was a caution," says another man, coming up behind.

Marse Jim chuckles indulgently, lowers his hands without being told to. "Ah, leave the boy alone," he says. "Better he be too careful than not careful enough."

"My sentiments exactly." The man who has come out on the porch has a mop of yellow hair, as thick and lustrous as any woman's. His uniform is crisp as a morning in fall, with the exception of a neatly sewn patch on one knee. His belt buckle is a gleaming oval of brass with the inscription CSA. He holds himself as erect as if he were marching at the head of a grand parade, not standing on a porch among a ragtag group of men, half of them in their undershirts.

He extends a hand to Marse Jim. "I am Colonel Jackson Moody, sir, at your service. And you are?"

Instead of accepting the handshake, Marse Jim salutes. This seems to amuse some of the men, who grin and poke one another. But if Marse Jim notices or cares, Tilda cannot see it. His eyes are moist and earnest. "Captain James McFarland, sir, late of the Mississippi Infantry Regiment." And only now does he pump Moody's hand.

"Captain, what brings you into these woods?"

Marse Jim swallows. "Man come by my place, told me the war was over. I could barely believe it. He said we's been whupped by the Yankees and need to accept that. Sir, I told him I *can't* accept that. So we been walkin' ever since, me and her." A nod toward Tilda. "She's my last slave. Only nigger ain't run off from me. She asked me just the other day"—and here, he hunches his shoulders and makes his voice slow, his words mushy and

indistinct and Tilda realizes with a shock that this is his imitation of her—
"'Marse, where us goin'? Where you got us walkin' to?'"

The men around them laugh in appreciation of the mimicry. All at once, Marse Jim yanks himself out of his slouch, makes his posture as vertical as a pole. He is not her anymore, cringing and quivering slave woman, but himself, noble and courageous white man. "I told her I *refuse* to live under Yankee domination," he says and here, he lifts his chin in defiance. "I told her, by God, we will walk and keep walking til we find someplace where white men are still willing to fight back against tyranny."

He stares. Moody stares. The men all stare. And Tilda realizes that something has happened here, something she doesn't understand and cannot name. But she knows with a deep and sudden foreboding that it is powerful to them, that it puts a glitter in their eyes and sets their Adam's apples to bobbing.

After a moment, Moody puts a hand on Marse Jim's shoulder. "Congratulations, Captain. You've found that place."

Marse Jim nods. "Yes, sir. Thank you, sir."

"Why don't you join me? I was just sitting down to a meal. Virgil, you come, too, since you're the one who found the captain. Judkins will take your place on watch." He leads them inside.

She doesn't know what she is supposed to do, so she follows them up to the porch and into the big cabin. Inside is one vast room. Bedrolls line the walls and there is a long, roughly constructed table at one end with benches on either side. Moody motions and all three men sit down. Tilda stands behind Marse Jim.

This annoys him. "Don't just hover there like a moth!" he snarls, flicking at her as though she were, indeed, a flying pest. "Get away! Go sit yourself down somewhere!" As she moves away to the other side of the room, she hears him say, "Damn niggers. Stupid as the day is long." There is laughter and general assent. She sits on the floor, far away enough to be unobtrusive, close enough to hear every word.

Moody says, "So, you walked here from Mississippi, Captain? That's impressive. 'Course, you're not the only one. Most of these boys have been with me through the whole war, but we've got a few that just sort of wandered in, like. Grissom out there is from Texas. Delacroix came up from Louisiana. But they're all like you—all refuse to live their lives under Yankee domination."

"So what do you propose to do about it?" asks Marse Jim.

Moody gives him a level look. "We propose to fight, of course."

Marse Jim's eyes look as if someone has lit a lantern inside his skull. He is giddy as a boy. "Colonel, that's all I've wanted to hear, that there are still white men in this country who refuse to knuckle under."

"Well, sir, you have found them. Moody's Raiders—the men chose the name, not I. We've already been fighting, in fact, and we have managed to bloody the Yanks' noses a few times. You ever hear the term, 'guerrilla warfare?' It means sabotage, hit and run strikes and the like. We don't have the manpower for a frontal assault, yet."

The boy chimes in eagerly. "We blowed up a bridge at Beaver Creek. Caused the Yanks no end of consternation. And we raided their armory. Got a whole passel of weapons and ammunition. Going to shoot them down with their own guns next time."

One of the men walks in balancing three bowls of some dark stew. The smell of it makes Tilda's stomach clench like a fist inside her as he sets one each before Moody, Virgil and Marse Jim, who seems not to notice. "Colonel, I'd be honored if you'd let me join you." His voice is grave and low.

Moody smiles at Marse Jim's earnestness. "We're glad to have you," he says, clapping Marse Jim on the shoulder. "Welcome."

Marse Jim looks as if he might cry. The boy speaks around a mouthful of stew. "What about her?" he asks. He is nodding toward Tilda. She snatches her eyes away as if they had touched something hot.

"What *about* her?" she hears Marse Jim ask.

"You trust her?"

Marse Jim chuckles. "Don't trust a one of 'em," he says. "But she won't do nothin'. I was laid up ten days, flat on my back in some little town east of here. She could have run off any time, but she didn't."

"She's loyal, then," says the colonel.

She stares at the floor. She can feel their eyes appraising her, feel it as surely as a touch grazing her skin. Marse Jim says, "Yes, I suppose."

"Good," says the colonel. "We've got a nigger woman who does the cooking and sewing and like that. This one can help. She any good at that sort of thing?"

"Mostly she been a field nigger," says Marse Jim, "but she'll learn."

Hearing her labor promised, hearing her loyalty vouched, she feels a hatred for her very self spreading like warm poison from the center of her body. Why didn't she leave? Why couldn't she make her foot cross that threshold? But she knows the answer. She is not the woman she used to be before Marse Jim, before the war. That woman was brave. She was sassy sometimes and impertinent with a mistress who found those traits amusing. Then she was sold. And this man began to hit her. And he knocked the sass and impertinence right out of her, made her this shameful thing she has become.

The boy is watching her closely. "She ain't half bad-looking," he says.

Marse Jim glances over without much interest. "I suppose she ain't," he says. "I guess I stopped noticing things like that so much after my wife died."

"Never had a wife," says the boy. "Don't get to see too many women, living as we do. You wouldn't mind if me, maybe some of the boys, gave her a tumble every now and again, would you?"

He is giving her an easy smile as he speaks. She swears she can feel her heart grind to a stop, her blood stand still as midnight in her veins.

Oh, please.

Oh please, God, no.

I have been through so much already.

Marse Jim's head comes around and he looks at her with more interest this time, stares at her for one heartbeat, then two. She can hear him, lying in the gathering darkness of a farmer's loft, asking if she is tired. She can remember herself thinking, you don't ask a chair if it is tired. She moves her head from side to side, a small motion and she does it just once, hoping he will see, hoping he will have mercy and spare her. She has been loyal. He said so himself. Doesn't that count for something?

Marse Jim grins, but his eyes are dead like fish. "Sure," he says, "you want to give her a ride sometime, you go right ahead."

So now her labor has been promised and her body has, too. And she curses the sliver of hope she allowed to bloom in her that night in the loft. Because she knows now, knows with a crushing certainty, that it was but the cruelest of lies.

She is not a person, only a thing.

She will never be anything more.

Jesse Washington stood at the side door, bidding good night to the evening class as another long day at the Cafferty School for Freedmen drew to a close.

He was a behemoth, well over six feet, with hands so large that Bonnie, watching from the stairwell just inside the door, thought he could probably pick up a watermelon in each. But the softness of his smile and the bashfulness of his demeanor belied his fearsome size. When the old women kissed his cheek or the men shook his hand on the way out the door, he touched them in response—a pat on the back, a hand on a shoulder—with porcelain caution, as if afraid they might break if he were not careful. Jesse was, she thought, a giant who had spent his life learning to tiptoe in a Lilliputian world.

Most of those who had volunteered to guard the school against vandals were old men with gray beards and baggy skin. This was to be expected, she supposed; younger men would need to work to support their families and would not have the time. But Jesse was the exception. He was the youngest of seven brothers, each as large as he was if not larger, and his family, hoeing cotton on a plantation north of town, had decided it could spare him a few nights a week to help protect the school.

He stood now, towering over the evening class adults, some of them hunched and toothless, who filed past him after another two hours bent low over books of reading and mathematics. Bonnie always found it a poignant sight, these elders struggling so mightily to learn enough that they might read a favored passage of the Bible for themselves, or simply sign their own names, and finally seize for themselves some fleeting scraps of human dignity from lives that had offered them so little.

Miss Ginny was the last to leave. Bonnie watched as she squeezed Prudence's arm affectionately. "You comin', sweetie?" she asked.

Sweetie. The old woman was fond of both of them, Bonnie knew, but for some reason, she had a particular attachment to Prudence.

"I will be along momentarily," Prudence said.

"Don't be too long now," said Miss Ginny. "And if it be dark when you leave, you get Jesse there to walk you."

"I shall be fine," Prudence assured. "He should walk you, if anybody."

Miss Ginny made a show of rolling her eyes and pursing her lips and they all laughed. As the door closed behind her, Jesse gave Prudence one of those humble smiles and aimed his eyes not quite at her. "Be happy to walk you if you want me to, ma'am."

"Now Jesse," said Prudence, "you know I hardly require protection from the ruffians of this town. Of course, if you should feel the need to protect them from me…"

She allowed the thought to dangle there playfully. Prudence loved to tease the big, soft-spoken man and sure enough, he ducked his head and began to stammer.

"Oh, no, ma'am, I… I don't…"

They laughed at his discomfort, but Bonnie could not escape a faint flicker of guilt that they were enjoying themselves at his expense. She was about to apologize, about to tell Prudence to leave the young man alone, when he stiffened all at once, his head coming up sharply like a hound that has caught a scent.

"I heard something," he said.

"What did you hear?" Prudence was still laughing.

But he did not answer. Instead, Jesse disappeared from the doorway. Bonnie looked at Prudence, saw her own confusion reflected in her friend's face. Together, they followed Jesse out the side door.

Bonnie recognized the four white boys at once. They were the same ones who had blocked the sidewalk the day she, Prudence, and Paul walked to the other end of Main Street to buy rice. Now they stood confronting Jesse in the alley behind the building. The one with the dirty blonde hair was holding himself conspicuously erect, trying to make himself taller than he was. Still, his chin came up only to Jesse's chest.

"I ain't scared of you, nigger," he declared. His voice, splintering like rotted wood, suggested otherwise.

There was nothing bashful in Jesse's eyes now. They were narrowed and hard, watching out of the fortress his face had become as he loomed over the boys like a mountain. "Done asked you," he said, in a stiff tone that somehow managed to offer both respect and threat, "what y'all doin' 'round back here?"

"Ain't got to explain nothin' to you, nigger!" cried the boy in that same cracked voice. "It's still a free country, ain't it? Yankees ain't took that from us, did they?" He looked around at his companions for support. "We can still walk where we want to walk, can't we?"

Jesse nodded his head toward the boy's right hand and Bonnie realized for the first time that he was carrying a pail. "Y'all always go walkin' around with a bucket of whitewash?" he asked.

"Told you I ain't got to answer no questions from you, boy," snapped the boy.

"Come on, George. Let's get out of here." One of the other boys had a hand on his friend's upper arm. His eyes were sizing up the situation and not liking what he saw.

"We got a right to walk where we want to!" insisted George, his voice careening toward falsetto.

A third boy said, "Fine. *I'm* going to walk somewhere else. You do what you want." He was looking up at Jesse as he spoke.

"Are you all cowards?" demanded the boy named George.

But two of them were already gone. He stared at the fourth boy, who took Jesse in with one round-eyed stare, then shrugged at his friend and trotted to catch up with the other two.

Alone now, George stared up at Jesse. People had come into the alley, drawn by the noise of the confrontation. The woman who lived in the house on the other side of the alley stood in her yard next to a chicken coop, drying her hands on a towel. George gulped. He drew himself up. "Fine then," he announced in a voice much too loud. "You want us to go? We'll go. But this ain't over, not by a long shot. You mark my words."

He had been backing away. "Mister George?" Jesse spoke in a cool voice and the boy stopped with almost comical obedience.

"What?"

"Why don't you leave the pail here?"

It sounded like a request, but it wasn't, Bonnie knew. The boy did, too. He let the bucket down carefully, his humiliation complete. He gave Jesse Washington one more long look. Then he wheeled and ran to catch up with his friends.

Immediately, the alley was filled with laughter and applause. Men patted Jesse's broad back.

"Look at that rascal go!" someone said. "He ain't gon' stop til he reach the river."

"Might not stop then," someone else said, and the laughter renewed itself. "Might not stop til he halfway through Arkansas."

"Good job, Jesse," a woman said.

Jesse lowered his eyes, smiling his embarrassment. "Aw, I ain't done nothin'," he said. "Weren't nothin' but a boy. Scared boy at that."

"I know his family," said Paul. He had come up behind Bonnie without her realizing. "They not too bad for white. I talk to his pappy tomorrow if you like."

Prudence said, "I would like that very much, Paul. Please see to it." She gave Bonnie a meaningful look. They had quarreled over the wisdom of setting up a guard at the school. Prudence felt vindicated now, Bonnie knew. If Jesse hadn't been here, there was no telling what mischief the boy would have accomplished.

Bonnie couldn't deny that. But she still felt a faint unease bubbling up from the very center of her. She could not place it, but she couldn't deny it, either. Bonnie touched Paul's arm. "Come," she said, "let's go read." She said this softly, for his ears only; he would not want the crowd in the alley to know she had been teaching him privately for weeks.

Together, they slipped away from the knot of people still laughing and congratulating Jesse Washington. She was aware of Prudence's eyes upon them, watching them go.

"What's wrong?" asked Paul, as they climbed the stairs to the loft where Bonnie and Prudence had their office.

"Nothing is wrong," she told him.

She felt him smile behind her. "Bonnie, you need to tell that lie to someone don't know you. You might fool them, but you don't fool me. You still worried 'bout havin' them guards in here."

"'Those' guards," said Bonnie. "'Them' is incorrect."

"Don't change the subject," he said.

She turned on him. "What do you want me to say? Of course I am worried. But what can I do?" She stood on the landing. He was a step below, looking up at her, his eyes full of sudden gravity.

"You can talk to her," he said. "Tell her you think puttin' a guard in here make things worse. It's like askin' for trouble."

"You think I do not know that?" she snapped. But the anger wouldn't hold. It passed like an April storm. "Oh, Paul, I'm sorry," she said. "The truth is, I do not even know what I think. Part of me is happy to see us standing up for ourselves. But another part is fearful of where that's going to lead."

"That the part you need to listen to," he said.

"I am not the one who needs to listen," she told him, moving to the wooden table that stretched lengthwise between the two desks. "It is Prudence. And you know her. She does not listen. She is stubborn and headstrong. She always has been."

"That Prudence a caution, all right." Paul sat opposite her at the table.

"Indeed. She is the most stubborn woman I have ever known," said Bonnie, reaching for a McGuffey primer.

"But that ain't all there is to it, is there?" said Paul.

Bonnie looked at him. "No," she said finally. "She is brave, too. She is also the bravest person I have ever known." She pushed the book across to him.

"Sound like you of two minds," said Paul, not reaching for the book. "You love her, but sometime you wish you could strangle her."

Bonnie surprised herself by laughing. "Yes," she said. "Something like that." She tapped the book. "Come," she said, "I believe we left off at page 56."

Still Paul didn't reach for the book. For a long, uncomfortable moment, he did nothing except stare. She felt herself shifting anxiously on the rough bench. "What is it, Paul?" she asked.

"I was just wonderin'," he said. "What about you?"

"What do you mean?"

"When you gon' get to do what Bonnie want? When you gon' get to live your own life? Way you tell it, only reason you come down here in the first place is 'cause it's what she want. Get the feelin' you done that a lot in your life, doin' things just 'cause she want."

"I am not angry about that," said Bonnie. "After all, if Prudence hadn't insisted we come down here, you and I might never have become friends."

"Friends," he said. His smile was faint as a mid-morning moon. Bonnie felt herself blushing. "Well, 'friend,'" he said, "that still don't get to the crux of the thing, do it?"

"What do you mean?" she managed to ask.

"What I mean?" he repeated, still smiling that barely there smile. "What I mean is, you got a life of your own, ain't you? You ain't tied to her with no string, is you? Only thing I ever hear you say is what Prudence want. I ain't never once heard you talk about what Bonnie want. You a person too, ain't you?"

"Of course I am. But right now, Prudence needs me."

"Ain't doubtin' that. And you's a good friend to be there for her. But what I want to know is: what do *Bonnie* need? Seem like you should be askin' that sometime. And if you won't, I will."

She looked at him, he looked at her. All at once, Bonnie felt as if she was standing at the rim of a cliff. "What I need," she said, forcing a laugh, "is for you to open this book and stop putting it off." She pushed the primer to him.

He took it, turned it, opened it, looked at her. "Seem to me, I ain't the one puttin' off," he said.

Without another word, he lowered his eyes and began to read, struggling laboriously through the simple words. Bonnie hardly heard him. Instead, she heard him asking again and again what she wanted for her own life. And she heard her own emptiness in response, a silence deep as a graveyard at dawn. It was the silence of absence, the silence of having no answer. She did not know what to say.

And how could that be? She was 26 years old, an educated woman. How could she not know what she wanted in her one and only life? Was he right? Was she truly so intertwined with Prudence, so beholden to Prudence's vehement sense of mission that she had no wants or aspirations of her own?

Questions she had never thought to ask herself before poked through Bonnie's mind. If you had no wants of your own, what did that make you? Were you even a person? Weren't you really just a shadow of one? And what mortified her even more than the sudden questions surfacing in her thoughts was the fact that this man of all men had put them there—this rough, unlettered man she barely knew, but who somehow understood her well enough to articulate truths so painful and private she had hidden them even from herself.

What did those truths mean? What did they amount to? In order to separate from Prudence, to detach herself and carve a life of her own, was she required to leave the school they had built? Did it matter that she loved teaching, that teaching had taught her and fulfilled her in ways she had never realized it would? Did it make sense to abandon that in order to prove a point? And if so, prove it to whom? The more she considered it, the more confused she became.

"Did you hear that?"

It took her a moment to swim up from the depths of her own thoughts. She was almost surprised to find herself in the loft across from Paul, who was staring at her, his eyes urgent and bright.

"What?" she asked, feeling disconnected and slow.

"I said, 'Did you hear that?'"

"Hear what?"

He slammed the book closed. "I think it was a gunshot," he said. He was already on the stairs, taking them two at a time. By the time she managed to get to her feet, he was already out the door.

She ran behind him, holding up her dress so she did not trip on it. She rounded the building into the alley—and stopped.

The boy had a squirrel gun so old she was surprised it had not exploded when he pulled the trigger. Jesse was holding his left bicep, blood trickling through his fingers. The woman from across the alley was trying to hold Jesse back—"You ain't hurt bad, but let me see to it," she pleaded—but it was like trying to restrain a steam engine. His teeth bared in a feral snarl, his eyes twin bonfires burning gentleness and bashfulness like paper in a hearth, Jesse Washington advanced on the white boy, who gulped and fumbled, trying to reload the rifle.

"Boy, if you smart, you get your ass out of here," Paul told him.

But the boy was rooted and Jesse was not to be held back. He tore free of the woman's restraining grip, grabbed the boy's throat in one massive hand and lifted him til the rifle dropped from his useless hands and his raggedy shoes were pedaling air. "Why you all the time got to mess with us?" demanded Jesse in a voice that seemed to issue from some dark cavern in his soul. "We ain't doin' nothin' to you all! Why you can't just leave us alone?"

The boy made gurgling sounds, his hands prying hopelessly at Jesse's grip. "Jesse, please!" Bonnie rushed forward, took hold of a bicep that seemed made of iron. "Jesse, don't do this!"

Paul and the woman were pulling at him from the other side. He seemed not to notice either of them, staring up at the struggling boy with a volcanic fury. Bonnie was dimly aware of Prudence approaching at a run from Miss Ginny's house on the far end of the alley. She was yelling something unintelligible. And that was the problem, Bonnie realized. Everybody was yelling at once. Nobody was being heard.

Standing on tiptoe, she touched Jesse's cheek. He looked down at her as if he had never seen her before, his face unrecognizable, streaked with tears. Recognition took a moment. "Miss Bonnie," he said, "I ain't done nothin' to him. Just sittin' back here, mindin' my own business, just watchin' over the school like I'm s'posed to."

"I know," she said, conscious of the white boy's feet still churning the air, but sluggishly now.

"Why they got to be so mean to us? Ain't done nothin' to them. Just tryin' to live, Miss Bonnie."

"I know," said Bonnie, "but if you do not put this boy down, you are going to kill him. You don't want that, do you? You don't want that on your conscience."

"Miss Bonnie…"

"Think of all the trouble that will bring down on the school. They will shut us down. That would hurt everybody—particularly the children and the old people. We won't be able to teach anymore."

For an agonizing moment, he stared as if she were yelling at him in some foreign language he could not understand. Then something like surrender crept into his eyes. "All right," he said. And he flung the boy as a smaller man might fling a wad of paper. George flew through the air and did not stop until he slammed the wall of the school. He crumpled to the dirt, hacking and vomiting and holding his throat.

"Just want 'em to leave us alone," said Jesse softly, his gaze encompassing them all, Bonnie, Paul, the woman, and Prudence, who was just now coming to a stop. "Just don't want 'em to bother us no more. Ain't nothing wrong with that, is it?" The gaze was focused on Bonnie now, his voice that of a lost child.

Her mouth opened upon a silence. She did not know what to say. The woman from the house across the alley saved her. "Need to dress that wound," she said. "Look like it just nicked you, but we should stop the bleeding."

She pulled at him to go with her. He gave Bonnie a look that broke her heart with its helplessness. Then he allowed himself to be led away.

"The boy came back," said Prudence, apparently needing to give voice to the obvious.

Bonnie nodded. "Yes, he did."

"He shot our guard," she said.

"Yes," said Bonnie.

"Got more than he bargained for with ol' Jesse," said Paul, glancing over at the boy, still on his knees in the dirt. Paul's laughter was bitter.

"There is nothing funny here," said Bonnie.

"I agree," said Prudence. "And what if it had been one of the other men? Jesse is big. He's young and he's strong. But what if it was Rufus? What if it was Lemroy?"

Bonnie didn't speak. The answer was too obvious for speaking.

"And there is no law we can approach," said Prudence. "There is no one who will make them leave us alone."

She was working up to something. Bonnie knew this with a sudden chill certainty. "Prudence, what are you thinking?"

Her sister's face was mysterious and cool. "I know what we need to do," she said.

"What?"

"Not now," she said. And then, to Paul: "Paul, I want you to open the school tomorrow. Have the children practice their penmanship until Bonnie and I return." She looked at Bonnie. "You and I are going downtown," she said. "We are going to send a telegram."

"What are you talking about?" asked Bonnie.

They paused as the boy scrabbled painfully to his feet and walked away, his gait hobbled and crabbed.

Prudence gave her a direct look. "I intend to make sure this never happens again," she said.

And without another word, she turned and walked back toward Miss Ginny's house, passing the limping boy at a brisk step without giving him so much as a glance.

She marched in much the same way down Main Street the following morning, her head held high, her eyes looking neither right nor left. White people gaped at her. None tried to impede her progress. But they paused in their commerce and gossip and stared after her, muttering in disbelief. Bonnie caught snatches of it.

"Ain't that the Yankee schoolteacher?"

"What she doin' here?"

"I heard one of her niggers beat Georgie Flowers up somethin' fierce."

Prudence must have heard, but she gave no sign, head still up, still striding at that same imperious pace. Bonnie had to struggle to keep up. She felt like a raft tugged in the wake of a steamship. It was, she realized ruefully, an apt metaphor for her entire life with Prudence Cafferty Kent. What was it Paul had asked?

What do Bonnie need?

The question pinpricked at her conscience.

But there was no time. Prudence turned in at A.J. Socrates's store. The sallow man was slouched upon a stool, his face buried in a dime novel. He looked up at the sound of them and a scowl pinched his face.

"Thought I told you you wasn't welcome here," he said.

"Nevertheless, I am here," said Prudence. "And I am sending a telegram." She produced a folded paper from her bodice and held it out to him.

He made a show of folding down a page in the dime novel before accepting the paper. Seconds later, his body had become an exclamation point. "Do you realize what you're doing?" he said.

"I am sending a telegram," repeated Prudence. He gave her an odd look and she stared back, daring him to object or even say another word.

A cold dread shivered Bonnie. "Miss Prudence," she said, "what is going on? What are you doing?"

"She is kicking a hornet's nest barefoot!" snapped Socrates. "*That's* what she is doing!"

A thin smile curled Prudence's lips. "I am making certain our people are protected," she said.

Bonnie looked at her a moment, then snatched the message from the man's unresisting hands. "She's trying to raise an army," he said. He spoke in a whisper, his eyes never leaving Prudence.

"Oh my God," said Bonnie, reading.

It was a message to David, Constance's husband in Boston, describing the attack on Jesse and asking him to procure eight rifles and ship them to her without delay. From now on, her guards would be armed.

Bonnie felt her heart kick hard. "You cannot send this," she breathed.

"Of course I can," said Prudence, airily.

Now Bonnie was yelling it. "You *cannot* send this!"

It seemed to catch Prudence by surprise. "Do you not understand?" demanded Bonnie. "Do you not understand *anything*?"

"I understand we can no longer allow them to bully us," said Prudence, and her voice was icy.

"Bully us? Sister, they will *burn us down*. Do you really think these people will sit still for you arming the Negroes of this town?"

"I am only trying to protect my property," insisted Prudence. "I have a right to do that."

She reached for the note. Bonnie held it away, then ripped it into pieces that fluttered to the floor like snow.

"What are you doing?" demanded Prudence.

"I am saving you from yourself," said Bonnie. "Saving us all. For once in your life, would you stop and *think* before you act? You do not understand these white people. You do not understand how this would provoke them."

Prudence's laughter was filled with air and light. "Do not understand white people? Have you forgotten that I *am* white?"

"It is not the same," said Bonnie.

"You should listen to the nigger," said the sallow man.

Prudence looked at him. Bonnie looked at him. All at once, she simply felt tired, fatigue soaking her bones like water in a sponge. "Yes," she said, "listen to the nigger."

Prudence gaped. Bonnie didn't care. She walked out. After a moment, she heard Prudence following. Bonnie glanced back and chanced to catch sight of the sallow man watching after them through the window of the store. She swallowed hard. Hatred burned in his eyes.

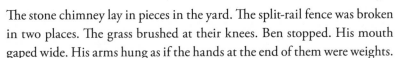

The stone chimney lay in pieces in the yard. The split-rail fence was broken in two places. The grass brushed at their knees. Ben stopped. His mouth gaped wide. His arms hung as if the hands at the end of them were weights.

"This here yard was her pride," he said in a soft voice. He pointed. "Over there, that was the flower bed. I still remember, she make Hannah get out there with her and they pull ever' last weed show its head above the dirt. Old colored man name of Hanks, he be out here once a week in the summer with that scythe, mowin' the grass on down."

"That grass has not been mowed down for a long time," said Sam.

"Not since forever, look like," said Ben. He led Sam through the side yard to the back door, and rapped on it. Ben's face was tight. He was anxious and Sam couldn't blame him. Ben had escaped these people seven years before. Now he was appearing at their door at the end of a ruinous war. Who knew how they would respond? They might press a rifle in his belly. They might spit in his face. They might do anything.

But the short, stout woman who opened the door only squinted at him through her glasses. "Yes?" she said. She had fine, white hair drawn up in a bun.

Ben gave her that smile that threatened to split his face along its seams. "Mistress, it's me," he said. "It's Ben."

It took her a moment. "Ben?" she said. "*My* Ben?"

"Yes ma'am," he said. "Once upon a time."

"You rascal! You run off from us."

"Yes, ma'am," said Ben. "I did."

"You know how much Albert paid for you? We trusted you, Ben. We treated you almost like family. And you up and run off? Why, Ben, that's just like stealing!"

"Yes, ma'am," said Ben, and no smile marked his face now. "I reckon you right. I stole. I stole myself."

She sighed elaborately. "Well, I suppose it's too long past to hold a grudge now. All the niggers left us after a while, when the war came. You were just the first."

"Yes, ma'am."

"Now you're back?" She was hopeful.

He shook his head. "No, ma'am. Just come to find Hannah."

Her face brightened. "That's right! You were sweet on Hannah. I remember that."

"Yes, ma'am. More'n sweet, actually. We jumped the broom, had us a little baby girl together. I'se real anxious to see them."

"Well, like I say, once the Yankees come through here, most of the niggers run off. There was a big fight in these parts just before Christmas. Oh, Ben, it was terrible. She left us right after that."

Concern clouded his eyes. "Do you know where they run off to?"

She scratched her chin. "Not for certain. But I hear a bunch of the niggers settled in town. Maybe you could look there."

"Yes, ma'am. Thank you."

To Sam's surprise, he did not walk away. "Place in terrible shape, Mistress."

"I know," she said, her voice rueful. "But what can I do? All of you all left me and Albert died in the war."

"You out here all by yourself?"

"I'm afraid I am. Don't know what I'm going to do, either. That war was a terrible thing, Ben. I suppose you all think different. I know all the slaves say 'Marse Linkum' gave them their freedom. But look at the cost, Ben. So many of our boys and men dead, niggers all run away, our whole way of life destroyed."

Ben said, "I make you a bargain, Mistress. If you don't mind feedin' a couple hungry men, we give you a day's work. See what we can do to get this yard back in order for you."

Sam was thunderstruck. "*Ben!*"

Ben lifted a hand. His eyes never left the old woman's face, which was lit like the dawn sky. She clasped her hands together. "Ben, you'd do that for me? Oh, thank you, Ben. Thank you. It's good to know the old feelings are not entirely gone."

"Tools still in the same place?" asked Ben.

She pointed. "Right out in the little shed in back."

He nodded. "We get to work then," he said.

She nodded. "Thank you, Ben."

As the door closed, Sam hissed at his friend. "Are you out of your mind?"

"You don't have to help," said Ben, leading the way to the tool shed. "I just felt sorry for her, is all. Poor old woman, out here by herself."

"She is a poor old *white* woman who calls you a nigger and thinks you ought to be ashamed for 'stealing' your own self."

"I know," said Ben, "but she weren't the worst of 'em. I seen plenty far worse."

"What about your wife? What about your daughter? Have you forgotten about them?"

Ben paused, his hand on the tool house door, and gave Sam a look. "You know better than to ask me that," he said. "Ain't never forgot about them. Not for a minute. Like I say, she just a poor old lady out here by herself. I just feel bad for her, is all. I sleep better if I put in a little work."

Sam shook his head. "This makes no sense. You were always the one haranguing me to move on. Now you want to stop and spend a day putting this old woman's house in order?"

"Told you," said Ben, "you ain't got to help. I understand if you don't. I really will."

"That is foolishness," said Sam. "Let her do her own work." But even as he spoke, he laboriously undid the buttons on his shirt and hung it on the door.

They worked the rest of that day. The woman had a sack of crushed lime and sand left from before the war. Ben mixed it with water and spent the morning and early afternoon carrying stones up and down the ladder, rebuilding the chimney. Sam handled the scythe, trimming the wild grass down to finger length. Raking it was difficult with one hand, but he managed it, using long, even strokes to pull the grass into a pile. Late in the day as the grass burned, the two men repaired the split-rail fence.

When it was done, Sam stepped away, dragging his forearm across his brow. It came away muddy with sweat and dirt. "You and your soft conscience," he told Ben. But there was no rebuke in it. He was too tired for rebuke.

Ben grinned. "Yeah," he said, "but admit it: you feel better than if you just left her out here to fend for herself."

Sam didn't answer and Ben nodded, taking it for assent. It wasn't. Sam had done this work for *Ben*, because he knew it would make his friend feel better. But Sam could happily have left the old woman out here to rot and spared not a second thought. Why should he give her his labor or even his concern? What had white people ever given him? What had they ever done except take?

Mary Cuthbert had treated him decently, yes. The memory rode in to him on wings of conscience. She had read to him, written letters for him, employed him. But was that enough to make up for all that white people had *taken*? Did it make up for Luke lying dead in that bog? Did it make up for Josiah hanging in that tree? Did it make up for Sam, reduced to stealing a dead man's shoes and finding even that difficult because he had only one arm to work with, white people having taken that, too? Did it make up for losing Tilda?

No, it didn't.

Damn them.

No, it did not at all.

They slept that night on the porch. The woman gave them breakfast in the morning, biscuits and eggs. As they were preparing to leave, she asked Ben if he might consider staying on. "You could help me get the place in order," she said. "I couldn't pay you much, but…"

She left the words hanging there. Ben didn't reach for them. He smiled and there was pity in it. "I got to find my family," he said.

He nodded a farewell and they set out for town. The walk took them downhill through a pine forest where trees had been broken and felled in great swaths. Then, for a while, they followed a river curling in great, wide loops along the valley floor. Ben, ordinarily a voluble man, kept a dogged silence this morning. Sam imagined he himself would not feel much like speaking if he were about to see Tilda again. Too much to think about it. Too many things to fear. And what words existed for that? After all these miles and all these mountains, what was there to say?

It took them three hours. The town that rose before them was a grid of clapboard buildings and dirt streets that hunkered in the shadow of two heavily forested hills. Sam and Ben entered on the main street. The signs of fighting were everywhere. They passed the smashed remnant of a general store, then a barber shop. They circled a huge crater in the middle of the street. Workmen were hammering together the skeleton of a building rising on a vacant lot between the scorched remains of a feed store and a hotel. At the end of the block stood a blacksmith shop, where hammer meeting anvil formed a song of industry that felt somehow hopeful in the bright, hard light of the morning. The blacksmith was a strapping young Negro man. Ben approached him eagerly.

"Do you know a colored woman named Hannah?" he said. "Got a daughter named Leila, be about seven." The man shook his head.

It took Ben three tries more before he found a woman who knew Hannah. Her eyes narrowed dubiously when Ben asked her—Sam figured he and Ben must look a sight—but she gave them directions: go to the end of West Street, turn right at the hog pens, left on Laramie and then a quick right in a little alley without a name. It was the house at the very end, just before the railroad tracks. Ben rushed out a word of thanks and took off at almost a sprint. Sam had to hurry to keep up.

"Oh, Lord," said Ben, speaking to Sam, speaking to the morning. "Oh Lord oh Lord oh Lord oh Lord. You believe this? I done found her. I done found her at last! Oh, thank you Jesus!"

At the mouth of the nameless alley, Ben paused so abruptly Sam almost plowed into him. As promised, there were three houses, tall clapboard structures with common walls. Two little dark-skinned girls with plaited hair sat on the steps of the last one playing hull gull. The first girl held out her fists. "Hull gull!" she sang out and her voice was sweet and thin.

"Hand full," came the second girl's voice and it, too, was falsetto music.

"How many?" asked the first girl, a challenge rising in her voice.

"Three." The second girl spoke with a smugness.

The first girl's features fell like a rock. "How you know that?" she demanded, as she opened her hand. Three seeds were nestled inside her chubby palm. As the first girl claimed her prize, Ben edged forward.

"Beg your pardon," he said, and to Sam, his voice sounded hollow as a cave.

The girls had not noticed the two men watching them. Now they turned wary eyes and did not respond.

"Is one of y'all named Leila?"

The two girls shared a look. After a moment, the first girl stood. "How you know my name?" she demanded.

Ben's legs deserted him then. He staggered like a drunk, then crumbled in sections until he was on his knees. His mouth moved, it even croaked sounds, but he seemed unable to construct a sentence.

Sam stepped forward. "Leila, is your mother around?" he asked. The little girl nodded, her eyes never leaving Ben. Sam said, "Would you fetch her out here, please?"

The girl spun around and ran inside. The second girl stepped down off the stoop. "Why he cryin'?" she asked, pointing.

At that, Ben mashed impatiently at the tears on his cheeks. Sam reached down to touch his friend's shoulder. "He is just happy," he said. "He has been trying to find his way here for a very long time."

The girl's mouth drew up in skepticism. "He don't look happy to me," she said.

The door slammed open. A slender, pretty woman with arms folded protectively about her waist spoke Ben's name in the way you would speak a ghost's. He looked up, then clambered to his feet, unsteady as a toddler. "Hannah," he said. "It's me. I come home to you."

She said something stricken, something that was not quite a word. And then she was in his arms, crying into his chest and the girls were watching with wide, scandalized eyes. "Oh, Ben," she sobbed. "I thought you was dead. It's been so long. I thought you was *dead*!"

He held her back from him so he could get a look. "Ain't dead," he said. "Ain't nearly dead. And ain't passed a day I didn't think about you—you and my baby. Soon's the war ended, I took off walkin'. I *walked* all this way here, Hannah, all the way from the North, just to see you. There were days I thought I'd never find you. But praise the Lord I did and we's together now and I ain't never gon' leave you again."

He leaned forward to close the distance between them with a kiss. She stopped him with a hand on his chest, and turned away from the questions that pooled in his eyes.

"Hannah? What's wrong?"

"I thought you was *dead*, Ben." It was an accusation now, and it made her voice tremble.

"But I ain't dead."

"I can see that," she said. "Oh, Lord, I can." She caught her tears in her hands, took a definitive step back from him. He reached for her. She flinched from his touch.

"I ain't dead," he said again.

She lifted her eyes. "You might as well be," she said, the accusation sharper now, her eyes glittering like wet stones. "For seven years you might as well been dead. You can't stay away for seven years, then come back and expect ever' thing gon' be just like you left it. Time move on, Ben. Time move on!"

"Hannah? What you mean?"

But that was when the door opened and a man appeared on the steps. He was tall, thick in the chest, had skin the color of crow's feathers and wore overalls with no shirt. "Hannah, what's going on out here? Who this?"

She looked back at him helplessly as a drowning woman looks at a far shore. Ben's chin came up, a primal challenge. "I'm her husband, that's who I am! Who the hell are you?"

The big man stepped down, his giant hands fisted. "The devil you say!"

Hannah pressed her hand into the other man's large chest. He stopped advancing, but his eyes never left Ben's. "Henry," she pleaded, "it's all right, sugar. It's all right. He just don't understand, is all. He just don't know."

"Understand what?" Ben screamed it with a rawness of pain.

Sam pulled at him with his one good hand. "Ben," he said, "come with me." His friend shoved him off with surprising violence.

"Understand *what?*" demanded Ben. His voice was gravelly and urgent and Sam realized he needed to hear her say it, needed it even though he knew—*had* to know—what was coming.

Hannah faced him. "Ben," she said, "this Henry. *He* my husband now."

The nakedness of his confusion was painful to see. Ben looked like a man who has suddenly learned that snow falls out of the sun. "How he gon' be your husband?" he asked. "*I'm* your husband."

"Ben, when you run off, you said you'd come back and get me in a year, two at the most. Ben, it's been *seven* years."

"But the war come. You can't blame me for the war!"

"Ben, ain't nobody blamin' you. And I hope you know, you can't blame me, neither. Can't nobody blame nobody for nothin'. It was never our choice to be slaves, and it was never our choice to be separated for so long. All we wanted was to be free to love each other and raise our babies. But seem like what we wanted ain't mattered a whole lot. So we got to make the best of it. That's all we can do."

"What?" Ben laughed his disbelief. He turned to Sam, as if for confirmation this odd new equation made absolutely no sense.

Snow falling from the sun.

"What?"

But he was talking to the back of Hannah's head. "Henry," she said, "this the man I told you about. Me and him was owned by Marse Albert and Miss Sue. We was together, before."

Henry nodded. The anger in his eyes had melted down to a dull pity. His fisted hands had fallen open.

She turned to the little girls, standing transfixed by the confrontation between the adults. "Leila," she said, and her head nodded toward Ben, "this here is your real father."

The little girl's eyes raked over Ben and she spoke with a scorn accessible only to children. "Nuh *uh*," she said. "Daddy's my daddy." And to emphasize it, she hugged the man named Henry around one of his massive legs. He made a half-hearted effort to push her off, knowing what the sight of it would do to the stranger in front of his home.

Ben didn't even see them. *Snow tumbling out of the noon sun. And rain leaping up out of the ground. And horses conversing like men. And...oh, God, the entire world turned upside down, all his expectations, all his hopes, spilling out on the ground like water from a broken jar.*

Ben's head went down. His shoulders rounded. They waited for him. It took a moment. They waited. Even the little girl. Finally, Ben lifted his head like a weight and spoke in a voice rusty with pain. "You was the only thing kept me alive," he told her. "Runnin' through bullets, lyin' in that hospital cot spittin' up blood, walkin' all those miles, crossin' rivers and mountains and valleys and woods, you and her was the only thing kept me alive. 'Cause I knowed I was comin' back here to you. Y'all kept me goin'. I thank you for that, at least."

He turned from her. She touched him and he looked back. "I'm sorry, Ben," she said. "I'm sorry."

He smiled without smiling. "Me, too," he said. "I won't trouble you all no more." Turning to go.

She touched him again, he looked back again. "You still got a daughter here," she said. An invitation.

He looked past her to the little girl, flesh of his flesh, blood of his blood, clinging to another man's leg as to driftwood in a flood, clinging to him as though her own father was a threat, as though her father who loved her more than he loved water and air, who had just walked across half a country on the mere hope of seeing her, would hurt her. "That ain't what she say," he said. And he walked away.

She called his name. He didn't stop. She looked at Sam. Her eyes implored him but toward what, he could not say. He lifted his shoulders— *what do you want me to do?*—and followed his friend.

They didn't speak. They walked without aim, walking itself being the entire point, putting distance between themselves and the nameless little alley where Ben's life had broken to pieces. After a few minutes, they reached the river. Ben sat on a grassy bluff overlooking the water. Sam sat next to him.

"So," said Ben, and his voice was quiet, "you got a quote for me?"

"What do you mean?"

"Ain't you gon' tell me what some dead white man got to say 'bout this?"

Sam faked a smile. "You will be happy to know that I have lost a great deal of my faith in the ability of dead white men to explain what happens to us in this life."

"Hallelujah," said Ben. "Thank you, Jesus."

Sam looked at him. "So what are you going to do?"

A sigh. "Don't rightly know," said Ben. "Maybe walk on with you. See if you have better luck when you find *your* wife. Lord know ain't nothin' for me here."

"There is your daughter." Sam spoke quietly.

"What daughter?" Ben snorted. "You heard her. She think that other man her daddy."

"Then tell her otherwise," said Sam. "She is still your daughter."

He didn't respond at first. The words just sat there between them like stones. From far away, they could still hear the faint sound of hammer tapping anvil. After a moment, Ben said, "She kind of look like me, I thought."

"She does," said Sam. "Around the eyes."

"Maybe I might stay," said Ben after a moment. "Mistress said she needed some help 'round her place. Maybe I go hire on with her. Leila the only family I got left in this world. Might maybe be good I stay around her for a while, see if she come around, let me be her daddy. Her other daddy, maybe."

"I think that is a good idea," said Sam.

Ben cut him a sharp look. "But what about you?"

"What do you mean?"

"What you seen, don't it make you wonder if maybe the same thing ain't waitin' for you?"

"You mean that Tilda might have another man?"

A shrug. "Might have another man or be moved on or even be dead. How you gon' know? I was gone seven years and you see what happen. You been gone fifteen. That's a long time, Sam."

Sam watched the sunlight at play on the ridges of the water. The morning had gone still. But for the blacksmith's song, they might have been the only people in the world. "I think about it all the time," he admitted. "I think about it every morning when I wake up, every night when I lie down to sleep. But you know the only thing worse than finding out something like that has happened?"

"What's that?"

"Not finding out. Living the rest of my life without knowing."

"You say that now," said Ben. "You might sing a different song, somethin' happen to you like it done to me. Lord, ain't nothin' never hurt me that bad, Sam. *Bullets* ain't hurt me that bad."

"I know," said Sam.

"Walked all that way, all them miles. And for what? Lord, it was bad enough Hannah say she married, but then Leila hug that man's leg and say *he* her daddy? Lord. My heart like to drop out my chest when she said that."

"I know," Sam said again.

Again, silence filled the space between them. It was the silence of knowing what came next, but being in no great hurry to get there. For two months they had walked together. For 600 hard miles, they had walked, tracing the progress of war from the capital city out through the southwesternmost tip of Virginia, through the mountains of Tennessee, just to reach this moment on a morning by a river with disappointment sitting on the air like a smell. But the long journey, for one of them at least, was at an end.

After a time Ben stood up, clapping his hands decisively against his thighs. "Well that's it, then," he said. "Guess I'll walk back up that hill and see if Mistress still want to hire me on."

Sam stood. "So I guess this is where we part company." A pause, remembering the impossible smile that had saved his life on a bridge two months and a forever before. "You have been a good companion, Ben. I have no idea what I would have done without you." He extended his hand. "I wish you good luck."

"Same here," said Ben, pumping Sam's hand in both his own. "You made the miles go by a lot faster. You be careful out there. Hope you find what you're lookin' for," he added. "Seem like one of us ought to."

At that, Ben turned abruptly, moving off at a brisk pace, and Sam knew he was crying. It was not yet noon. With luck, he could get another fifteen miles in before he lost the light—another fifteen miles closer to whatever was going to be.

Sam waited until Ben had disappeared. Then he turned in the direction opposite his friend and walked away. It wasn't long before he couldn't hear the blacksmith's hammer at all.

George Flowers was almost 14 years old and that, he felt, was too old for a tanning. Yet Pa had tanned him anyway, but good, on hearing from that nigger how George had stolen Pa's squirrel gun and shot that other nigger, the big one, in the arm.

With that, George's mortification was complete. Not only had the fellows seen him forced to back down from that highfalutin Yankee strumpet on Main Street, not only had they seen him tuck tail and run from that big nigger in the alley behind the warehouse, but now they also knew he had been taken over one knee like some baby still in short pants. After all that, how could he ever hold his head up in town again?

He could not.

So last night, George had slipped down to the water, untied Pa's raft, and struck off down the river to seek his fortune. This, he knew, would only make Pa angrier; he used his rafts to barter and trade and occasionally earn a few pennies providing transport to towns too small or too ruined to be served by the steamboats. But George didn't care. He would go to Vicksburg, maybe even all the way down to New Orleans, and start his life anew.

At least, that had been the plan. But now, a day and a half later, lying on his back lulled by the late afternoon sun and by the gentle rocking of the raft down the center of the big river, George's intentions had begun to soften around the edges. He thought of how distraught Ma would be at the thought of her oldest child adrift in the world, heaven only knew where. He thought of Seth, his seven-year-old brother, and how lost he would be

without George to show him how to play base ball or shoot marbles. He
even thought of Pa a little and how maybe he wasn't really the worst father
in the world. After all, Dewey Jacobs's father drank all the time and beat
the tar out of Dewey on a regular basis. Pa only tanned George when he
misbehaved.

A bank of clouds slid across the face of the sun. Maybe, thought George,
he should just go back and take his medicine. It might not even be as bad
as all that. They might be so happy to see him that all would be forgiven.
And besides, he was beginning to get hungry.

George had about talked himself into beaching the raft and beginning
the long walk home. But the sun felt so good upon his face and the current
was so slow and peaceful. The river, when it was in a good mood, had this
way of making you feel contented within the moment, making you feel
that all was right with the world. Surely, he told himself, there would be no
harm in resting here a few minutes more.

He slept without knowing.

He woke without knowing at first what had wakened him. He was
surprised to see that darkness had pulled itself across the sky and the shore
had become a region of shadows broken only here and there by pinpricks
of light. Above, the moon was a crescent shape, painting the ridges of the
water in a pale white gleam. He reached for the lantern, cursing himself for
not having lit it before.

The sounds came all at once, freezing every part of him except his bladder, which, to his horror, released its contents in a free-flowing stream
he could not control. Because he knew those sounds, the warning bells,
the frantic shouts and cursing, the chopping of blade against water and
underlying it all, the deep groaning of the mighty engine. He knew those
sounds all right, and when he wheeled about, he was horrified but not at
all surprised to see the blazing lights of the steamboat towering over him.
And all at once he remembered his father's voice, all those times he had
talked about how you had to hug the bank when you were piloting a raft
downriver, because the steamboats owned the main channel. George had
never quite listened.

He was pushing himself to his feet when the collision came, logs and
bindings snapping with a grinding cracking sound as the boat rode up
overtop the raft, splintering it like toothpicks. The boy went backwards into
the water, arms flailing. He gulped a mouthful of river, went down into

the murky depths, then kicked hard toward the surface. His head broke the water and he found himself in the middle of a maelstrom, the steamboat towering high above him, somebody still cursing up a blue streak, the air still filled with the noise of collision. George spluttered and hacked, desperately treading water. He brought a hand up to rub his eyes and managed to clear his vision just in time to see a dark shape—a piece of broken timber—hurtling across the moon-streaked water, coming toward his face.

And that was the last George Flowers ever knew.

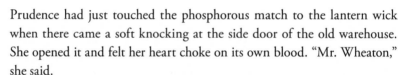

Prudence had just touched the phosphorous match to the lantern wick when there came a soft knocking at the side door of the old warehouse. She opened it and felt her heart choke on its own blood. "Mr. Wheaton," she said.

He was leaning easily against the door jamb and to her surprise, he gave her a smile. "My friends call me Bo," he told her.

"Which is why I shall call you Mr. Wheaton," she replied, her hand going automatically for the reassuring lump of metal in the pocket of her skirt.

He saw her and laughed. "Told you before: you ain't got no need for that little pea shooter of yours. 'Least, you don't need it for protection from me. The rest of the town might be another matter."

There was, she had to acknowledge grimly, some truth in that. For the last two days, white people had made it a point to walk past the school. They walked in twos and threes and larger groups down this end of the street where whites were rarely seen, going no particular place for no particular reason. Sometimes, they even stopped to mark the big building with hard glares. Making sure they were seen.

One grizzled old woman had approached her boldly just the day before as she stood at the door with Bonnie bidding the children goodbye. "You the one trying to raise the nigger army?" she demanded without preamble, her voice dripping vinegar. Bonnie had given her a pointed, meaningful look and Prudence had struggled to hold her temper and explain as politely as she could that she had no intention of raising an army and that any suggestion to the contrary was just a misunderstanding.

The woman had grunted and walked away, unconvinced.

"What do you want, Mr. Wheaton?" Prudence asked the smirking face before her. All at once, she felt tired.

Bo Wheaton heaved a theatrical sigh. "You are a purely contrary woman, Mrs. Kent," he said, though to Prudence, he seemed more amused than truly annoyed. "Always straight to business, that's you. Don't they believe in a little friendly small talk where you come from?"

"I have classes beginning in less than an hour, Mr. Wheaton. I haven't time for small talk."

A sour look. "Yes, well actually, I suppose that brings us to the business at hand." Reaching into his vest pocket, he produced a folded sheaf of papers. "This is for you," he said. "My father asked me to deliver it."

Mystified, she accepted the papers, unfolded them and read what someone had penned in a spidery hand:

> WHEREAS we, the undersigned citizens of Buford, Mississippi, have been more than forbearing with the Yankee woman Mrs. Prudence Kent who, without asking or receiving an invitation has come to our town to open a school for our negroes and
>
> WHEREAS we have been forced to put up with her strange and alien customs of social mixing between white and negro and
>
> WHEREAS the aforementioned Mrs. Kent has not responded to patient attempts by our leading citizens to instruct her as to the deep offense she has given to the citizens of Buford by her behavior and
>
> WHEREAS Mrs. Kent has repaid our patience by ordering weapons from the North with which to arm our negroes and inspire a servile rebellion among us and
>
> WHEREAS this behavior has excited a fervor amongst our citizens that is inimical to the maintenance of good order
>
> NOW THEREFORE, we demand that Mrs. Kent quit the area immediately for her own safety and for the continued peace of our town, selling the building that houses her so-called "school" and taking with her the negress Bonnie Cafferty who is her assistant in this enterprise, as well as all supplies and furnishings appurtenant to the aforesaid school.

The rest was signatures, hundreds of them. The first name, signed with a defiant flourish, was Charles Wheaton's.

Prudence glanced through the names, then looked up at him. She didn't bother to hide her amusement. "'Appurtenant?'" she said.

He colored a little, covered it with a shrug. "It means something that belongs to something else. They had lawyer Goodrich draw it up. They wanted it to be all nice and legal."

"I know the word's meaning," she said. "I am simply surprised to find such lawyerly language in so blatantly illegal a document."

"I told 'em you wouldn't agree," he said. He half mumbled this, as if to himself.

"Is your name here, Mr. Wheaton? I did not see it."

Again, she had caught him off guard. She could tell in the way he blinked twice, then stammered. "No, I ain't signed it," he said. "Not yet."

"Why have you not?"

He lifted his hat from his head, brushed a hand back through his hair. "Well, doggone it, I thought, see, you don't understand how things are down here, you being from someplace else and all. I know my pa tried to tell you, but he can be a hard man on the subject, especially since losing his legs in the war. And I know you're a spitfire yourself. You get your back up if you think anybody is tryin' to push you too hard. And I just thought if somebody was patient with you and took their time and explained it real gentle like, maybe then you'd see our side of things."

"And would that someone be you?"

"I thought we could go for a ride along the river, maybe this evening after supper, just the two of us, and we could talk. You know, get an understanding."

An incredulous laugh. "Mr. Wheaton, are you trying to woo me?"

He reared back. "No," he said, "no, I just thought...that is, I hoped maybe..."

She laughed at him. It was the gayest, freest laughter she had known in a very long time. She tried to make herself stop, especially as the coloring in his cheeks turned a deeper plum red, and she saw icebergs swimming in the pale blue lakes of his eyes. It took her a moment.

"I am sorry," she said. "It's just..."

"I'm sure there's no need for you to apologize," he said, and now his voice was stiff as new denim.

"It is just the last thing I would have expected," she said.

"Mrs. Kent, I assure you, you read me wrong," he told her. "I only thought to extend a kindness to you, you being from Yankee country and having no idea of our customs down here. I only thought to help you, but I see my intentions are misread…again. Anyway, I have done what I came to do. You have the petition now and…"

He paused and then, as if on sudden thought, he jammed the hat back on his head and snatched the papers from her. From his vest pocket, he produced a stubby pencil. Bracing the papers against the door jamb, he flipped to the last page and there, he inscribed his name.

"There," he said, handing the petition back to her. "My oversight is corrected."

He lifted his hat, gave her a formal bow. "Good day, Mrs. Kent."

Bo was glad to get away before she could say something else to make him hem and haw like a beardless boy. He walked down the middle of Main Street feeling small, shrunken by her laughter, not seeing much of anything, though he did absently mark the two little colored girls walking toward the school, books pressed to their chests, chattering excitedly about whatever it was that excited people like that. It angered him all over again and he was seized with an urge—he knew it was childish even as he thought it—to pick up a rock and chunk it at them. How could anyone, even a Yankee down from Boston, think anything good would come of trying to teach the slaves? His father was right. All it did was leave them unfit for their natural work and give them pretensions they would never be able to fulfill.

He didn't chunk the rock. He settled instead for kicking at a stray cur that came sniffing at his heel. The dog's yelp followed him down Main to the white section of town.

Vern was where Bo had left him, standing next to the wagon tied up outside A.J. Socrates's store. Horace, Socrates's colored man, was just unlocking the door. Apparently, Vern had said something amusing and the both of them were laughing companionably about it as Bo walked up. For no reason he could name, the two of them laughing together made Bo angry all over again.

"Little late opening your master's store this morning, ain't you, Horace?" he snapped.

The Negro's smile went away and he shook his head gravely. "No, sir," he said. "Ain't never late. Ain't late now." He produced a battered old pocket watch. "Ain't but 7:30, sir. Marse Socrates, he give me til 8:00 to open."

"Are you contradictin' me?"

A strange expression. "No, sir."

"Very well, then," said Bo, and he moved to follow Horace inside the store. Vern stopped him with a hand in the center of his chest.

He waited until the Negro was out of earshot. "I take it things didn't go well with Miss La-di-da?" he said.

"What do you mean?"

"Well, you are obviously in a fouler mood than when you went down there, the way you picked on poor Horace for no reason. So I take it you couldn't entice her to come for a ride with you while you explain the facts of life."

Bo pursed his lips, annoyance blowing out of him in a great snort of air. "Vernon, I tell you, she is just the most aggravatin' woman."

His brother was watching him closely. "Uh-huh," he said. "Well, I told you, didn't I? Told you and Pa both. There is only one way to get Miss La-di-da's attention. 'Course, you don't want to believe me, 'cause you're halfway smitten with the bitch."

Bo's head came up sharply and he poked an index finger in Vern's chest. "I have told you about that," he said. "Don't make me box your ears right here on Main Street, little brother."

It was the slow creak of wagon wheels that stopped them. Coming around the corner toward them was a mule-drawn cart. George Flowers was leading the animal. His wife and his youngest son were walking alongside, their faces downcast, their eyes fixed on some distant point of inner space. Shrouded in the back of the wagon was a body. A small body.

"My God, George," said Bo, approaching. "Who's this?"

"It's Georgie," said the man.

Bo peeled back a piece of the shroud and wished he hadn't. One whole side of the boy's face was crushed, an eye was missing, the skin was ragged and purple. Vern, standing next to his brother, gave a low whistle.

"I was too hard on him," said George, his eyes still fixed on things Bo could not see.

"What do you mean?" asked Bo.

"Whupped him for messin' with that Negro down at the school."

"That's right," said Vern, remembering. "George was the one shot big Jesse."

"Yeah, and I whupped him good for it, too."

"Did Jesse do this?" demanded Vern. "Did the niggers do this?"

"What?" The man seemed surprised. "No. Georgie done this hisself. Stole my raft. Out there on the river like a dang fool in the dark in the main channel with no lights. Got run over by a steamboat."

"We're goin' to get Preacher now," said the woman, and she seemed hollowed out by grief. "Goin' to get my baby buried."

"Well, we're purely sorry for you," said Bo. "You all let us know if there's anything we can do. All you need do is ask."

George Flowers gave a barely perceptible nod, tugged on the mule, and the sad procession continued grimly down Main Street. "That's terrible," said Bo. "We'll have to get Sass to bake 'em a cake or somethin'."

Vern didn't answer right away, just watched the sad family recede, tugging idly at the stray hairs of his whiskers. After a moment he said, "You know, when word gets around, everybody's going to naturally assume it was the niggers did that to poor Georgie."

"Yes, but you heard what his father said. Wasn't them. Boy got hit by a steamboat."

Vern's eyebrows lifted and he affected innocence. "Was that what I heard? I ain't rightly sure."

The brothers regarded one another for a long moment. Bo was about to speak when a thump of boots and a jangle of keys cut him off. A.J. Socrates had come up from behind him. "You boys need somethin'? Horace is in there, ain't he?"

"Horace is in there all right," said Vern, with a glance toward his brother. "We were just discussin' somethin' we saw."

"What's that?"

"You remember Georgie Flowers? Shot that nigger?"

"I ought to know that worthless little rascal. Lollygags out here on the street in front of my store 'most every afternoon."

"Well, he's dead. His family just went by, takin' him to the preacher to be buried. We saw the body. He's beat up somethin' awful. Look like somebody took a hammer to him. Half his face is gone."

"Who done it? Was it the niggers?"

"Can't rightly say," said Vern. "Logical to think so, I suppose. Tell you the truth, we were so shocked at the sight, we didn't even get around to findin' out all the details."

"Vern..." There was a warning in Bo's tone.

Vern glanced back at him and his eyes held a warning of their own. They shone with a dark malevolence Bo had never seen. For just that shadow of a second, he regarded his little brother and did not recognize him. Bo flinched from what he saw and did not speak again.

That same night, there was a meeting at the school. Twelve of them sat together by the light of a single oil lamp in the loft above the schoolhouse floor: the eight guards who took turns watching over the school by night, Paul Cousins, Preacher Lee, Prudence, and Bonnie.

Prudence had just finished telling them all about the visit from Bo Wheaton and the petition he had shown her. Closing the school, she had told them, was not an option. Nor was running away.

"But I am not unreasonable," she said. "Nor am I blind to the danger. And it occurs to me that perhaps there is something we can do to ease the tensions short of just giving up."

"What you have in mind, Mrs. Kent?" asked Preacher Lee.

She looked at Bonnie. They had discussed this. "Perhaps," she said, "we ought to discontinue the guard."

This brought groans of disbelief from most of the men. Prudence waved them down. "One at a time," she said, "please." She faced Preacher Lee. "It was your idea in the first place," she said. "What do *you* think?"

Preacher Lee scratched his chin thoughtfully. "Well," he said, "we done already made our point, that's for sure."

"Is that all this was about?" A man named Rufus had jumped to his feet. "Makin' a point? I thought we was guardin' this here place so our babies and even some'a us could get a education and come up a little in the world, now slave times is over. I ain't knowed it was only about makin' a point, Preacher."

Lee's tone was mild. "All I'm sayin', brother Rufus, is we got to be careful how we go 'bout this thing, whatever we do. White folks done got het up now, all this talk goin' 'round 'bout some nigger army, so-called."

"They het up?" Rufus's old eyes glowed. "So what. I'se het up, too. We all het up."

"Rufus," pleaded Preacher Lee, "be reasonable. Like Mrs. Kent say, I was the one had the idea to organize this here guard system in the first place. But we got to be realistic about this thing, now."

"What you want us to do?" The old man's voice was scathing. He had dark skin, blunt, heavy features, and his gleaming scalp was ringed by a horseshoe of white fuzz. "You want us to tuck tail and run? Done had enough of that. Been tuckin' tail to white mens my whole life."

"He want you to act like you got some sense!" Paul yelled it so suddenly Bonnie jumped. "We got to shut down this guard. That's what we got to do." Rufus swatted the words down as he would a fly and turned his back on Paul. "You think I don't know how you feel?" cried Paul. "We all feel the same way, don't we? All feel like we want to be treated like men for once in our lives?"

He stared around at the assemblage, some sitting, some standing, all their eyes upon him, shining up from the darkness of faces. "All I'm sayin'," said Paul, and his voice was husky, "is there ain't no need of *dying* for it."

Rufus turned. "Some of us don't care 'bout that," he said, his eyes level on Paul's. "Some of us ain't *scared* of it."

Paul's face dropped like a stone. Bonnie could only guess how deeply the insult cut. "Ain't no need of that kind of talk, brother Rufus," said Preacher.

"You callin' me a coward, Rufus?" Paul came to his feet, took a step. "Is that what you think? I ain't no coward and you know it. I'se just tryin' to help you, is all. I'se just tryin' to get you to *think* about what you doin' before it's too late."

And suddenly they reached a silence so deep Bonnie could hear the soft clucking of chickens in the coop across the back alley. She had been sitting quietly in a chair behind Paul. Now she surprised herself by standing. "*None of us are fearful*," she heard herself say. "None of us are cowardly. If we were, we would not be here. And shame on anyone who says otherwise." She stared at Rufus. His eyes flickered and he found something on the floor to look at.

Satisfied, Bonnie took in the faces gazing up at her. "All we are saying," she said, "is that we need to be smart in how we go about things. Perhaps the guard has outlived its purpose. Perhaps Preacher is right. Perhaps we have made our point. If we have, then keeping a guard on the school is just a useless provocation."

"Yeah, but while we busy bein' smart, they busy shootin' us." This was Alex, a thin man with a dignified bearing. "Look what happened to Jesse," he said, and the men nodded and murmured their agreement. "Ain't nothin' wrong with bein' smart, Miss Bonnie. But you also got to protect yourself. That's what I like about Mrs. Kent," he added, nodding in Prudence's direction. "No offense, Miss Bonnie, but she a *fighter*. We needs to be fighters like that."

Automatically, Bonnie glanced toward her sister. She would not have been surprised to mark a smirk of satisfaction on Prudence's face just then, a tiny show of vindication for Bonnie's benefit alone. But to her surprise, Prudence's face remained clear as water. She sat in uncharacteristic silence.

"How we gon' fight a whole town?" demanded Paul.

"Who said anything about fightin'?" retorted Rufus. "All they done is bring that there petition around. All they done is frown up they faces and mumble behind they hands. We s'posed to tuck tail from that? What kind of men that make us?"

"You do not understand," said Bonnie, exasperated.

Now Jesse stood. He still wore a dressing on his left bicep. "Beg pardon, ma'am," he said in that soft, deferential voice, "but it's *you* who don't understand."

"What do I fail to understand?" asked Bonnie, turning to face him. The calmness of her own voice surprised her.

"What I mean to say is, you's 'most white yourself, ma'am. Oh, I know you's colored, sho'nuff, but way I hear, you come down here from somewhere up North. Folks say you grew up right alongside white folks, right there in Mrs. Kent's house, and they always treated you like family. Is that true?"

Bonnie swallowed. "Yes, it's true," she said.

"From what I heard, you ain't even wanted to come down here in the first place, but Miss Prudence asked you to. Not that I blame you for that, ma'am. Don't know if I'd a' wanted to come here myself, I had a choice."

If she could have closed her eyes then, and then opened them again and been anywhere else, Bonnie would have done it. Instead, she forced herself to look up at the giant, his face slack with unspoken apology. "What is your point?" she asked him.

"Well, ma'am, it's like I say. You can't understand how we feel about this here. Man come through, gather us all together and say, 'Y'all niggers free. Ain't got to slave no more, 'cause you free.' And we say, free to do what? You got to do somethin' to give it meanin', or else, it ain't nothin' but a word. How you gon' know you free if you doin' the same things you was before, if you still jumps when they calls you or act like you scared to do what you got a right to do?"

"How you know you free if you *dead*, fool?" Paul yelled it.

Again, silence intervened. The big man lowered his head. Bonnie felt sorry for him, so gentle a man lashed like a whip by Paul's anger. "We just don't want any of you to get hurt," she said. "What would happen to your families if you were hurt?"

"Be hard on 'em, I expect," Jesse said.

"But at least they know we died as men!" hissed Rufus. "That got to mean somethin' too, don't it?" He looked around at the assembled men and repeated himself. "Don't it?"

Bonnie allowed herself an inward smile. She had tried to convince them. They were dangerously close to convincing her. She had assumed they were driven only by impulse and emotion. She had assumed them to be unthinking. But these men understood the stand they were making in guarding this school and they had given it—this was plain to see—a great deal of thought. They moved from motives deeper than just passion.

But did it really make a difference? The result was the same either way. The result was suicide.

Preacher Lee stood. "Don't see why we gettin' all excited," he said. "Ain't our decision to make, is it? Mrs. Kent, this your place. What you want us to do?"

All eyes turned to her. Prudence came to her feet in the middle of an expectant silence. Her eyes traveled the room before she spoke. Finally she said, "You are mistaken, Preacher. This is *our* place, not mine. I came here to listen. And what I think is that the decision should be made by the men who do the actual work of guarding this place. I will abide by whatever you all decide is best. How many of you think we should maintain a sentry on the school?"

The hands went up immediately. All eight of the guards.

"So," said Prudence, "I suppose it is unanimous, then. No need to ask if any of you think it a useless provocation." And now, she did regard Bonnie with just the flicker of a smile.

"You are making a mistake," said Bonnie. "All of you, you are making a mistake."

Another man spoke now—light skin, a high forehead, a thick mat of black hair. "We understand you worried about us," he told Bonnie. "And don't think we not grateful. But you need to worry 'bout your school and all them chil'ren you teachin' to read and write and cipher. That's what make this worth it. And 'side from that boy shot Jesse, you ain't had no more problem with white folks messin' with y'all since word got out we was watchin' this place. No more busted windows, no more dead cats. They ain't done nothin' since then but talk. Ain't that right?"

Bonnie nodded. "Yes," she admitted, "that is right."

He drew back in satisfaction. "Then that's all you need to worry about. Don't worry about us. We be fine."

The men's laughter was loud and easy. And triumphant. Bonnie realized it all at once: there was nothing they could do here. Nothing she or Paul might say would persuade these men. She smoothed down the wrinkles in her skirt just to give her hands something to do. "Well," she said, "I suppose it is settled then. I've papers to grade at home. Good night, gentlemen."

Bonnie ignored the alarm in Paul's eyes. He wanted to stay and fight it out. Could he not see there was no point? All at once, Bonnie felt older than her years.

"Miss Bonnie?"

She turned and Jesse was gazing down on her with buttery eyes. "Yes?" she said.

"Ain't want you to think we didn't appreciate you worryin' about us. We surely do."

This brought nods and noises of assent from around the room. "I know," she said. "And I understand why you are doing this. I still think you're making a terrible mistake, but I understand." And then, to Paul: "Mr. Cousins, would you see me home?"

Bonnie went down the stairs. After a moment, she heard him following. She could feel the questions brimming inside his chest but he didn't speak until they were outside and away from the building. Then he said, "Why you do that? Why you walk out?"

She stopped. The moon was a useless sliver of white slipping between the clouds and all she saw of him was shadow. But she did not need it to know the look on his face. Stricken indignation. "What else was there to do?" she said. "We had lost the argument," she said. "You saw that as well as I."

"We could have tried," he said.

"We would have failed," she said. "We already had."

"White folks scared, Bonnie. They do terrible things when they scared."

"I know," said Bonnie.

"No, you don't," he told her. "You think you do, but you don't." She didn't answer. She couldn't. The dark shape that was Paul spent a moment just breathing, almost as if he had forgotten she was there. Finally he announced, "I can't do this no more."

Alarm spiked Bonnie's chest. "What do you mean?" she asked, though she already knew.

"Can't work for y'all. You tell Miss Prudence I won't be comin' 'round no more. It's too dangerous. I *ain't* scared to die, you understand, no matter what that fool up there say. But I can't feature dyin' for no reason, dyin' for something that's already lost. That don't make no sense to me."

"I see," said Bonnie slowly. And it brought her to the edge of a question she did not know how to ask.

What about us? What about the shy glances we have exchanged as I have taught you to read? What about you meeting me to walk the half block home after a hard day at school? What about us sitting on Miss Ginny's porch together for hours on a Sunday afternoon, watching the street pass by? What about this soft, sweet thing that has been growing slowly between us?

"I shall miss our friendship," she said. She could not ask those questions. This was as close as she could come.

"I'm gon' miss that, too," he said. His voice was husky again.

Bonnie gazed at the shadow above her, wishing she could see his eyes. But they were as enwrapped by darkness as the rest of him. Miss Ginny's house was only a few feet away. She moved toward it. Paul moved with her.

Her life had changed so much, so fast. The woman she had been in February, laughing and gay and living in a wealthy white family's mansion, would not have known what to make of this woman she was in June, a tired schoolteacher walking a dirt street in a Mississippi river town escorted by a rough man barely removed from slavery.

How imperiously she had sat in the wagon as it stood before the abandoned warehouse the day Prudence addressed a crowd of Negroes pressing close. How regally she had looked down on them. In every word and deed and stray look, she had made clear that she was here only from a sense of moral duty—and not even her own. It was Prudence's determination that had brought them here. Bonnie had simply trailed along like a wagon after a horse.

She was so uncomfortable with these Southern Negroes, with their outlandish voices and unfettered laughter, their raucous worship and unlearned minds, their ignorance of words and places and ideas she took for granted. And she had never understood until, perhaps, just this night, the simple strength of them, the abiding courage of them, the unadorned wisdom of them.

Beg pardon, ma'am, the soft-voiced big man had said, *but you don't understand.*

And she had felt, in that moment, transparent, seen-through, revealed. All pretensions and assumptions laid bare.

You got to do somethin' to give it meanin', or else, it ain't nothin' but a word. How you gon' know you free if you doin' the same things you was before?

Could she, could Prudence, could some philosopher with the gift of eloquence, ever have explained the meaning of freedom quite so well? But then, who understands freedom better than a slave?

It had not occurred to her that she might learn from Southern Negroes. Or that she might grow fond of one of them in particular. But she had.

As if he knew she was thinking of him, Paul took her hand. He had never done this before. She felt something electric move through her blood and she was unnaturally aware of the feel of his hard and calloused skin. They paused again, standing at Miss Ginny's gate, and when he spoke, anxiety had gnawed his voice down to the bone.

"Miss Bonnie," he said, "I know this the most foolish thing I ever done, but if I don't do it, I'm gon' hate myself."

Somewhere, a dog was yapping. Looking down toward the river, she could see where the gaslights began, a yellow glow illuminating the other end of the street, the end where white people lived. In the darkness on this end, she waited, dreading.

"This real forward of me," he said, "and if you offended, I can't blame you. I got no right saying it and I knows that."

"Say it," she said and her heart crouched in her chest, bracing for impact.

"I'm goin' away," he told her. "Don't know where, but I know I got to go. Trouble comin' to this town, comin' to them mens we just left, sure as we standin' here, and I don't want to be around to see it. But before I go, I just wanted to tell you, well…I like you, Miss Bonnie. I like you in a special way. I know you's educated and got your pick of fellas and me, I can't read, nor write, got no prospects, don't even know for sure where I'se goin' when I leave here." He paused, as if suddenly hearing himself, hearing the hopelessness of what he said. "Lord, this so foolish," he muttered.

Bonnie said, "Paul, I—"

"No," he said, "let me finish, please. What I'se tryin' to say is, these few weeks I spent with you, well, they 'bout the best few weeks of my whole life. And when I go, you the only thing I'm gon' miss. The *only* thing. I hate to leave you. And I just wish, well, they was some way you could come with me. You be welcome. More'n welcome, in fact."

Bonnie was amazed how close she came to saying yes. How much some part of her wanted to say it. The woman she had been in February would have been appalled at the idea. The tired woman she was now in June stood in a darkness pricked by lightning bugs, and allowed herself to wonder for the fraction of a sliver of a moment if it were possible, if maybe she could…

But she could not, could she?

Prudence needed her. Bug and Adelaide needed her, too. Besides, something sensible and stolid whispered from behind her ear, she barely knew this man. Yes, she was fond of him, but was fondness reason enough to take so reckless a leap from the precipice of her very life?

He spoke into her hesitance. "You gon' say no," he said. "I don't blame you."

"I haven't any choice," she replied.

She felt him smile. "I know," he said. "Knowed it when I asked you. But like I say, I had to just the same." He opened his hand. She drew hers away.

"Paul, it is not that I am not flattered."

"You ain't got to explain."

"And it is not that I am not fond of you."

"I said, you ain't got to explain." His voice had hardened. "I knowed it was foolish when I asked you, but I couldn't help myself." He fell silent. She still couldn't see his eyes. She wished she could.

"Paul," she said, and then didn't say any more.

"Good night, Miss Bonnie," he told her.

And what could she do, but move away? He waited while she let herself in to the tiny house. When she closed the door behind her, she heard the soft scuffing of his shoes going away. She stood quietly in the darkness, waiting behind the door, until the sound of him faded in the distance.

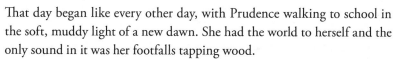

That day began like every other day, with Prudence walking to school in the soft, muddy light of a new dawn. She had the world to herself and the only sound in it was her footfalls tapping wood.

Prudence loved early morning. The day stood still and gave you time to gather yourself without regard for the fears and worries of other people. There were few things more paralyzing than fear and worry, and she could not understand why other people—even Bonnie—withstood them so readily. The world was what it was, the future would be what it would be, and there was not much you could do to change either. So you did what you knew was right, you accepted the consequences, and you did not look back.

It vexed her sometimes when people called this rashness. It was the only way she knew, the only way that made sense in her mind. Life could be lived in but one direction. Forward. Always, forward.

How else had she absorbed the jarring revelation that Cyrus Campbell was someone other than the genial savior of lost boys whose example was the bedrock upon which her family was founded? She had allowed it to slide to the bottom of a mind filled with more important things to think about, the same place she stored the pain of losing Jamie and Father.

It wasn't that the loss of them had not left a scar upon the truest part of her. Rather, it was that she could not allow those things to deter her. To do so would be to double the loss because it would mean losing not simply the men—a fate over which she'd had no power—but losing also the things they had stood for and cherished.

And that she could not allow. She had a mission and she would not fail.

Prudence paused as she always did when the big building at the end of the block rose above her, the unpainted wood just becoming visible in the light of a sun that still lay half-hidden in the cotton fields to the east. A splash of whitewash still spread itself across the front wall. Perhaps, Prudence thought, she would have the whole building painted once school was out and the children were picking cotton. Some gay color that lifted spirits instead of squashing them down.

She opened the side door and stepped in. At the top of the stairs, a shadow detached itself from the other shadows and came down toward her. "Good morning, Alex," she said.

The thin Negro stopped well short of her, his hat in his hands, the space between them measuring the width of his deference. Prudence had given up explaining to Southern Negroes that she did not need or desire these tokens of submission with which they came into the presence of whiteness. The habit was too deeply ingrained for them to stop.

"Mornin', Miss Prudence," he said, speaking to the tops of his shoes. Then he glanced behind her. "Miss Bonnie not with you this mornin'?"

"She will be along shortly."

Alex nodded and gave her his report, the gist of which was that the night had passed uneventfully. Then he bade her good day and slipped past her out the door. Prudence lit a lamp. It guided her to her desk at the front of the classroom where she sat down to begin grading papers. Soon enough the students would arrive and the long day would begin.

"Is it true? Did one of your niggers kill Georgie?"

Prudence jumped at the thin, reedy voice from her doorway. She lifted the lamp so she could get a better look. Its light fell upon a white boy with dark, unkempt hair and brown eyes round and suffused with sorrow.

"I beg your pardon?" she said.

"I asked you if your nigger killed Georgie."

"Georgie? Who is that?"

"Georgie *Flowers*," insisted the boy. "He shot big Jesse that day."

Prudence came to her feet. "That boy is dead?" This brought a nod. "What happened to him?"

"Got beat up real bad," said the boy. "Way I hear it, your niggers done it."

"No." Prudence came around the desk, the lamp held high so the boy could see her face. "*No*," she repeated. "No one at my school would have done anything like that."

"That ain't what I hear," said the boy. He took a cautious step inside, eyes traveling the walls. "This here is your school?"

"Yes," Prudence heard herself say. Suddenly, her mind was spinning in a dozen different directions.

"Ain't never been in no school," he said.

"You could be in this one if you wished," said Prudence. "We would be happy to teach you." She knew her mistake before the echo of her words had faded.

"Me come here?" The boy laughed in scandalized disbelief. "With the *niggers*? No thank you, ma'am."

"You know, I do not like that word," said Prudence. The admonition had become a reflex.

The boy's face was innocent as snow. "What word?"

"That word you use for the Negroes."

"Niggers?"

"Yes, that one."

He laughed. "Shucks, ma'am, that's what everybody calls 'em. That's what they call themselves." He gave another cautious glance around the room. The tables and chairs were neatly arranged, the books were stacked just so, a map of the world adorned one wall. "You give 'em a nice school, an' all, I'll say that much for you."

"Thank you," said Prudence with an automatic politeness that felt ridiculous.

"You know," said the boy, "Georgie ain't meant no harm. He was just funnin', is all. Weren't no cause to kill him."

"We *did not* kill him!" Prudence was surprised to hear herself yell.

The boy shrugged. "People say you did."

"*Who* says?"

He looked at her. "Everybody."

And a coldness shivered through her. The boy seemed not to notice. He shrugged and said, "Bye, ma'am," but she was barely aware of his leaving. Prudence made her way back around her desk and fell heavily into her chair, stunned by the implications of that one pregnant word.

Everybody.

She was still sitting when Bonnie arrived, 15 minutes later. Prudence looked up as her sister entered the room. "We have a problem," she said.

Bonnie was silent as Prudence recounted the boy's visit. She was silent for a long moment after. Then she sighed. "Paul said there would be trouble."

"He did?"

"Yes, last night as he walked me home. He is leaving, you know. He asked me to go away with him. I was going to tell you."

Prudence's mouth opened and surprise fell out. After a moment she said, "Gracious. I knew he was smitten with you, but I had no idea. What did he say? What did you tell him?"

"He does not even know where he's going, but he wants me to accompany him."

"You told him no," said Prudence, and it was less a question than a request to confirm what they both already knew.

"Perhaps I should have told him yes," said Bonnie. "He said these people are scared and they do dreadful things when they are scared."

"You do not think he exaggerates?" asked Prudence. She was, she knew, grasping for hope.

Bonnie gave her a level look. "Do you?"

There was a silence. Then Prudence asked, "What shall we do?" It struck her that she could not remember asking that question since she had first made plans to come to Buford.

Bonnie thought for a moment. Then she said, "The men. That is the provocation. We must get word to the men that they are to stay away for their own safety."

"I shall do it," Prudence said, coming to her feet, happy to have a course of action to follow. Forward. Always, forward.

Bonnie stopped her. "No," she said.

"What do you mean?"

"*I* shall do it," said Bonnie. "You are something of a provocation yourself, sister. You stay here and watch over the school."

Prudence wanted to disagree. It offended her to hide away like some dirty secret. But she knew Bonnie's logic was sound.

"You're right," she said at last. "Devil take you, but you're right. I will stay here. I will keep watch over the children."

So it was Bonnie who, a minute later, slipped out of the old warehouse by the side door. The street was still quiet, the rising sun cutting long morning shadows on the ground. She walked east where Main Street gave itself over to cotton fields. White flowers were blooming on the plants, petals fluttering gently, stirred by an early morning breeze. The fields seemed to extend themselves forever.

Bonnie tried not to think. She feared that if she allowed herself to consider their predicament, she would be paralyzed by terror. There was too much to contemplate. The boy, dead. The rumors, apparently flying. The simmering anger of white people who felt themselves willfully insulted, humiliated, robbed of their natural prerogatives. But of all that, nothing struck Bonnie so forcefully as a single, stunning realization:

Prudence was shaken.

She had tried to hide it, but she was. Bonnie had never seen her sister shaken, had never considered her shakable. And if Prudence was shaken, what should she herself feel, who lacked Prudence's iron will? It was, thought Bonnie, a question best avoided, even in the private chambers of her mind. So she walked east through the cotton fields and, to the best of her ability, thought nothing.

It took her an hour and a half. She found Preacher Lee on his knees in a row of cotton plants, his hoe thrown down beside him as he wrestled weeds out of the soil by hand. She came up behind him and spoke without preamble. "Preacher," she said, "we must talk."

He whipped around, startled, shading his eyes. "Miss Bonnie?" he asked, confused.

"A white boy came to the school this morning," she said. "He told Prudence that another white boy, the one who shot Jesse Washington in the arm, has turned up dead. He said the boy was beaten to death and there is a rumor going around the town that one of our guards did it."

"What?" asked Preacher Lee, climbing slowly to his feet.

It was as if he couldn't quite take it in. It made Bonnie impatient, though she knew she had no right to be. "Do you not understand?" she demanded. "There is a rumor in the town that our men killed this boy."

"They wouldn't do that."

"Of course they would not." Bonnie was finding it difficult not to snap at him.

"But if white folks think they did..." He didn't finish. Preacher had finally arrived at the crux of the thing. Now he met her gaze, his eyes wide.

"We need to reach the men and tell them to stay away from the school."

"I can't leave," said Preacher. The words seemed to shrink him.

"What do you mean?" demanded Bonnie.

"Marse Joe Hunsacker, he the man I work for. I signed the contract. I can't just leave. He get the dogs on me. He send the law after me."

"But the men must be warned!"

"Yes'm, but Marse Joe, he won't like…"

"He is no longer your master!" Bonnie heard herself yelling, couldn't make herself stop. "Do you not understand? There are no masters anymore. There are no slaves. You are a free man! You are *all* free men! That is the entire point!"

Preacher absorbed all this without response. His expression, thought Bonnie, was that of a man waiting out a storm. Which, perhaps, he was.

Nor did he bother to answer her tirade. Instead, when she was done, he said simply, "You gon' have to warn them men yourself. I can tell you how to find them." Feeling suddenly spent, Bonnie only nodded.

She spent the next four hours tramping through fields of cotton. She found the men on their knees like Preacher, or wielding hoes or sipping water from tin dippers or slopping hogs or mending fences, and it occurred to her how little the landscape of this place had been changed by the supposed new order of things. If you didn't already know there were no more slaves, you wouldn't know it by traveling these fields watching black men and women and children toting and hauling, stooping and bowing, and chopping cotton as they had, always.

To a man, the men expressed surprise. To a man, they all said they'd had nothing to do with the death of George Flowers, Jr.

"Why any us want to hurt that fool boy?" Jesse asked in his soft voice as she stood in the shade of him, looking up.

"I know you did not hurt him," she said.

She begged him, as she begged all of them, to stay out of town, stay out of sight for the next week, at a minimum. To a man, they all asked if she and Prudence would be all right.

"We will be," she said. "It is you all they want."

"Did you know I fought for the Union?" Jesse had asked her as she turned to go.

"Beg your pardon?"

"Run away to Union lines when the soldier boys come through here. Ended up walkin' north to Washington. When I heared they was gon' raise a colored regiment, I made my mark on the paper and they sent me off to the war. I done my part, Miss Bonnie. But I swear, I thought things be different, after."

She allowed herself the tiniest of smiles. "I suppose many of us did," she said.

She turned again to go. "Miss Bonnie?"

Bonnie came back around. His eyes were serious and sober. "Yes?" she said.

"You *sure* you and Mrs. Kent be all right?"

"Yes," she said with a certainty she did not feel.

It was close to noon when Bonnie came back in sight of the school. She was thirsty and staggering from fatigue, so it was a moment before she noticed the people standing across the street. When she finally registered them, her feet stopped moving and her heart stammered in her chest like an adolescent boy. There were seven of them, white men, standing there across from the big doors, talking together, watching.

All at once, Bonnie was not tired anymore. Exhaustion had been crowded out of her by panic. She gathered herself and walked forward. Their eyes tracked her. She felt the touch of them as surely as she would a hand on her arm. Their conversation reached her in bits and pieces.

"...heard that boy's head was near tore off his shoulders..."

"...now you see what the Yankees have loosed on us..."

"...there go one of 'em now..."

"...nigger army..."

Bonnie didn't stop at the school. She continued west down Main Street, still feeling the touch of eyes upon her, people pausing, talking, pointing.

Bo Wheaton was coming out of A.J. Socrates's store as Bonnie approached it. He did not acknowledge her with so much as a glance. Bonnie found herself grateful to be ignored.

She went into the store and took up a scrap of paper and a stubby pencil from the counter. Her hands shook as she wrote out a message. They were still shaking as she handed it to the sallow white man. "Please send this," she said.

He read the message, then looked up with a smile that made Bonnie's stomach lurch. "I don't think I'll be sendin' this," he said. "Don't think I'll be sendin' anything of the sort."

"But you must!" said Bonnie.

"What is it?" asked a voice behind her. She turned and was surprised to see Wheaton standing there. "What does she want sent?"

Socrates's grin turned conspiratorial. "It's to the provost," he said, "askin' him to send troops. Seems she's worried somethin' bad is fixin' to happen."

Wheaton didn't return Socrates's grin. Instead, some shadow Bonnie could not read flickered in his eyes. Then he said, "I think you ought to send it."

Socrates's smirk puddled into a frown of confusion. "Really?"

Now Wheaton smiled. Or at least, he appeared to. To Bonnie, the smile seemed an act, a mask he pulled on for Socrates's benefit. "Yes," he said in an easy voice. "Might as well be on the safe side."

Prudence glanced up at the knocking on the side door. Her heart was hammering. "Who is there?" she asked, fearing the response.

"It's me," said Bonnie.

"Oh, thank God," said Prudence, flying to the door to unlatch it. "You took so long, I was so worried about you."

"I had to go around to all the plantations where the men are scattered."

"Preacher Lee could not help you?"

She shook her head. "Preacher Lee was unable to be of service. He had to work and said he could not leave. I also sent a telegram to the provost. I asked him to send soldiers."

"I see," said Prudence. "So you believe we are at that point?"

"I do," said Bonnie. "There is a small group of them out there already. That horrible man Socrates was not going to send the telegram, either, but the oddest thing—"

She stopped, as if suddenly aware of the children, staring up at them. She tried to reassure them with a smile. "Do you think we should send them home?" she whispered.

"When the soldiers come," said Prudence.

"If they do," said Bonnie. She widened her smile and moved out among the children. "Who is ready to read for me?" she asked. Prudence thought her voice a poor imitation of gaiety.

The afternoon passed gently. Prudence lost herself in the familiar rhythms of question and answer, of furrowed brows and comprehension dawning like the sun. Occasionally, she would find herself watching Bonnie on the far side of the room laughing with a student, or bending down to explain something, and their eyes would catch. Prudence saw her own uncertainly reflected back at her. It was a novel feeling, uncertainty.

The hours bled into one another. Mathematics, recess, reading. Arms waving like a field of cornstalks when children knew the answers and wanted to be called upon. Two boys arguing because one made fun of other's poor reading. Geography. Spelling. Then it was almost dismissal time.

Prudence was leaning over a boy, helping him decipher the word *mother*, sound by painful sound, when a fist rapped against the side door heavily enough to make the windows shudder in their frames in the loft overhead. Her head came up and she saw her own confusion mirrored in Bonnie's eyes. Had some contingent from the town come to attack them in broad daylight? What about the children? Moving toward the door, Prudence smoothed down her skirt, fingers passing inadvertently over the lump the derringer made in her pocket. For once, it was not reassuring.

When she opened the door, Prudence found herself facing a Union soldier with sad, deep-set eyes under unruly brows. She felt herself breathe for what seemed the first time in an hour. "Have I the honor of addressing Mrs. Kent?" he asked, his voice issuing from beneath a thicket of russet-colored beard.

"I am Prudence Cafferty Kent," she said.

"Ma'am, I am Sergeant Gideon Russell. I was sent here by the provost marshal's office. I believe you sent a telegraphic message?"

"Bonnie did," she said. Prudence's knees felt weak with relief. She blessed her sister's foresight.

Russell might have smiled. It was difficult to tell with the beard. "Well, ma'am, whoever sent the message, we were detached by the provost, Colonel Leonard Sharpe—I believe you met him several weeks ago. Folks down here seem to believe you're planning some sort of servile insurrection amongst the Negroes."

"We have Negro guards to protect our school from the vandals that have attacked it in the past," said Prudence. "And the people in the town have it in their heads that the guards killed a little boy."

"Yes, ma'am," said Russell, "I already know the Negroes did no such thing. The provost asked that we come and take a look."

She caught it that time. "We?"

In response, he gestured behind him. She had to step through the doorway to see. Eight Union soldiers stood together in the middle of the thoroughfare, their horses tied to a hitching post at the abandoned livery across the street. But that was not what rounded her eyes and stilled her breathing.

It was that the entire white population of the town seemed to be standing there, too, a mass of folded arms and righteous stares, facing her building as if it were responsible for all the misery and barrenness of their lives and the day had come finally to hold it accountable for its crimes. She had never seen faces like these, never seen anything like the loathing that stretched their mouths and fired their eyes.

Prudence surveyed them. She saw shopkeepers, clerks, housewives, little children, drunks, A.J. Socrates, the woman Millie and her friends, Vernon Wheaton, and beside him, his brother Bo, wearing a deep expression she could not quite read. She thought it might be sorrow. She thought it might even be pity.

"My God," she said.

Prudence felt an unfamiliar something spreading out from the center of her and it was a moment before she could identify it. Helplessness. She could not remember ever feeling it before.

"We were planning no insurrection," she told the sergeant.

He leaned close. "I know," he said in a voice meant only for her. "I believe your only intention was to uplift the little pickaninnies. But look at these people. Do you believe soft words will convince them? They are frightened, Mrs. Kent. And they will not stop being frightened until we prove to them they have nothing to be frightened about. Just do as I ask."

Prudence gazed across at the hatred mirrored in a hundred pairs of eyes. "They are not just frightened," she said.

But Sergeant Russell was no longer leaning close. He stood back now and in a voice meant for the whole street to hear, he said, "Mrs. Kent, I need you to open the loading bay doors so my men can do a thorough inspection."

"But the children," she began.

His voice was stern. "Mrs. Kent, please do as I ask."

Prudence looked behind her to where Bonnie stood in the middle of the classroom, several of the children gathered to her.

She swallowed, pulled the massive key ring from her skirt pocket, and stepped onto the sidewalk. As she came into clearer view, an angry murmur lifted from the crowd like smoke from a fire.

"There's the Yankee whore!" someone cried.

"Ought to string her up right now!" someone else cried.

The soldiers watched impassively. Prudence's skin seemed to vibrate. She tried to swallow and couldn't. Her tongue tasted like metal. She opened the latches.

Two soldiers came then, brushing her aside and pushing at the big doors. They squeaked as they fell open. And then the whole interior of the school stood revealed. Vulnerable. The children had gathered in a tight knot around Bonnie, hugging her, hugging one another, crying soundlessly.

Russell addressed one of the soldiers, his voice still intended for the crowd. "Parker," he snapped. "Take three men and search this place top and bottom."

"Yes, sir," said the soldier.

As Parker called out three men and moved to follow orders, Russell grabbed his arm and spoke in a softer voice. "Gently, Parker, gently. It is not necessary to destroy the place."

Parker glanced from his sergeant to Prudence. "Yes, sir," he said. And the small group of soldiers brushed past her and entered the Cafferty School for Freedmen.

"What about the children?" asked Bonnie.

Russell glanced behind him. "Quite right," he said.

And then, to the crowd: "Make way! Make way, so the children can leave." He addressed one of the remaining soldiers. "Schultz, make a path through the crowd."

"Bonnie, you leave with them," said Prudence.

Indignation lifted Bonnie's chin and for a moment, she seemed taller than she was. "I will *not*," she said.

"Make way!" cried Russell again. The one called Schultz and the remaining three soldiers waded into the mob like swimmers breasting a wave, pushing, yelling. With palpable reluctance and angry protests, the people moved back.

Now, all eyes swung expectantly toward the children. They seemed to shrink in the sudden glare of attention, pressing back against Bonnie. "Go on," she told them, gently pushing a bright-eyed little boy who had fistfuls of her skirt.

"I'm scared," he said, his voice a high-pitched whine.

"I know," said Bonnie, "but you must be brave. All of you: you must be brave."

"You need to hurry those children up," said Russell.

"They are children," snapped Prudence. "They are afraid. Wouldn't you be?"

She didn't wait for an answer, stepping past him and into the school. She knelt before the little boy clinging to Bonnie as to the edge of a cliff. "I know it is frightening, but you see those soldiers with their guns? They are here to protect you."

Someone in the crowd cried out, "Hurry up and send the little niggers out!"

Prudence closed her eyes. She felt her blood rushing through her like a river. She opened her eyes. "You will be perfectly safe," she said, wondering if she were not telling a lie she would regret every day for the rest of her years.

Not that the boy knew this. She was his teacher, and who can you trust if not your teacher? He regarded her closely, then nodded solemnly and said, "All right, then." And without another word, he turned and ran. Other children followed him.

A tall girl turned to run, then turned back. "Miss Prudence, you didn't give us our homework."

Prudence smiled. "No homework tonight, Janey. Go."

She patted her back and Janey went, bringing up the rear on the line of children sprinting single file through the slot the soldiers had opened in the heaving mass of people. Just before she reached the other side, she paused in stride, one foot still hanging in mid-air, and looked back. The girl's gaze was unreadable. It was only a moment, then she wheeled back with a child's heedless grace, and ran.

Prudence never saw her again.

With the children gone, the soldiers stepped back and the mob flowed together like water. There were so many of them. Screaming. Jeering.

"I should have brought more men," said Russell.

Prudence had drawn a measure of security from knowing the nine soldiers with guns were there to protect them. This quiet admission made her gasp. Russell looked down at her as if surprised she had heard him, as if he had not realized he had spoken out loud.

Corporal Parker came down the stairs in that moment, holding a rusty old Enfield by the barrel. "Sergeant," he said, "this is the only thing they have. It doesn't even work."

Prudence recognized it. The rifle had been there the day they arrived. Russell snatched the weapon, inspected it for a moment, then stepped forward, holding it out before him like a peace offering. "Here is your 'nigger army,'" he said. "One old rifle with a broken hammer."

At the sight of the Enfield, a noise swelled from the crowd, an undistinguished roar of angry cries and shouted taunts. Anger flamed in Russell's cheeks. "Go home," he cried. "All of you people, go home. There is no servile insurrection. Go *home*!"

"What about the boy?" someone yelled. "What about Georgie Flowers?"

"Nobody at this school hurt that boy!" called Russell. "He took his father's raft down the river without permission and had a collision with a steamboat!"

"You're lying!"

"I've spoken to his parents myself! They say it was a steamboat!"

"Yankee lies! Goddamned Yankee lies! We know what happened to that boy!"

"It is the *truth*!" cried Russell.

In reply, a large rock came arcing in from somewhere in the ocean of arms and mouths and rage. It struck Russell on the right temple. He cried out, stumbled back, brought a hand to his temple. It came away bloody. Laughter lifted from the crowd.

Russell roared at them. "Go home! I am ordering you to disperse immediately."

"Not til we kill that nigger army, sarge!"

It was Vern Wheaton, weaving drunkenly, a blissful smile on his face. Somehow, he had worked his way to the front of the crowd. His brother stood at his side. Bo's expression was haunted and grim.

The cry went up. "Kill the nigger army! Kill the nigger army! Kill the nigger army!"

The soldiers edged back, rifles up. Bonnie had gone gray. Her eyes were lanterns in the shadows of the old warehouse. Russell seemed at a loss, looking to his men as if they might have the ideas he did not. Prudence lifted her hands. "*Please!*" she cried. "Please listen to me. We did not harm that child. I know we come from different worlds, you and we. But are we really so different? Do you really believe me so callous and inhuman as to kill a child? You heard the sergeant: George Flowers was killed by a steamboat. If you are skeptical, there is a simple remedy: go ask his parents yourself."

The crowd stilled. Emboldened, Prudence took a step. "And I promise you, there will be no army of insurrection to come out of this place. There was never any such plan. When we posted a guard here—when I very briefly and foolishly thought of buying guns for them—I was only trying to protect the children and this school, which have been the targets of threats and vandalism from its very beginning. It was not my intention to anger you. I was only seeking to help in the uplift of the colored people. I apologize if I gave offense. And I am begging you: please leave us alone."

They were listening. She could see her words striking home, like rain-drops pelting dry soil. A man gave her a tight little nod of indignation, her soft words validating his rage. A woman looked around as if waking from a dream and surprised to find herself here. They were *listening*.

And then Jesse Washington came down the street.

Prudence saw him before they did. He was coming out of the cotton fields to the east and now he stopped, puzzled, obviously surprised at the mob that had gathered in the street.

"Oh, my God," whispered Bonnie, suddenly standing at Prudence's elbow.

"I thought you told the men to stay away." Prudence's voice was an urgent hiss.

"I did," said Bonnie. "But he was worried about us. He asked me twice if we would be all right."

There was a terrible moment when time itself seemed suspended. Prudence urged Jesse, willed him, *prayed* him, to run, hide himself away, before...

Before.

Someone cried out, "There's one of 'em now!" Every eye swung toward him.

And Jesse stood there. It was as if disbelief had locked his knees in place. He watched as that swell of people rushed toward him. Finally, at the last moment, he got his legs to work, wheeling around, trying to run. He managed two lumbering steps. Then they were on him, climbing that big body like like ants on a sugar cube. Jesse Washington disappeared beneath them til all that was left of him was his voice, high and pitiful and plaintive, crying "No! *Please*! No! Oh, *Lord, please*!"

Prudence shrieked something that wasn't even a word. Bonnie turned away, tears tumbling down her cheeks.

Russell gave the order. "Close the doors," he cried. "Hurry!"

She awakens with the boy's arm draped across her from behind, his thighs and his damp, spent sex pressed tight against her. His breathing is soft and regular in her ear.

For a moment, she simply lies there, listening, assessing, as the world stirs itself to life, birdsong drifting down from the trees. After a moment, she raises herself up, glances over. The boy's face is almost sweet in repose, mouth sagging open, eyes closed, unaware of himself.

She wishes she had something sharp to plunge into his neck. Would she have the gumption to do so?

Probably not. Gumption is only a remembered thing.

She lifts his arm from her and gives it back to him He snuffles noisily and shifts in his sleep. They are on a thin mattress on the ground, inside a tent just back of the main house. She wriggles into her drawers and petticoat, then into the thin muslin dress she has worn every day for the past year and a half. She lifts the tent flap, then looks back on the boy. She wonders again how it would feel to kill him. Then she asks herself what good that would do. Better to kill Marse Jim, who lets him use her.

But these are just foolish dreams, she knows. She lowers the tent flap and steps outside. It is so early the sun is still whispering gossip to the eastern horizon, but already the air is steam. So she knows she is in for another day of awful heat.

The smell of cooking draws her to the building behind the house that serves as a kitchen. When she walks in, Honey is sitting in a chair near the door, reading a newspaper by lamplight. Honey starts at the sound of her and has the newspaper half hidden behind her back before she realizes who it is. "Shoot, girl," she says in a voice of mild reproach. "Don't sneak up on a body like that. You like to scared the dickens out of me."

"I'm sorry," says Tilda.

They are the only two women in the camp. Honey is plump, with skin the color of butter and a smile you could warm yourself by. Tilda judges she must be close to 70, though she is so spry she could easily pass for twenty years younger. She was a slave—still is, Tilda supposes—to Colonel Moody. He doesn't know she can read.

"Biscuits smell good," says Tilda. Several rows of them are browning on a tray in the hearth. A pot of gravy is warming.

"Wood pile gettin' low," says Honey, nodding to the log stack at the side of the fire.

"I'll chop you some later," says Tilda.

"Gon' be hot as all get out later," says Honey.

"It wouldn't do for me to have an axe in my hands right now," says Tilda.

Honey gives her a look. "That boy after you again?" she asks. Tilda nods. Honey says, "I hate 'em when they that age. Seem like they ain't never got but one thing on they mind. Want to stick they prick in any thing don't get away fast enough."

"Ain't that the truth," says Tilda.

"Make me glad I'm an old thing," says Honey. "They don't bother with me no more."

"Be glad when I'm an old thing, then." Tilda sits herself on a stool near the door.

"You spoke to your marse about it?"

Tilda's laugh is hard. "What good will that do? Who do you think told the boy he could have me in the first place?"

"Maybe he change his mind, he find out you don't like it?"

"How you talk? Marse Jim doesn't care what I like or don't like. Besides, he's too busy off playing soldier. I have not seen him so pleased in a long time."

"I don't know why they be happy," says Honey. "Ain't like they doin' nothin'. Nothin' that's gon' change nothin', I mean. Way I hear it, they caught a Union boy out ridin' by himself last week and beat him tolerable bad, stole some rifles off the back of a Yankee wagon. I mean, I'm sure the

Yankees don't like it none, but I can't imagine it's more than just a little bothersome to them."

"They won the war," says Tilda. "It is not as if stealing a few rifles is going to change that."

"That's what I mean," says Honey.

"But if it keeps them happy, what do we care? It simply means fewer problems for us."

Honey laughs. "Chile, ain't that the truth?"

Tilda has been fanning herself. Now she stops. "How long do you think it will last?"

"What?"

"All this. These men out here playing soldier, acting as if they can overturn the defeat. They have to accept it sooner or later, don't they?"

This makes Honey laugh again. "Chile, don't get me started talkin' on what white men will accept or how they think. 'Fore I understood that, I expect I could understand how many stars God hung up in heaven."

"So you think we could be out here for a long time? For months?"

Honey shrugs. "Maybe for years. We already been out here two, three months 'fore you arrived. I expect we be out here til the Yankees get tired of bein' annoyed and come clean this camp out—or the mens just start driftin' away 'cause they realize this ain't nothin' but foolishment. Might already be happenin'. Grissom left yesterday. Said he was tired of living out in the woods with a bunch of mens. Wanted to get back to his farm and see about his wife and young ones."

Tilda sighs. "So all we can do is wait and see if the Yankees get tired or these sorry rebs do?"

Another shrug. "Either that, or strike out on your own, I expect. Might have a fair chance to get away, someone young like you."

Her eyes hold Tilda's a beat too long. Tilda marvels that anyone might still think her young. She changes the subject. "What are you reading?"

"This?" Honey holds it up. "Colored paper out of Little Rock. *The Freedman's Voice.* They got all these notices in the back. Mothers lookin' for their children, husbands lookin' for their wives, brothers and sisters tryin' to find each other." Her voice trails off.

Tilda takes the paper and studies it.

Information Wanted of Hessy Carter, who was sold from Vicksburg in the year 1852. She was carried to Atlanta and she was last heard of in the sales pen of Robert Clarke (a human trader in that place) from which she was sold. Any information of her whereabouts will be thankfully received and rewarded by her mother, Lucy Pickens, Nashville

$200 Reward. During the year 1843, Donald Hughes carried away from Little Rock as his slaves, our daughter Betsy and our son, Thomas, Jr., to the state of Mississippi, and subsequently, to Texas and when last heard from they were in Lagrange, Texas. We will give $100 each for them to any person who will assist them, or either of them, to get to Nashville, or get to us any word of their whereabouts, if they are alive. Thomas and Georgia Smith

Carl Dove wishes to know the whereabouts of his mother, Areno, his sisters Maria, Neziah, and Peggy, and his brother Edmond, who were owned by Richard Dove of Jackson, Mississippi. Sold in Jackson, after which Carl and Edmond were taken to Nashville, Tenn. by Joe Mick; Areno was left at the Eagle Tavern, Jackson. Respectfully yours, Carl Dove, Utica, New York

Tilda looks up. "You think somebody might be looking for you?" she asks.

Honey purses her lips thoughtfully. "I can't feature it," she says. "Ain't got no kin left, near as I can figure. Never had no luck with babies. Had four, but they all died 'fore they could get growed. Had three sisters and a brother, but they all older than me. I expect they gone on to glory by now, or near about. What about you?"

Tilda ignores the question. "Why do you read these ads, then?"

A frown. "Don't rightly know. I reckon I just likes the idea of people lookin' for they chil'ren and they loved ones. Tryin' to get back to one another. Wish 'em all luck, tell you the truth. Hope they find the ones they lookin' for." She gives Tilda a wise look. "Noticed you ain't answered *my* question, Missy. You think anybody lookin' for you?"

Tilda thinks for a moment, then she shakes her head. "Had a son," she says. "Luke, his name was. He died many years ago. There was a man, Luke's father. I don't know where he got off to."

She folds the paper and is handing it back to Honey when the headline on the front page catches her eye:

Rampage in Mississippi!! Scores Flee!! Colored District Leveled!! Many Dead!!

Tilda reads. Honey watches her. She says, "Some place called Buford, I think that was."

Tilda nods. "I know where that is. Marse Jim's place was in the next county. The woman that used to own me before him had a place right outside of town. We came through there on the way here." She reads some more. "Oh, my Lord," she says. "It says here they were fighting over some school for colored and a rumor that Negroes with guns were guarding the place against vandalism. It says more than a dozen people were killed, some of them children. The military governor has sent soldiers to keep the peace."

"Ain't that always the way?" says Honey. "White folks don't never want us to have nothin'."

"It says they killed *children*," repeats Tilda.

"Why you surprised?" demands Honey, and her voice is sharp. "Why you think they won't kill children? Why they won't kill any one of us they takes a mind to? Especially now. Slave nigger, that's one thing. They know that that cost somebody some money. Free nigger, that's, well...just like it say, that's free. Ain't cost nobody nothin'. Kill all of them they please." Her voice has filled with ashes, her face is stony.

After a moment, Tilda hands her the paper, comes to her feet. She feels the boy's hands mashing at her breasts. She feels his semen trickling slowly upon her thighs. She feels filthy, slimy with sweat.

And she feels tired. So tired, Lord, she can barely stand. "Going down to the lake," she says. "Going to wash."

Honey isn't looking at her. Her eyes are on the paper. "You chop me some wood when you get back?"

"Yes," says Tilda. Her voice feels like a dead thing lodged in her throat.

She sees Honey glance up at the sound, makes herself turn away before the other woman can ask her questions whose answers she does not know. Tilda makes her way through the woods. She can barely see. The world has gone gray and watery. And that is when she realizes she is weeping. She is surprised there are still tears in her.

But then, what other sensible response is there to a world where children are killed because they went to school? Or ran away one time, trying to be free? What other response makes sense in a world where you wake up with some strange boy's hands upon you, his wet prick burrowing itself against you, and there is nothing you can do and it is forbidden for you even to cry out in your grief and rage and shame?

She is running. Then she is running faster. Then she is tearing at the flimsy, stained dress that sits so heavily upon her skin, tearing it off her, flinging it behind her, plunging through the woods. When she finally reaches the edge of the lake, she is wearing just her petticoat and drawers and she can hear herself breathing.

For a moment, she simply stands there and watches the water. The trees on the distant shore are fuzzy and indistinct, the still water nearly black in the shadows of early morning. She glances back. The woods obscure the house and the kitchen. A thin plume of smoke from Honey's cook fire lifts lazily above the tree line.

She finds herself remembering the night she stood in Agnes Lindley's door, Marse Jim snoring, the moon watching, unable to make herself take a step. Unable to make herself seize freedom.

But freedom takes many forms.

The thought propels her forward and she puts one foot in the water. Then the other. She does not hurry, but neither is there hesitation in her step. She walks forward, deeper. The water is blessedly cool, swirling around her ankles, then her knees, then her thighs. She keeps walking. She walks with purpose. She can feel the soil beneath her feet going down, taking her down with it. She can feel fish brushing her knees.

Then there is no more soil beneath her feet and she is floating. The water is up to her neck. She looks around her, turns her body so that she can see it all. The trees stand silent witness. Dragonflies skim the water, searching for breakfast. The sky is half and half, one side blushing pink, the other black as an ink spill. The sun dawns upon a life she hates in a world she cannot abide.

But freedom takes many forms.

Tilda closes her eyes. She stops treading the water and allows herself to sink. She opens her mouth, forcing herself to breathe the water in. The lake closes over her.

He put 20 miles behind him every day, striking out when the first glimmer of pink brushed the sky, ending his days with the sun half-submerged in the western horizon. He walked with great eagerness now, a fatalistic dread driven by watching his friend's life fall to pieces in an alley in a small Tennessee town. Sam just wanted to get it over with. He had spent weeks in anticipation and that was enough. Whatever was to be, he wanted it to be.

So the miles piled up behind him, pushed him through the hilly country around Chattanooga, down across the northwest tip of Georgia, across northern Alabama into the red dirt hills at the very top of Mississippi and from there, east toward the river. Pine forests gave way to cotton fields. Negro men and women with hoes bent and rising like automatons, chopping weeds from the precious cotton stalks. Just as if there had never been a war, he thought. Just as if they still were slaves.

He walked with a limp now and his foot hurt all the time, even with shoes, even with rest. He had decided the dull ache would be with him the rest of his life, a reminder of the hundreds of miles he had walked on a bare, infected foot before stealing a dead man's shoes.

He ate what he could beg, slept where he could find whatever meager shelter, slipped invisibly as air past white people driving wagons down dusty roads or congregating on plank-board walks in war-smashed towns barely deserving of names. They didn't see him. He was a one-armed Negro with bad feet. What was there to see?

Sam watched them from the shelter of his own anonymity and was startled by the nearness of his fury for them. Something got in his throat when they laughed, mouths thrown wide like braying donkeys, slapping one another on the back with percussion you could hear from a block away. Something stung his eyes when they slipped their thumbs under their suspenders and reared back to take a stand on this subject or that. It was as if even in defeat, even in dejection, subjugation, and abject humiliation, it had not yet dawned on them that they were not in fact masters of the known world, the highest expression of God's art.

Ben had been right. The silence in which he had spent the weeks since they parted gave Sam plenty of time to think while he walked. It was, he came to believe, a sour joke that he had once quoted dead white men to explain life to himself. Now, he simply walked through life and left the explaining for others.

He had changed. Maybe it was the miles, maybe it was wearing Josiah's shoes, maybe it was having his arm shot off for no good reason. He couldn't say. All he knew was that he was not the man he had been just a few short months ago. Something had calloused inside him. Some hope, some expectation, some...*thing* had hardened and scabbed. The realization made him sad.

He had survived two years of war without a change, without even a scratch, really. Oh, he had taken a fever and almost died, yes. But it had not marked him, had not *changed* him in any fundamental way. Other men had left pieces of themselves lying on the field to rot under the sun, other men had charged forward only to be hurled back by explosions, other men had been reduced to weeping and drunkenness by the nearness and inevitability of death. He had come through Minié balls swarming thick as bees without ever being touched, raced past explosions without a scrape, beheld carnage without tears.

He had never truly been wounded, whether in body or in spirit, and had never understood why. He was no better than other men, no different from other men. Why had the great Maker spared him?

And an answer suggested itself. It was a bitter thought as he walked unseen down those country roads watching colored people bend their backs to the hoe in this first summer of freedom, but he thought it anyway: maybe God was only just now getting around to him. Maybe—and was God really this cruel?—this was the price he owed, the penance to be paid, for losing Luke, for leaving Tilda.

And maybe, bad as it was, all this was only a precursor to what was yet to come. He had worried that she might not be where he had seen her last, or that she might have herself a new husband or new children like Ben's wife Hannah. But even that was not the worst, was it? No, the worst was that she might be right there where he had known her last, that she would not have a man, not have a child, be perfectly free to be his Tilda again—and choose not to. Because she would hate him.

That day in April when he had started out, he had stood there at the Schuylkill River wondering if this were not the most foolish thing he had ever done in his life. But here in June, there was no longer a need to wonder, because he knew it was.

But he walked anyway.

And three weeks after he and Ben parted at a river in Tennessee, Sam's walking brought him at last to a big yellow house that had haunted his memory for a decade and a half. It stood at the end of a long, sun-dappled lane lined with trees, wending back from the main road. There was a sense of lonely inertia to the place, and he recognized it for what it was almost at once: the slaves were gone, taking their industry with them.

Sam forgot himself for a moment. His feet began to move without command and they wandered about the property, carrying him along like a passenger on a train. He remembered this place so well.

Over there was the coach house where he had lain in the back of a wagon and heard a white woman declare that henceforth, his name was Perseus. Down there were the quarters where the slaves had lived, where he had sat eating cornbread and greens and had his first glimpse of a woman who walked like beauty. There was the tree, a regal oak, where he had stood with his back exposed and the whip coming down. And there were the fields where he had last seen Tilda, who would not look up as the wagon took him away, not soothe him with so much as a glance. Sam staggered under the weight of all that he recalled.

"Stop right there, you scalawag!"

The command drew him around slowly. The old woman stood partially concealed in a copse of magnolia trees that grew around one of the out-buildings. Her face was pinched shut, her hair was a tangle of silver strings falling to her shoulders, and her eyes were made of fire. Sam lifted his one hand before being asked. It was a moment before he recognized her.

"Miss Prentiss?"

She gestured with the rifle. "Are you one of them?"

"One of which, ma'am?"

"You know which!" Her voice was brittle as dried corn husks.

"Ma'am?"

Impatiently. "The army! Abe Lincoln's nigger army!"

For a moment, he thought he might be mistaken. He had never heard Louisa Prentiss use that word in all the years she had owned him. People who did use it, she always said, were coarse and unrefined. So perhaps this was not her.

But no. A decade and a half had taken their toll, had shrunken her down and whitened her hair, but he was not mistaken. She was definitely his old mistress. But what did she mean by a "nigger army?" Had one of the colored regiments of the Union marched through here? Was one garrisoned nearby? If so, surely it had been here for months, if not years, plenty of time for her to get used to the idea.

He spoke cautiously. "Miss, I was one of your people, a long time ago, before the war. Don't you remember me? It's Perseus."

The gun barrel moved, fractionally. "You're lying! I don't know any nigger named Perseus!"

He was surprised to feel himself smiling broadly to reassure her and was glad Ben was not there to see. "Of course you do," he said. "I was here for fifteen years."

"Perseus?" She stepped out from the shelter of the trees, walking cautiously as if the ground might give way any second. And then she remembered. "You ran away," she said. The words were coiled tight around a bright hard knot of accusation.

"Yes, ma'am," he said. "I took my son"—he stammered, trying to remember which Greek name she had given the boy; finally gave up—"Luke. You sent the slave catchers, but they shot him down when he tried to run. I told the boy not to run, but he got scared and ran anyway. Then they brought me back and you had me whipped." He pointed with the nub of his left arm. "Right against that tree."

"I remember," she said. She came closer. The rifle barrel was down now, menacing only the grass. "I never believed in whipping my people. You were the first one. I hated that."

"Yes, ma'am," he said, lowering his hand. "I hated it, too."

"Then why did you run off?"

"I wanted to be free."

"'Free.'" She spoke it like something dirty, like something you pick up with thumb and forefingers and hold at arm's length.

"Yes, ma'am, free." He said the word in order to reclaim it. "Now that the war is over, I've come back in search of Danae. Do you remember her?"

"Of course I do," she snapped. "You called her Tilda."

"Yes, ma'am, I did."

"It hurt her when you ran off. I expect you know that."

"Yes, ma'am."

"It hurt me some, too, to say the plain truth. I never understood how you could be so ungrateful to me. I treated you all well. There were no beatings on my place, I did not allow the overseer to work you to death. I even taught you to read. I was a good mistress, was I not?"

"Yes, ma'am, you were."

"Then how could you do that to me?"

And what could he do but shrug and repeat it? "I wanted to be *free*, Miss Prentiss."

She made a scornful sound. "Well, you are free, all right. All of you are free. But if you are not careful, you will get yourself killed, I expect. It's only God's own mercy that you got here safely. But you can't stay, Perseus. You have to turn around and go back where you came from."

He shook his head. "I cannot do that, Miss. I need to find Tilda."

"She is not here anymore, Perseus. I had to sell her right before the war began. I sold a lot of them, in fact. I had some…reversals. And then, when the Union came near, the others ran off." The admissions made her voice small.

"I have to *find* her!" The force of his own words surprised him. It surprised her, too. Her eyes rounded and she took in a short, sharp breath. "I love her," he said. The confession made him feel helpless.

Louisa Prentiss laughed at him. It was an airy, musical sound. "Love," she said. "That there is a mighty big word, Perseus."

He could feel the anger trying to squirm its way into his voice. He wrestled it down as best he could. "I know what love is, Miss Prentiss. I love Tilda. I always have."

"Go back where you came from, Perseus. Find another woman there. I am certain there are lots of pretty colored girls who would be happy to be courted by a buck like you, even with one wing. It's dangerous in these parts. You are going to get yourself killed insisting on one woman in particular."

"I must take that risk," said Sam. "That one woman in particular is the only woman I want. Can you please tell me where you sold her to?"

Exasperation snagged on her lips. "I do not recall you being this stubborn," she said. Then she sighed. "It was a man named McFarland. James McFarland. He had a big place in Kendricks. But the way I hear it, he abandoned it two months ago and took his last slaves with him."

"Do you know where they went?"

"No one does," she said.

"*Someone* does," he assured her, turning to leave.

"You cannot just walk yourself down there, Perseus. Have you not you heard a word I've said? It's *dangerous* right now."

He did not hear her, in fact. He heard only his own racing thoughts. Kendricks wasn't even fifty miles away. He could be there in two days. He might see Tilda in *two days*. "Thank you," he said, and to his surprise, his voice shook. "Thank you." He stepped away from her. And stopped.

There were six of them coming down Miss Prentiss's lane single file on horseback, lean white men in tattered cavalry gear, their faces overgrown with beards, their iron eyes fixed on him. The one in the lead brought his horse to a stop just a few feet away and climbed down. The animal nickered softly as the man looped the reins around a magnolia branch. He tipped a cap back from his brow as he stepped forward. "Louisa, I see you got one of them."

"One of what?" said Sam. He felt himself smiling again. Nobody even looked his way. The other men were dismounting.

"No, Zachariah," said Miss Prentiss, in an odd, fluty voice, "he is not one of them. He's one of my people from a long time ago. He come back to see me, is all."

"Is that so? Well, you can't be too careful, Louisa. Some of 'em can be pure deceitful." His gaze came around to Sam. "What about it, boy? What you know about that army of niggers?"

He wanted to draw himself up then, wanted to reach for some long and daunting word, pronounced in icy correctness, that would make this white man shrink from him in confusion, make him realize that Sam Freeman was a free Negro man, dignified and unafraid. To his horror, Sam felt the opposite happening, felt his smile stretching itself across his face, unfurling itself like a flag of impotence and fear. "Suh, I don't know nothin' 'bout no army of niggers."

How easily the old language had come back to him. Thanks to Louisa Prentiss, Sam Freeman was an educated man, a reader of books, a student of history and literature who prided himself upon his command of words, on the way he could use them to lash white men with the whip of their own ignorance. Yet how easily he had slipped into the broken grammar of the merest field hand. How easily he had said "niggers." It had happened without even conscious thought, and in that moment, Sam hated himself. He knew he'd had no choice, knew he had done the only smart thing, but that simply made it worse.

Not that it mattered. The one Miss Prentiss called Zachariah stepped directly in front of Sam. He had depthless gray eyes. His breath was warm and smelled of stew meat. "Is that so?" he said. "Well, boy, I'm afraid I don't believe you."

Sam lowered his eyes. This, too, felt appallingly natural. "It's the truth, suh," he heard himself say.

A rushing river thundered in his temples. The men had closed around him, a wall of beards and cold stares, and he could no longer see Miss Prentiss. Her voice came from somewhere far away.

"Leave him alone!" she commanded. "I told you, he just came back to see me, that's all."

"To rob you and cut your throat, more likely," said one of the men.

"No suh," said Sam, shaking his head emphatically. "No, *suh*."

"Zach, what are we wastin' time for with this one-armed nigger? You know how to make him talk. Tie him to that tree yonder and give him a few licks. That'll loosen his tongue."

"But I ain't *done* nothin'!" cried Sam. Indignation spiked in his voice and he knew instantly it was a mistake.

"Yeah, boys, I think you're right," said Zachariah, regarding him closely. "This one needs to be taken down a peg." He grabbed Sam by the stump of his missing arm. Sam wrenched away. Then three of them had hold of him, pulling in opposite directions as if to rip him like paper. He struggled to pull himself free. One of them hit him, a fist to the jaw that swung his head hard to the left.

"That's showin' him!" someone yelled. "Hit him again."

Far away, Miss Prentiss cried out. And then he lost track, because all at once, the blows were coming too fast and hard. They hit him in the stomach. They smashed him in the eye. He felt his shirt torn away. Blood filled his mouth.

Someone kicked him in the knee. It buckled with a popping sound and he went to the ground. He tried to stand, but a foot in the chest pushed him into the earth. Then all their feet came down hard, stomping him like a snake. They kicked his head. They kicked his face. Pieces of tooth lodged in his throat, choking him. They kicked his stomach and agony corkscrewed through him. They stomped his ribs like a board and he felt the bone give under their heavy boots. They kicked his back. They kicked his legs. Someone yanked out a great fistful of his hair. They stomped his groin. He curled himself tight around his own suffering. Hurt fell down on him like rain. Voices flew up from all around.

"Ain't so sassy now, nigger, are you?"

"You gon' tell us where that nigger army is, nigger?"

"Don't kill him yet!"

"No, let's string him up like the others!"

Someone grabbed him by the stump of his arm, tried to draw him upright, but it was as if his legs were gone like his arm. He couldn't stand. "Get up, nigger!" someone cried.

And Sam, who had called himself Freeman, knew with a sudden chilling certainty that he would die here, just two days from his goal, a fitting fate for a foolish man on a foolish quest that had been doomed from that day he stood above the Schuylkill River and bid Philadelphia farewell. As if in answer to that realization, someone pushed a knife into him just then, the blade going into the lower right side of his back, easy as a baby's sigh. Standing half-erect, all their hands upon him, he arched himself against the pain and knew that he was finished. He gave himself over to death. Welcomed it.

And then a blast of rifle fire filled the world.

It was a moment before he realized he was no longer being hit, that he was lying on his back in the dirt. The men had melted off him like snow from the grass. From somewhere above, a man's voice said, "Now, why don't you put that down before somebody gets hurt?"

Sam managed to pry his eyes open. Through sweat, tears and blood, he saw Louisa Prentiss open the breech and shove a second shell into place.

"Louisa," Zachariah was saying in the tone of voice you'd use to reason with a stubborn child, "you don't want to shoot us over some nigger. Now put the gun down!"

"No," she said, and there was leather in her voice. "You've done enough. I told you already: he doesn't know anything about it. I will not stand here and watch you beat this boy to death. Now I'll thank you to get off my property, Zachariah Monroe, or the next one goes through you."

He was incredulous. "You'd shoot me?" he demanded in a breathless voice. "You'd shoot a white man over some nigger?"

She appeared to consider this for a moment. Then she said, "I don't want to do it, Zachariah. It would pain me to no end. But look what you've become, all of you. Not soldiers. Not defenders. Just a mob of cowards, about to beat this boy to death for no good reason."

"I never thought I'd see the day," one of the white men said. His voice was a scandalized whisper.

"Neither did I," she said. She motioned with the rifle. "Now *get*."

There was a moment. Then one of the other men reached into the dirt for his hat. He smacked it twice against his thigh. "Ah, hell," he said, slapping it back on his head, "let's go, boys. She loves niggers so much, let's leave her to it." He mounted his horse.

Zachariah didn't move. He stared at the little woman holding the gun. His lip curled and Sam wanted to yell out for her to stand back from him before he slapped the rifle aside. But Sam could not produce a sound.

It didn't matter. Zachariah didn't try to take the gun. He stared long and hard at Louisa Prentiss, as if to make his contempt plain. Then, with exaggerated leisure, he went to his horse and mounted it. "Come on, boys," he said, "let's go. It smells like nigger around here."

The barrel of the rifle tracked them all the way down the lane. Only when she was sure they were gone did Miss Prentiss allow the weapon to fall. Her hands trembled as thought caught in a January breeze. She took a deep breath and for an instant, Sam thought she had forgotten him. Then she turned. "They will return," she said. "You must go."

"I don't know if I can walk," he said. His voice was like gravel.

"Then you can take one of the horses in the stable. Ride out of here as fast as you can."

"Miss Prentiss, I do not even know if I can stand." He had his hand to the wound in his back. It was oily with blood.

"You haven't any choice," she said. "You *must* ride."

He winced at the thought. If the beating and stabbing didn't kill him, bouncing his wounded body on a horse surely would. But she was right, wasn't she? No choice at all.

"Give me your hand, Perseus." Her hand was stretched out before him. He hesitated *(had they ever so much as touched before?)* then reached for it. Their hands clasped, their grip slippery with his blood. She braced him. It was difficult—he had just the one arm and now, for all intents and purposes, just one leg—but after a moment, he struggled upright. The world reeled around him and he gripped the trunk of a magnolia tree to make sure he didn't fall. His back was burning. Blood drenched the seat of his pants. He could not straighten himself and stood slightly bent at the waist.

"Come, we must hurry."

He tried. The knee that had been kicked would not bear any weight, his infected foot was still filled with pain, so his gait was an ungainly cross between a hop and a skip. She walked briskly ahead of him toward the stables behind the house. He followed as best he could, his entire body a nest of cuts and bruises and pain. He considered again how he had managed to get through a year of the war without a scratch. The thought was good for a small, humorless laugh.

In his awkward gait, Sam reached the barn minutes after Miss Prentiss did. She was saddling a big roan when he got there. She glanced at him, then went back to work, buckling the straps. "This is Bucephalus," she said. "He is the fastest I have. He will get you out of here."

Sam grimaced as he walked toward the horse. The animal looked worn and thin. "You did love your Greek," he said.

Her smile was tight as she finished the straps. "Greece was where civilization began," she said. "Of course, if we are not careful, Mississippi is where it will end." She looked at him, looked quickly away.

"Miss Prentiss," he said.

"Yes, Perseus?"

"Why are you doing this?"

She sighed, checked the saddle, then turned to face him. "They are frightened, Perseus. We all are. Some fool Yankee woman in town smuggled in fifty rifles to arm the colored men. They mean to finish off what the Union didn't, get revenge on white people for what happened in the time of slavery. Some of our men have been patrolling the roads, looking for them. It's gone hard for the ones they catch, Perseus, I don't mind telling you. Harder than it

went for you, I mean. There have been some terrible things done. Just terrible.
I cannot allow that to happen to you—even though you ran off from me."

"Thank you," he said.

"You can thank me by climbing up on this horse and riding out of here."

It was easier said than done. Between the arm he no longer had and
the leg he could no longer use and the pain that spiked in his back every
time he twisted or reached, climbing atop the horse posed a challenge not
readily solved. Finally, Miss Prentiss had to retrieve an old milking stool
from the cow stall at the far end of the building. He stood on that, the little
woman braced him from below, he took hold of the pommel, and somehow,
managed to lever himself up into place.

The exertion spilled fresh blood out of him.

"Perseus, you are hurt very badly. You need a doctor, but you dare not
go into town."

He was leaning into the horse's neck, waiting for the barn to stand still.
Oh, he hurt. He hurt like he had been rolled in broken glass and dipped
in fire.

"I know," he whispered and could barely hear his own voice.

"I regret I can't do more to help you," she said.

"You have done…plenty," he said. It was harder to breathe. "Thank
you."

He pushed himself as near to upright as he could manage, gave her a
shaky smile, and spurred the horse. Bucephalus moved forward at a trot.
Every bounce of the horse's flanks was a fresh punishment. He tried to ignore it. He held the reins in his teeth, pulled on them with his hand to guide
the horse. Soon enough, he was out of Miss Prentiss's lane and back on the
main road. There was no sign of the six men, but Sam knew she was right.
They would return. He should give up this foolish quest. He should run.

Instead, Sam turned the horse west toward the town where Tilda had
been sold, toward Kendricks.

He never got there.

Tilda shook her head.

"You're dying now, Sam. Are you happy?"

Tears stood in her eyes. He was moved.

"You could have escaped," she said. "You could have *lived*. Now look at you. You're cut to pieces, you're all beat up. There is so much blood, Sam. Lord, look at all this blood."

I had to reach you. He tried to say.

I had to find you. He tried to say.

She laughed a little as she wept. "You are such a fool, Sam. You are such a mad fool."

He was vaguely aware of hands on him, dragging him off.

Tilda. He tried to say. Tried to scream.

But it was no use. Tilda shook her head again, shook her head with all the pity in the world. He watched her. She grew smaller, slipping further and further away.

And then he was gone.

"You goin' down there to punish yourself again." From the door of her bed-room, Miss Ginny accused Prudence's back. She held a single candle that painted the walls with shadows that quivered out of the deeper blackness.

Prudence didn't speak. Her hand was on the handle of the back door, which she held slightly ajar. It was still dark out. Crickets serenaded the waning night. She had hoped to be gone without the old woman hearing.

"This ain't doin' no good," said Miss Ginny.

"I know," said Prudence.

"Ain't no point in you going down there to sit in the dark and cry, child."

But Prudence had already closed the door behind her.

Ten days after, it still did not feel real. Her soul still refused to believe.

So she rose every morning, as if that awful night had never happened, dressed herself in teacher's clothes, and left Miss Ginny's by the back door, walking along the alley so as not to be seen walking on the street. There was little real danger she would be attacked—too many Union soldiers patrolling the town—but still, she preferred the back way. She hid herself so the town would be spared the sight of her.

Miss Ginny was right, of course. There was no reason to go out. But she could not stop herself. She rose in the mornings and walked down the block as if there were still classes to teach and papers to grade—as if she didn't know all that was over and done with, as if she didn't know the old warehouse would never be a school again.

But she *knew.*

Walking down to the school—and how hard it was to stop using that word—was just what Miss Ginny had called it: an act of penance for all her sins of folly, arrogance and, yes, Lord, *imprudence.* So every day since it happened, she had walked the alley, come up the side of the building, unlocked the door, and entered upon a scene even *her* soul could not deny.

Shafts of sunlight tunneled the shadows, entering through the holes that bullets had punched in the walls. Glass still crunched under her feet, desks were still overturned, tables were still splintered, and papers still littered the floor from the brief struggle that had ensued when a few of the townspeople managed to force their way inside before the soldiers repulsed them. They had seized her. She still felt their hands upon her, still felt herself being carried away, her feet not touching the ground. And they had seized Bonnie. She still heard her sister scream.

Then Sergeant Russell lifted his rifle and shot and a white man fell dead with a bullet hole in his cheek and they melted off of her and she crawled back into the shelter of the school—*crawled!*—as soldiers swung the big doors closed, and she looked around for Bonnie.

And she looked around for Bonnie.

"Where is Bonnie?" she cried.

And Sergeant Russell lifted his shoulders. "We could not save her."

"You must save her! You must go get her!"

"There are nine of us," Russell told her. "There are hundreds of them."

"You must save her!"

But they weren't listening to her. The dead white man's body was impeding the path of the door. Two of the soldiers rolled it into the street outside, and now the doors were being closed and the lock secured and chairs being used as barricades.

She heard a scream arise from somewhere outside. Then hail—no, *bullets*—coming through the door. Russell cried, "Get down!" She was slow to obey. A soldier tackled her to the floor, covering her body with his own. She could smell tobacco and onions. She could hear him breathing. Another soldier yelled, "I am shot!"

When the hailstorm ceased, Russell ordered them all upstairs. Someone scooped her up and carried her. Two others helped the wounded soldier, whose backside was squirting blood. They cleared a table, lay him atop it on his stomach, and one of them began attending to the wound.

There were windows in the loft overlooking the street. A rock sailed through, and a spray of glass splashed the floor. She heard, quite clearly, Bonnie's scream. It did not sound human.

"Please," she said. She was talking to Russell, who stood at the window watching the scene below, his face ashen and still. "Please save her."

He looked at her. "Mrs. Kent," he said, "I am not certain we will be able to save ourselves."

Through the shattered glass, they watched the crowd mill about aimlessly for a moment. Then, as if they all decided at once, they moved south, toward the colored section. If they could not have the school, they would have the town and every colored face in it.

Prudence searched the mob for Bonnie. She did not see her.

They spent the night in the loft, for the most part too terrified to speak. Prudence could see the glow of distant fires, hear shrieks of pain that seemed like nothing a human throat could ever produce.

She thought of the mob not as a collection of maddened people, but as a single entity, a beast that prowled the colored section of the town, visiting devastation on anyone luckless or foolish enough to confront it. Because the animal did not listen to reason, the animal was insensate to pleadings and lament. The animal existed only to rend and tear.

And she had created it and set it loose.

She should have listened. She knew that now, walking the alley to the building that once had housed her school. But she had not listened, had she?

Up until that awful night now ten days past, her life had repeatedly taught her one lesson: too much time spent listening only allowed voices of timidity and cowardice to turn you from doing what you knew needed to be done, *demanded* to be done. In her experience, listening was too often just an excuse for fearfulness and inaction. If she had listened, after all, she would never have spirited a family of runaways out of Boston in a wagon with a false bottom, never have spoken out for the cause of abolition, never have known Bonnie as her sister.

And yet...

If she had listened, her sister would still be alive.

And then that next morning came, a dazed, hung-over morning wreathed with tendrils of smoke, and she finally ventured out from shelter with the company of soldiers, leaving the wounded man behind, and it felt very much as if they were the last people in all of God's creation. Noah walking forth from the Ark could not have felt more lonely. Silence oppressed the town, clamped down on it as tightly as a lid to a jar so that she started a little when Russell ordered three of his men to go down to Socrates's store, to break in, if need be, and send for help. His voice seemed unnaturally loud, an affront to the stillness.

As the soldiers ran to comply, Prudence asked Russell if she might check on Miss Ginny. He agreed with a curt nod and they moved up the street to the little house with the garden blooming in a riot of color out front.

Prudence knocked on the door. A taut voice answered her from the other side. "Get away from here, you devil. I got a gun and I'll shoot you. Swear 'fore Jesus, I will."

"Miss Ginny, it is Prudence."

"Prudence?" The door opened just a sliver and the old woman peered out hesitantly. When she saw Prudence and the five Union soldiers standing behind her, she breathed a long sigh. "You all right," she said, opening the door wider. "Thank you, Jesus."

And then confusion creased her brow. "But where Bonnie?" she asked.

It was the hardest thing Prudence had ever said. "They took her last night."

The old woman's eyes filled. "She dead then." Her voice wobbled like a child learning to walk. "God help her soul, but she dead."

Prudence tried to reply, but her throat constricted, squeezing tight against the words. Nothing came out.

Miss Ginny grabbed her hand. "You need to get in here."

"No," Prudence managed to say. "I need to go and see for myself what has happened."

"I would prefer it if you stay behind, Mrs. Kent," said Russell. "The sights we are likely to see will not be fit viewing for a lady such as yourself."

"No." Winter snows lay thick upon that single word. "I need to see, sergeant, and I will. The only question is whether I shall be in the protection of Union soldiers when I do."

He sighed. "Pity the man that marries you. You are a handful, you are."

It was a grumble of defeat in which she once would have taken immense pride. But there was no pride left in her that morning. So she just waited for him to turn away and followed when he did. Together, Prudence and the soldiers wandered in silence through the remnants of mass madness.

The streets were littered with the detritus of other people's lives. Prudence's feet scuffed against other people's papers, pieces of other people's furniture, dolls belonging to other people's children, ambrotype images of other people and their families staring up with solemn pride from fractured glass and broken frames. Houses were smashed and burned, the wood left blackened and deeply scored. In one house, flames still burned low, slowly dying for lack of fuel.

They found the bodies hanging in a single tree before the remains of someone's home. There were twelve of them, tongues protruding, rope biting into their skin, necks elongated, heads turned to unnatural angles. No one spoke, or needed to. The only sound was the occasional creaking of a rope or angry buzzing of a fly. Prudence's knees turned to water. Horror rushed up from her gut and she went to her knees to vomit in the dirt. One of the soldiers fell down beside her and did the same.

These people were not simply dead. They were ruined. They were desecrated. Burned. Gouged. Skinned.

There was Paul, head on his chest, face smashed in on itself, covered with a crust of blood.

There was Rufus, peppery old Rufus, deep wounds marring the smooth black crown of his scalp, creamy white bone showing through at the shoulder.

There was a man she didn't know. Or maybe she had once; there was no way to tell. His body was only a husk, a hollow-eyed black thing so badly charred she feared the merest touch would turn it to ash.

Lord, there was poor little Bug, the big eyes distended now in the horror of his own grotesque death.

And there was Bonnie, the only woman, her hands empty and limp, her dress torn, her skin gray, her face bloody, her tongue between her lips, her eyes mercifully closed.

Oh, sister. Oh, Miss Bonnie.

Prudence took Bonnie's hand. It was cold and rough with scars, the fingernails broken. She brought the hand against her forehead, closed her eyes and wept as she had not even wept when the news came that her husband had been killed at Gettysburg.

How many thousands of nights had they lain awake in the same bed, one having snuck into the other's room? How many hundreds of childish confidences had they shared? How many dozens of arguments had they had? How many smiles and pouts and walks in the square and summer evenings on the front stoop watching the sky turn to gold and then to black as fireflies winked at them from the gathering shadows?

How many? Too many for it all to come down to this, a brutal death in a godforsaken Mississippi town.

"Cut them down," said Sergeant Russell. "Someone find a Bible and give them a decent burial."

He put an arm around her shoulder. "Come," he said, and his gruff voice was oddly gentle. "That's enough."

A soldier had clambered into the tree and was using his knife on the rope that held Bonnie. Another braced her from below. The man in the tree sawed through the rope and Bonnie's body folded itself over the shoulder of the soldier below. Prudence allowed herself to be led away.

She did not know what to do. For the first time in her entire life, she had no idea, no plan, no sure and certain sense of what came next. It was as if she no longer knew herself, as if she no longer *was* herself, as if something essential to who she was had died that same awful night.

Maybe just surety and certainty themselves. Maybe it was as simple as that.

The soft nickering of the horse drew her up out of herself, pulled her out of that morning and back into this one, ten days later. She glanced up and saw it by the light of the swiftly paling moon, a horse's muzzle poking out from behind the building. It was a big roan and its one visible eye watched her with an almost human intelligence. When she paused warily, the horse whinnied again, as if urging her closer.

Prudence came forward slowly, until she was standing in front of the animal. She placed the flat of her palm on its forehead. "Where did you come from?" she whispered. And then she saw the dead man.

He was colored, lying with his face in the dirt, clothing torn, face bruised, and blood everywhere—even, now that she looked, smeared on the horse's flanks. She knelt gingerly, seeking his face. She would be surprised if she knew it. Most of the colored men in town—most of the colored *people* in town—were still hiding in the woods and fields where they had fled the night the rampage began. This man was probably from someplace out in the country. She wondered if he was another victim of white people who had lost their minds. She had been told that the rumor of a marauding colored army had now spread far from town.

Prudence touched his face and something that could not happen did. The dead man moved. It was just a flicker of his eye—as if something unwelcome troubled his dreams—and for a moment, she tried to convince herself she hadn't seen it. But there was still warmth in his skin, and his chest—she could see this even in the meager light of the newborn day—rose and fell in a frail rhythm. The dead man was alive.

She flew down the alley and back through Miss Ginny's door, crying out her name. The old woman came out of her bedroom, eyes wide and shiny. "Land sakes, child. What's wrong?"

"There is a man out there. He has been injured! We must help him!"

Moments later, Prudence rushed back down the alley, Miss Ginny as close behind her as age and infirmity would permit. The horse was still where she had left it, as was the man. Prudence was almost surprised. She had half expected to come back and find nothing at all, proof she had hallucinated the whole thing. Miss Ginny came up behind her. She looked closely. "You sure he alive?" she said.

Prudence nodded. "Yes, I am certain of it," she said. "He has been dreadfully injured, though."

"Yes, he has." She pointed. "You see that?"

Prudence came closer and saw what she hadn't before. The stranger was missing an arm. "My God," she said, "what happened to him?"

"Time for that later," said Miss Ginny. "Got to get him off the street. Whoever done this to him might be lookin' to finish it off."

Prudence hadn't thought of that. "How can we do that?" she asked. She could look at him and know there was no way she could lift him, much less carry him back down the alley.

"Got to drag him," Miss Ginny said. "Use the horse. Take him into the warehouse."

Warehouse. Even distracted as she was by dilemma, some part of Prudence caught the word and it pricked her like a needle. *Warehouse, not school.* She shook her head, impatient with her own thoughts. "Dragging him could worsen his injuries," she said.

Miss Ginny pursed her lips. "Can't get too much worse than it already is," she replied.

Prudence found a rope inside the warehouse. She tied one end to the pommel on the horse's saddle, the other to the man's shoes. Then Miss Ginny led the horse, slowly as possible, gently as possible, while Prudence supported the man's head, and they dragged him inside. Prudence had the sense they were hauling not a man, but a thing—a sack of flour or beans. At one point, Prudence paused and knelt to check him, convinced the ordeal meant to save his life had taken it instead.

"He dead?" asked Miss Ginny, and Prudence almost thought she detected a note of hope. But she shook her head no. "Stubborn man," Miss Ginny said. And now the note in the old woman's voice was of admiration.

It took them a few minutes, but finally they had him in the old warehouse. Prudence ran down to Miss Ginny's house for some linens and they made him a pallet on the floor. Then they knelt beside him and got to work.

From a cabinet in the loft, Prudence retrieved medical supplies left over from the days when the old warehouse had served as a military hospital. They cut his clothes away, gently dabbed the blood and grime from his skin, and dressed his wounds. The worst of them was a gash in his lower back.

Miss Ginny made a small fire in the potbellied stove from pieces of paper and splinters of desk, heated a knife blade, and then pressed it to the skin. There was a hissing sizzle that made Prudence wince. But Miss Ginny's hands worked with a deft dexterity that magnetized Prudence's eyes. "You have doctored wounded men before," she said as the older woman lifted the blade to survey her work.

Miss Ginny glanced at her. "Too many times," she said. "In the war."

She applied the hot metal to bare skin again. The man barely flinched and Prudence found herself wondering, and hating herself for the thought, if all this effort would not prove itself wasted. He had been through so much—you could see the map of his sufferings in the bruises and scars that covered him to the very bottom of his feet. How much could a man take and still live? Or want to?

After a moment Miss Ginny said, "I'm finished. How is he?"

Prudence lay her ear against the stranger's broad back. After a moment she said, "He is still breathing."

"Too stubborn to stop," said Miss Ginny. She beckoned to Prudence. "Come here, gal, and help me up."

Prudence stood, then braced Miss Ginny as the older woman came to her feet, grunting with the effort.

Prudence nodded toward the figure on the pallet. "Do you think he will live?"

"That's betwixt him an' God," Miss Ginny said. "I expect they arguin' over that right now."

"I hope he does live," said Prudence, still looking down. "There has been enough dying here."

"Lord know that's true," said Miss Ginny, one hand massaging an ache in her right flank. "I'm going down to the house, rest a bit. You stayin' here?"

"Yes," said Prudence.

"Expected you would," said Miss Ginny. "Tie the horse up yonder," she added, pointing to a corner of the room. "Get him some water. I get some oats for him later."

"I will," said Prudence.

But she didn't move, not at first. For a long moment after Miss Ginny was gone, she simply stood there watching the half-dead man. Something familiar tugged at her and it took a while before she knew it for what it was. For the ten days since the rampage, she had wandered about without it, and for a woman whose life had so long been marked by moving forward, always forward, toward definable goals, the absence was disconcerting. *Purpose.* She felt it again. It was a small purpose, perhaps, in the grand sweep of things, but it was purpose nevertheless—and she held to it with a fierceness and a firmness.

Purpose.

She would keep this stubborn man alive.

The day sat on the verge of twilight, but you could not tell by the heat. It still shimmered in angry waves off the dirt road, glanced painfully off window glass and the belt buckles of passersby. On a chair in front of the warehouse sat Prudence, her blouse wet and gray, sweat drooling off her brow. She fanned herself miserably with an ornamental fan her father had once brought home from Philadelphia.

Inside the warehouse, she knew, the temperature was even worse and she felt guilty for sitting out front while the half-dead man lay insensate on a scavenged cot inside. But she had spent the last half hour trying to ensure his comfort. She had changed his dressings, then raised him into a sitting position and spooned water and soup broth into him.

It felt like doing chores. It felt like watering a plant. It had been three days now. He had not died, but he had not improved. She had begun to believe he never would. If anything, he was getting worse. His skin was damp and hot to the touch and though it was hard to be certain in this diabolical heat, she believed he had a fever.

Something else to fear. Her life had become full of such things.

The streets were quiet this afternoon but for the occasional colored man or woman straggling past. It was only a few days since colored people had begun returning to the town, and they still walked through as if crossing a high and rickety bridge.

They never looked her way, much less spoke to her. They pretended she didn't exist, she whose grand plans had led them to ruin. And she couldn't blame them for pretending. There were days she wished she didn't exist, days she wished the soldiers had not saved her and she had instead been carried out the door to join her sister in the arms of oblivion. Even better, she wished her father had been like other fathers, able to keep at a distance the inhumanity of what was being done to colored people in Dixie, able to regard it as something terrible happening to someone else somewhere far away and leave it at that, not teach his children that they had an obligation to advocate for those who could not do it for themselves.

Look where that had gotten her. Look what it had done. These colored people hated her and there was nothing she could say in response. They had every right.

She was surprised, then, when she saw a man and a girl approaching from across the street. Prudence's fan paused in its steady, useless motion. She knew the girl—dark skin with lively eyes, hair jutting from her scalp in pigtails. She remembered the way her hand leapt into the air every time Prudence or Bonnie posed the class a question. Adelaide.

Prudence stood. She was so unused to being approached, or even noticed, she didn't quite know what to say. She was thankful the man spoke first. "She wanted to see you," he said, shrugging an apology. "Wouldn't let nobody rest until I brought her over here."

"Wanted to make sure you was all right," the girl said.

Prudence's lower lip snagged on her teeth. She had to pause, concentrate on breathing, to make sure she didn't break and cry. It had been weeks since anyone except Miss Ginny had shown her anything like simple human concern. Not that she deserved it, not that she had a right to expect it.

But still…the note of caring in the girl's voice was welcome to hear.

"I am fine, Adelaide," she said. "They did not hurt me."

"I heard about Miss Bonnie," said Adelaide. The girl paused. "I liked her. She was real nice."

"I know," said Prudence. "I liked her, too." She tried to smile, but didn't quite.

"And poor Bug. You know, he tried real hard to learn to read."

"Yes, Adelaide. I know."

"Are you gon' open the school again?"

The question surprised her. "No," she said, and she realized it was the first time she had said it out loud. "I do not think it would be safe."

"Done tried to tell her that," said the man. There was still an apology in his voice. "I think she just need to hear it from you."

"But *why?*" insisted Adelaide. "I *like* going to school."

"I know you did," said Prudence, "and I enjoyed being your teacher, but we have to be practical in our considerations. The people in this town will no longer allow me to teach you."

"The *white* people you mean." Her features had collected themselves into a scowl.

"Adelaide!" The man—her father, Prudence assumed—was scandalized.

Prudence simply nodded. "Yes," she said, "the white people."

"It ain't fair," said Adelaide.

"There is no such word as 'ain't,'" said Prudence, automatically. "You are right, however. It is not fair at all. Sometimes, Adelaide, that is just the way life works."

The man put a hand to the girl's back. "All right, Adelaide. You done had your chance to see her like you asked. Now it's time for us to get on and leave Miss Prudence be."

The girl held Prudence's eye for a moment, then made a sound of disgust and turned away. The man turned to follow, then turned back. "Miss Prudence, I want you to know somethin'," he said. "It ain't worked out right—I mean, it *didn't* work out right—but it ain't your fault these people act the way they do. And we want you to know we appreciate what you tried to do for us."

"We?"

He lifted a hand to encompass the whole town or at least the colored remnant of it. "All us," he said. "We all thankful for you comin' down here, tryin' to teach our chil'ren an' us."

It was too much. "You should not be thanking me. It is because of me that half your town was burned down."

He shook his head. "Ain't the way I see it, Miss. Ain't the way most folks sees it, I reckon. Wasn't you run through this town killin' folks for no good reason and settin' they houses on fire. That was..."

He paused and Prudence finished the thought. "That was white people," she said.

"Yes, ma'am." He gave her a serious look. She smiled at him. He sighed, then added, "Color ain't nothin' but color, ma'am. People just people, just actin' how they been taught."

"I wish I could believe you," said Prudence.

"You should, ma'am. Save you a peck of heartache, I expect." He touched the brim of his hat and led his daughter away. Prudence sat. Five minutes later, Miss Ginny came down the street carrying two glasses of lemonade, sweat trickling down the sides. Prudence went inside to get another chair and they sat together in companionable silence, watching the shadows lengthen over Main Street. The lemonade was blessedly cool and just tart enough. Prudence had to fight a temptation to drink it all in one long pull.

"Hot," Miss Ginny said.

"Extremely," said Prudence.

"They be makin' contract for the freedmen to harvest the cotton 'fore too long. You want to try somethin' bad, you try pickin' cotton in this heat."

"I cannot imagine how difficult it must be," said Prudence.

Miss Ginny sipped her lemonade, nodded toward the building behind them. "How that man doin'?"

"He is the same as he ever was," said Prudence. "There has been no change."

"You gon' sleep in there again tonight?"

Prudence nodded. "He may need me."

"You doin' the best you can for him, you know."

"I know."

"Ain't your fault, it don't work out. Ain't your fault he hurt."

Prudence only looked at her. She didn't trust herself to reply.

They sat together without speaking. A wagon ambled by. Prudence finished her lemonade.

"Bonnie wouldn't want to see you like this," Miss Ginny said, finally.

"Actually," said Prudence, "Bonnie would likely welcome my newfound introspection and humility, but she would find them a tad belated."

They were silent together a moment. Miss Ginny glanced off. "You be leavin' soon, I expect. Once that man in there get on his feet. Or if he die. You be leavin' after that."

"I had not given it much thought," said Prudence. "I suppose I will."

The old woman swung her eyes around. There was something accusatory in them that took Prudence by surprise. "You be leavin'" she said, "and I won't see you no more. Never no more."

"Miss Ginny..." But Prudence didn't know what words came next. She stammered into an awkward silence.

Miss Ginny sighed. "You know, they's something I should have told you a long time ago. Just couldn't figure out how. Or when. Now I s'pose I ain't got no choice."

Prudence stared, waiting. Flies buzzed at a pile of fresh droppings in the middle of the street. A stray breeze lifted a few wisps of Miss Ginny's thin hair that had escaped being tucked neatly into a bun. After a moment, the older woman said, "I knew your daddy."

"Yes," Prudence said. "I know. From when he came down here to buy the slaves he used to set free."

Miss Ginny shook her head. "No. I mean, I met him the first time he come down here, 'fore he bought anybody."

"I do not understand."

"He come down here to see the land—Cyrus's land. As you know, Cyrus ain't had no chil'ren, so when he died, he left the land to your daddy, same as he done the furniture company. Saw your daddy 'mos like a son, I expect. And after Cyrus died, your daddy come down here with two little girls—the oldest, she weren't no older than four—and his wife. I reckon these be your sisters and your mama."

"I never knew he brought them here."

"Probably your sisters be too young to remember. And I expect it ain't the kind of story your daddy gon' want to tell his baby girl."

"What do you mean?"

Her smile was sad. "You got to let me tell this my own way," she said. "Done argued with myself for weeks 'bout whether I should tell it at all."

Prudence could hear the soft clucking of hens from behind the warehouse. A group of soldiers walked by, arguing loudly. "Go on," she said.

Miss Ginny gave her a direct look. "Your daddy were a good man, mostly. Better than most, in fact. Want you to know that. He come down here thinkin' he might keep the land, run it like Cyrus done—hire somebody to take care the house, keep the slaves in line, like Cyrus done. But he ain't really knowed what it was like to own no slaves, you see? Done lived up in Boston, most his life, and he ain't knowed. And first day he get here, first thing he see is this little gal get whipped 'cause she hungry and done stole a peppermint from the overseer's wife. Weren't nothin' new to us; overseer used to give out these terrible whippings. But it seem like that just offended your daddy. He fired that overseer on the spot, kicked him off the property.

"Then he call a meetin' of all the slaves, say he gon' make us a deal. He say, 'Pick one'a y'all to be overseer instead. Y'all work my land for me, and I pay y'all a share of the crop.'" Miss Ginny chuckled. "You should of seen the looks on them folks' faces when he said that. 'Is he serious? Is this white man funnin' us?' What he was talkin' 'bout, it was 'mos like bein' free. But he were serious. We seen that after a time. So we voted for a ol' fellow name of Bob—had a bad eye, but he was the best worker you ever seen. And he was fair. That's all we ever asked. We ain't never mind workin', just want to work for somebody treat us right."

Prudence smiled. "Well, my father always believed—"

Miss Ginny went on as if Prudence had not spoken. "Anyway, they was a girl at that meetin'," she said. "Pretty thing. Long hair, sassy eyes, smile remind you of the sun comin' up some bright, clear morning. Course, I might be a touch slanted on that. She were my daughter, see. Elizabeth her name. All the mens fancied her, but she ain't give no more than a hi, howdy do to none of 'em."

The spindly little woman paused. She lifted her head and gave Prudence a look so direct that Prudence blinked. "Your father fancied her, too," she said. "And I don't mind tellin' you, she fancied him right back."

Prudence did not breathe. "What are you saying?"

"I'm sayin' they spent time together. I'm sayin' he slept with her."

"No." It was a plea.

Miss Ginny nodded, slowly. "Yes'm," she said. "Your mama and your sisters up to the house and your daddy down in the quarter with Lizzie."

Prudence's whole world lurched violently on those words. "My father was not that sort of man," she said.

Affection embraced pity in the eyes that looked up at her. Miss Ginny smiled. "Honey," she said, "they all that sort of man."

"Why are you telling me this?" Prudence asked.

"Got my reasons," Miss Ginny said. "You'll see. And they's more. After your daddy finished his business and went back to the North and left ol' Bob to run the place, we found out Lizzie pregnant. By the time your daddy come back down to inspect his land, she done had the baby. In fact, the baby about a year old. A little girl. Pretty little thing with real light skin, just beginnin' to toddle. And he fell in love with her, your daddy did. Told

Elizabeth he was takin' her back to Boston with him. He wouldn't have no child of his raised as a slave."

Prudence's voice caught. "Bonnie," she whispered.

They had always been so close, each the earliest companion the other could remember, sharing one another's secrets and hopes, more like sisters than friends. Now she understood. They really were sisters after all.

But Miss Ginny's face creased in confusion. "What?"

"You are saying Bonnie was his daughter. You are saying she was my sister, my real sister."

Miss Ginny pitied her with a smile. "No, that's not it," she said. "He didn't get Bonnie til two, three years later. Took her and her mother up to the North, just like he told you. Bonnie weren't the first slave he freed. His own daughter were the first."

"Well, then, what happened to her?" asked Prudence.

Miss Ginny didn't answer. She regarded Prudence as if waiting for her. Willing her. Prudence did not understand. Then, all at once, she did. Adrenaline drove a spike hard through her chest. "No," she said. Another plea.

"I ain't sure what happened to that child," Miss Ginny admitted. "Maybe he did what he said he would, took her to a convent in Boston for the nuns to raise. Maybe he done that. But if you want to know what I think, if you want to know what I *believe*…"

A pause. A direct look. "I believe he probably took that baby into his home and raised her, never told her who she really was nor what she really was. I believe she grew up to be a woman with more heart sometime than common sense. And I believe right now, she sittin' on a chair next to me, tryin' to convince herself ol' Ginny crazy, and maybe she right about that. All I know is, when I seen you that first time right here on this street, I thought you looked so much like my Lizzie. And then, when I got to know you, good God. She had that same fire inside her, wouldn't let nobody tell her what to do, same as you. That's how she wound up with your daddy. I begged her not to, but you couldn't tell her nothin'."

Prudence had the odd sense that if she stood up, she would just keep going. "My mother," she said, and then she stopped. She could not get enough breath.

She tried again. "My mother died in childbirth."

"Is that what he told you? Well, if she really were your mother, maybe she did. Or maybe she walked out on him when he come home with some other woman's child in his arms for her to raise. Or maybe she died of somethin' else altogether. I can't tell you what happened to her. I can tell you what happened to Lizzie. She shriveled up after he took her daughter away. Like she ain't cared no more 'bout livin'. She wanted to fight him, but how she gon' fight him? He a white man takin' his property. He got every right to do that and she ain't got no right at all, 'cause she his property, too."

A pause. Her eyes lost focus. "Lizzie died," she said. "Weren't even a year after she lost that baby. I think it were heartbreak that done it. Just plain as that."

"I do not believe you," said Prudence.

"Yes, you do," said Miss Ginny. "That's why it hurt so bad and I'm sorry for that, Prudence. I truly am. But I couldn't stand to look at you no more, grieving and tearing yourself to pieces and not knowing the truth. You had this picture of your daddy, like you had this picture of Cyrus, doing the right thing for the right reasons and here I come and throw dirt on the picture. I knows how you must feel. But see, I think all us deserve to know where we come from, if we can. I think that's important."

"My father was a good man! He hated slavery. That is why he came down here once a year and set a slave free."

"Yes, he done that. That started about two, three years after Lizzie died. He come down here to check his property and found out she were dead. And I told him what I told you: him takin' her baby away is what killed her. That really seem to hurt him, and I ain't minded at all. See, I wanted to hurt him. Far as I was concerned, he were the reason my only child was gone. That's when he swore off slavery. That's when he freed ever' slave he owned. Some of us went away, some of us stayed and tried to work that land. But white folks here about, I expect I ain't need to tell you how they is. We soon come to see, weren't no use, they weren't never gon' let us farm in peace. Land been just sittin' there ever since. Good land, too.

"But your daddy, he ain't seem to care. And ever' year after that, he come down here and set somebody else free, took them up to the North if they wanted to go. He started with Bonnie and her mother. They was the first. He tried to take me, but I wouldn't go. I ain't wanted to be in the same town with him. So instead, he give me that little house I got. Must have sat empty for six months 'fore I finally decided to move in to it. I hated him that much."

"I never knew these things," said Prudence, helplessly.

"I know," she said. "Must be 30 people runnin' 'round up North owe they freedom to your daddy—and his guilt. And you know the day he come down ever' year?"

Prudence nodded. "He left every year on June 21." Then she started. "Today," she said.

"Lizzie's birthday," said Miss Ginny. Her eyes shone with tears waiting to be cried. "Oh, my God," said Prudence. She did not trust herself to say more. For a shadow of time, she hated this little woman sitting next to her, this woman who, from the moment they first laid eyes upon one another, had shaken and undermined Prudence's understanding of her very self. It was bad enough she had told Prudence that Cyrus Campbell was a monster who hated and tormented his own. Infinitely worse, she had told Prudence that the father she loved and adored and wanted more than anything in life to make proud had been a slave owner, had fornicated with some poor slave woman, just like all those dealers in human chattel he had taught her to loathe.

None of what the old woman told her contradicted the fundamental truths Prudence had been taught to believe: her father had been saved by a colored freeman who took him in and treated him like a son. Her father had gone South every year to buy the freedom of some poor man, woman or family held in slavery, and he had loathed slavery. All of it was true and yet, all of it was now a lie.

And the biggest lie, she realized, might be herself. She herself might be colored, and this wizened little woman with chestnut skin might be her grandmother.

"Who knows about this?" she asked.

"Some of the old folks," said Miss Ginny. "Not so many of the young ones. Some of the older ones, they wanted to tell you, but I ain't let 'em. Had to think on it, first. Ain't everyday you tell someone she might be colored. Or part colored, which is the same thing."

The sound of her own voice surprised her. "But I am white," whispered Prudence. "For goodness sake, Ginny, look at me and you will see not a trace of African blood. I am white as paper. I have red hair. There is no chance my mother could have been colored."

Miss Ginny shrugged. "Maybe," she said. "I suppose that's what make this such a pickle, child. We'll never know for sure."

The awful truth of that settled over Prudence like a shroud. Miss Ginny saw. "Do it bother you," she said, eyeing Prudence closely, "knowing you might be part colored?"

"Of course it does," said Prudence. "It is a lot to consider."

Miss Ginny reflected on that for a moment, then nodded to herself and stood. "Then I leave you to it," she said. Pause. "Are you sorry I told you?"

She wanted reassurance, Prudence knew. And that was surely odd, because Prudence did, too. "I do not know," said Prudence, and there was a new helplessness in her voice. She was grateful when the little woman didn't speak again, just hobbled back down the street, empty lemonade glass in her hand.

Prudence felt Bonnie's absence with a knife blade's keenness. If only her sister were there, she would know what to say, would know how to push and cajole and even vex Prudence in a way that helped her to understand the mysteries of her own heart.

"Honey," the old woman had said, "they *all* that sort of man."

But not John Matthew Cafferty, she had wanted to insist, wanted to cry. Not her father. Not the man whose teachings had been the very *cornerstone* of her. Not him, too.

They all that sort of man.

But maybe she was right. Maybe they were.

Look at him: He had not acted from lofty principle. He had not acted from noble ideals. No, he had only acted from the guilty conscience of a small man whose misbehavior led to a tragic thing. And for all those years, he had allowed her to believe otherwise, had accepted accolades from the abolitionist societies, preached with fire for the cause of freedom, beamed in the adoration of his friends, his daughters, her.

So long had he lived this lie, she thought, that he probably forgot it was not true. No, he had passed the lie down to his daughters like some loathsome family trait and they, unknowing, had lived it as well. Her confidence, her sense of self and of place, seemed relics from another life. She knew nothing. She was no one.

Prudence had no idea how long she sat there. But when next she became aware of herself and her surroundings, the long shadows were melting together. In a few minutes, the light would be gone. Mechanically, she took the chair and the empty glass inside and lit a lamp.

Pushing absently at the tears that trailed down her cheek, Prudence went to check on the half dead man. She would make sure he was still breathing before she went upstairs to her makeshift bed in the loft and tried to read herself to sleep.

The circle of light fell on him. She leaned over to take a look and her heart kicked painfully. His eyes were open.

Her hand went to her mouth. "Oh my Lord," she said. "You are awake."

He answered her in a rasping whisper. "Who are you?" he asked.

And Prudence could only laugh.

"My name is Mrs. Prudence Cafferty Kent," the white woman said.

"Where...?" His voice had become a mere rumor of itself. He was so weak. And Lord, the pain. His every joint and limb and square inch of skin pulsed with echoes of the same angry throb. Yet apparently, he was alive. The idea rather surprised him.

"Do not try to speak," the woman said.

He had a sense of having lived this episode before. It took him a moment to place it. Then he remembered the day he had awakened in the hospital in Philadelphia to find another white woman, Mary Cuthbert, leaning over him. He had always marked that moment as his restoration to life. Apparently, life still was not finished with him. Sam swallowed dust. "Where am I?" he asked.

"You are in Buford," said the woman. "We found you outside. You were beaten badly. We did as much for you as we could."

"'We?'"

"Ginny. A freedwoman. She is a friend."

"You saved my life," he said.

"We did what anyone would have done."

He doubted this, but did not say. "May I have water?" he rasped.

"Yes, of course," she said.

She disappeared from his sight for a moment and returned with a glass of water. She lifted his head—God, how it hurt—and brought the glass to his lips. The water was warm, but he drank it greedily, then automatically brought his left hand up to wipe his wet cheeks. Instead, the stub of his ruined arm came into view and he remembered. He sank into the cot with a grunt that had nothing to do with physical pain.

"Are you all right, Mr....?"

"Freeman," he said. And saying it, he could not help reflecting how haughtily he had once pronounced that name. How proud it had made him then. Now it was only a name. "Sam Freeman," he said. It was only then that he caught it. She had called him "mister." No white person had ever called him "mister." Not even Mary Cuthbert had ever called him "mister."

He looked at her with new interest. "You are not from here," he said.

"I am from Boston," she said softly. "I came two months ago when the war ended to start a school for the freedmen."

"That was a noble gesture."

"The school is closed now," she said.

"Closed? Why?"

She straightened. "We will talk about that another time," she said. "For now you must rest. I will go and tell Ginny you have awakened. She will be pleased to hear."

The white woman stepped away from him, closing the door on further questions. Sam had the impression she was in a hurry to get away. He lay there in the stifling heat, every movement a torture, questions with no outlet circling in his mind. What day was it? How long had he been here? How badly was he hurt? Who was this woman and why had she seemed in such a hurry to get away? What was this place?

He turned his head—about the only movement that did not cost him pain—and allowed his eyes to rove the vast room by the light from the lamp Mrs. Kent had left behind. In the corner, in some kind of makeshift stall, Bucephalus dozed. The big doors looming above were pocked with holes. They could almost have been bullet holes. The vast room was filled with broken and overturned desks. The floor was a carpet of papers covered with childish scrawls.

And he realized with a start that this was it. This was the school she had spoken of.

My God, what happened here?

He resolved to ask her when she returned. But he was so weak, so tired. After a moment, he dozed.

Sam's screams rang through the old warehouse, wordless shrieks of mingled rage and fear that jolted Prudence out of a light sleep and sent her trotting down the stairs from the loft. She found him, the shadow of him, just visible in the thin white light of the moon, sitting upright on the cot, his breath pushing in and out of him in great, fast gusts, his entire body trembling as if wracked by some arctic chill. She paused a few feet short of him.

"Mr. Freeman?"

He did not look her way, did not answer, seemed to have concentrated his whole will simply on the act of being.

"Mr. Freeman?"

"I apologize for having wakened you," he said finally, still not looking at her. "I did not know you were up there. I had a bad dream."

"You had a nightmare," she said. She sat on the cot next to him.

He nodded. "I had them often when first I left the Army. I have not had one for a very long time."

"What did you dream?"

He looked at her. "I dreamt of the men who attacked me."

"You were attacked? Well, I feared as much from your injuries. What happened to you?"

He didn't speak. She waited. It took a long moment. She waited. "I went back to the place where I was…owned," he said. He paused before the last word as before a hostile door.

"Why would you do that?" she asked.

"I went looking for my wife," he told her. "I have not seen her since I left that place 15 years ago. I was hoping she might be there still."

"But you did not find her?"

"No. I found only my old mistress and a gang of white men who set out to stomp me to death because they thought I was part of some Negro militia."

At those words, Prudence felt some unspeakable cold shiver her blood. "Is that what they called it, Mr. Freeman? A Negro militia? Were those the exact words they used?"

He glanced at her with sudden interest. "Well, no," he said. "They called it a…"

She spoke into the pause. "They called it a nigger army," she said. "They used that odious word, did they not?"

"Yes," he said, "they did. But how did...?"

Prudence did not hear. "Damn them," she hissed, stabbing to her feet. She felt fire in her cheeks and tears in her eyes. "Damn them all to hell."

"Mrs. Kent? Mrs. Kent, what is wrong?"

She mashed at the tears. "I am sorry, Mr. Freeman. I am so very sorry."

"I do not understand."

"I am afraid I am to blame for the attack upon you."

"I still do not understand."

Prudence sighed. "I told you I had opened a school here, did I not? The people hereabouts—the white people, at least—sought to frighten us off. And when the attacks became too much to bear, I allowed some of the freedmen to establish a guard here and very foolishly sought to arm them, though I never did. It was from this that rumors grew that we were raising, as you call it, a Negro militia, and planning an insurrection. Once begun, the rumor took on a life of its own. It spread throughout the countryside, far from town."

"This was your school," he said, "this building."

"Yes," she said. "They destroyed it. They destroyed half the town. Many people were killed, many injured just as yourself. All because of me."

"Do you really believe that?"

"I know it," she said.

"You are wrong," he said. "These people require no excuse for violence. Their own wretched anger and bitterness are all the reason they need. Had it not been your so-called Negro militia that inspired them to attack this place, it would have been something else, trust me. Look at me if you do not believe that. Look at my arm."

"I had assumed you lost it in the war."

Sam shook his head. "I lost it just some weeks ago."

"What do you mean?"

"Someone shot me in Tennessee. A white man mistook me for another Negro man he was hunting."

"You rode here from Tennessee?"

He shook his head again. "No, I *walked* here, from Philadelphia. My former mistress gave me the horse to help me escape the men who tried to kill me."

Prudence's mouth came open. "You walked from *Philadelphia*? Why, that must be a thousand miles. That is the most astonishing thing I have ever heard."

"I told you," he said. "I was looking for my wife. I needed to find her."

"Needed? Past tense?"

Sam didn't answer the question and she was embarrassed to have asked it. After a moment, Prudence sat back down on the cot.

"Such devotion is inspiring," she said. "What is your wife's name?"

"Tilda," he said. "Her name was Tilda. Is Tilda, I suppose, assuming she still lives."

"You have suffered a great deal searching for her. We could see in the marks on your body."

Sam's head came up and he regarded her with eyes that seemed to see all the way through her. "Yes," he said, "I have. But then, many of us are suffering just now, each in his or her own way. I suspect you know this as well as anyone. Suffering is hardly unique these days, is it?"

She felt the sting in her eyes and willed it back. He had spoken more truly than he could ever know. "No," she said, after a moment, "there is nothing unique about suffering."

She allowed him two more days to regain his strength. On the morning of the third, she came to him and told him he must get up, must exercise if he ever hoped to recover. He protested that he was not yet ready. She insisted he was. He pointed out that he knew his own pain better than she. She listened for an impatient moment, then to his surprise grabbed his forearm and pulled. Biting back a shriek of pain, Sam came to his feet.

Alone in the stifling warehouse, they practiced walking. She told him to lean on her, but Sam shook his head and said he would use a walking stick. She was a white woman and this was Mississippi. He knew better than to even stand too close to her, much less to put his arm around her.

Sam thought that was the end of it. But she made an impatient sound and to his horror, circled her left arm around his waist. Sam was alarmed at her sudden closeness, her cheek pressing against his chest. "Mrs. Kent!" he cried. His heart punched heavily and his arm didn't know where to go.

She looked up at him. Her eyes were green and annoyed. "What is it, Mr. Freeman?"

"I cannot do this," he said. "I am a colored man and you are—"

"You are a colored man and I am the white woman who is trying to help you walk again. Or do you propose to spend the remainder of your days lying on the floor in an old warehouse? Shall we train the horse over there to bring you water and empty your chamber pot upon your beck and call?"

Sam pushed an angry gust of breath through his nostrils. "There is no need for you to mock me," he said. She was an exasperating woman.

"Do you think I care that you are angry?" she said. "If so, please be assured that I do not. Your fears are unfounded. We are behind locked doors. No one can see you inside here with your terrible brown hand touching my precious white skin. Now, you will lean on me, Mr. Freeman, and you will *walk*."

He stared down at her, searching her face for something that wasn't steel. He didn't find it. Sighing, muttering in anger, he draped his confused arm upon her shoulder and took a step. A bolt of lightning shot immediately from the small of his back. He squeezed his eyes shut and concentrated on breathing as the flash of fire was seconded by smaller eruptions from the healing contusions that covered his entire body. His knee rebelled at the full weight of him and he could not straighten his leg. Sam had not known it was possible to hurt so badly in so many places and yet still live.

In the darkness of eyes closed, he heard her voice at his ear. "That's the way, Mr. Freeman," she said. "Keep going. Do not give them the satisfaction of leaving you a cripple."

He opened his eyes. "The satisfaction they sought was to make me dead," he said.

"Then you have already frustrated them once," she said. "Consider how gratifying it will be to do so again."

"The most gratifying thing," said Sam, "would be never to see them again." The pain was ebbing. He steeled himself, knowing the lightning would come again with the next step. And then he took that step.

"So you intend to leave Mississippi?"

"Yes," he said, "just as soon as I am fit to travel." Tears were leaking down his cheek. "What of you? Have you not had your fill of Dixie?"

"I have not decided," she said. "Perhaps I will return to Boston. I truly loathe the thought."

"Why is that?"

"I hate to let them run me off," she said. "We do not know each other well, but if we did, you would know that is not in my character."

"I believe I am coming to know something about your character, actually."

The shadow of a smile passed her lips. "Come," she said, "let us take another step."

She braced him and he lifted his foot and brought it down, grinding his teeth as pain cut a jagged path down the length of him. For a minute, he exhaled his agony in winded gusts. Not long ago he had been a man who could and did walk a thousand miles. Now he had become a man who had to measure the steps and suck in his breath even to make it to the end of an old warehouse and back. It was a humbling thing.

"Tell me about Tilda," said Mrs. Kent.

He gazed down into her disconcertingly direct gaze.

"What do you mean?" he asked.

"I mean that it is not every woman a man would walk a thousand miles to find. You must have loved her a very great deal."

"I did," he said.

"I once had a man who loved me a great deal," she said. "My husband Jamie. He died in the war."

"I am sorry."

"I would like to think he would have loved me well enough to walk from Philadelphia to Buford as you did, Mr. Freeman, but I honestly do not know."

"Please call me Sam," he said.

"I will, Sam, if you will call me Prudence."

"Well, Prudence, I am certain your husband would have walked those miles. When you love someone, distance is immaterial."

She gave him a dubious look. "That is an easy thing to say, Sam. It is much more difficult to imagine yourself actually doing it. Especially after 15 years. So much can change in so many years. Many men—I daresay, most men—would not have undertaken what you did."

"I had no choice," he said.

"I see," she said. "And now?"

"Miss Prentiss—that is the woman who once owned us—said she sold Tilda to a man who has since left the state, taking her with him. There is no way of knowing where she has gone. At any rate, I am in no shape to continue searching for her. My decision has been made for me."

"So it would seem," said Prudence. "It is a circumstance I have regretfully come to know all too well, having decisions made for me. How will you feel, returning to Philadelphia?"

He gave it a moment, but no answer came. "I do not know," he confessed.

She nodded thoughtfully, then said, too brightly, "Let us try another step, shall we?" From its makeshift stall in a corner of the warehouse, the big roan whickered as if in encouragement. Sam took another hesitant step. His wounds screamed and he felt blood creeping on insects' feet from the dressing on his back.

She allowed him to rest, saying nothing. He was grateful for the silence. It gave him space to contemplate the momentous thing he had just heard himself speak. Something about it made him feel guilty, and something in him rebelled against that. Didn't he have the right to give up? Wasn't the final verdict on this foolish errand heard in the painful scrape of his feet on the floorboards? Wasn't it felt in the pain grinding through his body? What more was there to say? What more could he ask himself to do or to suffer through? Was not this enough?

"All right," said Prudence, "let us turn now and go back." Awkwardly, he made the turn. She had provided him an old army cot, salvaged from what place he could not guess. It came toward him now at a gradual pace.

When he finally lowered himself, Prudence bracing him to provide counterbalance, Sam was breathing heavily. Pain shimmered through the arm that wasn't there. He trembled as he lay back. Prudence stood over him with arms akimbo. "You will rest," she announced. "We will walk again this afternoon."

Then she said, "What is the matter?" and he knew his disbelief must have shown on his face.

Sam laughed despite himself. "I was just thinking that you remind me of the sergeant who used to drill us in the Army. I believe, however, that you are a little tougher than he was."

Her cheeks painted themselves a rosy pink. "I am only trying to help you get back on your feet, Sam."

"I know you are," he told her. "And I *am* grateful for it."

That was surprising enough that it made her smile. He was such a grim

and taciturn man. And she had the sense he had been this way long before
he was injured. Perhaps not when he was with this Tilda who seemed to
mean so much to him—perhaps then, he had been a different man. But
yes, she thought, certainly for a very long time, he had been this man who
faced life as though walking against the wind.

She was about to answer when there came a heavy fist against the side
door. Questions congealed in her eyes as she went to answer.

She pulled the door open and was shocked at the sight of him. Not
simply his presence at her door after all that had happened, though that was
shocking enough, but also his appearance. All the time she had known him,
he had carried himself as a feckless ne'er-do-well, overly impressed with his
own charm. But he seemed to have aged overnight. His gaze was somber,
his mouth set in a grim line. His hair, usually combed into place with a
fastidious, almost womanish care, straggled from beneath his hat at odd
angles. He did not bother to remove the hat or even touch his fingers to it.

"What do you want, Mr. Wheaton?"

"I have a business proposition to share with you, Mrs. Kent. I also bring
news. I promise, both will be of the utmost interest to you."

"I cannot imagine that anything you would have to say would be of any
interest to me, Mr. Wheaton. Good day."

"I am afraid I do not have the patience today for your usual obstinacy,
Mrs. Kent. Shoot me with your little pea shooter if you like. I am coming in."

He brushed past her without another word, then stopped short at the
sight of the wounded Negro lying flat on the old army cot. "Who is this?"
he demanded.

Prudence's anger sparked like struck flint. "I will tell you who he is, Mr.
Wheaton. This is Mr. Freeman. Mr. Sam Freeman."

He regarded her with a sour smirk. "'Mister,'" he said. "Even at the price
you've paid for the lesson, you still do not learn."

She ignored him. "Mr. Freeman is another victim of the mob law you
and your friends instituted when you burned down half this town."

Wheaton had been gazing down at Sam, but now his eyes came up
sharply. "I was there," he said. "I'll not deny that. But I burned nothin'. I hurt
no one. I tried to stop the ones who did the hurtin' and burnin', if you want
to know the truth. Socrates didn't even want to send your message to bring
the militia here. I was the one told him to do it. *Me.* But things had gone
too far by that point. I am sure we both know who is responsible for that."

She ignored the rebuke. Or pretended to, at least. "Mr. Freeman was set upon by a gang of ruffians at a farm outside of town. They beat him very nearly to death. He barely managed to make it here on his last legs. We found him collapsed in the dirt outside."

"And you have been nursin' him back to health like the angel of mercy you are."

"Mr. Wheaton, I beg you: This poor man has been through enough. Please do not compound his sufferings by revealing his whereabouts to the ruffians who did this."

"Mrs. Kent, once again you misjudge me. You delude yourself if you think I care enough about this boy one way or another to spare him another thought once our business here is concluded. Though I will give him a piece of friendly advice." He looked at Sam. "Heal up fast as you can and get out of town, boy. Things are changin' hereabouts, and it would not be in your best interest to spend more time here than necessary."

"What are you talking about?" asked Prudence.

"Well, as it happens, Mrs. Kent, that has to do with the business proposal I mentioned to you a moment ago. Is there somewhere we may speak in private?"

"We can speak here," said Prudence.

Wheaton glanced at Sam, then shrugged. "If you insist," he said. "You see, the late unpleasantness has convinced my father and some of the other men that for the future happiness of the town, measures must be taken to expel the Negroes and troublemakers among us."

"Expel?"

"Yes. But only from the town proper, you understand. After all, the Negroes are still our primary labor force. The planters will need to make contract with workers soon to harvest their crops, accordin' to the new rules imposed upon us by our Yankee masters. But thank the good Lord, we still have the power to decide some things for ourselves. And one thing we've decided is that all the niggers will be required to make their homes outside of town from now on. Buford is going to be exclusively white."

Disbelief left her mute. There was a moment. Then Sam spoke for the first time since Wheaton had come through the door. "You said, 'Negroes and *troublemakers*,'" he said.

Prudence glanced toward Sam without seeing him. "He means me," she said.

"Indeed I do," Wheaton said. "The ordinance is being drafted now that will give Mayor Alexander powers to expel anyone who is deemed a menace to public safety."

"You cannot do that," said Prudence.

"But we will," said Wheaton. "Lest you think us unfair, though, let me hasten on to share the business proposition that brought me here. You see, my father recognizes that you and your family own certain properties in this town and he proposes to rob no man"—a fractional bow—"or *woman* of what is rightfully her own. So he stands ready to buy this buildin' and the abandoned farmland I understand your family still owns outside of town, at a substantial profit to you."

"I am not interested, Mr. Wheaton. You may leave."

There was bitterness in his laugh. "I knew that would be your first response, Mrs. Kent, but for your own sake, I urge you to reconsider. Do you really want to insist upon your right to stay in a place where you are not wanted? Frankly, many in our town are surprised you are still here, after the unpleasantness. One often hears people speculatin' about it: 'What does she want? What is she tryin' to prove?'"

His eyes softened and there was something like fondness in his smile. "As someone who has ample experience with it, I am well aware of your spirit, the fact that you will not allow anyone to dictate terms to you. I respect that about you, Mrs. Kent. I do. But your point has been made. After what happened here, most young ladies would have hightailed it out of this town on the next train. You did not. You stood your ground.

"But now that your point is made, you must consider the rest of your life. They'll never allow you to teach the Negroes here, Mrs. Kent. Surely you must understand that by now. So the question is: do you really intend to spend years in this stalemate? Is it really in your interest to try and hang on in a place where you are not wanted and you accomplish nothin'? After all you have been through here, after all you have lost, wouldn't it make more sense for you to return to the comforts of your home and consider... pursuing another course? I know what you think of us, but you should not let that prevent you from actin' in your own interest. My father has offered you a dignified way to extricate yourself from this situation. I implore you not to dismiss it out of hand."

Prudence was silent. She said, "You..." And then she stopped, impatiently flicking at the tears that had begun dripping from her eyes. A deep breath. She looked at him. "You make a persuasive argument, Mr. Wheaton. I will give you that."

"I know we haven't…gotten along, Mrs. Kent. I know you do not trust me and I understand that I bear some responsibility for that. But I truly do believe this course of action *is* in your best interest."

"Do you?" she asked. Then she sighed and something in her deflated. "Well maybe you are right after all, Mr. Wheaton. I will have to think about it. And I will have to write my sisters. They are as much heirs to my father's estate as I, which makes them part owners of this property."

"Do you think you will have any difficulty convincin' them?"

She shook her head. "No, if I tell them it is for the best, they will agree."

"And do you believe it is for the best?" asked Wheaton.

"I do not know," she told him. "Perhaps. As I have said, I'll have to think on it."

Wheaton touched his hat. "Excellent," he said. "Take all the time you need. But the thing you must understand—and forgive me if this sounds like a threat, but it is only the truth—is that there is no question of whether or not you will be leavin' town. That has already been decided. The only question is what will happen to your properties once you do."

"I understand," she said.

He nodded. "Very good. I will tell my father to have legal papers drawn up in anticipation of a happy conclusion to this business. Thank you for your time, Mrs. Kent. Good day to you, ma'am."

He nodded to her, moved toward the door, then paused and looked back. "You get better quick, now," he told Sam. And then the door closed behind him.

She stood watching the door a long moment, hating Bo Wheaton for being who and what he was. Hating him all the more for being right.

Sam spoke from behind her. "So," he said.

"So," she said. She did not turn.

"It appears we both will soon be leaving."

"Yes," she said. "Damn him, but he is right. He made no argument I had not already considered, but…"

"You hate to let them run you off," he said, finishing the thought for her.

"No," she hissed, and now she turned to face him. "I hate to let them *win*."

Sam pulled his cot toward the wall, tossed some miscellaneous scraps of broken wood to one side, and limped back to lift the water pail out of the path of the loading doors. Then he pulled the doors open.

Prudence was standing there with a colored boy she had hired to muck out the makeshift stall. She gave Sam an appraising glance. "You would not have been able to handle that door just a few days ago," she told him. "You have made great progress these last two weeks."

"Yes, Sergeant Kent, thanks to you, I have."

Sam Freeman was not ordinarily a playful man, but he had been calling Prudence "Sergeant Kent" for two weeks now, first as she walked him up and down the floors of the old warehouse, then as she stood off to the side encouraging and cajoling as he walked himself. The name was not only a tease, but also a salute of sorts. He knew now that had she not pushed him, he might never have gotten up from that cot.

She had not let him leave the old warehouse yet. The town was still too dangerous, she said, and he was in no position to defend himself. But she had brought him books and he had passed the time in reading. He enjoyed losing himself on the pages of great works, but it did not give him the same pleasure it once had. Once, words had been his shield. Now they were simply words.

They talked sometimes when he was sweating with exertion and sitting heavily on the edge of the cot. He learned that she was from a wealthy family of abolitionists in the North. Her father had once owned slaves here in Buford, she said, but had come to realize what a detestable practice that was. He had dedicated himself wholeheartedly to the antislavery cause and had taught his children likewise.

"What made him change?" Sam had asked.

She had been perched on the edge of a desk slightly above him and she gave him a look he could not read. "He just did," she said. "He just came to understand that it was not a fit practice for a Christian man." She held his eyes. She turned away.

He had never known a woman like Prudence Kent. He had known many abolitionists after he escaped from slavery, had attended their gatherings and even spoken at their meetings. But he'd never known a woman—he'd never known *anyone*—who called him "mister." That stayed with him. He mentioned it to her one day as he hobbled gingerly across the floor, leaning on a walking stick fashioned from the remains of a broken desk.

"You know, Sergeant Kent," he said, "I must say that you startled me the first time we met."

"Oh?" She was standing with arms folded, marking his progress. "And how did I do that?"

"You called me 'Mr. Freeman.' No one has ever called me that. I never thanked you."

She made an impatient sound. "You should not thank me for paying you the courtesy any person owes another person to whom she has not been properly introduced."

He grunted with the exertion of a step, then paused. "Yes," he said, "but we both know not everyone believes a Negro is a person to whom one owes such small courtesies. It is a pity more white people do not emulate your example."

She smiled, again with that look he could not read.

"Your sergeant thinks you give her entirely too much credit," she said. "Your recovery is entirely of your own doing. I only facilitated it."

"Yes," said Sam, "well I would beg to—"

Then he saw the boy. It stopped him.

The child gripped the handles of a wheelbarrow full of clean straw. He was tall, perhaps 15 years of age, lithe and sinewy as only a boy-man can be. The sight of him made Sam's heart lunge for the bars of its cage. Because the boy was Luke. For a sliver of time, over before it was begun, he glanced toward Sam with the face of his long dead son.

Then the instant was gone. Sam blinked and the boy was no longer his son, had *never* been his son, but was only himself, a medium-brown boy with the shadow of a moustache overtop full lips glancing with mild interest toward the crippled man standing in the middle of the floor. He nodded politely, then maneuvered the wheelbarrow around Sam toward the corner where the horse was kept. Sam watched him closely as he crossed the room.

"Is something wrong?" Prudence was at his shoulder.

"What do you mean?" Sam asked, eyes still tracking the boy as he set the wheelbarrow down and approached the horse, stroking its neck and murmuring soothing words.

"You look as if you have seen a ghost," she said.

And that was near enough to the truth that he turned to search her eyes for mockery. He found only concern. "The boy reminded me of someone," he said. "That is all."

"I see," she said. "And who might that someone be?" she asked.

"Just someone I once knew," said Sam. "It does not matter. He has been dead a very long time."

Just then, the boy stripped off his shirt and laid it aside. His back was a mountain range of black scar tissue, shining dully. It made Prudence gasp. "Devil take those who could inflict such marks on a child," she said, and her voice had reduced itself to a thin hiss of outrage. "Devil take them all."

"We are agreed in that much," said Sam, turning away. He could not bear to watch the boy work, the scars on his skin riding up and down as he used a pitchfork to empty the wheelbarrow. Without a word, Sam hobbled through the big doors and went instead to stand outside and watch Main Street pass by.

Somewhat to his surprise, Prudence followed. "I pray you do not mind my company," she said, when he looked down at her. "The boy's injuries affect me."

"I do not mind," said Sam.

A welcome breeze stirred a stray wisp of bright hair across her face. Absently, she brought a hand up to smooth it back into place. Her eyes were somewhere else. "Devil take them all," she whispered in that same scorched voice.

And then, just as if her words had somehow conjured it, Bo Wheaton, mounted on a black mare, came up the street from the direction of the river. He stopped directly in front of them, not bothering to dismount. He touched his hat to Prudence, spared Sam not so much as a glance.

"Mrs. Kent," he said.

"Mr. Wheaton," she said.

"My pa sent me to ask if you have come to a decision on sellin' your properties."

She gathered herself. "You may inform your father that I am willing to sell," she said. "I am simply awaiting confirmation from my sisters so that we may commence our negotiations."

"Splendid," said Wheaton. "That is most welcome news."

"I wish I could be as pleased as you," she said.

"I understand that you cannot," he told her. "But I am confident you will eventually see this as the best possible outcome. We are of different stock, you Yankees and we Southerners. You do not understand us and we surely do not understand you."

A pause. Wheaton's expression closed, his face turning reflective, and for a moment, Sam thought he might have more to say. But Wheaton only touched his hat again, wheeled the horse around without another word, and headed back at a trot in the direction of the river.

"Devil take *him*, especially!" hissed Prudence, and the fury in her eyes was awful to behold.

Sam regarded her for a moment. Then he said, "I have lost much to men like that over the years. White men like that."

Prudence met his gaze with eyes he could not read. "Yes," she said, "I feel the same. I, too, have lost much to white men like that."

He had a moment to wonder again if she was mocking him. A moment to decide that she was not. He allowed a silence to intervene, as he pondered what he was about to tell her—and why. He could find no reason to do so. Still, he said, "You asked a moment ago if I had seen a ghost. I suppose I had, after a fashion. When I first saw him, that boy in there reminded me of my son."

Now she looked at him. "You have a son?"

Sam swallowed. "I *had* a son," he said.

"He died?"

"Yes, he died, though I suppose it is more accurate to say he was killed— shot. He was about the age of that boy in there when it happened."

"Oh, Sam, I am so sorry." Her hand went to her mouth. "How awful. How long ago was this?"

"Fifteen years ago," he said, and paused. She waited, looking up at him. He looked away.

"It was my fault," he continued.

"How was it your fault?"

"I insisted on running away to freedom. He wanted to go with me and I allowed it, even over his mother's protests. You see, we did not have to run. As mistresses go, Louisa Prentiss was far better than most. She did not allow her people to be beaten, she did not work them inhumanely, she did not break up families. She even allowed us to read. But for some reason, my soul still rebelled against the idea that I was owned by this other person, that I was required to accept the notion heaven had placed her in a station superior to my own. So I took my son and ran. The slave catchers caught us and he was killed."

Sam paused a moment, reminded himself to breathe. "I should never have done it," he said when he could speak again. "It was not so bad there. I should have been content and told him to be content as a slave."

Her next words shocked him. "How dare you," she said. "How dare you say a thing like that? Look again at that child," she demanded, wheeling to point into the warehouse where the boy, oblivious, had begun mucking out the makeshift stall. "You saw those marks on his back as well as I did. But to be a slave does not simply leave marks on the skin. It leaves a mark here," she said, tapping her chest. "I should think I, a white woman, would not have to explain that to you. I should think you would know it better than I."

He stared down into her angry eyes. He felt his shoulders drop. He breathed. "You are right, of course. It is just as you say, and I should not need you to remind me of it. I don't really. It is just…"

He stopped. He breathed again. When he spoke, his voice was hoarse, grainy like unsanded wood. "I am empty. Do you understand that? Do you know how that feels? I am tired and I am *empty*."

Sam swallowed hard. He looked up into a sky he saw only dimly, through the blur of tears. "You made a great fuss over the fact that I was a man who would walk a thousand miles to find his woman. But what I never told you, Prudence, is that that man is gone. He is a stranger to me now. He is something I vaguely remember, but can no longer understand. I told you I was not going to continue my quest because I believe it is hopeless and physically, I am unable. But that is only part of the reason. The rest of it, which I have hesitated to admit, even to myself, is that I have nothing left inside me, no dream of finding her, no hope for any sort of future. It is as if my soul has been hollowed out. Can you understand how that feels?"

He fell silent all at once, brought his eyes down to hers. They regarded one another for a moment. When she spoke, it was in a rasping whisper he barely heard. "More than you know," she said.

"What do you…?"

But she wasn't listening anymore.

"Calvin," she called out to the boy, "I shall be at Miss Ginny's house. Come get me when you are finished and I shall inspect your work." She walked away without waiting for an answer. Her steps were lively.

Sam had just managed, clumsily, to get the saddle up on the horse's back when there came a knocking at the side door. He opened it and Prudence was there.

"Good morning," she said.

"Good morning," he told her.

"May I come in?"

In reply, he stepped aside. She entered, her right hand nervously rubbing her left upper arm. "I wanted to apologize," she blurted, turning immediately to face him.

"There is no need," he told her.

"Yes, there is," she insisted. "I had no right to speak to you as I did yesterday, to lecture you that way. I do not know what had gotten into me."

"If anyone should apologize, it is I," he said. "I acted as if I were the only one who understood loss. That was foolish of me. You have lost your entire school."

She gave him an odd look at that. He went back over to Bucephalus to confront the challenge of cinching a saddle with one hand. The cot stood in the center of the warehouse. He had stripped the bedding and left it folded neatly on the edge of the old desk.

"You are leaving us today?" said Prudence.

"I would have come to say farewell," he said, fumbling at the straps.

"Do you think you are equal to hard travel again?"

"My knee tires easily, my foot still aches some, but yes, I am up to it"—a pause—"thanks to you."

"At least you will not have to walk," she said, watching dubiously as he stood there, trying to decide how to cinch the saddle. "Come," she finally said, crossing toward him, "let me help you with that."

"No," said Sam. He spoke more curtly than he'd intended and she pulled up short. He sighed. "No, thank you," he amended. "It's not that I do not appreciate the offer of help. It is just that I won't have any help getting to Philadelphia. I shall need to be able to do this myself."

She nodded. "You are right, of course."

She came and stood above him as he bent down, trying to manage the two straps with one hand. Knowing she was there somehow made the fumbling worse. He pulled uselessly on the strap in his hand, then gave up with a sigh. "Keep trying, Sam. You will find a way."

He looked up at her. "I have been a fool," he said.

"What do you mean?"

"I thought of it after we spoke yesterday. This quest has always been useless, and it is not just because I do not know where Tilda is and do not know if she still lives and do not know if she still wants me. Even if I knew she was alive and I knew precisely where she was, it still would not matter. Even if she still wanted me, that, too, would not matter."

Her brow furrowed. "I do not understand."

"It is simple, really. I have come to realize it was not just her I was trying to get back. No, I was trying to get back what was. I was trying to get back the life we once had. But time does not work that way." He sighed. "In Virginia," he said, "I saw an old colored woman. She was looking for a baby that was taken from her 20 years ago. She asked everyone if they had seen her daughter. The poor wretch could not bring herself to understand that the baby was no longer a baby, that if she yet lived, she was a grown woman by now, likely with children of her own. You cannot go back to what was."

Prudence smiled her sorrow. "But perhaps you will find something new."

"You don't know," he said. He turned from her, not wanting to see the pity in her eyes.

"I do," she said. "Finding something new is the best hope you have. It is the best hope either of us has."

His eyes came back around. "What do you mean?"

"Leave the horse a moment," she said. "Come with me. There is something I want you to see."

And so it was, moments later, he found himself walking down a ruined street on the far eastern end of the town. She walked several paces ahead, her back arched, her shoulders square as a box. He limped behind, leaning on a walking stick like a man 30 years older.

Every house on the block was a blackened cavern gutted by fire, the yards strewn with the burned remains of family life—pots and pictures and shoes and lamps. The stuff of people's daily existence, gone over now to debris, to pieces and relics owned only by the sun and the breeze.

Prudence stopped. She spoke to him without turning around. "I had many students who lived on this block," she said. "Of course, the rioters said they only sought to disarm the Negro militia they thought I had armed with rifles."

"Nigger army," he corrected. "That's what they called it."

She turned. Her face held a sad, beautiful dignity. "Yes," she said, "that is what they called it, but I wish you would not use that word."

It made him feel small in his bitterness. "I suppose you are right," he said.

She turned again without a word and again he stared at her arched back and squared shoulders. They walked for a moment, then Prudence stopped. "This is the tree," she said, standing before a twisted old oak guarding the end of the block. Sam went to her, stood a few feet behind.

"They hanged twelve people in this tree," she said, her back still to him, her arms folded tight. "They did terrible things to them, things I cannot speak of, but I still see them in my mind whenever I close my eyes. They hanged Rufus, who was one of the men helping us guard the school. They hanged Bug—that's what everyone called him, a little boy, so eager to learn, as they all were. They hanged Jesse, who worked for us at the school. And they hanged Bonnie."

All at once she gasped, then lowered her head, and he knew she was weeping. Her body shook with the force of it.

"Who was Bonnie?" he asked softly.

It took a moment. "Bonnie was…a colored woman. As I told you, my father became an abolitionist. But he did not just demand that the slaves be set free. He would actually buy slaves and set them free on his own. He bought Bonnie when she was but a little girl and brought her to Boston.

We were raised together, she and I. She was my very best friend. She was my sister, in all but actual fact."

A sigh. "You asked yesterday if I knew how it felt to be empty, to have your very soul hollowed out."

"'More than you know.' That's what you said."

She nodded. "More than you know," she said. She started to weep again.

Sam's hand went to her shoulder. He didn't tell it to, it just went. He was acutely conscious of the wrongness of what his hand had done, but he couldn't pull it back. "I am sorry," he said. "For you, for me, for all of us."

After a moment, she looked at him. "We should go," she said.

He nodded. He let her get a few steps ahead, then fell in behind her.

She said, "I was not taught to think that way, you know."

"What way?"

"Just now, when I was in distress and you put your hand on my shoulder, just to comfort me as anyone would do. I could tell it made you anxious, your terrible brown hand touching my precious white skin. It was the same the first day I helped you walk." Her laughter was bitter as smoke. "That is not how my father taught us, and sometimes I forget the rest of the world sees things quite differently."

"Especially here," said Sam.

"Especially here," she agreed. "Here, it is as if the war never ended. Yes, the fighting stopped, but only because it had to. But nothing was settled. That is the thing I have found most astonishing in my sojourn here. These people are so haughty and prideful one gets confused sometimes about who actually surrendered to whom. I simply do not understand them."

"And you are white," said Sam.

There was a pause. "And I am white," she finally agreed. Another silence.

"Yes, you are," said Sam, "but you are not like these people."

"Perhaps I am," she said. "Perhaps they are what I would be had I been raised in a place where I was taught to view my skin as proof that I was a higher order of human being. Oh, do not mistake my meaning; there are some in Boston who do feel that way. There are many, I suppose. But there were also those like my father, who came to believe that such beliefs were ignorant and low, and would not tolerate them in his presence."

"Your father sounds like an exceptional man," said Sam.

"He was an imperfect man," she said. "I told you what he once was. But yes, once he understood the error of his ways, he embraced equality with a fierceness. And on that point he was absolutely unbending."

"It must have made for a difficult childhood."

The question seemed to surprise her. She stopped and turned, a tiny vertical consternation line creasing her brow. "What do you mean?"

He paused in his hobbling gait. "All the other children," he said. "They must have thought you some kind of oddity."

She turned back, walking again. "My father taught us to endure."

Sam didn't move. "Is that what you are doing here in Buford? Enduring?"

She stopped again, turned again. "I suppose you could say that. Why?"

"It seems a lonely existence," he said, "just enduring. You have no business among these white people. You are not like them. I am glad you accepted that man's offer, though I know it was difficult for you. But I would hate to think of you staying here among them."

"Do you hate white people, Sam? It is perfectly all right to say so if you do. Sometimes, I hate them myself."

Sam came forward, his bad leg scraping awkwardly on the baked dirt. "I do sometimes," he said. "Sometimes, I hate them with a passion. Then I meet someone like you, who has treated me so kindly, or I remember Mary Cuthbert who nursed me to health in Philadelphia when I became ill in camp and the Army sent me there to die, and I am reminded all over again how foolish that is. It is simply that I get...*frustrated*. I once believed that if I learned to speak as well as they do, better than they do, if I carried myself with scrupulous dignity, they would see the folly of looking at my skin and presuming from that to treat me like dirt. I have since come to understand how naïve I was. But I am naïve no longer. They have beaten and shot and stabbed all the naïveté out of me."

Prudence nodded, slowly. "I understand," she said. "Look around you. I thought that with my family's fortune, and my own stubbornness, my absolute refusal to give in to them, I could change things for the Negroes, at least in this tiny corner of Dixie. What you see before you is the only change I managed to make."

A mangy orange dog loped out of the front door of a burned-out house. It stopped in the middle of the mud street and watched them for a moment. Then it put its head down and went on its way.

"So I feel much as you feel, Sam," she said. "I, too, have had much taken from me. They took my illusions. They took my sister. And what is worse, I have no one to blame but myself."

It was a moment before Sam spoke. "So," he finally said, "we are passengers in the same boat. What can we do now? Where do we go from here?"

Something helpless stole into her eyes just then, something vulnerable and small. "Well," she said, "that is the heart of the matter, is it not? I have been asking myself that same question for a month and I still have no idea."

She looked at him with her defenseless eyes. It was a sight too painful for seeing. He found something over her shoulder to stare at instead. After a beat, she said, too brightly, "Come on, then, let us get you off your feet. You can rest for a while and then return to saddling your horse." She moved to the right side of him and reached for his arm, draping it across her shoulder. He knew she was waiting for him to flinch. He did not. So she braced him as they made their way slowly down the dirt street, as the blackened houses and the gnarled oak slipped further behind.

He knew someone might see this, might see them walking together this way, might think them a couple instead of a crippled Negro man being helped by a thoughtful white woman. Someone might take offense. Someone might raise the alarm.

He tried to care. But something had gone out of him. Whatever it was that allowed him to worry and fear, whatever it was that allowed him to give a damn, had seeped out of him like sweat, leaving him listless and hollow.

He was empty.

So, although he tried to care, he could not. What could they say to him that they hadn't said? What could they do that they hadn't done? What could they take that was not already gone?

With his arm draped across her shoulder, her arm looped around his waist, they walked at his slow and painful pace down the street. At the far end of the block, Main Street crossed like the top bar of a T. On the opposite side of Main stood a cotton field, flowering white. Soon, crews of Negroes would stoop and bend there, twisting the fiber out of the hard bolls under the late-summer sun.

They turned at the corner. The warehouse was down on the left. From behind them, a wagon pulled by two rangy mules slowly overtook them. The driver was a dark-skinned colored man with a heavy beard. He looked at them from under the brim of his hat, nodded with a face that gave away nothing. The wagon clattered off into the distance.

"So now we are discovered," said Prudence. "A white woman helping a crippled colored man. Oh, the horror."

He didn't answer. A rivulet of sweat trickled down the center of his back. It was early yet, but already he could tell it would be another day of infernal heat. They crossed in the wake of the wagon, walked alongside the field, the cotton plants whispering together in the breeze.

They entered the warehouse moments later. It was pungent with the smell of the horse. She braced him as he made his way over to the cot, his bad leg scraping behind him like some remnant of another life. "Are you all right?" she asked.

"I am a little tired, is all."

"That is my fault. I should not have made you walk such a long way."

"No," he said, "I needed to see."

At the bed, he had to turn slowly to position himself. She clung to his stump as he did, counterbalanced his weight with her own as he lowered himself gingerly down to the canvas. There was a moment, her face close above his, her eyes watching his.

And she kissed him.

Almost before their lips touched, he pulled back, sick with horror. He fumbled for words, but his mind was empty. He simply could not believe what she had done.

Nor could she. You could see that. The green eyes were perfect ovals, pools of shock in a face where every muscle seemed to have failed simultaneously, her features hanging slack as a flag on a windless day.

A moment came. A moment went.

Then she came forward and now she was kissing him again, pressing her lips to his with a need that obliterated his mind, that drove him slowly back upon the canvas. He was sick with horror, yet scalded by need. He fumbled again for words, for resistance, for reason. Instead, his one arm came up, encircling her, pulling her closer. He kissed her until she pulled back from him. For a moment, she simply watched him, saying nothing. Her face was flushed. Her hair had come loose.

"Prudence," he said.

And she kissed him again.

What came next was awkward, as how could it be anything else between an injured man with one arm trying to unbutton his scavenged pants and shirt while lying on an army cot beneath a woman shrugging out of a dress and a whalebone corset? It took a while, took enough time, he thought, for them to come to their senses, change their minds if they'd wanted to. He half-thought she would. He half-wished she would.

Then he was naked and she was naked above him, sweat gleaming on her skin in the near-darkness of the old warehouse. And he stopped thinking. He put his hand on her

terrible brown hand touching precious white skin

and drew her to him.

He wanted to be on top of her, to take her as a man should take a woman. But he knew it would be awkward trying to brace himself with the one arm, knew he had no choice but to lie there beneath her. And though he barely dared admit it even to himself, there was something deliciously wicked in that, some crossing of uncrossable lines, some inversion of the natural order. Why not? With all the lines they were crossing now, all the inversions of the natural order they were committing, what did one more matter?

He felt absent from his body and yet, at the same time, furiously at one with it. He felt…loosed, felt like a balloon, the string released from an errant child's hand, floating above the trees, floating into the sky.

She pushed herself against him with a hard urgency and he thrust back with an answering fierceness. His bad leg and residual injuries howled their protest. She was weeping. He wept without knowing.

After, she lay atop him, her breasts mashed into his belly, her moist cheek turned against his chest. His hand was buried in her October-colored hair.

They should get up from there. Someone might come to the door. Someone might peek through one of the bullet holes in the wall. Someone might see. But he did not say this and he did not move. Could not. The moment was its own universe, and it held them fast, safe in mutual embrace, sweating and breathing together, her ear pressed to the drumming of his heart.

But reality would not long be denied.

"What have we done?" he said.

"Shush," she said.

"What have we done?" he repeated.

"I do not know," she admitted.

"I should know better," he told her. "You should, too. They will kill us if they find out. They will kill both of us."

She lifted her head and turned her eyes upon him. "And how will they find out?" she asked. "Will you tell them?"

"Of course not," he said. "I am only saying that—"

"Stop," she said.

"I am only saying it is a dangerous thing we have done. Foolish, too."

"Do you regret that we did it?" she asked.

He thought about it. He tried to locate regret somewhere within him, scanning for it as a sailor scans the sky for a navigational star. But he could not find it. He didn't answer her. Which was, he knew, an answer in itself.

"I will not apologize," she said. She turned her cheek to his chest again. "I will *not*. You said it yourself: they have already taken so much from us. Will we allow them to take this, too?"

"But what does this mean? What happens next?"

It took her a long time to answer. "I do not know," she finally said, her breath stirring the hairs on his chest.

"I do not know either," he said.

A moment passed. His chest rose and fell, the weight of her upon him pleasant and warm. When she spoke, her voice was small. "You do not know, or you have not the courage to say?" she asked.

She waited for him, but he couldn't answer. She lifted her head again and watched him for a moment. He tried to read in her eyes what she saw in his, but he couldn't. She lowered her head back to his chest.

"What will you do when you leave this town?" he asked.

She sighed. "I will return to Boston, I suppose, where I will try to content myself with giving money to charities and schools that are set up to help the freedmen. What about you, Sam? What will you do? Will you return to Philadelphia?"

"Yes. Maybe. I suppose."

"There is another option," she said. A hesitance had entered her voice. It made him lift his head and look at her. All he could see of her was her hair.

"And what is that?" he asked.

"You could come to Boston," she said. "With me." Now she looked up and her gaze touched his.

He had trouble forming words. "I cannot..." he began.

"Why not?" she asked.

Why not, indeed? He didn't know.

"You could come to Boston with me," she repeated. And then she blinked. It seemed to take all day.

Could he really do that? Could he really? Travel with this woman he barely knew to a city he'd never seen? And then what? Marry her? Simply be with her? Glare back at all the Brahmins of Boston society who glared at him and demanded with their eyes to know what place he had in her life? Leave behind the agonies and miseries his life had become, leave behind this fruitless walking toward an impossible place?

She was watching him closely and whatever she saw in his face at that moment put a smile on hers. He was wondering what it was, when he realized that he was nodding.

"Yes?" she said.

"Yes," he heard himself say.

She rose above him, her face so close he could feel her soft exhalations upon his check as she breathed. She filled his vision, the beauty of her blotting out every other external thing. "Yes," she whispered and there was a finality to it, a door closed, a bolt turned.

She kissed him. Her hair covered him. It hid him away.

What had she done?

A day later, and she still did not know. She sat on Miss Ginny's back porch, the sun sliding down the sky. But she didn't see that. She saw only herself astride Sam Freeman, surrendering to a sudden rash passion that had come over her like fever. She saw herself casting off restraint, normalcy, even simple decency as if these things were but winter garb in a room grown suddenly stifling.

For so long, her impulsiveness had been a family joke. They had chided her for it and she had always pretended to be upset, but they knew and she knew that it made her proud. She said what others feared to say and did what they were scared to do.

But even she had never done anything like this, never given herself over to ungoverned passion with a man she barely knew. Yet there she had been, naked and shameless, straddling him as a man straddles a horse, riding him with tears in her eyes. *Tears.*

A day later, she was still trying to understand why she had done it. And how she felt about it now that she had. But answers eluded her. Instead, only questions rushed in.

Would they marry? She had, after all, invited him in the afterglow of the act to come with her to Boston. Would he think she had proposed? Had she? Would they simply be together without benefit of clergy?

And dear God, what if she was pregnant? What if nine months from now, she gave birth to a little mulatto baby?

And what about the fact that he was a Negro? She hated the question, hated herself for asking it. But she couldn't stop. After all, she was—Miss Ginny's revelations notwithstanding—white. Could she simply go to Boston with this black man, marry him, and live there in her father's house as if it were the most natural thing in the world?

What had she done?

The answer was simple, she supposed. She had finally gone too far, even for herself. She had done an awful thing.

But what confused her was that she did not feel awful. In truth, she felt good. Opening herself to this man had felt...*right*. It had made her feel human again.

How could that be wrong?

And now, as if on cue, here came Sam Freeman walking down the alley, leaning on his stick.

She sat up straight. For some reason, she thought of her last day in Boston, her exhilaration at seeing the house in Louisburg Square disappearing behind them, her sense that each clop of horses' hooves against cobblestones was taking them closer to a great and noble adventure. She had laughed at Bonnie, who sat stiffly, worriedly, beside her. But Bonnie had been right to worry, of course.

She regarded Sam as he grew closer. A sober-faced man, his blunt and handsome features set as if he were embarking upon some mission of grim importance. As, perhaps in his mind, he was. He still limped, she noted absently, but he was moving with greater ease now. His recovery really had been remarkable.

And then he stood before her.

A silence followed. Sam kicked at a pebble. He cleared his throat. She looked up at him.

"I wanted to talk to you," he said. His voice was a whisper of recrimination. "I wanted you to know that I am sorry for what happened between us. I did not mean for...you know. I did not mean to take advantage of you. I hope you can forgive me."

It had not occurred to her that he might feel...was it *guilt*? Prudence cleared her own throat. "You did not...I was not..."

I kissed you first. I wanted it to happen.

And there it was, the truth of the whole matter, a truth so embarrassing, so downright *shaming*, she barely dared confess it even to herself—much less speak it out loud.

"It is all right," she heard herself say instead. As if she were granting him absolution. As if she were validating his guilt. What a coward she had become.

He looked at her. She reached across and took his hand. "It is *all right*," she repeated, trying to say with the fervor of her voice what she couldn't with words. "I am very fond of you, Sam," she said. "Very fond. Nothing has changed that."

There was a silent moment, a pregnant moment. She saw him wrestling with her words, translating them. "Are you saying—"

He never finished the question. The door behind her opened, he yanked his hand away. Miss Ginny said, "Surprised to see you here, Sam. You feelin' better, then."

"I am feeling much better, Miss Ginny. Thank you."

"Good to see you healin' up. I was just about to send Prudence down there with your supper. But since you here, I s'pose you can just come on in and eat with us at the table." He grimaced and Prudence knew he was looking for a way out. But Miss Ginny held the door wide and in the end, he could do nothing but follow Prudence up the stairs and into the tiny kitchen.

His plate was already on the table, heaped high with hog and hominy. Miss Ginny spooned a plate from the pot in the hearth and handed it to Prudence, who reflected absently that one thing she would not miss about Mississippi was the food. Then Miss Ginny made a plate for herself. The kitchen was tiny and there were only two seats at the table. "You two take the chairs," said Sam. "I can eat standing up."

Prudence said, "Sam, you cannot do that."

Confusion. "What do you mean?"

She waited for him to realize why on his own and when he didn't, she nodded toward the stub where his arm had been. Prudence saw his face fall as he realized his mistake. "Sit down," she said. "I shall stand."

Sam's features hardened. "I still forget sometimes," he said.

He took his seat and for long moments, the only sound in the kitchen was of metal utensils scraping meal plates. Then Miss Ginny said, "Pleasure to have you join us here, Sam."

"Yes, ma'am. I appreciate your hospitality, and your welcoming me into your house."

"Oh, it ain't so such a much," said Miss Ginny. "My old master give it to me when I got too old to work." She gave Prudence a meaningful look. "He weren't such a bad master, all around."

"But he was still a master," said Sam.

"Yes, he was that," said Ginny.

"Yes, he was," Prudence added.

Another silence. Then Miss Ginny brightened. "Forgot to tell you," she told Prudence, reaching into a cubby on the wall behind her. "You got a telegram."

It could only be from her sisters. She had sent a long letter the day Bo Wheaton came to her door. Distraught, she had poured her grief onto the pages. She had told them of her ordeals, told them of the night Bonnie died, told them of Wheaton's offer. And she had all but begged for permission to accept it, to sell father's properties and return home.

Prudence was embarrassed by the memory of it. How pitiable she must have sounded.

Sure enough, the message A.J. Socrates had scribbled out on the flimsy white form with the name Western Union on top was pointed and simple in its urgency. "Awful news. Terrible about Bonnie. Worried about you. By all means sell immediately. Come home soonest."

She folded the paper carefully. "They are worried for me," she said, meeting Miss Ginny's concerned stare. "They gave me permission to sell everything and wish me to return home. I suppose I must now send word to the Wheatons that I am free to negotiate in earnest." A rueful laugh. "Although, given that this was transmitted through Mr. Socrates, I am certain they already know."

Miss Ginny said, "That's what you wanted, ain't it?"

"Yes, I suppose it is."

"You s'pose?"

A sigh. "I do not like seeing the Wheatons get their way. I do not like having to turn tail and run. And I do not like abandoning all these people who counted on me. I made *promises*, Ginny. I told them I would educate them and their children."

"Child, ain't nobody hold that against you. They seen what happened sure as you did. They know you ain't got no choice."

"*I* hold it against myself," said Prudence, and the force of her own anger took her by surprise. "I must say that I dislike running away from this fight, especially knowing what they intend to do in this town after I have gone, how they mean to drive out all the Negroes."

"You oughtn't be so hard on yourself," said Miss Ginny.

"I do not enjoy losing, Miss Ginny. And I hate that this town will not pay for what it did to Bonnie and all those other people." At the thought of it, she felt tears lurking behind her eyes.

"I understand that," said the old woman. "I do for a fact. But I don't know what you can do about it."

Prudence sighed. "Nor do I," she said.

A moment passed. And then Sam said, "I do."

She turned toward him, surprised. Apparently, he had also surprised himself. He sat there with a fork frozen in flight to his mouth, his eyes wide with sudden insight. He looked at her. "I know what you can do," he said.

"Well?" she said. "Spare us the suspense. Tell us."

So he did, sketching out in a few bold strokes the idea that had come to him. She asked him some questions. He answered them. She asked some more. He answered those, too. When he was done, a slow grin unfurled itself across Prudence's face, like a flag in a languid breeze. She came to her feet. "Sam, you are a genius," she said. "What an audacious feat that would be."

"Them white folks be mad as a hive of bees," said Miss Ginny.

Prudence looked at her. "Yes, they would, wouldn't they?" And they both laughed. "It would take a great deal of work," said Prudence, "but that would be a pleasure."

"Cost a pile of money, too," said Miss Ginny.

Prudence waved at the caution as if it were a housefly. Her gaze was turned within. "Money is not a problem," she said. "And it would be worth both the work and the money if we are able to pull it off." She looked up at Sam. "Do you really think we can do it?"

He considered her question for a moment, then nodded. "Yes," he said, "I believe you can."

"Need to be careful," warned Miss Ginny. "If word get out, they be even madder than they was before. Only us three knows for now, but when you start talkin' 'round to people, you can't be sure."

"Miss Ginny, surely colored people are more than practiced at keeping secrets from white people," said Prudence.

Ginny pursed her lips, thinking. Then her mouth opened in a toothless grin. "I reckon they is at that," she said. "And you right. Gon' be a sight to see when white folks figures out what you up to."

Prudence paced anxiously. "I need to send some telegrams. I shall have to go to Memphis and send them from there. For that, I will need to hire a wagon. I will start off first thing in the morning." She glanced up at the clock on the wall. "Is the livery stable still open at this hour?"

"I believes so," said Miss Ginny.

"While I am in Memphis I should also buy supplies."

"You should make a list," said Sam.

"And I will still need to send word to the Wheatons that I am prepared to sell."

Miss Ginny laughed. "Slow down, gal. You movin' twelve directions at once."

"I cannot help it," said Prudence. "There is so much to do. And the time is not long." Another glance at the clock. "I need to get to the livery stable," she said, rushing out of the room to get her bonnet. Halfway down the hall, she stopped, seized by a sudden impulse that turned her and flung her back into the kitchen, where she threw her arms around Sam's neck, surprising him so badly he dropped his fork. She was aware of Miss Ginny's eyes upon her as she squeezed him, but she didn't care.

"Thank you, Sam," she said. "You are brilliant. Thank you."

And then she rushed from the room, hurriedly pinned a bonnet to her head and, for the first time since the awful night they had taken her sister and strung her up in a tree, left Miss Ginny's by the front door and marched down Main Street, heedless of the intrusive staring of others' eyes.

Let them stare. What did she care? Prudence had a mission and it impelled her down the street with her head held high. And yet even so, even in this moment flush with new purpose, some small part of her dwelt yet again in that awful thing she had done just a day ago.

Except that again, she wondered…was it really so awful? Was it *really*? She'd had any number of chances to turn away from the edge.

Yet she had not turned. To the contrary, she had flown like an arrow. And immediately afterward, she had felt *joy*. Recrimination had come later, yes.

Regret and fear and second-guessing, too. But in the abandon of the moment when she gave herself to him, there had been nothing in her except joy.

And how could joy be wrong?

She did not know that it could.

So maybe it was her fears that were wrong instead.

Maybe it would be all right, then. The thought of it made her decide to write her sisters again. She would mail the letter tomorrow from Memphis. There was one thing she had to know, one question she had to ask.

But however they answered, she knew that she was finally done with doubt. All was possibility now.

Prudence was smiling as the livery stable came in sight.

Tilda looked up, her smile soft and sad. Luke, tugging peacefully at her nipple, gurgled his satisfaction. "Greedy little boy," she said. "Never gets enough."

Sam said, "I suppose he takes after his father." He stood by the door, the grime of another long day coating him, watching his son pull at the ninny, watching Tilda gaze down on their baby with all the love in the world. It made him feel cleansed. It made him feel new.

She looked up again, still smiling that smile. "So, are you going to do it?"

"Do what, Tilda?"

"Go to Boston with that white lady."

He swallowed. "I do not know," he said. "Perhaps."

Her eyes shone. "You should go, Sam. You need to go back to the North. That's where you belong. There is nothing but misery for you down here, nothing but sorrow for all of us. I told you that, didn't I?"

"Yes, you did. You were right."

"I'm glad you finally understand. Only…"

"What?"

Her gaze became pinched around the edges. "Don't hurt her, Sam. All right? Don't hurt her the way you hurt me."

The words knifed through him, but what could he say? He *had* hurt Tilda, hadn't he? Wasn't that what this was all about?

Sam swallowed. "What about you?" he asked, his voice flinching. "What about us?"

"Don't be foolish, Sam. You said it yourself. You are chasing something that ended 15 years ago. You are chasing time. No one ever catches time."

"But..."

"No one ever catches time," she repeated. "No one ever does."

"It is more than time," said Sam.

But Tilda was gone. And he was speaking aloud in the darkness of the old warehouse. He sat up, confused, knowing something had wakened him, but unsure what it was. Then he heard it again, a soft rapping on the door.

"Sam?" Miss Ginny's voice.

"Coming," he said. His mouth felt filled with cotton. He got to his feet and pulled on pants and a shirt, marveling at the ease with which he moved, an ease that would have been unthinkable just days before. All that time spent walking with Prudence had done wonders for him.

His feet bare, he padded to the door and pulled it open. Miss Ginny smiled up at him. She handed him a plate of eggs. "Thank you," he said as he took the plate.

"How long you and Prudence been sleepin' together?" she asked, still smiling.

Sam almost dropped the plate. "*What?*" he sputtered.

"You heard me," she said.

Stalling for time, he stepped back, placing the plate on Prudence's old desk, which he had been using as a table. Any number of replies chased one another through his thoughts, replies of anger, indignation, denial, confusion. But his heart was too exhausted for any of those.

"How did you know?" he asked.

"I ain't no fool," she said, following him into the room. "Anybody with eyes could see."

"Have you spoken to her?"

"No. Wanted to talk to you first. 'Sides, she left this morning. Goin' up to Memphis to send that telegram. She be gone most of the day, I expect. So: how long?"

"Miss Ginny, that is rather a personal question."

"Love that girl like she my own," said Miss Ginny. Her voice was taut. "That make it my concern, I expect. How long?"

He swallowed past the lump in his throat. "It was only once," he said, "two days ago."

A tight nod of satisfaction. "Didn't figure it could be much more than that. You ain't been in shape for such foolishment too long."

"Miss Ginny, this is a matter I would rather not discuss."

She ignored him. "You love her?"

"Beg pardon?"

"You heard me. Do you love her?"

"I do not think you have the right—"

She shouted it. "Do you *love* her?"

"I am very fond of her. We are fond of each other."

"You very fond," she sniffed.

"Yes," he said.

"You walk a thousand miles for her?"

"What?"

"You say you love her, then she deserve that much, don't she? Don't she deserve a man walk a thousand miles to find her? This Tilda I hear tell about, you done walked pert' near that far for her, way I hear. You walk that far for Prudence?"

"It is not the same."

"Oh, it ain't?"

"No, it is not!" he snapped. "Tilda and I were together fifteen years. We had a son together and we lost him."

"So now you give up."

"Do not do that," said Sam in a warning voice. "Do not make it sound as if I did not try. You said it yourself: I walked a thousand miles. I had my arm shot off. I ruined my feet. I got beaten and stomped nearly to death, and I could not find her. She is gone and I have no idea what else you expect me to do. Shall I keep walking through Mississippi the rest of my life to please you, Miss Ginny?"

She didn't answer. He looked down on the tiny woman for a long moment, weighed his next words, then decided to say them. "Are you sure you are not asking me all this just because she is white?"

He had expected to get a rise out of her. Instead, an expression he didn't understand passed over her face like a cloud between sun and soil. And then just as quickly, it was gone. "She been through a lot, Sam. That's all I'se sayin'. She don't need to be hurt no more than she already been. Don't hurt her."

Sam started. It was the same thing Tilda had said in his dream.

"It is not my intention to hurt her. That is the last thing I seek to do."

"Intention ain't got nothin' to do with it sometime."

He didn't reply. He couldn't.

After a moment, the old woman said, "I know you think ol' Ginny meddlin'."

It was an opening, but he couldn't take it. He still had no words.

She sighed. "Suppose I am," she said. "I knows y'all ain't no chil'ren. But I can't help carin' about her, Sam. You can't ask me to stop. And Tilda…"

He looked at her. "What about Tilda?"

"Expect I care some about her, too, and I ain't even met her."

"You care about Tilda."

"Yes."

"Do you care any about me?"

"What you mean?"

He was surprised to feel tears welling and he mashed them away, embarrassed.

"Sam," she began.

"Never mind," he said.

She looked at him. He looked at the floor. After a moment, she said, "I reckon you right. I know what Prudence need. I can guess what Tilda need. But I don't know what *you* need. Do you?"

He tried to reply, but his mouth had glued itself shut. He turned away, not wanting her to see his face, afraid it told secrets he did not want told. "I see," she said. "Well, then, I expect that's the question you need to get an answer to, ain't it?" She put a hand on his shoulder. He half turned, looking into her ancient eyes. "I leave you to it," she said.

He still couldn't speak. So he simply watched as she left by the side door, which closed softly behind her. When she was gone, he stood there alone in the darkness of the old warehouse, his thoughts blurring through his mind too fast to catch or hold. He was not sure how long he had stood inert when he heard the soft nickering of the horse.

"Yes," he answered, softly. "That would be an excellent idea."

He crossed the room, leaving his breakfast untouched, and lifted the saddle from a bench near the makeshift stall. "Let's go for a ride," he said.

He had to swing the saddle high and drop it heavily onto the horse's back. He had finally figured a method to cinch the girth, painstakingly passing the length of one end of the belt through the metal buckle on the other end, bracing it awkwardly with the nub of his left arm and pulling it tight. It took a long time. When he was done, he stood up, a sheen of sweat covering his brow. He went over and shoved one of the loading doors open, leaving just enough of a gap for the horse to pass through.

Then Sam went back and untied the animal from the upended school bench he had used as a makeshift post. He had to mount from the right, grabbing a fistful of the horse's mane and levering himself up into the saddle. Sam had cut the reins into two pieces, nailing them to the ends of a piece of chair leg about a foot long, making of it a bar that he could use to mimic the motion of two hands. He lifted that bar now, and nudged his mount around.

They rode through the open door. Sam paused just long enough to shove it back into place with his right leg, then urged his horse into a slow walk down Main Street. He felt the animal's powerful flanks moving beneath him, saw the storefronts and homes passing him by, the river shimmering in the distance. He breathed the morning gratefully. It felt as if he had not breathed for a very long time. The blur of his thoughts slowed and lessened into one.

What have I done?

He had not meant for this thing to happen, had not even known the thought of it was there, lurking somewhere below consciousness. One moment, he had been himself and she had been helping him lower his body gingerly onto the cot. The next moment, she had been kissing him. And then he had kissed her back. And his life had turned itself inside out, all in that one inexplicable moment.

Not that his life contained much of value. He had no money, no home, no child, no woman, not even a friend, unless you counted poor Ben, trying to sort out the wreckage of his own life up in Tennessee. No, all he had in his life were the joys and regrets of another day. If he continued through Mississippi searching for a woman who wasn't there, that was not likely to change. Until the end of his days, he would be what he was today: a man with nothing, chasing a life once lived fifteen years ago.

No one ever catches time.

And now, here was this woman who was not a phantom of his dreams, who was not a ghost of his past, who was *here*. And he wanted her. Did he not deserve that? Had he not earned it by the years he had spent, the miles he had walked, the blood he had shed?

She had been as shocked as he by the impossible thing that happened between them. But she wanted him too, *needed* him too. He could *feel* that in the impulsive arms she had thrown around his neck, in the way she had squeezed him close.

If he wanted her and she wanted him, why should they deny themselves that? If she was a free woman and he was truly a free man, who had the right to tell them no?

"I know what Prudence need," the old woman had said. "I can guess what Tilda need. But I don't know what *you* need."

The answer was simple, wasn't it? He needed to be at peace. He needed to be free. He needed to move forward.

And for that, he needed Prudence.

It was the sound of the moaning man that drew him back out of himself. He had ridden out from town and now found himself in a field of tall grass within sight of the brown river. Ahead of him crouched a man, folded over as if to hold his very self together. He looked up at Sam's approach, and Sam saw that the man was barely more than a boy, his skin brown, his face streaked with tears, the expression in his eyes desolate. Sam wanted to turn away and leave the boy to grieve in private.

But the eyes had seen him, so there was nothing he could do but walk the horse forward. "I'm sorry," said the boy, as Sam reined up near him. "I didn't think anyone would come this way."

"It is I who should apologize," said Sam. "I did not mean to intrude." A pause. "If you do not mind my asking..."

"My mother's dead," said the boy. The saying of it brought fresh tears.

"I am sorry to hear that," said Sam. "How did it happen?"

"I don't know, mister," said the boy. "They won't tell me."

"They?" Sam lowered himself from the horse, patting its neck as it bent to graze in the summer grass.

The boy nodded. "Marse and ol' Miss. They run me away from they front door just now. Said they don't want nothin' to do with none of their old slaves never no more. Like I done something wrong to *them*. Like I was bad or somethin'. They the ones sold *me* away."

"I see," said Sam. He knelt beside the boy.

"I told them I come lookin' for my mama. I'm the onliest thing she got in the world and she the same for me. I told her when they sold me off seven years ago, I would find her again. I weren't but 10, she cryin' her eyes out and that made me bust out, too. And I *promised* her I would come back and we be together again."

"And you came back today and they told you she was dead."

A nod. "Wouldn't tell me how it happened, wouldn't even tell me where she buried. Just closed the door in my face. Wouldn't open it, no matter how I cried out to them."

A dark rage howled to life within him then and for a moment, Sam saw himself going to them, to these lordly dealers in human flesh, and beating them until they begged to give this boy the simple human courtesy of a report on his mother's death. Sam swallowed the urge down. There was a stickiness in his throat.

"I am sorry," he said.

The desolate eyes turned to him. "Why white folks got to treat us so bad?" he said.

"I do not know," said Sam. He would have put a consoling hand on the boy's shoulder, but the boy was sitting to his left. Instead, Sam watched the horse chew grass for a moment. Then he said, "So what are you going to do?"

The boy looked down. "Walked all the way here from Alabam' lookin' for her. Suppose I'll just walk back. Leastways, I still know people there. Maybe get hired on for harvest."

Sam looked away. Was this what they were to be now? Once a slave people, now a wandering people, rootless and itinerant, searching for one another and for connections that used to be? It was as if to be forever incomplete was the Negro's awful destiny.

The boy's smile hung awkwardly from his forsaken eyes. "I used to take care of her, you know? My mama? She weren't well and I would look after her. Make root tea when she was feelin' poorly, put cotton from my sack into hers to keep the overseer from gettin' on her. That was the main thing that troubled me when they sold me off: I wondered who would take care of her. So I was lookin' forward to comin' back here. I thought, well, that's one thing I don't have to worry about no more. I could take care of her myself, just like I always done. And then I get here and they tell me this."

Sam's gaze was on the river. "You can't catch time," he said. "No one ever does."

The boy's eyebrow arched. "Beg pardon?"

"Nothing," Sam said.

He sat a long time with the motherless boy, both of them watching quietly as the river passed them by.

Once again, they sat on the gallery overlooking the river. Once again, Colindy brought them lemonade. "Thank you, Sass," said Charles Wheaton without looking at her. "That will be all." And Colindy nodded and went away.

The negotiation went quickly. Wheaton made her a generous offer: $4,000 for the building, $75 an acre for 180 acres of farmland—more than either was worth. Prudence accepted it, conditioned on one stipulation. She told him what it was and he knotted his lips in obvious distaste. But Prudence told him she would not sell the building unless he agreed, so he did.

The only remaining sticking point was time. Wheaton desired to take possession of his new property within the week; he wanted to see her gone quickly. But Prudence could not agree. There was still much work to do and she needed time to do it.

And what could he say? Loathe to stand too firmly and jeopardize the deal, he relented on this point, too. She would have one month to vacate the building. With that decided, he extended his hand and they shook on it.

"Well," he said, not bothering to hide his pleasure, "I suppose that concludes our business in as satisfactory a manner as possible, under the circumstances."

"I suppose it does," she said.

"You will be returning to Boston, then?"

A querulous edge had entered his voice and Prudence immediately knew it for what it was. She smiled, very faintly. "Yes, Mr. Wheaton. I have no intention of taking your money and using it to set up a new school in the next county over."

He reddened. "This whole thing has unsettled the town terribly," he said. "It is a pity we could not have come to an accommodation sooner. A great deal of grief might have been avoided. A great many lives might have been saved."

She thought she might gag on the sanctimony of it, and a half-dozen sharp retorts leapt to her tongue. But she knew what Bonnie would have told her: keep her mouth shut for once and bide her time. How often, when they were girls, had she led Bonnie into some rambunctious misadventure against Bonnie's cautious advice? Finally, Prudence was listening.

She made herself smile again. "Yes," she said. "But at least we have reached agreement now, before any further hardship can come."

"Yes," he said, "quite."

Prudence expected him to conclude their business then, but instead, he simply gazed out over the river for a time without speaking. There was silence but for the sawing of insects in the trees. Then he said, "We are different people, you Northerners and we Southern folk. It would have been better had you simply allowed us to go our own way. It is beyond my comprehension how any of you can expect that we will ever be one country again."

"But we must try," she said. "What other option do we have?"

He looked at her. He looked back at the river. "We in the South must be left alone to manage our own affairs," he said. "That is the only way the thing can possibly work. But if you all insist on imposing upon us your values and your ways of doing things, well..."

She waited for him to finish the thought. When he didn't, she said, "Well, that is business for another day. Our business for this day is concluded, is it not?"

"Yes," he said, "it is, indeed. Good day, Mrs. Kent. Sass will show you out."

He wheeled his chair back through the open door without another word or even a nod of farewell. She was surprised to find herself feeling sorry for him. There was a melancholy about the man, thought Prudence, as if he understood that for all his machinations, for all the violent resistance his town had raised, they were only delaying the inevitable.

"We will resist," he had told her, the first time they sat on this porch, "if it takes a hundred years."

And maybe, she thought, he had been right. It might take time to truly understand the shifting of the ground, the turning of the tide, might even take a century, as he had predicted. But the change was begun. Of that much, there could be no doubt. The change was begun, and it was irrevocable. And he knew it.

Of course, Charles Wheaton was thinking in the long term, was gazing out upon a far horizon. Prudence's concerns were more immediate.

Not a hundred years from now.

Not fifty years from now.

Not twenty years from now.

Now.

What hope was there for the 412 Negroes in and around Buford, Mississippi *right now*, if left to the mercies of white people who had burned down half a town rather than allow a school to be set up for their benefit?

After a moment, Colindy appeared on the porch. "Marse Bo bring the wagon around directly, Miss," she said. Her dark, moon-shaped face was as impassive as ever, her feelings and opinions, her *self*, not daring to so much as peek through the windows of her eyes.

Coming to her feet, Prudence heard herself say, "Colindy, may I speak with you for a moment?"

Now surprise entered the expressionless eyes. "What you want to talk to me about?" she asked.

In a few broad strokes, Prudence sketched out the plan she and Sam had hatched at Miss Ginny's table. When she was done, Colindy's eyes had widened still more. It was a moment before impassiveness remembered to reassert itself.

"So," said Prudence, "would you like to join us?"

"Can't do that, Miss."

"Why ever not?"

"Just can't is all. They ain't gon' never allow that."

"What can they do to stop us?"

"Ain't no tellin'."

"Colindy, please think about it. It could change so much for you."

"Done thought about it plenty," said Colindy. "It's foolishness, is all it is. Just foolishness."

Prudence was about to say more, but the heavy tread of boots coming through the house stopped her. Bo Wheaton appeared on the porch. "Sass?

What's this about? I thought you were goin' to get Miss Prudence here. I been waitin' out there fifteen minutes."

Colindy addressed herself to the floor. "I'se sorry, Marse Bo. Mrs. Kent an' me was talkin'."

He shoved his hat back on his head. "Oh?"

Prudence had time to wonder if her entire plot was about to come tumbling down before her very eyes. How perversely fitting it would be if once again she were the victim of her own impulsiveness.

Colindy said, "Yes, Marse. She keep askin' me what you and Marse Charles mean to use that old warehouse for. I done told her I don't know. I don't mix in white folks' business."

Without meaning to, Prudence breathed out a long sigh. It was an expression of relief, but she saw immediately that Wheaton took it for exasperation. "You done real good, Sass," he said. "You're smart not to put your nose in where it don't belong."

His gaze fell upon Prudence, and she tried her best to look contrite. "As for you, Mrs. Kent, if you were curious, why didn't you just ask my father or me? I don't know how it's done where you come from, but down here, if you want to know somethin', you ask somebody. You don't go sneakin' around behind folks' backs."

"You are absolutely right," said Prudence, lowering her head. "I apologize for my unseemly behavior."

"Well," he said, surprised. "You? Apologize? I didn't think you knew the word. I accept your apology, Mrs. Kent. And just to answer your question: we don't know yet what we goin' to do with that property. As I'm sure you can imagine, the most important thing to us was simply to take possession of it in a fair and legal manner, to assure that you have no further reason ever to return to Buford."

Prudence had had enough of pretend contrition. She met his eyes. "On that we can agree," she said. "When I leave here, it is my hope never to see you or your town again."

She saw a shadow of laughter flicker in Colindy's eyes, gone before it was truly there. "Goodbye, Sass," she said. "You take of yourself, now."

"Goodbye, Miss," said Colindy.

Brushing past Bo Wheaton, Prudence made her way through to the front of the house and climbed into the phaeton. He followed, climbing into his seat. Wheaton let the brake off, clicked his teeth, and the horses started forward. Prudence turned in her seat and saw what she had expected to see: Colindy, standing out front, following her with those impenetrable eyes.

Prudence and Bo Wheaton didn't speak during the trip back to town except once when she asked him to make a slight detour. He only grunted in response and she wasn't sure he would do it, but he did. He even slowed the wagon as it passed the ramshackle little cemetery behind the colored church. The twelve parallel depressions in the dirt were still clearly visible almost six weeks later, even though the grass had grown in. Bonnie's grave was third from the left. But soon, it would not be necessary for a visitor to count off the graves to find the victims of the massacre: Charles Wheaton had agreed to her stipulation that he furnish grave markers and see to the upkeep of the graves.

Prudence could not imagine who would ever need to seek Bonnie Cafferty's grave. She had told Bo Wheaton the truth when she said she had no intention of ever returning to this place again. Still, it cheered her to know her sister would not spend eternity lying in an unmarked hole. She deserved better than that.

The back door of the church opened just then, and the Reverend Davis Lee stepped out. He was smoking a pipe and had his head down, as if deep in thought. The sight of the wagon seemed to catch him by surprise and he started. Then he recognized her. Slowly he lifted his hand and nodded. His face bore an expression she could not read.

Still, she was grateful for the gesture, for the acknowledgment. In some part of her heart, Prudence was still convinced all the Negroes hated her for the ruin she had brought upon them. It was the one thing about Sam's plan that gave her pause. In order for it to work, she would have to ask them to trust her—again. What right did she have to ask? And even if she did, wouldn't they—*shouldn't* they—refuse?

Prudence returned Preacher Lee's solemn nod. Wheaton flicked the reins and the graveyard fell behind.

After a moment, the wagon rattled to a stop in front of Miss Ginny's. Finally, Bo spoke. "Well," he said, half turning in his seat, "I suppose this is the last we will see of each other, Mrs. Kent."

"Yes," she said.

"It's been a most interesting association. As I believe I told you once, you are the first Yankee I ever had a chance to know on a close-up basis."

"I'm certain you shall not be eager to repeat the experience," she said.

He gave her a thoughtful frown. "Oh, I don't know," he said. "Some of it wasn't too bad."

"It is a matter of perspective, I suppose. All of it was awful for me."

"Yes," he said, "I can imagine how you would feel that way. You've been through a lot. But we're not bad folks, Mrs. Kent. We're just like anybody else, I suppose. Just like you Yankees, come right down to it. We're just tryin' to get by, best way we know how."

She was seized with a sense of having lived this moment before. Then she remembered Adelaide's father, standing before her in front of the school one hot afternoon with his daughter. She met Bo Wheaton's eyes. "Another man," she said, "told me once that people are just people, behaving according to what they have been taught."

"I would agree with that," he said.

"So would I," she said, "but you see, Mr. Wheaton, that is no excuse for ignorant behavior. A man must not be defined solely by the things he has been taught. He must also be defined by his willingness and capacity to learn new and better things."

For a moment, she fancied she could see her words hitting home. Then he grinned at her. "Ma'am, you sure talk pretty," he said.

She regarded him for a moment. "Goodbye, Mr. Wheaton," she told him. She climbed down from the phaeton. The moment her foot was on the ground, the wagon rattled off. He could not wait to get away from her. The idea was distantly amusing.

Prudence waited until he was out of sight, then walked down to the warehouse, eager to tell Sam about the meeting with Charles Wheaton. The idea that Wheaton's money would help pay for a plan that would bring his town to a halt had her in a giddy mood and she couldn't wait to share the news with him.

But the warehouse was empty. Nor was the big horse in its makeshift stall. Sam was out riding, then, exercising the horse and testing the condition of his own battered body.

Prudence sat down to wait. It didn't take long. Fifteen minutes later, she heard the clopping of the horse's hooves growing steadily closer. After a moment, the big doors swung open and Sam led the roan in. Man and beast were both sweating. It had been a good, hard ride.

Sam stopped at the sight of her. "Prudence," he said.

Prudence had been sitting on his cot, but now she came to her feet. It was the first time they had been alone together since that day. "Sam," she said. And then: "I have been to see Charles Wheaton."

"Oh?" He was latching the door.

"It went well. Indeed, I daresay it went very well."

Limping slightly, Sam led the horse across the room to its makeshift stall. He looped the reins over the leg of the overturned bench, undid the saddle, and laboriously laid it aside, then picked up a brush and went to work on the horse's left flank. During all this, he was silent. Prudence approached him from behind.

"Sam, we need to talk."

She heard him sigh. He paused in his brushing. "Look," he began, "I need to—"

"No," she said. "Allow me to speak first, please. Three days ago, you apologized to me for what…happened between us, and I allowed you do it. That was cowardly of me."

"Prudence, I—"

"No, allow me to finish. I have been thinking a great deal about this. I allowed you to go on as if what happened was your fault, as if I had not kissed you first. I behaved as if I were granting you pardon. That was a dreadful thing to do, but I could not bring myself to face the truth. The truth is that it happened because I wanted it to happen. I wanted *you*, Sam. I still do."

Now he turned to face her. His eyes were unreadable in the shadows and half light of the warehouse. "I am leaving tomorrow," he said. His voice was thick.

"*What?*"

"I must go," he said. "I thank you for everything you have done for me, you and Ginny both, but—"

It was as if he were speaking another language. "You are leaving?"

"Yes," he said.

"But why?"

"I have to find her," he said. "I have to at least try."

"Tilda?"

"Yes."

"But what of our plan here?"

"You have no need of me for that."

She felt as if she were falling through space, nothing to hold to, not even an impact to look forward to. Just falling.

"I am sorry," he said.

Prudence couldn't breathe. "After we...and that is all you have to say? Sam, please, you must not do this to me."

"I know. I am so sorry."

And Prudence, who had solemnly promised herself to refrain from impulsive acts, slapped Sam Freeman hard enough to turn his head. He touched the spot. "You are sorry?" she said. She slapped him on the other cheek. The flat, sharp bang of flesh against flesh echoed in the cavernous room. "How dare you?" she cried and hated the tremble she heard in her voice.

"I am sorry," he said, yet again.

She held up her index finger as if to warn that his next word might be his last. Sam fell silent. Prudence regarded him as if he were some repellent bug. And then she ran away.

Watching the door slam behind her, Sam felt exhausted.

Stay with this white woman who had nursed him back from the dead, who had given him a home and healing and hope? Betray Tilda.

Go searching for his wife, for the woman he had loved from the instant he saw her, the woman whose image had gone before him in battlefields and a hospital ward and a thousand miles of walking? Betray Prudence.

There was no path without betrayal.

So how was a man to know what to do? He didn't know what was right. He didn't even know if still believed such a thing as right existed.

Morning came.

Sam had saddled the horse and was on his way to the loading door when he heard a knock at the side door. Hoping it was Prudence and yet *fearing* it was Prudence, he flew to answer. But it was Ginny who was standing there.

"Heard you leavin' us," she said.

"Yes."

"Thought you might need these." She lifted a haversack and a canteen. "Put you some biscuits and salt meat in there," she said. "Ought to carry you a couple days, at least."

"Thank you," said Sam.

"You goin' lookin' for Tilda?"

"Yes, I am," said Sam. "Miss Ginny, please…tell Prudence…" And then he stopped, because how he could he finish that sentence? What words could encompass all that was churning in his heart? He looked at the old woman, helpless.

She told him, "I'll tell Prudence you said goodbye."

Sam nodded, unable to do much more.

Miss Ginny touched his arm. "You a good man, Sam. I want you to know that. We all doin' the best we can."

Sam kissed her cheek. "Goodbye, Miss Ginny," he said.

"Goodbye, Sam. You take care of yourself."

"Yes, ma'am." She watched as he secured the haversack and canteen to the horse's saddle. Then he led the horse toward the big doors. They swung open upon a morning perfect and blue. He stepped through, leading the horse. His right knee thudded in protest as he swung his leg up over the horse from the right. Sam barely noticed. He was used to the pain.

Sam lifted the reins, regarded Miss Ginny for a moment. "Thank you for everything, ma'am," he said.

He gave the horse the spurs and it walked slowly forward. He heard the big door close behind him. And then he felt his heart knock painfully at the walls of his chest. Prudence was standing out in front of Miss Ginny's little house, her hands clasped before her. When the horse drew abreast of her, Sam reined it to a stop.

Without a word, she handed up a canvas sack, closed with a drawstring at its neck. Mystified, Sam accepted it. He sat it on his saddle and was using his one hand to work the drawstring open when she spoke. "It contains about $25 in Union coins. There is also a derringer pistol."

He considered the gift. Then he pushed the sack into his pants pocket. "Thank you," he said.

She regarded him with hurt, defiant eyes. "I wish you good luck, Sam. I hope you find her."

With that, she turned away. He watched her go. When the front door had closed behind her, he spurred the horse gently and it moved away at an easy pace. Only once did Sam look back. No eyes met his. Miss Ginny's door was still closed, her curtains drawn. The morning he had first started out from Philadelphia came back to him then. He had stood on the bridge, wondering if he were not making the biggest darn fool mistake of his entire darn fool life.

He wondered the same thing now. And yet, as before, he had no choice.

Sam spurred the horse into a trot and in just a few minutes he had left the town, and Prudence, behind.

Abandonment hung over Jim McFarland's place like a pall of smoke.

The fields were so overgrown with grass and weeds they were hardly recognizable. The house was nothing but a burn spot on the soil, and the barn slumped as if ready at any moment to collapse in on itself. An awful stench of death drifted toward Sam and made him gag.

He climbed down from the horse, covering his mouth. Fearing the worst, he went inside the barn to investigate the stench. It turned out to be a dead mule. The carcass had gone black. Rats had been at it.

Hand still clenched firmly to his mouth, Sam backed out of the barn and went back to his horse, which nickered with soft urgency. "I know, boy," he said.

He didn't begrudge the horse its unease. This was a haunted place.

A snarl of determination issued through clenched teeth as he one-armed his weight back into the saddle.

They picked their way through the pine woods back to the main trail and continued west. After a few minutes, they came across an old Negro man in a battered silk top hat resting by the side of the road. Sam asked if he knew Jim McFarland. The man said he reckoned he knew most everybody in the county; before the war, he had been a driver for his own master. Sam asked if he knew what had happened to McFarland. The man smiled a sunny smile through a scraggly beard and said he did not. He tipped the old top hat back from his brow and shaded his eyes as he regarded Sam.

"Why you lookin' for that scalawag anyway? Ain't nothin' but trouble, that one. My old marse used to say so all the time."

"It is not him I am concerned with," said Sam. "I am looking for a woman who was once a slave on his place."

"Well, way I hear it, he ain't had but two, three of us'n left by the time he lit out," said the man. "Used to have near 'bout fifty, but the rest, they up and left during the war. Tell you who you ought to talk to. You ought to talk to Nick."

"Who is Nick?"

"Nick use' to belong to Marse Gus Chambers. Stayed on Marse Gus's place after the surrender. He told me him and Marse Gus stopped at Marse Jim's place on the way home from the war. Said it was a powerful strange sight to see Marse Jim holdin' on to them two, three slaves like don't none of 'em know the war over. Nick and Marse Gus was probably the last ones seed Marse Jim 'fore he up and disappeared."

Sam asked directions and the other man gave them. He said, "Thank you, Mr.—"

"Walker," said the other man. "That's what most folks calls me. They used to call me Driver on account of that was my job. Now it's just Walker. 'Cause that's what I does, since the surrender come. I walks."

"I know the feeling," said Sam.

He found Nick three hours later, mending a pasture fence with another Negro man. When Sam called out to him, he drew a forearm across his sweaty forehead. "What can I do for you, mister?" he asked. He was a tall, thin man and when he approached, Sam saw that he walked with a pronounced limp.

"I am hoping you can help me," said Sam. "I am searching for a woman who used to be a slave on the McFarland place. I hear you stopped through there a few months back, before McFarland disappeared."

"Yes, I reckon we did. Me and Marse Gus. Wasn't but three colored on his place by then, though. Two women, one fella. Tell me about the one you lookin' for."

"She would be about 45," said Sam. "I have not seen her in many years, but when I knew her she was..." A pause, remembering. Then he sighed. "Well," he said, "she was about the most beautiful thing you ever saw. She had dark skin and long, thick hair."

Nick smiled. "They was one there like that. The other one, she were pretty, too, but she were a young gal."

Sam felt hope fluttering in his chest. He pushed it down. "Did you get the name of the older woman?"

Nick frowned. "I did," he said, "but I'm durned if I can remember it."

"Please try," said Sam.

"Been tryin' all the time we been talkin'," said Nick. "It won't come."

"Do you know where they went?"

"Not exactly."

"What do you mean?"

"What I said. Don't nobody know 'zactly where they gone, but I expect I know what direction."

"What direction would that be?"

Nick gave him a surprised look. "Why, think about it," he said. "If they go south, what be the point? They already south. North or east and they gon' run into more of them Yankees, and them the ones they tryin' to get shed of."

"West," said Sam.

A nod, an easy smile. "That's it. Way I hear, that's where a lot of them rebs is goin' that don't want to give up the fight."

Sam's response was cut off when a white man sitting astride a horse in the middle of the pasture yelled out, "Nick, am I paying you to lollygag with every tramp who wanders through, or am I paying you to work?"

"Be right there, Marse Gus," yelled Nick over his shoulder.

"You all wanted to be paid for your work," groused the white man. "Well, if you don't work, you don't get paid. That's how it goes."

"Yes, sir, Marse Gus."

Rolling his eyes for Sam's benefit, Nick turned to go. Sam itched with the frustration of it. It was so close to proof that Tilda was alive—or had been as of three short months ago—and was headed west with some stubborn rebel who refused to believe his cause was lost. But at the same time, it really wasn't proof at all, was it? A vague description that could fit her, or a hundred other colored women: 45 years old and beautiful. Based on that, he might chase this McFarland down, find the woman he was traveling with, and then she might not be Tilda at all, might be some other poor woman entirely. And then where would he be?

The same place he was now, he supposed, sighing. It surely couldn't make things it any worse. He clicked his tongue at the horse, ready to continue this fool's journey.

Then Nick turned back. "One thing I do remember," he said. "Something she told me."

"Beg pardon?"

Nick grinned. "Well, like I say, she were a pretty thing and I was feeling flirtatious, but she weren't interested. And I told her, I say, 'Gal, I'm gon' *make* you love me.' And when I said that, she said the durndest thing."

Something hot stabbed Sam's chest. He stopped breathing without realizing it. "She said, 'Love is long suffering,'" he said.

Nick's grin fell. "That's right," he said. "That's exactly what she said. How you know that? She said it was from the Bible."

"It is," said Sam.

Memory.

Sitting on the stoop in front of his cabin on a Saturday night. Tilda, looking up at him, laughter in her eyes. Him, vaguely annoyed that she is amused, vaguely hurt that she has refused, yet again, to jump the broom with him. How many times has he asked her? How many times has she told him no?

"Gal, how many times you gon' turn me down? I feel like I'se fit to bust."

A smile that knows. "Love is long suffering,'" she says.

"What? What that mean?"

"That's in the Bible," she says.

"Where? Show me."

So she gets a Bible and reads to him. When she is done, he can only look at her and marvel. "Ain't never seen no nigger could read."

"Negro," she says. "And you can learn. I can show you."

"How?"

"Come here," she says.

And he scoots closer so that she can open the Bible across both their laps. She points to the unfamiliar symbols on the page and explains how they join together to make sounds. He can barely pay attention. He is uncomfortably aware of the closeness of her, the warmth of her bare arm brushing his, the smell of sweat in her hair.

It is their first reading lesson. The first of many.

"It's in the book of First Corinthians," he told Nick. "Chapter 13." And then he closed his eyes and read the words off a page in his mind.

"'Love is long suffering; it aboundeth in kindness. Love is not envious. Love is not insolent: it is not puffed up. It doth not behave itself unbecomingly. It is not self interested. It is not easily provoked. It placeth not the evil to account. It rejoiceth not in iniquity, but shareth in the joys of truth. It beareth all things. It believeth all things. It hopeth all things. It endureth all things patiently.'"

When he opened his eyes, he was almost surprised to find Nick still there, looking at him. The words had taken him elsewhere.

"That's in the Bible?" asked Nick.

Sam smiled. "She read it to me one day when *I* was feeling flirtatious," he said.

The white man cried out again. "Nick, didn't you hear me, goddamn your black hide?"

"I *said* I be right there!" shouted Nick, half turning. The sharpness in his voice surprised Sam. From the look on his face, it surprised Nick, too. The white man looked especially shocked. He blanched and swallowed, but did not speak.

"I expect you will have some grief from that," said Sam.

"He get over it," said Nick. "But you right: I better get back to work 'fore he lose his mind." He regarded Sam closely. "Good luck findin' her, you hear?"

"Thank you," said Sam. And he spurred the horse into a trot.

His thoughts moved even faster. She was *alive*. Somewhere to the west of him, she was alive.

Love endureth all things patiently. It perseveres.

He had forgotten that, hadn't he? Forgotten her voice reading that to him in the gathering twilight of a warm evening in spring. Forgotten the wonder of sitting next to her, listening. Forgotten the awe of jumping the broom with her. Hand in hand before an old straw broom someone held low, eyes upon them, Miss Prentiss watching from the back porch in tolerant amusement, their legs tensing and then springing them high, together, still hand in hand, across that old wooden stick into the land of matrimony. He had forgotten how he had leapt with her and felt as if he might never come down.

The horse raced past unseen trees.

Sam made camp that night in a field off the main road not far from the river. He ate for the first time all day—biscuits and cold chicken from the haversack Miss Ginny had fixed. He worked open the sack Prudence had given him and ran his hands through the coins. At the bottom, he found the derringer and pulled it out. A tiny thing. Unless fired at close range, it was more apt to make a man mad than really hurt him. Or miss him altogether.

Of course, it had been a weapon just like it that killed Lincoln, so obviously the little gun could be deadly. Sam slipped it back into the bag. He slept that night without dreams.

When the morning light woke him, he saddled his horse and rode down to the riverbank. He traveled along it for half an hour before finding what he sought: a ferryman. Sam paid passage and the man took him and his horse across the wide, solemn Mississippi into the state of Arkansas.

He rode at a leisurely pace, not really seeing the sugarcane fields as he passed them by. Instead, he found himself trying to envision the ending of this quest. For weeks now, for *months*, he had pictured it as tragedy and disaster—Tilda with a new man, Tilda rejecting him, Tilda dead. For the first time, he allowed himself to imagine it as something else: Tilda joyous. Tilda rejoicing and praising God for reuniting them. Tilda as amazed to see him as he would be to see her, her arms thrown around him, her tears wetting his neck.

Was that possible? Did he even dare allow himself to hope?

He rode for two days, covering 150 miles. The trail grew cold. He asked at the back doors of farmhouses, stopped mule drivers and fence post diggers. None recalled seeing a white man and three Negroes making their way west.

There was a moment when he thought he might have uncovered a sign of them. A Negro blacksmith in a little town called Beckman told him a white woman named Mrs. Lindley had taken in a white man some weeks past. The blacksmith believed the white man was traveling with at least one Negro woman.

Sam followed the blacksmith's directions and soon found himself standing at the back door of a Mrs. Agnes Lindley, who told him she had indeed taken in a white man, a Captain McFarland, C.S.A., who had fallen ill with pneumonia. But she could not remember his first name. He had been traveling with a colored woman, but she couldn't remember that name at all. And there had not been three Negroes. The woman had been the only one.

Some other McFarland, thought Sam bitterly. It was not them. It was not *her.*

He nodded to the white woman and backed away, began the laborious process of hauling himself up on the horse. She watched with interest.

"How did you lose your arm?" she asked. "Was it in the war?"

"Yes," he said, regarding it as not quite a lie.

"Were you fighting for our side?" she asked. Her voice lifted toward hope.

He thought idly and for no particular reason of what it would be like to placate this white woman's need to believe the improbable. Then he thought about Nick snapping at "Marse Gus." He realized he was tired. When had he become so fatigued?

"No, ma'am," he said firmly. "I fought for the Union."

Her mouth mashed itself down to a nearly invisible line. "I see," she said.

She would get over it, he thought.

He swung the horse around and trotted off. On the way out of town, he passed the same blacksmith, standing next to a well, drinking from a dipper of water. He was stripped to the waist, his dark skin oily with sweat. "Did you find the house?" he called.

Sam reined up. "I found the house," he said, "but I do not believe the woman who stayed there is the one for whom I search."

"So what are you going to do now?" asked the blacksmith.

"I do not know," said Sam. "Would you mind if I have some of that water?"

The man spooned the dipper full from the well bucket and handed it to Sam. As Sam drank thirstily, the man said, "You know what you ought to do?"

"What is that?" asked Sam.

"Place a notice."

"What do you mean?"

"In the newspaper. There's a colored paper out of Little Rock, *The Freedman's Voice.* It runs notices all the time. Husbands looking for their wives, mothers looking for their children, that sort of thing."

"Do the notices work? Are people reunited?" He handed the dipper back.

"Don't know," said the man, shrugging his shoulders. "Only been doing it since surrender, after all. But seems like it might be worth a try, unless you got a better idea."

Sam didn't have a better idea. He didn't have *any* idea. All he had was the gnawing frustration of knowing he was closer to seeing Tilda than he had been in 15 years and yet not close at all. She was here, somewhere, waiting to be found. He was certain of it.

"How far is Little Rock?" he asked the blacksmith.

"About a day's ride," said the blacksmith. "That way." He pointed the cup of the dipper north.

"Thank you," said Sam. He turned the horse and spurred it down a street of clapboard houses.

Some pragmatic voice in the back of his head whispered to him, told him he could not live the balance of his life engaged in this foolish chase. And he almost pulled up on the reins and surrendered to practicality. He had done it before, he supposed. He could do it again.

Except for...

Tilda scooting close to him on the front stoop one warm evening in spring.

Except for...

That laughter in her eyes.

Except for...

The sound of her voice, reading the Bible to him.

Love is long suffering; it aboundeth in kindness. Love is not envious. Love is not insolent: it is not puffed up. It doth not behave itself unbecomingly. It is not self interested. It is not easily provoked. It placeth not the evil to account. It rejoiceth not in iniquity, but shareth in the joys of truth. It beareth all things. It believeth all things. It hopeth all things. It endureth all things patiently.

And there was one other line in that passage, one he had forgotten until just now.

Love never fails.

Oh, God, please. Let that be true.

With that prayer on his lips and anxiety gnawing his heart, he spurred his mount toward Little Rock.

Her body had refused death.

She had offered it death, told it to breathe death in like air and be released from the painful obligation of living. Her body had refused. Her legs had kicked, her arms had reached, her head had broken the surface, returning her to the world of sunlight, trees, and men. She had vomited water.

Only Honey knew. Honey, who came looking a few minutes later, driven by some preternatural sense, and found her lying in the wet grass, shivering despite the heat. Somehow, she just knew.

"Tried to kill yourself, didn't you?" Sounding angry.

Tilda nodded, shivered some more.

"Foolish girl," said Honey. "You gon' kill yourself because you tired of some randy little white boy and his prick?"

Tilda could barely get the words out, her body knocking like a steam engine. "It's not...just...that," she managed.

Honey softened. "Sweetie, I know. But you can't let them make you so sad you destroy yourself. You got to always have hope, child. Even if you ain't quite sure what you hopin' for. Just to hope, that's the whole point."

"That makes no sense," said Tilda.

Honey shrugged. "Maybe it don't," she said. "Or maybe it make all the sense in the world and you just too sad and tired to know. Come on."

And she had helped Tilda to her feet.

They had gone that very day to Marse Jim. Honey had stood behind her while Tilda made the little speech they had rehearsed. Told him she deserved more than to be used for the pleasure of some randy boy, said that if he did not put a stop to it, they would no longer cook nor sew for the camp.

She had braced herself to be hit, but Marse Jim had only regarded them with an amused smile. "Very well," he said. "You don't have to sleep in his tent no more. You can move in with Honey if you've a mind."

Surprised, she had smiled. "Yes, Marse Jim. Thank you, Marse Jim."

That was a month ago. She has moved into the cookhouse with Honey. And her life has settled back into a routine. She cooks, she gathers wood, she washes clothes. The men seldom venture out any more on what they once grandly called "operations" against the federal troops. Most days are spent flopping around the camp, drinking, arguing, and cursing Yankees and all their progeny.

It is not a good life, but it is a tolerable one. At this point, that is all she asks for, all she desires. A life she can tolerate. A life she can bear.

So she is not prepared for what happens this morning when Honey comes into the cookhouse and shakes her shoulder. Tilda, curled under thin sheets on the floor, grunts in her sleep, forces one eye open. It is still dark outside. Then the light from an oil lamp fills the tiny space. "What are you doing?" she asks.

Honey's eyes are bright. "You got to see this," she says.

Tilda's other eye comes open. She squints against the light. "See what?" she says.

Honey brandishes the newspaper like money. "This," she says.

Honey has a system. Once a week before dawn, a colored man leaves the paper for her in the hollow of a tree down by the river.

Tilda closes her eyes. "See it later," she grumbles.

Honey swats her with the paper. "See it now," she insists. "It's about you."

Tilda's eyes open. She sits up and accepts the paper from Honey's hands. Honey points to a notice at the bottom of the page, holds the lamp close. Disbelieving, Tilda reads.

> I am looking for Tilda, my wife. When I knew her, we were in bondage to
> Louisa Prentiss, near Buford in the state of Mississippi. At the time of the
> late rebellion, she was property of a James McFarland who, it is believed,
> has carried her into Arkansas. Information on her whereabouts and present
> condition will be gratefully received by her husband, now using the name

Sam Freeman, via the kind offices of *The Freedman's Voice* in Little Rock, Arkansas. Love never fails.—1 Corinthians 13:8

Tilda stares at the words for a very long time. It is as if symbols on paper have ceased to have meaning. She cannot process. She doesn't understand.

Honey is impatient. "That's you, ain't it? Louisa Prentiss, wasn't that the woman owned you? And he mentions Marse Jim. That's got to be you. He's lookin' for *you*."

Still Tilda stares. It makes no sense. She has not seen him in 15 years. She has not allowed herself to *think* of him in 15 years.

"Sam?" she says. She makes his name a question. It feels as if she is trying out a word in some exotic new language. And then: "Why?"

There is a tenderness in Honey's smile. "For you," she says.

"For me?" It is the most absurd thing she has ever heard. She tries to laugh, but it comes out tears. She has trouble swallowing the idea down. She has never thought of herself as a woman someone would come searching for.

"What you gon' do?" asks Honey.

"What *should* I do?" asks Tilda.

"Go to him."

"I can't do that."

"Why not?"

"Marse Jim would kill me if I tried to get away from him. I saw him do it to two others."

Honey looks at her. "You just tried to kill yourself," she says softly, "few weeks ago."

It is the first time they have spoken of it since that day. "That's different," Tilda says.

Honey sighs. "All I know is, they's a man out there lookin' for you. You asked me once if anybody was lookin' for me, and I told you I couldn't feature it. But if somebody was..." A pause, her thoughts creeping into silence. When she speaks again, her voice is whispered steel. "If somebody was, I'd go to them. You better believe that."

There is a moment. She can feel herself standing there so long ago in midnight darkness, one foot poised over Agnes Lindley's threshold, unable to bring it down. She can feel herself hating herself.

Then she comes to her feet. Grinning, Honey hands her her dress and shoes. "There you go," says Honey.

"This is foolish," says Tilda, climbing into the worn dress.

"It's *all* foolish," says Honey. "These men sittin' around all day pretendin' they still fightin' a war been over for months…talk to us like we's dogs or hogs. It's all foolish. Why should this be any different?" Then she frowns over the notice in the paper. "'Love never fails,'" she says. "Why he put that in, you suppose?"

"It's something from the Bible I read him one time," says Tilda. "It was long ago. We weren't much more than children."

She is dressed now and stands there regretting. "This is foolishness," she says again, emphatically. "Marse Jim will find me and he will kill me."

Honey purses her lips. "Maybe he will," she allows. "But seem to me bein' scared all the time ain't much different from bein' dead."

"How you talk!" hisses Tilda. "You're here the same as I am, still slaving for these people, even though you're supposed to be free."

"Yes I am," says Honey. "But you know what the difference is? *I* ain't got nowhere else to go."

They stare at each other. Honey doesn't blink. Finally, Tilda shakes her head. "Foolishness," she says. But she is moving toward the door. She pauses long enough to give Honey a brisk hug. Their eyes meet. Then she is gone. Honey hears the leaves in the woods behind the cookhouse rustling at her passage. The sound is soft, as if Tilda were no more than the merest breeze.

"Godspeed," she says.

It is too early for cooking, but Honey is too keyed up to sleep. She reads the paper by lamplight until a rim of pink appears in the eastern sky. Then she starts a fire and gets breakfast on.

An hour later, the men queue up at the door, plates in hand. There are fewer of them today. Fewer of them every day, she notes, ladling a meager portion of scrambled eggs into a plate. They are disgruntled, dispirited, shuffling their feet. She wonders, as she does on many mornings now, how much longer they can continue to hide out here, pretending their cause is not lost, pretending they are soldiers, still. Jim McFarland is one of the last in the line, hitching his suspenders over his ample gut.

He accepts his meal with a grunt. "Where's that other one?" he asks.

Honey has been rehearsing this moment. She keeps her face bored, her voice tensionless. "She went down to the water. Do some washing."

"Early for that," he says.

She shrugs. "Not so hot early," she says.

For a moment, she fears he is going down to the water to check. But he doesn't. He doesn't say anything, just takes his plate and walks away. She doesn't dare even to sigh.

Hours pass. It is late in the day when he approaches her again. She is before the cookhouse, splitting logs for the fire.

"Where's that other one?" he asks. "Ain't seen her all day."

Honey lowers the axe, dabs with her forearm at her sweaty brow. "Couldn't say," she says. "Ain't seen her myself."

She doesn't even see him move. The next thing she knows, she is on the ground and the side of her face burns as if it has been dipped in fire. She touches it gingerly. His shadow falls upon her. The sound of argument and movement in the camp falls away to silence. There is nobody in the world but the two of them.

"You think I am a fool?" he growls. "Where is she? Where is my nigger?"

Somehow, she still has the axe. Her grip tightens on the handle. She means to bury the blade in his stomach. As she is thinking this, a pistol appears in his hands. He draws the hammer back. "Asked you a question," he says.

She stares up at him. Spits blood. "You go to hell," she says.

The pistol comes up. She closes her eyes. She hears a gunshot.

Honey opens her eyes, surprised that she can. Colonel Moody is holding a revolver, the smoking barrel pointed to the tops of the trees. His gray eyes are fathomless. "That'll be *enough*, Captain," he says.

"My nigger's gone!" shouts Marse Jim. "My nigger's gone and this one knows where she went."

Moody turns those eyes on her now. "That true, Honey?"

Honey is surprised how frictionless and easy the lie feels. "No, sir. Done tol' the cap'n already, I ain't seed her all day. I'm just as surprised as he is that she gone."

Marse Jim's voice rises toward panic. "She's lying! Can't you see she's lying?" The gun in his hand waggles crazily.

Moody is cool. "Maybe she is," he says, "but you can't shoot the truth out of her, now can you?"

There is a moment, as a mad despair backlights Jim McFarland's shining, half-moon eyes, that she is certain he will try. "She's the only thing of value I still own in this world," he says, pleading.

"I understand," says Moody. "But Honey is the only thing *I* still own. Would you deprive me of my property because you have been deprived of yours? Where is the honor in that, Captain?"

She can see the words taking effect. His back stiffens. The gun comes down. The light in his eyes fades to a dull determination. "I've got to find where she went," he says.

"Maybe there's some clue in the cookhouse," says Moody amiably.

To Honey's horror, Marse Jim shambles into the little cabin where she lives. She can hear him banging around pans, throwing ladles aside. Then there is a horrible moment of silence and she knows. She just knows.

Belatedly she remembers to climb to her feet. As she does, Marse Jim appears, holding the newspaper above his head like a captured flag. "She's gone to Little Rock," he says. "Some buck put a notice in a nigger paper. She's gone off there to meet him."

Honey feels sick. She curses herself for not burning the paper.

"Are you sure?" asks Moody.

"Damn certain I'm sure," cries Marse Jim, holding the paper close to his eyes. "It's got my name in it and everything. Says big as life, 'She was the property of James McFarland.' That's me."

"So it is," says Moody. "Then your course is clear. You must go to Little Rock. Will you require assistance?"

"Against one runaway nigger?" Marse Jim's laugh is a bitter explosion. "No. I don't think so."

"Godspeed, then," says Moody.

Marse Jim turns and shambles off without another word. Moody holsters his pistol. He regards her for a moment. "I trust supper will not be unduly delayed because of this?" he asks.

In reply, she closes her eyes and conjures the image. The fear in Tilda's eyes that very morning as they stood in lamplight by the door. And then, the resolve. God grant that resolve will be enough to keep her safe.

Honey's body begins to shake. Tears sting the fresh bruise on her cheek. Her prayer is fervent and unspoken.

Run, Tilda.

Run.

Prudence's fingers lingered against the coarse stone, tracing the deeply ingrained letters. For years into the unknowable future, for decades of wind and rain and wear, they would tell the story of a life in a few spare, painfully inadequate words.

Bonnie Cafferty
Beloved sister
b. 1839 d. 1865

The tombstone stood among a long line of similar stones marking the resting places of the other 11 victims of what was already being called the Buford Massacre. Charles Wheaton had kept his word regarding the condition she set as the price of selling her property. It struck her that Wheaton was, in his way, an honorable man. It almost made her sorry for what she was about to do. But only almost.

Prudence sat on a bench facing the tombstone. She had paid a man to clean up the ramshackle little cemetery behind the church and he had done a fastidious job, clearing walkways, pruning trees, building benches. The graveyard might almost have been a park.

But it was indeed a graveyard, and she sat there, comfortably alone among the dead, the sun warm and welcome on her neck. It was a beautiful day. The sky was cloudless and endless. An occasional breeze moved playfully through the magnolia leaves above. Prudence withdrew her hand from the stone. She exhaled. It felt like the first time in years.

For two weeks now, she had spent every waking hour of every waking day going and doing. Up to Memphis to buy tickets from the steamship company and to negotiate with the Army and buy supplies. Down to the telegraph office, trading coded messages with her agent in Philadelphia.

In between, she had traveled the county, speaking to every colored woman or man who would give her an audience. She had addressed dozens at a time in their churches, had spoken to groups of three and four on back porches, in blacksmith shops, in fields.

Many of them tried to talk her out of it, told her it wouldn't work. She promised them it would. Some walked away shaking their heads at her foolishness. Others nodded contemplatively as if thinking maybe it could work, at that.

Prudence didn't know if it would work. She wondered secretly if the doubters were right, was gnawed by the fear that once again, she was asking colored people for their trust and once again, she would fail them. She kept her doubt hidden behind a determined face. Still, she wondered…

Prudence exhaled again. She regarded the stone for a moment. Birdsong drifted down from the magnolia branches.

"Hello, sister," she said. Her voice seemed unnaturally loud in the stillness. She cleared her throat. "Hello, sister," she said again, softer.

God, how she missed Bonnie. Doing this was hard enough. Doing it without Bonnie's help and wise counsel was almost intolerable.

"I suppose I simply wanted to say that I am sorry, first and foremost, for dragging you down here," she said. "Had I not done that, what happened to you would not have…would not have…it might have been I who…"

Her voice frayed and tore like rotted cloth. She stopped, took a breath, wiped at the tears. "Well," she said, "what I was going to say"—and she forced more energy into her voice—"is that I am sorry for everything that happened. And I am sorry, too, that it has taken me so long to come visit you. I simply could not bear it before. And now that I am finally here, I am here to say farewell. I am leaving in a few days. I do not believe I will ever return. I hate this place, Bonnie, and I hate leaving you here."

"But oh, sister…" Again, she had to pause, her voice trembling, going away from her. Prudence sniffled up tears. "Oh, sister," she said again, "know that no matter how far from this place I go, you will always travel with me in my heart."

A silence intervened. Prudence watched through glistening eyes as a tiny bird lit on a branch above her. It bounced under the weight. After a moment, the bird flew away. Prudence spoke again. "So much has happened," she said, "I barely know where to begin. I met a man—and lost him. It happened quite suddenly. Oh, Bonnie, you would have loved him. He was a colored man, if you can picture that of your sister. He was a good man, though. In fact, he was such a good man that he decided he could not be with me, decided he had to continue on with the mission that brought him here: to find his wife. He left me to go looking for her."

A sigh. "I tried to hate him for that, Bonnie. For a time, I believe I succeeded. But how could I, really? He gave me something I needed in a moment when I was at my lowest ebb. He gave me the caring touch of another human being. To tell you the truth, I feel I was blessed to hold him, if only for a few days.

"Besides," she added, "he was the one who gave me the idea for how to respond to the Wheatons and their ilk. It is such a good plan, Bonnie. It is bold and impractical...all the things you say that I am. I can imagine you would have had your doubts, you would have been cautious about it. But I think in the end you would have given in and been delighted to do so. I think you would have thought it fitting."

She laughed a little, still sniffling tears. From the front of the church, she heard the soft nickering of the horses. The driver she had hired was waiting for her in her new phaeton. A faint smell of pipe smoke drifted to her. Preacher Lee was in his church, poring over his Bible.

"And here is something I have not yet told you, sister, something Miss Ginny told me that I find so astonishing I have not even been able to make myself think about it. She says, if you can believe this, that I might be... colored or rather, part colored, I suppose.

"I know"—a melodic laugh—"is that not the most confounding thing you have ever heard? I do not know if I believe it. I do not know if I *want* to believe it. But at the same time, I cannot ignore the fact that it might be true. Ginny thinks my mother was not my real mother. Evidently Father sired a baby, a girl, with Ginny's daughter, and she thinks I might be that child. She says Father and this woman kept company for a time. To learn such a thing about your father, Bonnie, is...is..."

She was unable to fashion the words. Restless, her hands massaged one another. At length, she said, "I admired him so much, as you know. I thought him the most outstanding man in the world because of the way he fought against slavery. I wanted so much to be like him, Bonnie. I wanted so much to make him proud. Now I find what a hypocrite he was and I feel…"

She pursed her lips, gazed to the sky, made herself breathe. "Betrayed," she said finally. She chased it with a sigh. "I feel betrayed. I feel as if there is no longer anything in this world I can depend upon. It is a feeling I have had ever since we came here and learned that Cyrus Campbell was someone other than who I thought he was. And the feeling has only grown worse. I have lost my father—or at least, the man I thought my father was. I have lost you, I have lost Sam…"

Prudence wept without knowing. "I have lost myself," she said. "It is as if everything I love, everything I depend upon, I lose. I feel as if I am falling and helpless to make it stop. I do not know who I am anymore, Bonnie. I do not even know who I am."

The sound of her voice was pitiful in her own ears. Prudence had become the one thing she always scorned: weak. But she couldn't help herself. She no longer knew how to be anything else.

She remembered once when she and Bonnie had been girls, walking together in the Common on the first warm day after a wet and miserable winter. She had stopped, kneeling to inspect the carcass of a dead baby bird, now being swarmed over by ants. Bonnie, disgusted, had walked on. So absorbed was Prudence in watching the ants dissect the poor dead bird, chunk by tiny chunk, that it was a moment before the boys' voices reached her.

"Who said you could walk in our park, nigger?"

"What are you, lost? Get on back to your side of the Hill."

There were three of them, white boys surrounding Bonnie, their hands curled into fists, their little faces twisted by their own meanness. A few adults stood by, watching in tolerant amusement. It made her angry. But what absolutely infuriated 11-year-old Prudence was Bonnie's response. She was crying.

Prudence Cafferty, the terror of Louisburg Square, star hitter in a game called base ball, came to her feet running. She charged into the nearest boy, who never saw her coming. Even as he went down on his face, Prudence pivoted and decked the second boy with a roundhouse punch that would have done a dockworker proud. The boy she had tackled was coming to his feet, wailing through a bloody mouth. She gave a two-handed shove that sent him sprawling over his prone friend. Then she wheeled around for the third boy. He already had his palms raised in a gesture of surrender, his eyes twin moons. The boy took a few steps back, then spun around and ran for all he was worth. His friends stumbled to their feet and took off after him. Only then did Prudence unfist her hands.

Bonnie tried to hug her. "Oh, Prudence, thank you. I do not know what would have become of me had you not been there."

Prudence shoved her off. She raised a stiff index finger to Bonnie's hurt and disbelieving face. "You must never let them see you cry," she said. "*Never* let them see you cry."

And now, here she was, 15 years later, sitting at her sister's grave, crying. You could never tell where life would deliver you.

Time passed. Finally, when she knew she could avoid it no longer, Prudence rose. It was time to rejoin the day. One last time, her hand tarried on the stone marker beneath which Bonnie lay. Prudence pursed her lips, done crying for now.

"Farewell, sister," she said. And she walked away.

A stone path took her around the side of the little church to the yard in front where her phaeton was parked. Her driver, a rangy Negro boy of perhaps 17 named Curtis, was chatting with Preacher Lee. They stopped when they heard her coming. Preacher Lee, holding his pipe by the bowl, approached her. His smile was solicitous. "Are you all right, Mrs. Kent?" he asked.

"About as well as can be expected," she told him.

"I understands that," he said. "Ain' never easy, losin' a loved one." Pause. Then he said, "You know, I've heard some say you feel guilty for all that happened here. The riot and such, I mean. Is that true?"

She looked at him. "I suppose it is," she said. "Were it not for me, none of it would have happened."

He shook his balding head. "Uh-uh," he said. "You can't feel that way, Mrs. Kent. I can't let you. After all, weren't you had the idea of puttin' them mens in that school. If you remember, it was *me*."

It had been. Somehow, she had forgotten. "Well, yes," she began, "but—"

Another emphatic shake of the head. "No 'buts,' Miss. It was *my* idea. I'm the one give it to you. If anybody guilty for what happened, I expect it's me. And believe me, I done spent a many a night walkin' the floor and talkin' to Jesus about that. Expect I still got a few more to go. If it weren't for me, whole lot of trouble be avoided, whole lot of good people still be alive, startin' with your friend."

"You cannot take that all upon yourself," she said.

There was sad wisdom in his eyes. "Oh, but it be all right for you?" he said.

She didn't know what to say. She said nothing.

"Here's what I think," said Preacher Lee. "Maybe if we got to blame somebody, we ought to blame them what set fire to people's homes and hanged them in trees. That's who I think we need to blame, the same ones who even now pressin' forward to stir up more wickedness."

"You refer to the new ordinance."

"Yes, ma'am. They passed it last night, way I hear."

"It is a ridiculous law," said Prudence. "The provost will never suffer it to stand."

Preacher Lee shrugged. "He might. He might not. But here's the thing, Miss: what it tell you they even pass a law like that?"

"I do not understand," said Prudence.

"Well," he said, "think about it. Seem to me if I done been in a war and my side give out, I be bound to do what them who won the war want me to. Can't have my own way about things, 'cause I'se on the losin' side. Seem to me that's the natural way of things. But these rebs…" He shook his head.

"They seem not to realize they are the ones who were defeated, do they?"

"That's it exactly," said Preacher Lee. "Way they sees it, they just got beat. Ain't the same as bein' defeated." There was no amusement in his laugh. At length, he put the stem of the pipe in his teeth and gave a meditative pull. The boy, Curtis, watched them in big-eyed silence.

"Well," said Prudence, "as you know, I do not intend to allow them to get away with it."

"I knows about your plan," said Preacher Lee. "But it don't really change things, do it?"

"What do you mean?"

He allowed a puff of smoke to drift out of his mouth. "If you pull this thing off, it might teach this town a lesson sure 'nough, help the colored here in Buford. But ain't gon' do nothin' for the next town over or the town after that or the town after that."

Prudence was stung. "I cannot fix all of Dixie, Preacher. I am doing the best I can."

"I'm sorry, Mrs. Kent," he said. "Didn't mean to sound like I was findin' fault. You doin' the Lord's work. All I'm sayin' is, it gon' take more than that to cure what ails these rebs. They can't get it out they minds, can't get it out they *hearts*, that they's the ones God put here to rule over his dominion. If the Union Army couldn't get that out they heads, what you doin' ain't gon' change it."

"I am under no illusions about that," said Prudence. "But I am not trying to change them. I'm trying to pay them back."

"'Vengeance is mine, saith the Lord.' That's in the book."

"I know," said Prudence. "And I know it is unseemly. But if what I am doing inflicts a little discomfort on the lordly white masters of this town, I cannot say that I will lose any sleep over it."

He gave her a puckish smile. "Can't say I will neither." He drew on his pipe and did not speak for a moment, regarding her by the fading light of that mischievous grin. After a moment, the smile had burned itself out and he said, "You got a good heart, Mrs. Kent."

She felt herself blushing. "I do not know about that," she said.

"I do," he assured her.

Prudence was moved. She held out her hand. He grasped it lightly in his own. "You have a pretty good heart yourself, Preacher," she said.

He braced her as she climbed onto the phaeton. "Goodbye, Mrs. Kent," he said. "I'll see you soon."

She bade him farewell. Curtis turned the wagon back onto the dirt road that fronted the church and headed for Buford. In her mind, Prudence went wearily down a list of things yet to be done, even as her deadline ticked toward zero. She would make it, she promised herself. She had no alternative.

Twisting around in her seat, she watched the tiny church growing smaller, Preacher Lee turning to go back inside. And behind the humble building, the neat row of tombstones, 12 in all, names and dates carved deep to recall this story for generations not yet born.

Farewell, sister.

She turned in her seat, facing resolutely forward, and did not look back again.

Sam hitched Bucephalus to a railing outside the offices of *The Freedman's Voice*, which was housed in a little clapboard building where it shared walls with a general store on the one side and a law office on the other. He automatically put a kerchief to his nose; on the next block was a tannery whose stench hung over the entire area like a cloud. Through the paper's front window, he spied the man he was looking for: A.L. Jones, the publisher, sitting at his desk, poring over copy.

Abraham Lincoln Jones—until Emancipation, he had been just Isiah Jones—was an energetic young colored man with a wide, friendly smile, which he lifted toward the door now, as the tinkling of a bell fixed to the frame alerted him to Sam's entrance. Sam had come to like Jones in the week of their acquaintance. His naïve optimism reminded Sam of the man he himself had once been.

"Good morning, Sam," the younger man said.

"Morning, Abraham," said Sam. "Is there news?" He knew there wasn't, even before he asked. He had come here once a day now for seven days straight, ever since he placed the notice in the paper. Abraham knew how much finding Tilda meant to Sam. If there was news, he would have said it before Sam even opened his mouth.

Sure enough, a grimace curdled Abraham's affable features. "Afraid not," he said.

Sam nodded, stoic. Then the fatigue overtook him and he sighed. "Is there ever news?" he said.

"I don't understand."

"Of all the people who place notices in your paper, are any of them ever successful?"

"Occasionally," said Abraham, coming out from behind his desk. "Not very often. But what other choice is there? A small chance is better than no chance at all."

"You're right, I suppose," said Sam, feeling older than his very bones, "but I can no longer sit around Little Rock waiting."

"Where will you go?"

"I am not sure. I suppose I will go West."

"What should I do if we hear word?"

"I doubt that will happen," said Sam, "but if you do, I would appreciate it if you would wire a Mary Cuthbert through the Library Company of Philadelphia. I will write her to let her know I have taken the liberty of giving you her name and that I shall be checking in with her every month or so."

"You won't give up?" asked Jones, scratching the information down on a pad.

Sam shrugged. "I wish I could."

Abraham offered his hand. "I wish you good luck, then."

The handshake was warm. "Thank you," said Sam. "I wish you the same."

The bell on the door chimed again as Sam passed back through. Abraham felt a rare stab of melancholy as he watched his new friend lever himself laboriously up into the saddle, lift the special reins, and turn his horse west. He had a great hope for the future, did Abraham Lincoln Jones. It was why, when the Yankees took Little Rock, he used the money he had been saving to buy himself free to start the paper instead. He had an expectation that with shackles struck away, colored men would startle the world, achieve stupendous things, rise to heights scarcely dreamt during the time of bondage. It would happen with stunning speed, he believed, well within his lifetime. And he was determined to be part of it.

But all too often, his dream collided with a reality such as this, a good man wounded deep in his soul, doomed to spend the rest of his life locked into a quest that could not help but end in failure. How, Abraham wondered, could colored men achieve those stupendous things, rise to those heights scarcely dreamt, when slavery had left so many scars upon them?

Sam Freeman was an intelligent man with the potential for greatness. But that potential would never be realized because Sam had only one consuming passion: to get back what he had lost.

Abraham sighed. *Not all chains are visible*, he thought.

He was returning to his desk when the bell over the door chimed again. He looked up, already smiling, and found himself facing a colored woman. She was meanly clothed in a faded old dress. Sweat shone on her brow from some unknown exertion and her eyes were round with some unknown fear. "Can I help you, Miss?" he said.

She didn't speak. She looked around wildly, sweeping the tiny office with those panicky eyes. He had the impression of an animal in a cage. "Miss...?"

"There was a notice about me in the paper," she blurted finally.

"A notice?"

"It said Sam was looking for me. My name is Tilda."

He jerked to his feet like a puppet yanked by its master's strings. A moment. A moment to disbelieve, a moment to grasp for words, a moment to realize. And then Abraham Lincoln Jones was flying past the startled woman, through the door, racing down the mud-rutted street, screaming at the top of his lungs.

Sam thought he heard his name being yelled. He reined his horse and twisted around. To his surprise, Abraham was running full tilt after him. Sam tried to imagine what could be wrong, what dire thing could have sent the young man hurtling down the street so madly. When his friend reached him, Sam said, "What is it? What is wrong?"

Abraham tried to speak, but his voice came out of him in a gusty, indecipherable wheeze. He doubled over, hands on his knees, mouth hanging open like a fish, spittle dripping off in a long chain.

Alarmed, Sam said, "Abraham, are you all right?"

Still unable to speak, Abraham pointed in reply, his finger stabbing back toward the newspaper office. Mystified, Sam looked. He saw nothing. The tannery men in their rough jeans, going to work. The lawyer, waddling off in search of lunch. A wagon rolling away, muck flying from its wheels. A boy and his father walking together, talking animatedly. A woman standing in front of the newspaper office gazing their way. Nothing.

No, not nothing. A woman.

Sam squinted. He turned the horse.

A woman. Hard to make out at this distance, but she could have been, could almost have been... He urged the horse forward a couple of steps, stopped again.

He had grown so used to thinking of her as something remembered, something dreamt, and hoped, but not something real, something tangible and flesh. So he stared at her with the purposeful scrutiny you give a mirage. But she didn't waver like a trick of the heat. She was real. And yes, she looked like, she could have been, could almost have been...

Oh, God.

She was.

He stopped breathing.

She *was.*

Dazedly, he spurred his horse forward at a walk. He wanted to gallop, wanted to shout, but he felt as if he were floating through a dream. The street receded, the world went away. There was only her, drawing closer now, and him, his heart filled with feelings he didn't even have words to name.

He reined the horse a few feet short of her, climbed down, took the time to loop his reins over the railing.

"Sam?" she said.

"Tilda?" he said. "My God, is that you?"

He stood close to her, not daring to touch her for fear she might somehow prove to be a stray wisp of his mad imaginings. He did not trust that he was not really asleep in a field just outside of town, wrapped in yet another dream that would break his heart when he awoke.

But she was beautiful. Time and fears and stress and ache showed in her face, yes. It had been fifteen years. But she was beautiful, still.

"What happened to your arm?" she asked.

"My arm?" He glanced over, having completely forgotten, and was momentarily surprised to see the stump of a limb hanging from his left shoulder. "It was shot off," he said.

"In the war?"

He shook his head. "I came through the war without a scratch," he said. "This happened a couple months ago, while I was walking through Virginia, Tennessee, somewhere in there. Somebody shot me. They thought I was somebody else."

"You were walking?"

He nodded. "I walked all the way from Philadelphia, Tilda. I came down here looking for you. And oh God, I've found you!"

Then he couldn't stop himself. He took her in his embrace. And for all the hardship he'd had since being shot, for all the difficulty of learning to dress himself, open a bag, climb atop a horse with but a single limb, he had never felt the loss of his arm more painfully than he did right in that instant. Because he needed two arms to do justice to what he was feeling, two arms to pull this woman close, pull her into him, two arms for an embrace as enduring as his love.

Sam felt tears massing behind his eyes. Joy tears. Sorrow tears. Crazy, mixed-up tears.

Then he realized: she had stiffened at his embrace. Now she was pushing him gently, but firmly, away. Sam pulled back, mystified. She met his eyes.

"We've got to go," she said. "Now."

"I do not understand," he said.

"Marse Jim will be looking for me. He'll come after me."

"He is not your master anymore. Have you not heard? The war is over."

Her great beauty twisted itself into a smirk that derided him. "You think Marse Jim cares about any of that?"

"He must care! *The war is over.* There are no more slaves and no more masters."

Now she shouted it. "You're not listening to me! I said, *he doesn't care!* As long as I'm living, I'm his property, I'm his slave. That's how he sees it."

"Then we shall make him care," said Sam.

"No," she said, in a voice that did not allow for contradiction. "You shall get killed. That's what will happen. You'll get us *both* killed." She grabbed his hand in both of hers and her eyes were wild with pleading. "You don't know him, Sam, but I do. We've got to get away."

In his mind, Sam kept trying to work it like a math problem. But he couldn't get the sums to line up. The war was over. Emancipation was the law of the land. How could this Jim McFarland, or *any* man, still think he had the right to hold someone in bondage? It was madness. It made no sense.

In his confusion, Sam cast about him for help. He found himself sharing a look with Abraham Jones, who had come up without Sam's noticing. Jones's face mirrored Sam's own disbelief. Then the younger man shrugged.

And that, too, mirrored something in Sam: a recognition that ultimately, he had no choice.

"All right," he said. "We shall go. We shall go right now."

For the first time, she smiled. It was small and it was bruised, but it was hopeful, too, and relieved. All in all, thought Sam, her smile was one of the saddest and most beautiful things he had ever seen.

"Can you ride?" he asked.

She nodded. He braced her as best he could as she climbed into the saddle. When she was seated, he went to Abraham and offered his hand. "I want to thank you again," he said. "Thank you for everything. Were it not for you..." He let the thought peter away, unable to speak the words.

Abraham shook his hand. "Take care of yourself, my friend," he said, through his big smile. "Take care of *her*."

"I will," said Sam.

Abraham glanced up at Tilda. "I see why you were unwilling to give up on her," he said, and mischief had entered his smile.

Sam shook his head. "No you don't," he said. "There is more. There is much more."

He clapped Abraham on the shoulder, then went around and muscled himself up on the horse behind Tilda. Her face was tense, her eyes scanning the street. Well, soon enough they would be gone and she could put the fear behind her. He reached around and took the reins, turned the horse, and went down the street at a trot.

Abraham Lincoln Jones watched after them until they had disappeared and then for a few minutes more after that. Maybe he had been wrong about Sam Freeman. He had thought Sam too wrought up in a useless quest to ever be of much use to the race. But maybe there was no quest more important than to simply return to the embrace of love. And maybe, in his hopefulness and his stubborn perseverance, both of them now vindicated by the miracle Jones had just seen, Sam offered the race an example that would be invaluable in coming days.

At least, thought Jones with a private smile, that was how he would write the story. He pulled out his watch. If he hurried, he just had time to get it in the next paper.

For the next few hours, Jones worked at his desk, writing out the account of meeting Sam, helping him place his notice, secretly feeling that here was an impossible quest, then Tilda showing up in the offices of *The*

Freedman's Voice, his own mad dash down the street, and finally, the touching conclusion, the moment when the star-crossed lovers were reunited after 15 long years.

He would have to punch that part of the narrative up a bit, he thought, his pen flying across paper. Was it simply his imagination, or hadn't the woman Tilda seemed more filled with fear of this "Marse Jim" character than with joy of seeing Sam again?

No matter. In the narrative, her happiness at being unexpectedly returned to her one true love would leap off the page. He would see to it.

It was after six and the streets outside had cleared away to emptiness by the time he was done writing and typesetting. The headline told the tale:

Former Bondman Finds His Truelove (With the Help of The Voice).

It made him smile to think of how the story would give hope to so many people. He couldn't wait until it was in the paper. He was eager for their reactions.

Jones was reaching for his composing stick when he heard the door open. He came around the printing press, wearing the ink-smeared apron he always wore when putting the paper together, and found himself facing a smelly, unshaven white man who regarded him with naked malice from beneath the brow of his slouch hat.

The white man had a rifle cradled in one arm and with his free hand, he held up a copy of *The Freedman's Voice*. "You the one publishes this rag?" His voice was like rocks in a barrel.

Jones made himself smile. "I am A.L. Jones," he said, "just as it says on the window. And who might you be, sir?" But he already knew, instinctively, who this white man was, and his eyes grazed the pistol he kept under the counter. From where he stood, Jim McFarland couldn't see it. Jones wondered if he could reach it without arousing suspicion.

"I am Captain James McFarland," said the white man. "You took something that belongs to me, and I'll have it back."

Jones freshened the smile. "I'm sure I have no idea what you're talking about, sir," he said, coming forward as naturally as he could manage.

"That's far enough," said McFarland. He gestured with the rifle, not even bothering to move it from the crook of his arm, where it nestled in gleaming dark malice.

"I was just going to ask if you were sure you had the right place," said Jones, eyes darting toward the pistol.

"Don't toy with me, nigger. I got the right place, all right."

Still smiling, Jones said, "Well, then, perhaps you'd be good enough to tell me what it is I am supposed to have taken from you."

"Nigger wench. Goes by the name Tilda. Some buck looking for her put a notice in your paper. Next thing I know, she's disappeared."

Jones scratched his chin. "Tilda? I'm sorry, sir, name doesn't ring a bell."

Jim McFarland's voice was thunder from a cloudless sky, a blast that startles all the more for having come out of nowhere. "I told you don't *toy* with me!" he roared. "Think I'm a fool, nigger? Now you got one chance to keep your head on them shoulders of yours: tell me where they went. Tell me everything you know."

Jones swallowed, then found his smile again. "Well, sir," he said, "perhaps if you be kind enough to show me the notice." Desperate. Playing for time. The pistol under the counter just a step or two away.

McFarland gave him a look of dark suspicion, then slammed the paper down. Jones was grateful for that, because it gave him an excuse to come forward to the counter. His left hand finally closed on the reassuring shape of the pistol grip even as he studied the notice with feigned concentration.

"Oh, yes sir," he said. "I remember this. A Mr. Sam Freeman placed this ad a week ago. Said he was lookin' for this woman, Tilda. He waited around town for 'most a week, come in here every day to check if I heard any answer, which I haven't. He came for the last time yesterday, say he wasn't going to tarry 'round here any longer. Said he's going back home."

"Where's that? Home?"

"Philadelphy," said Jones.

McFarland pondered this. Jones wondered if there was a way to pull back the hammer of the pistol without the white man hearing. Maybe he could shoot him without the raising the gun, shoot him right through the counter. The pistol was slimy in his grip.

McFarland said, "You're lying."

"What do you mean, sir?" He gave the white man the roundest eyes he could.

"I mean, no buck comes all the way down here, goes through all that time and trouble looking for a woman, and stays for only six days. No, he's here. He's either in Little Rock or someplace close, but he sure ain't gone to Philadelphy. Not yet. She means too much to him."

"Well, sir, I can't say as I'd know. All I do is take the money and put the notice in the paper." Still smiling.

"What about the woman? She come in here?"

"No, sir. Haven't seen a woman in here all day. Sure would like to, though. Make the day go faster." He hoped his smile suggested lascivious thoughts. A certain kind of white man, he had found, liked it when colored men spoke sex to them. He was reasonably sure this foul-smelling reb was one of them.

But Jim McFarland barely seemed to hear him. To Jones's horror, he was picking idly through the items strewn across his desk. One of them was the tablet on which he had written out the new story for tomorrow's front page. He could still see the lead in his head: "Two star-crossed lovers, both former slaves, were reunited yesterday in Little Rock and your own *Freedman's Voice* played a critical role." And further down, it told how Sam had spent three months walking in the South looking for Tilda, how he had sojourned recently in a town called Buford, in Mississippi.

His lungs stopped sucking down air. He saw McFarland snatch up the tablet. He saw the white man's lips moving, reading the story. Then he saw the piggish eyes abruptly narrow. McFarland's head was coming up, the rifle was rising, his mouth was already curled around whatever cruel triumph he was about to yell.

Hurry.

Jones's hand fumbled for the pistol and he brought it up, cocking the hammer as it came. He managed to clear the desk, managed to sight the center mass of the man before him. He had time to see McFarland's eyes go wide. All he had to do was pull the trigger.

But the blast that filled the small space came from Jim McFarland's rifle instead.

The bullet ripped through Jones like fire. Felt like it had taken his shoulder off. His legs turned in a corkscrew motion, twisting around one another, and he went down to the floor, which was littered with scrap paper and stray pieces of type. He found himself at eye level with the spittoon he never used. There was blood everywhere. Jones thought he might vomit. His heart thumped heavily in his ears.

Then he heard McFarland's measured steps, coming around the counter.

All Jones could see of him was his boots, gray with age, brown with muck. Jones's left hand sought his right shoulder, the pistol dropped somewhere and forgotten. The hand touched something spongy and wet, embedded with sharp edges that he supposed were bone. If he lived, he thought, he would surely lose the arm.

But he didn't think he would live.

"Almost had me goin', boy," said McFarland, kneeling into Jones's field of vision. "Guess I forgot what natural liars niggers can be."

Jones's leg kicked, a spasm. "So he went back to Buford, eh?" said McFarland. "Well, that works out just fine for me, I suppose. Been thinkin' about goin' back home anyway. Be able to kill two birds with one stone."

Jones's leg spasmed again, and this time didn't stop. Lying on the floor, he danced a macabre jig to music only his leg could hear. He tried to speak, but the sounds he made were nothing like language. Blood bubbled, coppery and hot, on his lips.

McFarland stood. He prodded Jones's wrecked shoulder with the toe of his boot. "Could have spared yourself all this," he said. "Should have told me where they went."

He stepped out of Jones's view. Jones heard his feet scraping across the floor, doing what, he could not guess. For a moment there was silence, but for the knocking of his own leg as it bounced madly against the floor.

Then, in a distracted voice to himself, Jim McFarland spoke the last words Abraham Lincoln Jones would ever hear. "Need to get me a horse," he said.

"Where are we going?"

They were an hour out of Little Rock. This was the first time she had spoken to him unprompted since they left Abraham Lincoln Jones standing in front of his newspaper office. The realization that he had no answer took Sam by surprise.

For three months, he had been driven forward, whipped by a single imperative: *find her*. Thinking beyond that had never even occurred to him. Now here she was, real and in the flesh and *there*, asking the obvious question. He gave the first answer that entered his head, hoping it sounded like something he had planned all along.

"We are going North to Philadelphia," he said. "I was recently employed at a library there and perhaps I can get my situation back. That is," he added cautiously, "if you are of a mind to travel that far."

"Philadelphia would be fine," she said. "Marse Jim hates the North. He will never come looking for me there."

"What does it matter if he does?" asked Sam. "I keep telling you: the North won the war. He has no legal authority over you."

She snickered. "Legal authority," she said. And then, she said nothing more.

Sam's first thought was to ask what she meant. He chose silence instead. It seemed wiser. No, it seemed *safer*.

Silence had ridden hard between them all the way out of Little Rock. It occurred to him that he was riding with a stranger. Once, he had known her so intimately. Once, the contours of her face, her breasts, her mind, had been as familiar to him as the breath in his lungs. Now she had become this...*foreigner*, as distant and unknowable as the moon.

For this, he had walked a thousand miles, lost his arm, been beaten and stabbed? Sam pursed his lips to keep the questions inside.

They ambled east in the silence. Another hour passed. Sam lost himself in wondering where they would stop for the night. If they were fortunate, they would find an abandoned barn, or perhaps even a colored family that didn't mind taking in strangers. If they were not fortunate, they would be obliged to sleep in a clearing or a field somewhere.

"Would you be willing to take me to the place where Luke died?"

The sound of her voice surprised him. She had turned in the saddle and was looking up at him. Her eyes were disconcerting.

"Likely, it will be difficult to find," he said. The mention of their dead son unsettled him. He wondered, guiltily, if this was the moment she would cry and accuse him of getting their boy killed. He braced for it, but it didn't come. All she said was, "Would you be willing to try? I would like to see it."

He heard himself say yes. And he realized, somewhat to his surprise, that he wanted to see it, too.

They stopped for the night an hour later. For a dollar drawn from the dwindling supply of coins Prudence had given him, a colored widow in a little town without a name allowed them to use one of her two rooms, moving her two children into the other room for the night. She fed them a dinner of poke salad and beans.

In the room, Tilda went straight to the bed and stretched out on her back, eyes closed. Sam didn't even consider joining her. He used the haversack as a pillow and laid himself on the rough boards of the floor. After a moment, he heard Tilda snoring lightly. He lay awake, wondering if this were not all a mistake.

Love never fails.

He reminded himself of this. But still, he wondered.

Morning came. The woman fixed them corn cakes and eggs. Before Sam and Tilda set off, she stuffed a few extra corn cakes in Sam's haversack for lunch. They set out at an easy pace. Sam was worried about tiring the horse, which now had to bear the weight of two.

Another long, silent time passed. Finally Sam had had enough. He said, "I do not recall you being so quiet."

"Fifteen years is a long time," she said.

He waited for her. When she didn't say anything more he said, "And what does that mean?"

"It means what it says," she said. "Fifteen years is a long time. Many things change."

Many things change.

Three words and suddenly, it was if his heart had fallen out of his chest. From the first day he set out upon this quest, he had cautioned himself not to hope, even a little, that they could restore what had once existed between them, had told himself he was looking for her only because he owed her that much. But he realized now that he must have been hoping without even knowing he was doing it, because her words made him dizzy with pain. He wondered if he was about to become Ben standing in that alley, trying to laugh the truth away even as the hope that had sustained him for so many hard miles spilled like water around him.

It crushed him to think maybe now the same thing was happening to him. It crushed him to think maybe she did not love him anymore.

Sam swallowed. "'Many things change,'" he repeated, and his voice sounded log hollow in his own ears. "What does that mean?"

"Nothing," she said. "Never mind."

He persisted. He couldn't help himself. "I just wish to know to what you are referring. I believe I have the right to—"

That was as far as he got. She spun around, her face close to his in the confines of the saddle, her eyes hateful, her features razored. "I have been *raped* and I have been *beaten*!" she cried. "Do you hear me? Raped and beaten over and *over* again! I am *sorry* if I am not very amusing company for you, Sam Prentiss or Sam Freeman or whatever it is you call yourself now. But I am afraid I don't feel very sociable these days! Do you understand? Is that all right with you?"

Sam's mouth opened to release a stunned silence. It must have satisfied her, because she turned back, her hands pinned beneath her arms, her head hunched down as if against a stark, cold wind. She looked as if she wanted to curl up inside herself, crawl into the shadows, and die. A silence intervened. Then she spoke again.

"And if you were thinking we might lie together, if that is why you came after me"—her voice was stripped like bark from a tree down to some grim and plain essence of itself—"you can forget it. If that was your intention, Sam, we can part company here and I will walk. I swear I will."

"That was not my intention," he said. And it wasn't. He spoke these words absently. The truth is, he barely heard her. He'd barely heard anything—not words, not cawing of crows, not clopping of horse's hooves—since she'd spoken those stunning, poisonous words that should not have surprised him but somehow did anyway.

Raped and beaten. Over and over again.

And why not? Why should this be a shock? Miss Prentiss had never allowed that sort of thing on her place, but that didn't mean it didn't happen. Of *course* it happened. Only the fact that they had been spoiled by a mistress who believed in treating even colored people like people had ever allowed him to forget that. But then, Tilda had been sold to this James McFarland person and her luck had changed and she had lost the luxury of forgetting. Apparently, this McFarland had practiced every form of cruelty and mistreatment they had previously been fortunate enough to escape. And Tilda had suffered that without him. Suffered it alone.

He gazed down at her shoulders, wanted to touch them, but did not. She seemed…shrunken. Her chin was on her chest and she still held herself tightly as if afraid she might otherwise unravel, the shreds and tangles of her unspooling all over this delta land east of Little Rock.

"I am sorry," he heard himself say.

If she heard, she gave no indication. Seen from behind, she might have been carved from stone. Sam fell silent. And in silence, they passed the remains of the day. They rode past mangled train tracks and blooming fields. They forded streams whose cold, clear water grazed the horse's belly. It was just before twilight when they reached the broad brown back of the Mississippi and paid a ferryman to take them across. They made camp in a clearing that night.

Sam fashioned four poles from sapling limbs and set them out in the river. When he checked the lines an hour later, he'd caught three catfish. Sam gutted them and cooked them over a fire while Tilda watched. When they were done eating, Sam handed Tilda his bedroll, which he had purchased in Little Rock. He gave it without a sound and she accepted it the same way. Sam lay on his back in the summer grass, folded his arm across his chest, and slept.

He awoke in the morning to find her watching him. Her eyes were intent, as if she were struggling with a puzzle she couldn't quite figure out. When she saw him looking at her, she yanked her eyes away and busied herself scraping a mud spot on her dress.

"We should reach the spot today," Sam told her. Her eyes questioned him. "The spot where Luke died," he amended.

A hard look he couldn't read settled upon her face. He produced the last of the dried meat he had bought in Little Rock and they had it for breakfast.

When they were done eating, Sam began saddling Bucephalus. As he worked, his thoughts turned themselves toward practical matters. What kind of shape was Tilda in? Could she take a long, hard journey across country on horseback? Especially living hand to mouth, as such a journey would require?

He could, he supposed, go to Buford—it wasn't far—and ask Prudence for help. She would not have left for Boston yet, and she probably wouldn't turn them away.

But Prudence had already done so much. He already owed her more than he could ever repay. Could he really go now and ask her to help him and the woman for whom he had abandoned her? He played that conversation over in his head a half dozen times. He could not find a way to make it work.

So they were on their own then. Fine. He would figure something out. Sweating from the exertion of cinching the girth with his one hand, he stood, his hand absently stroking the horse's neck. Lost in thought, he didn't hear Tilda behind him, didn't know she was there until she placed her hand atop his. Startled, he turned, and nearly tumbled over into the brown eyes that looked up at him.

"I am sorry," she said. "I had no cause to speak to you that way. Yesterday, I mean."

"It is all right," he said. "I understand."

"Do you?" she took her hand away. "How can you? I am not sure I understand myself."

"I just meant that I took no offense. You have the right to be"—pause, reaching for a word that made sense, finding none—"vexed."

Her eyebrow lifted and he thought she almost smiled. "Vexed? Is that what I am?"

"Angry," he said. "Hurt, furious, sad…" A sigh. "You tell me, Tilda. I do not know."

"Nor do I," she said. "So much has happened. I barely know how to understand it all." Her gaze sharpened and she regarded him closely. "Why did you come down here, Sam?" she asked.

"You already know why," he said. "I came here for you. All those years, I tried not to think about you, because thinking about you hurt too much. I had to make myself believe you did not exist. But then, when I heard them firing off for the surrender, all I could think about was you. I could no more make myself stop than I could sprout wings and fly. That is when I knew I had to come down here. I quit my job the next day."

"How did you think you would ever find me?"

"I had no idea. I only knew that I had to try."

She didn't answer. She looked at him for a very long time and he had that sense again, of her eyes trying to work out a puzzle whose pieces just didn't fit. Finally she said, "That's a long way to walk."

"It was about a thousand miles," he said.

"Long way," she repeated. She shook her head and went to fold up the bedroll.

When she was done, Sam helped her climb into the saddle and they were off. They traveled east at a moderate pace. Sam walked part of the way, leading the horse, in order to give the animal a break. Sam's knee was stronger now, his limp barely perceptible. The ache in his foot remained, but it had become a normal part of his body.

Tilda still didn't speak much, so Sam spoke to her. He had the impression that she enjoyed—no, that she *appreciated*—his talking to her.

So he told her how Miss Prentiss had sold him to a speculator 15 years ago who, in turn, sold him to a planter in Louisiana. The planter, impressed by Sam's bearing, had made him a butler. Sam was on that place for seven years, holding coats, fetching cigars, dusting balustrades, serving soups. The planter had seemed quite fond of him.

It was a good life for a slave. Sam slept in the big house, supervised the household staff, ate the same food his master ate, albeit at a table in a corner of the kitchen. His new master trusted him, right up until the night Sam climbed out his bedroom window and ran for freedom.

"I never gave up on wanting to be free," he told Tilda, as he led the horse past a field where colored men chopped cotton, their arms gleaming with sweat, their hoes rising and falling in ceaseless rhythm.

He had known better what he was doing this time, he told her. He painstakingly made contacts on the underground railroad. And so it was, hiding in cellars and crates, riding in false-bottomed hay wagons, he slipped inexorably north until that dark, moonless night a ferryman took him across the Ohio River. From Kentucky into Ohio. From slavery into freedom.

He had stood there on the banks of the river facing south, facing the land of his lifelong captivity. He had listened as the water lapped at the ferryman's retreating barge, watched as the ferryman's lamp grew smaller until it was swallowed by darkness. He had wept.

For a few years, he told her, he had lived quietly in Ohio, where he found work as a stevedore. Then the war broke out. He yearned to fight from its beginning, but it took two long years before the Union began recruiting colored men. Finally, Sam had gone to Philadelphia to enlist, had seen action, then had taken ill with a wasting disease and been sent back to Philadelphia to die, but somehow lived instead, with Mary Cuthbert's help. And there his life had stood until the news came that the war had ended, and on a day's notice, he had abandoned everything to come looking for her.

"I should have come sooner," he said.

"How could you have done that?" she asked. "You were a runaway. They would have captured you and taken you back."

"Still, I should have tried," he said. "When I think of what you were going through while I was reading books in a Philadelphia rooming house…"

"It is not your fault," she told him.

"Yes, but…"

"It is *not* your fault," she said again, staring down at him for emphasis.

In his mind, he knew she was right. But his mind had no power to convince his heart. His heart had but one response to every line of reasoning he tried to put forward, one answer it gave with pitiless insistence.

Raped and beaten. Over and over again.

Raped.

Beaten.

Over and over again.

God.

He tried to imagine what she had gone through, but he couldn't. He realized that in some cowardly corner of his being, the failure made him glad. He hated this McFarland with a sudden intensity that vibrated him like a tuning fork. Look what he had done, this slave owner, this trader in human souls. He had killed Tilda in every way except actual body. Had killed the sureness, the quick laughter, the deep compassion and loving warmth of her, and left in their place only this cold, mute stranger who regarded the world with an almost animal wariness.

Sam had never felt this way about any man. He had not even known it was possible to feel this way, to be filled with so much loathing. And he knew with a sudden stark certainty that he would kill this man if he ever got the chance, would do it happily and without hesitation.

But he would never have that chance, would he? The realization left a hard little knot of disappointment in his throat. He swallowed. "Tell me about him," he said.

"About who?" she asked.

"This McFarland person."

She stiffened. "I would rather not," she said. "No good can come from talking about that one. It only makes me sad and reminds me of days I would rather not recall."

"All right," he said. He should have known better, he thought. He should have known she would find the thought of him too painful to bear.

A minute passed. Then she said. "I will tell you this much, because I think you need to know: he will not give me up without a fight. You keep saying how he has no legal authority to take me back, now the war is over and slavery is done. What you do not understand is that those kinds of things mean nothing to Jim McFarland. That is not the way he thinks.

"He was always bad, but toward the end of the war, he saw his little boy killed by a group of Yankee raiders, and I think it unhinged him. He is not right in his head, Sam, do you understand? He refuses to let go—maybe he *can't* let go—of the idea that colored people are slaves, always. *Always*, you hear me? No matter what the government or the law says. And if you will not be his slave, then he will kill you, pure and simple. I *saw* him do it, Sam. When we got word of the surrender, Wilson and Lucretia, two young ones sweet on each other, thought they might go away and have a life on their own. He tracked them down like some kind of bloodhound and shot them in cold blood, shot them down like mad dogs. I *saw* him do this, Sam."

He met her eyes, which were earnest and wide. "He is searching for me, Sam. I guarantee it. Do you have a gun?"

Sam said, "No." Then, remembering, he amended. "Well, I have a little derringer a friend gave me." He patted the bag hanging from his belt. "I keep it in here."

"If he comes upon us, you must be prepared to shoot him without hesitation. Do you hear me? Do not try to talk to him, do not try to reason with him. Just shoot him if you see him. Do you understand?"

Her intensity shook him. "Yes," he said. "I understand."

Her eyes questioned his. Then, apparently satisfied with what she had seen, she turned back, once again pinioning her hands beneath her arms. He left her alone with her thoughts.

It was early afternoon when they reached the Prentiss plantation. Orienting himself from there, Sam turned the horse off the road and into the woods. He was back in the saddle by now and the sun, when it managed to pierce the latticework covering of leaves overhead, warmed the left side of his face; thus he knew they were traveling north. The woods were different seen in daylight 15 years later, but he was certain this was the route he had traveled with Luke.

They rode in silence for hours into the deep woods, into a past that was never far enough from Sam's memory. His son, his handsome, spirited son in whom was met the best of Tilda and Sam, had paced him through these trees, following the North Star shining on the handle of the little drinking gourd in the sky.

How eager Luke had been to be free. How impatiently he had listened in the days before they ran, as his mother raised objection after objection, demanded to know why they couldn't just be happy with a mistress who treated them well.

Well treated or not, Sam would say, they were still slaves. Then he quoted the Frenchman: "'No man has received from nature the right to give orders to others.'"

She would just roll her eyes and say, "I'm sorry I ever taught you to read."

But their son, their beautiful Luke, would listen, enraptured, drinking in the words like icy water on a scalding day. And when they had run, he had done so with abandon, leaping ahead as if he could not wait to be free. He was every inch his father's son. And it had gotten him killed.

Here.

Sam had wondered if he would recognize the spot when he saw it. Now as he reined the horse in a sun-splashed clearing, he realized all at once that he need not have worried. The stain this place had made upon his memory was indelible. Awkwardly, he climbed down. The soil was spongy beneath his feet.

Tilda said, "Sam?"

He said, "It happened right here."

Her eyes rounded. She slipped down off the horse, stood next to him. Sam pointed. "We were sleeping right there," he said. "The slave catchers came through there and woke us. Luke tried to run and a trigger-happy fool shot him. He fell right there, near that log."

Sam half expected to see his son's bones still scattered about the spot where he died, his skull grinning at them as if in macabre greeting. But apparently, someone had retrieved the body and buried it. Perhaps Miss Prentiss had it done.

Tilda was walking slowly about the clearing as if in a daze, as if she no longer knew herself or her surroundings. She gazed around and Sam had the impression she was memorizing this place. Then she paused, facing him. "Did he suffer?" she asked.

Sam shook his head. "No," he said, "it was quick."

She nodded, paced around some more. Sam stood, holding the reins of the horse, watching her. None of it felt quite real. He had the odd sense of having stepped back through a rip in time. He half expected to see himself and Luke sleeping on the ground, to hear the thunder of hooves as the slave catchers came upon them, to watch Luke lunge for freedom, to live the most awful moment of his life all over again.

He found himself struggling to breathe. Then Tilda went to her knees on the spot where Luke had fallen. Her head sagged. After a moment, she began to cry. Her shoulders shook.

Sam went to her, stood behind her. He rested his hand lightly on the back of her neck.

"He was such a good baby," she said. "Do you remember?"

"I remember."

"He never cried nor fussed the way other babies do. But Lord, that boy was so busy, once he learned to scoot around on his own. He wanted to see everything, explore everything, get into everything. You had to be constantly looking out for that one, otherwise, there was no telling where he might end up." The memory made her laugh a little. Then laughter turned back to crying.

Sam heard himself say, "I am sorry." He didn't recognize his voice. It felt heavy and lifeless in his throat. Then he realized he was weeping.

"I am sorry," he said again. "I should never have filled his head with that foolishness about being free. I should have listened to you. Miss Prentiss was not so bad, really. There were many others who were a great deal worse. I should never have run and I should never have taken our boy. You were right. We should have stayed there with you."

She didn't answer right away and Sam wondered if he had hurt her by bringing up the old arguments of so long ago. He was braced for her to scream at him, to jump to her feet, wheel around and slap him hard. Instead, she spoke quietly and said something he did not expect. "No, Sam, *you* were right. You and that Frenchman you used to always quote. 'No man has received from nature the right to give orders to others.' I think I was just too scared to see."

She looked up at him, holding him with her eyes. "I don't blame you for what happened to our son," she said. "Oh, perhaps I did when it first happened. But I was so angry then, Sam, so hurt. I thought I was losing my mind with the pain of knowing my baby was gone. It took me *years*, but after a while, I realized: I cannot blame you, because it was not your fault. *You* were right. It is slavery that was wrong. Maybe belonging to Marse Jim helped me understand that."

After all these years of hating himself for what had happened, all these years wrestling with guilt and shame and now, to hear those words...

It was not your fault.

...he couldn't...he didn't...

You were right. Slavery was wrong.

His mouth fell open, his thoughts fell silent. And all at once, his legs went wobbly and loose until they gave way, no longer capable of supporting his weight. Sam Freeman felt something go out of him then, felt something lift off of him, and without meaning to, he sank to his knees next to Tilda.

Kneeling in the spot where their son had died, Sam held his wife, she held him, and together they cried for a long time.

Three hours later, their shadows dragging behind them, Sam and Tilda walked side by side down a dusty road, Sam leading the horse. They didn't speak much, but this silence was not hard and somber like what had sat between them since Little Rock. This was a silence shared, not imposed, a silence made of contemplation.

Sam felt so many feelings at once he couldn't even name them all. But they coalesced into a rough-hewn hope, a sense that maybe the future, which had always seemed so bleak and endless to him, might actually hold something else entirely, might even hold some hard-earned measure of happiness. They had done the thing that frightened him most, and they had emerged holding one another, giving one another strength.

It made him think, for the first time in a very long time, that anything was possible, anything could happen.

Anything at all.

"Nigger!"

It shattered his reverie like glass. A hateful word, a guttural voice.

Sam was still turning when the pistol barked and he felt something punch him hard in the ribs.

Tilda screamed, the horse bolted, and he heard himself thinking distractedly that the animal would never have made a good cavalry mount. Too easily spooked. Then, the ground came up to catch him. He found himself looking up at a slovenly white man in a slouch hat who stepped out now from where he had been waiting for them among the trees at the side of the road. This, then, was Jim McFarland. Sam realized bitterly that for all Tilda had told him about this man, *warned* him about this man, he had not truly listened. He had still managed to walk blithely into ambush.

He ordered himself up, ordered himself to his feet, but his body was not listening to orders anymore. It wouldn't move. He could only lie there watching as the man came forward. Tilda was kneeling at Sam's side now, pulling at him, tugging at him. Her mind was gone. She was screaming something that was no longer words. McFarland glanced at her with a terrible contempt. Then he swung the back of his closed fist at her head and she flew away.

Get up! Sam ordered. But still his body refused to obey. His wife was about to be taken from him by this animal.

Raped. And beaten. Over and over again.

There was not a blessed thing he could do about it. Sam had never known a sense of failure so utter and complete, not even when his son was killed.

McFarland stood over him, sighted down the pistol. "Nigger," he said again, in that awful, scraping voice of his. "You think you can take my property and get away with it?"

Sam's hand sought the bag tied to his belt. His fingers fumbled about looking for it, kept closing on emptiness. He sighed, felt death rattling in his chest as he did. It had been a long shot at best, a long shot bordering on wishful stupidity, the idea that he could open the bag, seize the little gun, and fire it before McFarland pulled the trigger. But he couldn't even feel the bag, and didn't that speak volumes about the uselessness of his entire goddamned existence?

Sam's fingers stopped fumbling for the missing bag. He met McFarland's burning gaze with open eyes and a strange calm and waited for the gunshot.

It came.

It was not what he expected, not an echoing blast that followed him down into oblivion. No, it was a flat pop, not unlike the breaking of a child's balloon. And now there was a tiny red hole in *McFarland's* face, just below his left eye. His hand came up to inspect the wound. He looked about him in dazed confusion. Then his eyes went blank, rolling back til only the whites were visible. He swayed and then, like a tree, toppled onto the dirt so hard he bounced. He lay still and did not move.

Sam craned his head, saw Tilda moving forward now, the little derringer gripped in her right hand, smoke drifting from its tip. And he realized: She hadn't been tugging at him; she had been tugging at the bag on his belt and screaming in feigned hysteria to cover it up. Tilda moved past him now, went to inspect McFarland. Sam saw her foot prod his ample belly and get no response. When she knew her tormenter was dead, Tilda flung the little gun away from her like something filthy and came to kneel next to Sam. Her face filled his vision.

"We must get you to a doctor," she said.

"No use," he said, and his voice rasped out of him like a rusted hinge. "Not going to make it. Hurt too bad."

Her face hardened. "Do not say that. You will not die on me, Sam Freeman. You get up right now, do you hear what I'm saying? You get up!"

And she grabbed his arm and pulled him to a sitting position, ignoring his gasp. Sam's shirt was matted to him by blood. The bullet had entered beneath his only arm. Working feverishly, she pulled off his shirt. She took her teeth to the cloth where it wasn't soaked with blood and shredded a long piece. She looped this around his chest and tied it so tightly he gasped again. Sam watched all this activity with a detachment bordering on amusement.

When she felt she had controlled the bleeding as best she could, she came around to the front of him. "Now, you are going to stand up, Sam, and you are going to get on that horse." And the amusement went out of him.

"I cannot," he said.

"Yes, you can!" The very force of it made him flinch. He gulped and did not respond. "You will get up," she told him, "and you will get on that horse, and we will go into that town and get you a doctor. Do you hear me, Sam Freeman?"

He nodded because he was scared not to.

She looped his arm over her shoulder, braced her own arm around his waist, and lifted. He had no leverage with which to push. He could only lean his weight on her and let her lift him.

It was impossible. It could not be done.

She bared her teeth, snarling with the effort. He felt himself rising.

Pain blinded him. He felt blood seeping from his wound, saw it soaking through her dress where her side was pressed to his. They were glued together by blood. She didn't even notice.

Impossible. Could not be done.

But then he had his feet beneath him and he was still rising, the world reeling about him like children dancing around a pole. He clung to her, and she led him, his steps weak and faltering, to McFarland's horse. She lifted his foot, placed it in the stirrup, lowered her shoulder to his backside and pushed, and *pushed,* and he took the pommel and pulled as best he could and somehow he was doing it, his leg coming up and over until he was seated in the dead man's saddle. Exhausted. Sam collapsed against the pony's neck.

Tilda was gone for a moment. When she came back, she was astride Bucephalus. She leaned over, took the reins of McFarland's pony. "You hold on tight," she told Sam.

He nodded, unable to speak. Tilda urged the roan into a walk, McFarland's horse following obediently behind. She glanced briefly down at the body of her former owner, then turned her gaze to the road ahead.

"Free at last," she whispered.

And Sam, his eyes closed in a world white with pain, heard this and smiled.

Ahead of them, the town of Buford rose out of the cotton fields. Tilda glanced back. Sam was unconscious, drooling into the horse's neck. She had to shake him hard to bring him back to her. It took a moment for his eyes to focus, to know her, to remember.

"We're here," she said.

He lifted his head, pain corrugating his brow, surveyed the street, then pointed to a big, dark building on a corner. "There is an alley behind that warehouse," he whispered. A pause, wincing, gathering his breath. "There will be a little house on your right. Look for a flower garden."

She was uncertain, but she nodded anyway, jabbed her mount lightly with the spurs. They moved forward under the cold white gaze of the moon.

Tilda found the alley. She found the house. She pulled Sam's horse up alongside her own. "There is a doctor here, Sam?" she asked.

"There are...friends," he gasped.

"You have no need of friends. You have need of a doctor."

"I do not know the doctor in this town. They will."

She was still uncertain, but she slid down from the horse, climbed the three steps to the back door of the little clapboard house, and knocked hard. There was a scuffle of movement from inside. The door opened and a white woman was there.

"I am sorry," said Tilda, stepping back in surprise, "we must have the wrong house."

"What house are you looking for?" the white woman asked.

"I do not know. Sam, he...that is, my husband, he said..."

"Sam?" Something Tilda did not quite understand lit the white woman's eyes. There was recognition, and something more.

"You know Sam?" she asked.

"You must be Tilda," said the white woman,

"Yes," said Tilda, wondering how this woman knew her name.

"He did it," announced the white woman, beaming. Her eyes were emerald. "He found you."

"Yes," said Tilda.

"Where is he?"

And Tilda realized that for just a moment, she had forgotten the urgency of her mission, lost it in her confusion over who this white woman was and how she knew things she couldn't know. "He is there," she said, pointing. "He has been shot."

The green eyes rounded. "What? Why did you not say so?" And she brushed past Tilda without waiting for an answer, calling over her shoulder to someone still inside the house. "Ginny! It's Sam, he is hurt!"

Now a wizened little colored woman appeared at the door. She appraised Tilda with a smile. "He found you," she said.

"Yes," said Tilda. Who were these people?

"Good," she said.

The white woman, her voice soaked with tears, was taking command. "Help me get him inside!"

She went to help. From the right side of the horse, the older woman pushed Sam's leg up and over until it cleared the horse's head. Tilda and the white woman caught the weight of him and lowered him, gently as they could.

"I am sorry," Sam kept mumbling, not quite conscious. "I am sorry." Tilda wasn't sure which of them he was speaking to.

They got Sam's legs under him as best they could. Tilda took his right arm over her shoulders, while the white woman braced herself under the nub of his left. They had to turn single file to go up the three stairs and through the narrow doorway into the house.

"Take him to my room," the white woman said. "It is through that hallway, the second door on the left."

Sam's feet scraped the floor, his head lolling forward. Occasionally, he moaned.

The room she led them into was filled by a four-poster bed with a faded print cover. At the foot of the bed, a steamer trunk sat open and full of clothes. Apparently, the woman was packing to go somewhere.

They backed Sam up against the bed. Tilda pushed him gently back while the woman lifted his legs. Sam landed in the bed with a groan. His skin was a dead gray. The makeshift tourniquet around his side was soaked with blood.

"What happened to him?" asked the white woman.

Tilda ignored her. "He needs a doctor," she said. "Is there a doctor in this town?"

The old woman spoke from the hallway behind them, as there was not space enough in the tiny room for all of them. "They's a doctor down the street," she said. "He don't mind treatin' colored, neither."

"The two of you go get him," the white woman said. She addressed herself to the old lady and added, "At this point, seeing me might just inflame matters."

The old woman nodded. "Yeah, you probably right about that. Don't want him to let Sam die just 'cause it's you askin' for help."

"I shall stay here and keep an eye on him," said the white woman.

"All right, then. Come on, gal," she told Tilda. And Tilda had no choice but to follow the little woman back out into the night.

"Who are you?" she asked as they cleared the house. "Who is that white woman? How do you know Sam?"

"He ain't told you?" mused the little woman. And then, softly, answering her own question: "No, I expect he wouldn't. My name Ginny Campbell. Used to slave down here, but I been free for years. Got the manumission papers from my marse before the war. That white woman, she Prudence Kent. Rich girl lived up North in Boston. Her daddy taught her to hate slavery and when the war ended, she come down here to start a school for colored. Run into trouble with the white folks here. They killed people, they tried to burn her school. So now she goin' back to Boston."

She regarded Tilda with an expression Tilda couldn't read. "That's who we is. Now, as to how we knows Sam: it was just like tonight. We found him in that alley yonder, face down in the dirt, more dead than alive. Bunch of white men had set on him, stabbed him, beat him near 'bout to death. Prudence nursed him back to health. He was here a few weeks."

"Was that when he lost his arm?"

"No. That was already gone when we met him. Got it shot off him in Tennessee, he said."

"He has been through a lot," said Tilda.

"Yes, he has. Still goin' through it, I expect. What happened?"

"My former master did not want to let me go. He came after us and shot Sam from ambush."

"Come after you?" She was opening the picket gate of a house. "Ain't he knowed the war over? Slavery done."

"He was not the type to care about such things," said Tilda.

"What happened to him? Your old marse?"

"There was a gun in this little bag Sam carried."

"I know. Prudence give it to him."

"I shot him with it. Killed him."

A sharp nod of satisfaction. "Good," Miss Ginny said.

They followed a brick path around to the back door. Miss Ginny knocked and after a moment, a white man appeared, rail thin and with a halo of silver hair flying in all directions. "Ginny?" he asked. He was hooking his spectacles over his ears.

"Dr. Brown, we need help," said Ginny. "They's a man at my house. A gang tried to rob him as he were ridin' into town. They done shot him up bad."

The doctor's eyes widened as they fell upon Tilda's blood-soaked dress. "Let me get my bag," he said.

Fifteen minutes later, the doctor shooed Prudence, Ginny, and Tilda out of the tiny room where Sam lay breathing heavily and closed the door behind him.

The three women stood together in the hallway in a moment swollen with awkwardness, looking at one another. Then, without a word, Tilda walked away. She went outside and sat on the back porch of the house, her knees drawn up to her chin. No one came to join her, and for this she was glad. She was blood-soaked, filthy, and exhausted, her mind aching from trying to think a hundred things at once. Tilda drew in a deep breath, released it slowly, made herself watch and think nothing as heaven circled slowly above.

She did not know how long it was—an hour, maybe—before the door opened behind her. The white woman—Prudence, she reminded herself—was standing there. "The doctor is still in with him," she said. "I drew you a bath. It's in Ginny's room."

She closed the door without awaiting a response. Tilda sat there a moment longer. Then she got up and went inside. There was no one in the kitchen; the two women were in the front parlor, and the door to Prudence's room was still closed.

The door to the next room, however, was open, and when Tilda peeked around, she found the metal tub at the foot of the bed, steam drifting lazily from the water. A scrub brush, a towel, and a bar of soap sat on a table. A dress—it was pale blue and so crisp she thought it might never have been worn—had been laid out on the bed.

Tilda stripped gratefully out of the filthy dress that was the only thing she had worn, day and night, for five months. It fell from her in a heap, like a blood-caked, sweat-stained, mud-spattered old skin. Her body itself felt not much cleaner, felt as if it were crusted with all that had happened to her, all the agony she had seen and felt, all the terrible things that had been done to her and that she had done, the life she had endured for these past five years.

Absently, Tilda wiped a tear that slid down her cheek. She stepped carefully into the steaming water, lowered herself slowly. It was like walking into the embrace of God. Gratefully, Tilda leaned her head back. She closed her eyes.

"The doctor just left."

At the sound of the voice, Tilda's eyes came open. At first, she thought only a moment had passed, but then she realized the water was cool. She had drifted. Now she twisted around. Prudence was standing in the doorway.

"He got the bullet out," Prudence said. "He said it is a miracle Sam survived." A tiny, private smile. "He is still sleeping, but I thought you would like to spend the night in the room with him. I made a pallet for you on the floor." She indicated the dress on the bed with her chin. "That belonged to my friend. It should be about your size. I thought you could fit it. What would you like me to do with your other dress?"

Tilda glanced at the dirty old skin lying on the floor behind her. "It is fit only for burning," she said.

Prudence nodded with a smile. "I was hoping you would say that," she said. She picked up the dirty thing and took it with her. As the door closed behind her, Tilda came up out of the water. She dried and dressed herself quickly and went into the room where Sam lay. The other two women were there, standing at the side of the bed. They turned when they heard Tilda behind them. "I think he gon' be all right," said Miss Ginny. She squeezed Tilda's shoulder as she stepped out of the room so Tilda could enter.

Something in her chest unclenched when she saw her husband. Color was returning to his cheeks and the bandage around his chest was clean and dry. His face was relaxed, no longer pinched by pain. "He looks peaceful," Prudence said.

"You nursed him to health once before," said Tilda. She didn't bother making it a question.

Prudence glanced at her. "Ginny told you about that? Yes. We found him down the block lying in the alley. He had been set upon." A pause. "That dress is very pretty on you," she said.

Tilda looked down, admiring the blue fabric that swirled around her ankles. "Thank you for letting me use it," she said.

"You can have it," said Prudence. "There are some other things I would like to give you as well."

"But your friend…"

"My friend…" Prudence paused. "My friend passed away," she said, "but I know she would join me in wanting you to have her things."

"Are you certain?"

"Yes," said Prudence. "In fact, you would honor us if you took them."

"Thank you, again, then."

Prudence touched Tilda's shoulder, moved past her to the door. "Get some sleep," she said. "It is after midnight."

Tilda spoke without looking at her. "You are fond of Sam," she said.

The white woman paused at the door. "Yes, very fond," she confirmed. "I nursed him back to health so he could go and find you."

Tilda's gaze lifted upon an expression she could not read. She was exhausted. "Good night," she said.

"Good night," said Prudence. And the door closed behind her.

Alone in the dark, Tilda stripped out of the clean blue dress and lowered herself to the pallet. She pulled the rough cover up to her chin. There was something reassuring about the sound of Sam snoring lightly above her. She found Sam's hand and held it.

The sun was high in the sky when Tilda awoke. It took her a moment to know where she was. The smell of bacon and eggs cooking in the hearth was so tempting she could almost have wept for joy and for a moment, she thought this was what had awakened her. Then she realized: it was Sam.

"M'thirsty," he mumbled, again.

She stood up where he could see her, took his hand in hers. Sam turned his head and to her joy, she saw him recognize her. "Tilda," he said. And then, "What happened?"

"You got shot."

"Again?" The distress in his face was almost comical.

"Yes," she said. "I brought you here to your friends, Miss Ginny and that white woman."

"Prudence?"

"Yes, I believe that to be her name," said Tilda. "They were very kind. They got you a doctor. He got the bullet out."

"McFarland?"

"He will not be bothering us again, Sam."

His brow creased with the effort to recall. Then he said, "I remember. You saved my life."

"No, Sam," she said. "You saved mine." She kissed him lightly on the cheek.

There was a pitcher of water on a table by the bed, and Tilda poured him a glass, then helped him sit up to sip it. When he asked for the slop jar, she held it for him so he could empty his bladder. As she was helping him back into the bed, there came a soft knock at the door.

"Just a minute," called Tilda. When she had her husband comfortably situated, she went to the door.

Prudence was there. "We have bacon and eggs," she said.

"Sam is awake," Tilda told her.

"He is?" Prudence's drawn countenance rose like Jesus on Easter.

"I think he is going to recover," said Tilda.

"Oh, thank God," Prudence whispered. And to Tilda's surprise, the white woman hugged her. To Tilda's surprise, she hugged back.

"May I see him?"

In response, Tilda only stood aside.

Prudence needed no further invitation. She went to stand at Sam's bedside. "We were afraid we were going to lose you," she told him. "How are you feeling?"

"My side hurts."

"That is probably to be expected," she said.

"Yes, it probably is," he agreed.

Silence. There was a hesitation between them Tilda couldn't quite place. Finally, Sam cleared his throat. "Is everything on schedule?" he asked.

"Yes. We have just a few more days. Everything is in readiness."

"Readiness for what?" asked Tilda.

Prudence turned, showing the surprise on her face to Tilda, but speaking to Sam. "You have not told her?" she said.

"I did not expect to come back this way," said Sam.

The tightening around Prudence's eyes was barely perceptible, but it was there. "I see," she said.

"Readiness for *what*?" Tilda repeated.

Prudence told her. When she was finished, Tilda laughed. "My goodness," she said, "are you seriously doing that? I cannot even imagine how much money an enterprise like that would cost. But then, Ginny told me your family was wealthy."

A smile. "Well, yes," said Prudence, "though I fear we are significantly less wealthy than we were before this little adventure. It has, indeed, been costly."

"Speaking of which," said Sam, "I know I have not the right to ask you this, but have you room for two late arrivals?"

"Of course, Sam. You know you have only to ask." And then, brightly and abruptly: "Well, if you will both excuse me, I must send a telegram to Memphis. I need to confirm the arrival of those wagons."

A nod to Tilda, and she was gone. Tilda thought something seemed hurried in her step. As the door closed quietly and they were alone again, Tilda contemplated her husband, lying there in the sheets of this other woman's bed. When she spoke, her voice was soft. "She told me she was quite fond of you."

Sam's gaze held her. "We are fond of each other," he said.

"Oh." She thought of other things she could say, questions she could ask. Instead she said, "Let me change the dressing on that wound."

And she knelt over the bed and pulled the dressing away. It was stained, she saw, with blood and a tacky pus the color of an egg yolk. The surgeon had left the wound open. The skin around it was swollen, angry, and red.

"I do not like the way this looks," she said.

"It will be fine," he said. "Just change the dressing." His voice was clipped. She looked up at him. She did as he said.

Later that day, Tilda inspected the wound again. This time, Prudence was with her. "You are right," said Prudence as Tilda drew the dressing away. She wrinkled her nose. There was an awful smell.

They sent Ginny for the doctor. He inspected the wound and confirmed their fears. There was an infection. He cleaned the site as best he could, then prescribed bed rest.

"What are we going to do?" asked Tilda, once the doctor was gone.

"We have only two more days," said Prudence.

"You will have to postpone it."

"She cannot postpone it," said Sam, still sitting up in the bed. "There are too many moving parts to the plan. It could never be done in time."

"Well, perhaps Sam and I can stay here in town until he is better," said Tilda.

Prudence shook her head. "The ordinance goes into effect three days from now. No colored allowed within the city limits."

"Surely, they will make an exception," said Tilda.

Prudence shook her head. "These people will not make an exception, I promise you."

"But they *might*," insisted Tilda.

"I do not *want* an exception!" Sam yelled it. Tilda looked at him. He seemed as surprised as she did. He repeated himself, softly. "I do not want an exception. I want to leave. I hate this place," he breathed. "I do not want to be here a second longer than necessary."

"I hate it, too," said Prudence.

They turned to her, waiting. "Very well, Sam," Tilda said. "No exception."

It made him smile. She smiled in return, but it felt like a forgery, like a crude imitation of a smile. Tilda turned away so Sam couldn't see what a fraud she really was.

In doing so, she found herself facing Prudence, who did not bother to fake a smile. Her eyes searched the other woman's face and Tilda knew they shared a single thought, a single fear.

It angered her. She had shared too much with this woman already.

On that Monday morning when all things changed, A.J. Socrates arrived at his general store on Main Street and was perplexed to find it still locked up tight at eight o'clock in the morning. Ordinarily, his colored man, Horace, got there an hour before he did, swept the floor, stocked the shelves, and made coffee. Socrates rattled the front door in frustration, then went fishing in his pocket for his seldom-needed keys as he wondered what could have happened to Horace.

Then his gaze strayed across the note tacked to the wall. He snapped it down and read it quickly. When he was done, he read again, more slowly. Then his head came up. His eyes were dark dots surrounded by white and his cheeks were scarlet.

That same morning, Mrs. Millie Baker awoke with a start. She checked the clock by the side of the bed and saw to her consternation that she had overslept by almost an hour. But that was impossible. She had a very dependable colored girl named Sue who woke her faithfully on time every morning and brought her breakfast. Mystified, Millie threw on a housecoat and padded downstairs. She found the house dark and silent.

Then she saw the note on the table in the front parlor. Mystified, she picked it up and began to read. As she did, her mouth fell open—and stayed that way.

That same fateful morning, Joe Hunsacker and his oldest son, Joe, Jr., took a table, two chairs, and a stack of contracts and set them up on a patch of dirt in front of the cabins where his Negroes lived. They sat there and

they waited. And they waited. Joe had reminded his people as recently as
the previous Friday that he would be here this morning with papers for
them to make their marks obliging them to pick his cotton crop for him.

After 15 minutes, Joe sent his son to bang on cabin doors and bring the
Negroes out. Instead, Joe, Jr. brought him a note he'd found. Joe Hunsacker read it, then looked up at his son and saw his own confusion reflected
back at him.

As all this was unfolding, Charles Wheaton sat in his wheelchair at a
table in his study waiting for tea. This was the way his day always began,
with a cup of tea and a biscuit brought to him by Sassafras. That routine
disrupted, he felt oddly unmoored. He had things to do today, had to meet
with his foreman, then with his attorney, then prepare for a trip to Memphis
to inspect a rail car he might buy. But how could he do any of that, until
he first had his tea?

After waiting fifteen minutes, Wheaton called his son Bo and sent him
to Sass's room to make sure she was all right. It annoyed him that Sass was
moving tomorrow to a house of her own outside the city limits. He would
miss the convenience of having her in his house, answerable to his needs, 24
hours a day. But it couldn't be helped. The trouble that woman—he never
called Prudence by name, even in the sanctuary of his own thoughts—had
brought down on Buford simply could not be allowed to repeat itself. And
clearing the town of niggers was the best way to ensure that. No exceptions.

Bo returned moments later. He didn't have Sass, but he did have some
sort of folded paper in hand. Wheaton had just taken it from him when
there came a sharp rapping at the door. Father and son stared at each other.
Vern came into the room then, scratching his armpits and yawning. "What
happened to Sass?" he demanded. "She usually wakes me up way before
this."

Wheaton didn't reply. He was waiting to hear Louis, the houseman,
open the door. Instead, he heard another rapping, louder and more insistent
this time. "Wheel me to the door," he said.

Vern looked at Bo as if their father had spoken to them in Greek. Wheaton slapped at the wheels of his chair. "Now!" he demanded.

And Vern took hold of the chair and pushed it. Bo went ahead of them
and opened the door. The man who stepped inside without waiting for an
invitation was known to them all. Silas Alexander, a man of grand gray
whiskers and prosperous girth, was the longtime mayor of Buford, known

since the war for never being seen around town unless wearing the dress uniform of his former rank in the Confederate cavalry. But there were no shiny brass buttons or crisp gray serge about Silas today. Today he wore jeans and a frayed old shirt, as if he had been in such a hurry he hadn't had time to dress properly.

When Wheaton rolled up, the mayor grabbed his chair by the arms, stopping it short, and began babbling, the words pouring out of him like water. "Oh, Charles, it is a disaster. What will become of us! What can we do? The bitch has ruined us!"

"Stop jabbering, man!" scolded Wheaton. "What are you talking about?"

Alexander drew himself up, pointing. "I see you have one those damnable notes," he said. "Read it for yourself."

Mystified, Charles Wheaton unfolded the paper in his lap. It was a form letter, professionally printed, except for his name in the salutation and the signature at the bottom, both of them printed in emphatic block letters. It said:

Dear Mr. <u>CHARLES WHEATON</u>

One of the ways you know you are free is that you have the right to come and go as you please. This note is a courtesy to inform you that as a free person of color, I have decided to do exactly that. I hereby resign my position in your employ.

I have come to this decision after many long hours of prayerful consideration. But the outlandish response of the white people of this town to our modest efforts to educate and improve ourselves, and the passage of a spiteful ordinance effectively barring people of color from residing within the town limits, ultimately made the decision an easy one.

If we are not good enough to live in the town, we are not good enough to live in the county. If we are not good enough to live in the county, we are not good enough to live in the state. So we are exercising our Constitutional and God-given right to go away from you.

A war was fought and a president was killed to secure for we people of color the simple right to be treated with the dignity to which all human beings are entitled. To remain another second in

this hateful and inhuman place would be to dishonor the sacrifice
they made.
   Very Truly Yours,
   <u>*COLINDY JOHNSON*</u>

Below this signature was printed a message in Colindy's hand:

   My name wasn't never no damn Sassafras!!

Wheaton looked up into the mayor's sweaty eyes. He felt as if he was going to be sick. "These notes are…?"

Silas Alexander answered the question before it was asked. "All over town," he said. "Every planter, every shopkeeper, every wife who employs a nigger for cleaning house or cooking, has gotten one of these damn notes."

"That Yankee bitch. This is her doing."

Alexander glared scorn at him. "Well, of course it is," he said. "What I want to know is: what are we going to do about it?"

Wheaton swallowed hard, fearing the answer even before he asked the question, but needing to ask it anyway. "How many of the niggers are leaving?"

Alexander looked at him. "As near as I can tell? All of them."

Prudence stepped out of the front door of Miss Ginny's house and surveyed her handiwork with a smile.

The street was filled with colored people and mule-drawn wagons, 57 of them in all, plain wooden contraptions with benches and a driver's perch. The line of them began behind her phaeton and stretched east down Main Street past the warehouse to where the cotton fields began. All of them were Union Army surplus and had been purchased at favorable prices, the military happy to be rid of them now that the fighting was over. Right on schedule, they had begun rolling in the previous night under cover of darkness.

The resulting scene was all cacophony and bedlam, mules grunting, babies squalling, children laughing, women crying, men shouting, families flocking back and forth loading bundles of clothing, cookware, and personal belongings. Through an agent, the Cafferty family had purchased four parcels of land totaling 1,700 acres in the central part of Ohio. Because much of it had not been cleared, they got it for the bargain price of $25 an acre. It was to this land that the Negroes of Buford were now embarking.

The coming fall and winter, she had told them, would be difficult. There would be time before the hard weather came to build only a few rough structures, and these would be used as dormitories to shelter the elderly and the infirm. The rest of the former slaves would live in surplus Army tents on provisions to be provided by a charitable foundation hastily set up by the Caffertys and several of their wealthy abolitionist friends. Each of the 47 colored families in and around Buford had been advanced a mule team and a wagon provisioned with food and farming implements. In the spring, they would begin to clear the land, break their new soil, and plant their crops, and when harvest time came, they would take those crops to market. A year later, when there was a second harvest, the Caffertys would receive 10 percent of any profit. They would continue this arrangement for 10 years or until the original purchase price of the land had been reimbursed, whichever came first. After that, each family would own its own plot of land, roughly 36 acres each.

Buford and the area around it were home to 1,398 souls, 412 of whom were colored. And all 412 stood gathered in the street this morning, packing their wagons. The town would get its wish. No more Negroes would live here. Buford would be—what was the phrase Bo Wheaton had used?—"exclusively white."

Prudence had not slept in two days. Yet she had never felt more alive. Satisfaction filled her chest the way air swells a balloon.

Standing next to her, Colindy said, "This a mess."

Prudence looked down at the plump little woman, who stood watching with arms akimbo, lips pursed, head moving slowly, pityingly, from side to side. "Are you sorry you changed your mind?" Prudence asked.

For the first time since Prudence had known her, Colindy smiled. "No," she said. "Most fun I ever had in my life was signing that note to Charles Wheaton. I be happy to go anywhere, long as it's away from him." Prudence laughed, and felt a ghost of guilt for doing so. After all, this was still the place where Bonnie had died. But she couldn't help laughing. It felt good.

Behind her, the front door opened and Willie Washington, one of Jesse's equally massive brothers, stepped out of Miss Ginny's house, cradling Sam in his arms. Tilda followed. Prudence and Colindy moved aside to give them room. Sam was unconscious, unaware of his very presence in the world. He had only gotten worse these last couple of days. A stubborn fever had claimed him, turning his shirt gray with sweat. Last night, he had returned to the war, awakening from a fitful sleep to order some unseen soldier to duck if he didn't want to lose his head. You could hear his cries all through the house. In the bed she now shared with Miss Ginny, Prudence had wept.

Sam was dying.

She hadn't yet spoken this belief aloud, hadn't wanted to put the poisonous thought into the air. She tried hard to hold faith in miracles. But faith died anew every time she looked at him, the feeble, watery eyes, the ashen skin, the oozing wound.

Prudence turned away as the big man carried Sam past, afraid her feelings might surface in her face. Indeed, sometimes she caught Tilda watching her with a hard expression that suggested her feelings were already too well known. And what could she do about that? She could respect this woman, and she did. But she couldn't make herself stop feeling. She couldn't make what had already happened not happen.

And she wouldn't have if she could.

"This is foolish," Tilda said to no one in particular as she trailed Willie Washington down to the street.

"Yes, ma'am," said Willie tolerantly, looking and sounding so much like his murdered brother.

"As bad off as he is," said Tilda, "this wagon ride is sure to kill him. It is madness to do this."

"It is what he wants." Prudence hadn't meant to say it, hadn't meant to say anything. Now Tilda stabbed her with her eyes. But, the thing having been said, Prudence met her gaze. She would not back down. Why should she? It was the truth. Sam knew his condition as well as they did or better. But this was what he had asked of them. And shouldn't that be honored by those who loved him?

After a long moment, Tilda turned her eyes elsewhere. She climbed into the wagon behind Prudence's phaeton and barked at Willie Washington to be more careful how he handled Sam as he stretched him out on a cushion in the back.

Prudence was conscious of Colindy's questioning gaze. She ignored her and stepped into the street to begin organizing chaos.

They were hours late. She supposed that was to be expected. The families had been asked to meet their wagons at dawn, to load them and form up a caravan. But some had brought more cookware or clothing than would fit in the meager space allowed, some were weeping at the thought of leaving the only homes they had ever known, some couldn't keep their children from scampering off. Prudence had hired a former Army scout as a caravan leader. He stood in front of the abandoned livery stable across the street, watching with unconcealed amusement as the unwieldy cavalcade sorted itself out.

Prudence was conscious of white people gathering on the sidewalk now to stare at them with folded arms and crimped faces. Some bore expressions of hurt disbelief, as if grievously wounded by some great betrayal. Occasionally, she heard one of them say something like, "Look, isn't that the Johnsons' Jim?" or, "Look, there's my Hattie big as day!" But they made no move to interfere, and that was all she cared about. Prudence ignored them.

Then the wagon came clattering down the street, such a rattle of wood and a thunder of hooves that people instinctively jumped out of the way. But Prudence stood her ground, watching it approach and draw to a stop next to her. She knew what was coming. Part of her relished it.

Sure enough, Bo Wheaton was at the reins. His brother Vern sat in the leather-upholstered seat behind him, bracing their legless father, who gripped the brass railing with knuckles that had gone white and leaned his choleric face as close to Prudence as he could without tumbling over. "You minx!" he cried. "You tricked me!"

And in that moment, it was all worth it, all the long hours negotiating for unseen land in an unknown place, haggling with Army quartermasters, begging trust from skeptical dark faces. Prudence hoped that wherever she was, Bonnie was watching. She mustered her sweetest smile. She even batted her eyes. "Why, Mr. Wheaton, whatever do you mean?"

Incredulity turned his features to ice; they did not move, except for a tiny, involuntary spasm of his lip. For a sliver of time, she wondered if he were having a stroke. Then he spoke in a voice cold and dead as yesterday's cook fire. "You bitch," he said. "Do not play the wounded innocent with me. We had an agreement and you deceived me."

Only statues filled the street. Nothing moved. Every eye stared. Prudence was distantly aware that a phalanx of the colored men had assembled at her back, looking on in silence. She knew this through some sixth sense other than sight, for she did not once take her eyes off the glowering visage before her.

"I did no such thing," she said. "You asked to buy a building from me." She swept an arm to her right, still not turning away from Wheaton. "It is right there, ready for your occupancy. In fact"—she lifted a key from her bodice and lofted it, so that it landed with a soft jangle on the seat between father and son—"here is the key."

"But you enticed our niggers—"

"These *Negroes*"—she paused, allowed air to fill the space between this word and the next—"are free men and women able to make their own decisions. That, I believe, was the outcome of the late war that your 'nation' lost so disastrously. And if, as free men and women, they have decided to accept my offer to help them resettle elsewhere, well, that is their right, is it not?"

"But what will happen to us?" It was a strangely plaintive cry, the bawling of an abandoned child. "You know very well, these people are our labor force. If you take them away, you cripple our tradesmen and shopkeepers! And what of our planters? It's almost time for the harvest! Who will work our fields? Don't you see? You will wreck our town!"

"And what is that to me?" asked Prudence, the flat calm of her own voice surprising her. "You should have thought of that before you passed that damnable ordinance, before you attacked my school, before you massacred a group of people who had done you no harm." She took a step that brought her so close she could have kissed him, if that had been her intent. "You should have thought of that before you murdered my sister."

Charles Wheaton blanched. "I have told you before: you cannot hold me responsible for what the rabble decides to do. It has nothing to do with me. Look at me!" he thundered, his arm falling to where his legs ended. "I am hardly in a position to do harm to anyone!"

"No," said Prudence in the same flat voice, "you only sit in your mansion and *allow* it to happen, when you could stop it with a word, because the entire town takes its cues from you. You let the rabble do what you have not the guts to do, so that when it is done, you can hold up clean hands and pretend you were never involved and continue to believe yourself a gentleman, even though you most certainly are not."

She stepped back. His gaze remained fixed on her. She had the curious sensation that there was no longer any animating intelligence behind those eyes, nothing beyond a feral rage at being challenged as he had never been challenged before. Wheaton seemed beyond even words.

Vern leaned across his father then. "Daddy, I don't know why you waste time arguin' with this highfalutin Yankee bitch." His eyes radiated a feverish heat. "She wants rabble? Give her rabble. Hell, you give the word and these niggers won't make it far as the river."

For the first time in long minutes, Prudence allowed her eyes to stray. They took in Vern Wheaton, his weak chin, his moist lips, his features gnarled as oak roots with hate. From there, her gaze traveled across to his brother, Bo, who regarded her with sad eyes and a strange little close-mouthed smile.

Now she returned to the father. When she spoke, there was something off-handed in her voice, something casual and unconcerned that made Wheaton's brow squeeze itself together. "Do you remember, Mr. Wheaton, how this town became enflamed by the false rumor I had armed a small group of Negroes who were guarding my school? You remember what they called it, do you not?"

"A nigger army," he breathed. "What of it?"

"Well, Mr. Wheaton, if someone were to spread that rumor today, it would not be false."

She actually heard his breathing stop. "You have armed them?"

Prudence nodded. "Every one of them, man, woman, or child, who is old enough to heft a rifle, yes."

Wheaton gaped. His gaze swiveled to the colored men massed at Prudence's back, to the women watching him with folded arms, to the families huddled together in their wagons. They met him with a wintry silence.

Then Wheaton's eyes found Colindy. "Sass," he said, drawing the one syllable out in a homey burr that made him sound like a disappointed father, "certainly *you* are no part of this foolishness?"

Colindy took a step forward, separating herself from the wall of women with whom she stood. "Mr. Wheaton," she said, "I think you need to go."

He stared at her as if she were some new and unknown thing. As perhaps, thought Prudence, she was.

"One other thing," said Prudence. "You may recall, or at least know of, Sergeant Gideon Russell. He was the Union soldier who sheltered in the school with me the night your rabble burned the colored people out of town. He sent a company of Union men to deliver these wagons. They are waiting to form up with my caravan about a mile north of here and accompany us as far as Memphis. So, should you be tempted to take your son's rather intemperate advice"—she looked at Vern—"you might wish to keep that in mind."

Again he stared. His mouth moved, but did not make a sound. It was as if he had used up his entire life's store of words. Prudence said, "Good day, Mr. Wheaton."

His father was still struggling to form language when Bo Wheaton settled the matter. He flicked the reins and the wagon rattled off. Prudence stared after them. The street was too crowded for Bo to turn the wagon, so Prudence had no idea what route they would take to return home. She had a sense of them driving until they fell off the side of the world. But that was their problem. She clapped her hands together and spoke loudly enough for the entire street to hear.

"All right," she said, "enough dallying. It is time all of us were on the road."

The late-day sun struck gold from the waters of the Mississippi. The paddle-wheel slapped at the river with a steady cadence Tilda had long since ceased to hear. Nor did she hear the hammering of the engines or the squealing, grunting, and lowing of the animals in the cargo hold one deck below. She sat with Ginny at a table on deck, watching.

Prudence had somehow found and purchased a wheelchair for Sam in Memphis. She had wheeled him to the railing so he could watch the riverbanks pass them by. Prudence sat next to him. They were talking, their heads close together. Tilda was too far away to know what they said. Occasionally, Prudence dabbed at Sam's brow with a cold compress.

A white man in a foppish hat happened to see her do this and apparently took exception. He said something to Prudence, whereupon her eyes flashed, and whatever she said in response caused him to recoil. He went on about his business at a quick step. She had a sharp tongue on her, this Prudence. Tilda felt an admiration she didn't want to feel.

"Who is she?" she asked.

Confusion creased the folds of the old woman's eyes. "What you mean, 'who is she?' You know who she is. She Prudence."

"No," said Tilda, "what I mean is—"

Ginny cut her off. "What you mean is, did she sleep with your husband? Was they lovers?"

Tilda looked at her, feeling transparent. "Yes," she said.

Ginny drew back. There was a moment she seemed to spend just contemplating her next words. Then she said, "When we found Sam, he was more dead than alive."

"Yes, I know," said Tilda.

"No, I don't think you do," Ginny told her. "I don't just mean his body was hurt. I mean, his spirit. He was near 'bout at the end of his rope. Done walked a thousand miles, been shot, stabbed, stomped on, done lost his arm, almost lost his foot, lookin' for someone he ain't seen nor heard from in 15 years. Lookin' for *you*. And after all that, he was near 'bout to givin' up. She felt the same way. She done come down here to start a school for colored, come down here with high hopes and big plans, and all it got her was death. They killed Bonnie. That was a black girl she called her sister, girl that she growed up with her whole life.

"So if you ask me what they done for each other, I tell you like this: they healed each other. They helped each other be whole again. That's what they done."

"Were they in love?"

Ginny's smile bore secrets and sorrows. "I asked him that once," she said. "He told me he was very fond of her."

"I see," said Tilda.

"No, you don't understand that, neither. He said he was *fond* of her. I asked him if that meant he walk a thousand miles trying to find her if she was ever lost. He couldn't give me no answer. And we both knowed that was a answer in itself. You see, he could have stayed with her. He could have said, 'I done enough to find Tilda, been through hell to find this woman and I ain't found her yet. Can't nobody in the world fault me if I choose to stay here and be happy my ownself.' But instead, he chose to keep looking for you. What you think that mean?"

Ginny's gaze was direct. Tilda no longer saw it.

Was it just a little more than a week ago that she had stood in the cookhouse with Honey in the predawn darkness, trying to get used to this mad new idea that she, beaten and tired old thing that she was, was a woman someone might come looking for? It had unsettled her, had seemed a thing too large and foolish to believe. She felt it again now, that same sense of disquiet, as if her entire understanding of herself, of who she was and what she meant, had somehow shifted right before her eyes.

Tilda had never thought of herself as a woman someone would *choose*. But apparently, she was.

And then, she was standing. And then, she was walking toward the railing where Prudence tended her husband.

They looked around at her approach. Prudence smiled. "There you are," she said. "Perhaps you can break the stalemate. Sam is not happy with the name I have chosen for the town we are founding in Ohio. Tell me what you think."

Tilda said, "Beg pardon?" Words seemed leeched of meaning somehow. "I want to call it Freeman," said Prudence. "Freeman, Ohio."

Tilda said, "I think"—she saw Sam grimace—"that is a wonderful idea."

Prudence nodded triumphantly. "Well, then," she told Sam, "that settles it. Freeman, Ohio it is."

"Fine, then," said Sam, and Tilda could barely hear his voice. "Apparently, I am unable to talk you out of it."

There was a moment. No one spoke. Then Tilda saw an understanding settle in Prudence's eyes. Prudence clapped her hands together as she stood. "Well," she told Tilda brightly, "I think I shall take a walk. Would you mind keeping our friend company?"

"No," said Tilda, "I would not mind that at all."

A squeeze of her arm. Then Prudence walked away. She went to the opposite side of the deck, stood at the railing. After a moment, she pulled a letter from her pocket. She had read it a dozen times in the week since it arrived, read it enough that she could recite it by heart, had no need to see the words on paper. But she opened it anyway and read:

> *My dearest sister:*
> *I can only imagine what you have been going through since that woman told you about Father's indiscretion. I am sure you feel great disappointment with him, but also, I would wager, you have endured a period of wondering about your own identity.*
> *Do not judge him too harshly, Sister. You saw him ever through the eyes of love as a favored youngest child and so perhaps you failed to realize it, but he was only a man and as such, heir to all the weakness of men. Yes, he owned slaves. But remember, he set them free. Once he really had a taste of what it meant to own human beings, he wanted no part of it. He saw that while the institution debases the slave, it also debases the owner. I am persuaded that while many men see that, very few have the courage to act upon it. Our father did. On balance, he was a good*

man, Sister. He did much good in the world. I implore you to
keep this mind.

I am glad you have chosen to share this burden with me. I
believe I may be able to ease your mind.

Fourteen years ago, when you were just a girl, a letter arrived
for Father. I used to watch him often without his knowing; he was
away so often, I think I felt that if we were not careful, one day
he might go and never return. For that reason, I developed the
habit of spying on him. As he read it in his study that day I was
watching secretly from the door, and I saw a great change come
over him. His shoulders slumped, his mouth drooped open, his eyes
became glassy. So alarmed was I that I contrived to pretend I had
just wandered into the room and I asked him what was wrong.
He told me it was nothing. I knew better. I bided my time until he
was distracted elsewhere in the house. Then I crept into his study
and read the letter.

It was from a convent in Springfield. A Sister Mary Catherine
was writing to let him know that some little girl he had placed
in her care had died suddenly of a fever. On reading this, I was
filled with questions: who was this girl and why had Father placed
her in the convent's care and why had he never spoken of her?
But there was no one I could ask—least of all, him. So there the
mystery remained.

As I grew older, I suppose I figured it out, but I kept the truth
from myself, kept it in the back of my thoughts where I need never
confront our father's deepest secret. Your letter forces me to do just
that and at the same time, removes any last smidgen of doubt I
might have had. As is your way, sister, you have stumbled headlong and heedless into the truth and I suppose I should thank you
for it. The Bible says the truth shall make us free.

Here, then, is the truth: our father had a fourth daughter, a
little mulatto girl he never claimed. She died in a convent orphan-
age when she was 12. Our sister's name was Hope.

Now, as for you—I was six years old when you were born,
and I do not remember much. But I do remember when they let
me hold you for the first time; I thought you were awful—such a

horrid, wrinkled little thing. And I remember the ghastly pallor of our mother's face and how she died not two hours later.

So if the revelations of this woman in Mississippi have left you questioning your own identity, wondering if you might secretly be a little mulatto girl whose mother was a slave, you may be at ease, Sister. Nothing of the sort of is true. You are who you have always been—my impulsive and imprudent and very much beloved Sister, Prudence.

I hope these words set your mind at ease. I very much look forward to seeing you again.

With all my love, I remain, your sister, Constance.

Prudence was gazing at her sister's signature when Miss Ginny approached. The wind was tossing her thin white hair all about her head. "What's that?" she asked, nodding toward the letter.

Prudence didn't reply at once. She could see her oldest sister, her brow furrowed, sitting at the writing desk in her bedroom scratching out these words she hoped would bring Prudence comfort and save her from any more time spent wondering about her own identity, wondering if she was who she'd always thought she was. But, thought Prudence, she need not have bothered. Somehow, an odd thing had happened. Somewhere in the month of preparing this mass exodus of every Negro in and around Buford, Prudence had stopped wondering. Prudence had stopped caring.

It was skin, she decided. Only skin. And it had no power to add or subtract or otherwise alter her fundamental understanding of her own self. She was who she had always been.

"It is just a letter," she told Ginny. "From my sister, Constance."

As she spoke, she opened her hand and allowed a breeze to take the paper. The letter sailed high, then began to fall, tracing looping curlicues in the air until it deposited itself in the waters of the Mississippi and, soon after, was gone.

"Why you do that?" asked Ginny. "You didn't want to save it?"

Prudence felt herself smiling. "There was no need to save it," she said. "There was nothing in it I need."

Tilda sat in the chair facing her husband, facing the man who had come looking for her. She dipped the compress in the pan of cool water, wrung it out, and placed it on Sam's forehead. His brow was on fire.

"We were just talking about you," he told her.

"About me? Why?"

"If I…" A pause, a cough. "If I don't make it, I want you to stay with Prudence and Ginny in Boston. At least until you get your bearings, decide what you want to do."

"Sam, shush. There is no reason to talk like that. You will be fine."

He shook his head. "It is important to me," he said. "I need to know that you are going to be all right. Please do this for me. *Promise* me."

His eyes held hers. She blinked away tears. "Very well, Sam," she said. "I promise."

"Good," he said. "That takes a weight off my mind."

"Are you thirsty, Sam? I could get you something."

His hand waved weakly. "No," he said, "I'm fine. Just want to talk. Haven't had much chance…just…talk." She could hear him breathing. "So," he said, "have you given any thought…what name you're going to use…now?"

It took her only a second. "Tilda," she said. A pause. "Freeman. Tilda Freeman."

Sam smiled. He felt a fullness. It was all gone then, all far away from him, all regret, doubt, blood, sweat, fear. Those were earthbound things and he was sailing far above them all.

"Thank you, Sam"—the tears in her voice slurred her words—"for not giving up on me. For not giving up on us."

He closed his eyes. His thoughts were cottony. From somewhere far below him, he could hear the sound of a steamboat making its way up the Mississippi, paddlewheels churning the water, engines banging, plates clinking as stewards prepared for the evening meal, a man complaining in angry Spanish. All of it so far away.

Sam opened his eyes. His vision was filled with her. "Do not cry," he said.

She took his hand. "'Love is long suffering,'" she said. "Do you remember when I read that to you for the first time? Love is long suffering. And you sure proved it, didn't you? You sure did."

"Love never fails," he added, and his own voice was ragged and breathy in his ears.

"Love never fails," she agreed. A sad smile tugged at her lips. "And I love you, Sam."

It made him smile. He closed his eyes, and this time, did not open them again.

His final thought was of her.

THE END

Acknowledgments

Another writer—I believe, but cannot swear, it was Stephen King—once said that as a novelist, one researches only to enable one to lie more effectively, i.e., to create a believable fictional world in which readers will be emotionally invested. This is particularly true of historical fiction, where you undertake not simply to create another world, but to recreate another time, a task that rests on nailing down answers to a hundred insanely arcane and specific questions.

To wit: What color and character is the soil in northeast Mississippi? How long did it take to repair a chimney in the mid-nineteenth century? Was the phrase "turn in" (as in going to sleep for the night) in use in 1865?

To whatever degree I have been not able to lie effectively on the preceding pages, I take all the blame. To whatever degree my lies do work, I must share credit with a number of individuals and institutions without whom this book would not be.

I am indebted to the staff of the Library of Congress, particularly those in the periodicals room and the map room. In the former, I spent hours reading old newspapers, trying to capture the feeling of the day the Civil War ended. In the latter, I spent hours devising feasible routes for my characters to reach their destinies.

Phil Lapsansky of the Philadelphia Free Library generously unearthed for me images of how Sam's workplace would have appeared in 1865. Kelly Rodgers, program director of Maryland Therapeutic Riding Institute in Crownsville, Maryland, invited me up there to show me how a disabled rider might handle a horse. Steve Depew and Tom Head of the U.S. Natural Resources Conservation Service helped me understand growing seasons and the nature of the soil in northern Mississippi. Historians Kathleen Thompson and Craig Pfannkuche gave me great assistance in understanding the appearance and mores of Chicago in the mid-nineteenth century. William C. Davis, author of *Portraits of the Riverboats,* greatly aided me in my attempt to recreate the ambiance of a steamboat trip down the Mississippi.

I should say here that Leon F. Litwack's Pulitzer Prize-winning book on the aftermath of slavery, *Been in the Storm So Long,* was a key inspiration for this novel when I first read it many years ago. A number of the incidents in my novel—including the mother searching for her lost infant daughter—are fictionalized versions of real episodes written about by Litwack and other historians of the period.

I am also indebted to my agent, Janell Walden Agyeman of Marie Brown and Associates, for her never-flagging patience, faith and persistence, to my assistant, Judi Smith, for always sweating the small stuff, and to my editor, Doug Seibold of Agate Bolden, for understanding—and occasionally reminding me—that good enough is never good enough.

Finally, I would be remiss if I did not mention my wife of more than 30 years, Marilyn, and our family, for their understanding, support and bottomless love.

For all those things, I gratefully thank all those people. For everything else, I gratefully thank God.

ABOUT THE AUTHOR

Leonard Pitts, Jr. was born and raised in Southern California and now lives in suburban Washington, DC, with his wife and children. He won the 2004 Pulitzer Prize for commentary for his syndicated column, which appears in more than 200 newspapers, and has won numerous other journalism awards. He is the author of several books, including the novel *Before I Forget* (Agate Bolden, 2009).